The Inn at Copper's Run

Frontispiece Photo by Ellen Harris Phillips

The Inn at Copper's Run

JENNY JOHNSON

Noble Theme Publishing

Noble Theme Publishing
ISBN-13: 978-1-7930-3508-0 (paperback version)

This is a work of fiction. Names, characters, businesses, places, events and incidents are either products of the author's imagination or are used in a fictitious manner for the purposes of story and not to the detriment of any person, place or event.

Definitions of Prelude and Encore derived from Merriam-Webster Dictionary https://www.merriam-webster.com/
"Away in a Manger" quotation in Chapter 13 thought to be written by W.J. Kirkpatrick, now in Public Domain.

Cover photo by Lynn R. Mitchell
Frontispiece photo by Ellen Harris Phillips
Author photos by Martha D. Evans

DEDICATION

To the men and women of the New York City Police Department and the Fire Department City of New York who served on September 11, 2001.

ACKNOWLEDGMENTS

Thank you to my friends and fellow writers in the Scribes Writers' Group: Katharine, Diana, Camille, Hilary, Jennifer and Laurie. Thank you also to the beta reader for this book, Jennifer Haynie. And always I am grateful for the support of my family.

CONTENTS

	Remember September	ix
	Prelude	1
1	September Morning	3
2	Sanctuary	17
3	Copper's Run	37
4	Unexpected Challenge	55
5	Revelation	75
6	Sam's Plan	87
7	Alaine's Response	101
8	Homecoming	125
9	Transition	135
10	Alaine's Story	147
11	Mowher's Story	157
12	In Conflict	175
13	Beautiful Star	189
14	Encounter	203
15	Warnings	221
16	History Lesson	241
17	Decision	253
18	Confessions	267
19	Missing	279
20	Jeopardy	291
21	Hide and Seek	303
22	Pursuit	319
23	The Way Home	335
	Encore	345
	September Twelfth	347
	About the Author	349

REMEMBER SEPTEMBER

Remember September, not for the harvest ripe with grain
But for the harvest of souls
Unleashed from earth's bonds by desperate acts of terror
As the world watched in horror at what could not be true
But was true.
And in two hours we all were changed forever

Remember September, not for the fear we came to feel
But for the dust covered faces
Of those who wiped the tears, held the hands, and gave us hope
As we covered our mouths in silence at what we watched.
And we knew
That those two hours changed us all forever

New scars were felt upon the face of our nation,
Upon a field where flowers had been growing,
Upon a place where great decisions were being made,
Upon the places where our brothers came and went about the business of their lives;
Scars that would mend but never fade,
Wounds, which would heal, but hurt for endless days.

But scars were ever part of the fabric of our nation
Upon the warriors who dearly bought our freedoms
Upon the dreamers who brought us new horizons
Upon the teachers who opened our eyes and lighted our way with understandings
Scars, which have healed, but are not forgotten
Wounds that have mended and have made us strong.

Remember September, not for the dread we have come to know
As we revisit that day, that time.
But for the chance for re-awakenings, new beginnings,
Quiet determinations to make our time on earth
A better time,
To make the earth a better place for us all. J.J.

Where can I go from your Spirit? Where can I flee from your presence?
If I go up to the heavens, you are there; if I make my bed in the depths,
you are there.
If I rise on the wings of the dawn, if I settle on the far side of the sea,
even there your hand will guide me,
your right hand will hold me fast.
If I say, "Surely the darkness will hide me and the light become night around me,"
even the darkness will not be dark to you;
the night will shine like the day, for darkness is as light to you.

(Psalm 139:7-12)

PRELUDE

[an event serving as an introduction]

Sampson MacDonald had his workspace at One World Trade Center in New York City. The steel, concrete and glass monolith rose 110 stories above lower Manhattan, and his office on the 87th floor offered a view extraordinaire.

One of Sam's pleasures, and they were pitiful and few of late, was to stand at the expanse of glass windows comprising the walls of the massive office structure and gaze over the panorama of the City, as he did on this Tuesday morning. He never stopped feeling vertigo from the exercise; he never stopped feeling a sense of his own insignificance when he saw the geography of The Big Apple spread around him. But he was moth-drawn to continue looking as he held his cup of bitter coffee and thought about the endless, mind-numbing day ahead.

One moment the sun's light warmed the ice blue sky. The spectacle of sights and lives being played out above and below almost gave him hope.

The next moment a shadow blocked the light as if a great bird bore down from on high.

The shadow of what?

The thought had barely occurred when the building gave an immense shudder that dashed the lukewarm coffee onto Sam's once-crisp white shirt as it tossed him across the potted plants near the windows and slammed him to the floor.

Spread-eagled on the dark gray carpet with his face burning from its contact when he fell, Sam felt a rush of vertigo as the building began to roll from side to side like a giant tree responding to a mighty wind.

Sam stopped breathing and waited for his demise.

So this, then, is to be the end? Am I to die in humiliation in a place I despise with people I hold in contempt?

1 SEPTEMBER MORNING

Sampson

It wasn't that he had a deep interest in pursuing a serious relationship with her. In any case, he doubted it would go anywhere. His experience taught Sam that women could be fickle and often followed the money, of which he had little at present.

Therefore, Sam wasn't sure what prompted him to loiter near Alaine's desk near lunch time on that particular Monday. Alaine wasn't the type who'd have accompanied him in his former life. Back in his money days, he liked his women flashy and showy, the kind who made an instant statement when they entered a room by his side. This in no way described Alaine. Pretty enough with her light copper hair and fair skin, she looked a bit delicate for his tastes. Maybe he'd just needed a distraction.

Likewise, it wasn't Sam's customary style to approach a potential date with adolescent artlessness. But to his chagrin, this defined his method as he mumbled to her a lunch invitation.

"I beg your pardon?" Alaine asked. "I'm sorry, I'm afraid I didn't—"

Her voice was low. So low he almost asked her to repeat her response.

"I was asking if maybe you'd like to join me for lunch? We might grab something out on the concourse? You could choose the place?"

His sentences ended as questions. This was not going well.

The Sam he'd been before his fall from economic and social power would have approached this simple transaction with arrogant confidence, expecting enthusiastic acceptance of his attentions. That Sam took for granted welcome by the young women to whom he showed interest, and by many to whom he didn't.

He knew the appeal of his six feet plus stature and his longish black hair slicked back and curling at the ends over his shirt collars. He understood the power of a well-placed wink from his smoky gray eyes. He got it that he was better than average looking, but he also suspected his popularity had once been well supported by a high end wardrobe and six figure salary.

That was the other Sam...but not this one. This Sam's confidence with women was off, his wardrobe was getting threadbare and his salary had suffered appreciably. It came, then, as no surprise when Alaine declined his invitation.

What did surprise him was the way she declined. Alaine, who rarely made eye contact with anyone, met his eyes for several seconds before responding so hushed he was forced to bend toward her to hear.

"Sam, that's the nicest and most tempting offer I've gotten in a long time. I would love to go with you, but please understand, I can't. I'm...engaged. Please don't ask me again." She was almost whispering now. "Trust me; if I went with you, I could--we could both be in--that would never work."

It was a long speech for Alaine. Sam had never heard her say more than about a three-word sentence. Immediately following its delivery, she reverted to the silent and unpretentious office assistant who avoided any hint of personal connection. He was at a loss for how to react. She'd given him a compliment and a rebuff. Without saying so, she'd also begged that he would understand her unexplained circumstances and make allowances for her behavior. That was odd.

So was his uncharacteristic response...he who normally made caring overtures to no one.

"Is there something--?" he started. She shook her head.

"Look, if there's anything--"

"No." She shook her head again. "There isn't. But thank you."

I think she's as miserable as I am, Sam talked to himself as he walked back to his own workspace. *We have that in common. This guy, her fiancé, must be a real jerk and maybe a dangerous jerk.*

# # #

Sam MacDonald hated how he made his living. He despised the early morning ritual of dark suits, white shirts and Dolce & Gabbana conservative, understated ties, which he now considered to be overpriced on his current budget. He hated his stylish but uncomfortable shoes. Sam especially detested the "*I'm-so-excited-to-be-working-here!"* hype and the stale challenges from management to stay on top of his game.

It didn't start out that way. There was a time when responding with "Investment broker" when questioned about his profession sounded edgy and seductive, even to himself. Especially to himself. It hinted at secret deals, insider knowledge, and big money. Terms like *hit the bid, paying for Beta,* and *levering up* rolled like oil slick off of his tongue, and he could *go long* or *go short* with the best of them. It was exciting back when he was lean and hungry, aggressive and ruthless--eager to live the life and make his mark.

And make his mark he did, back then, in the form of hard-hitting investments for his clients yielding healthy stashes for himself. He could do no wrong. When the profits seemed endless, his ears itched with epithets like *Bright Spark...High Flier... Wunderkind.* Excess was the word of the day, every day. The late nights, rich meals and nonstop partying gave even overindulgence a bad name.

Inevitably, it all went to his head...and to his decision-making ability. It didn't take many bad judgments, many miscalculations, to send both his rising star reputation and his bank account headed south.

The prestigious investment firm position gave way to a job he'd barely managed to get with a questionable company that charged its clients outrageous fees for mediocre service. When the status went, so did the confidence, the self-respect and the reason to care...about anything.

Still, he had to eat. So he went every day, faithfully, to the job he hated in the dark suit, white shirt, conservative, understated tie and shoes that hurt.

# # #

Alaine

Alaine Albert's most important goal in the office was not to call attention to herself. Due both to an innate shyness and purposeful reserve, she simply tried to be as invisible as possible. While she rarely initiated conversation with her office mates, she made sure her work skills and performance were unquestionable. Her inconspicuous capability became the wall that protected her from unwanted male advances and discouraged gossip-prone females from getting too close.

These facts, coupled with her tendency to avoid eye contact, were enough to cause all but the most imperceptive co-workers to steer clear. Therefore, Alaine had few she could even count as acquaintances in what she referred to, sarcastically to herself, as the Tann & Leisch *family*. She kept the few at a distance and all interactions on the surface. About the most personal conversations she was privy to were ones she overheard describing herself beginning, "She has a nice face..." and ending "...a sad but nice face."

She worked as an office assistant to an unlikeable man who had been with the company longer and was openly more loyal than most to its questionable practices. Because Sam MacDonald's assistant, one he shared with another broker, was on maternity leave, Alaine had been ordered to assist him when her time wasn't taken.

She considered Sam one of the safer men in the office. He was polite, considerate and, unlike her own boss, always a gentleman. Their encounters, brief and professional, failed to make her as nervous as those with other male coworkers.

But beyond recognizing his niceness and his business-like demeanor, she barely thought of him at all. She didn't dare allow herself to even consider getting to know him better, given the...difficulties posed by her current relationship.

# # #

Sampson

It wasn't just the job Sam loathed. He was surrounded by an office of co-workers who related to each other with caution and suspicion. There was no visible hostility, rather a subtle sense of paranoia and mistrust. On the surface, the obligatory social exchanges were in place, barely, but he felt no sense of functioning together for a common interest. There was no common interest, only individuals co-existing, each solely for his or her self-interest.

All except for Alaine Albert.

In her, he saw a trace of beauty without it being overpowering. She came across unworldly in the midst of feigned sophistication. Something genuine and soft caused her to stand out in contrast to most of the other women, young women displaying a cheaper version of trendy New York City cool. A vulnerability drew Sam, but he also sensed a melancholy making Alaine's quiet manner even more mysterious. That, and the vulnerability, made Sam give her a second thought.

Sam noticed details making him suspicious that circumstances of her life might not be good...details like darkened marks that appeared periodically on her arms, slowly yellowing over time before disappearing...details like the way she avoided personal references and close relationships. The more reticent Alaine grew, the more intrigued Sam became about why she shrank from personal scrutiny.

Sam was embarrassed for even bothering with the bumbling invitation she had refused earlier. She wasn't, after all, that special, was she? It had to be something else. Truth was, he was bored and disillusioned in general. Even a slight preoccupation with what someone else's dilemma might be gave a measure of relief to the monotony that was his own life.

At twenty-eight, he wasn't supposed to be working with this B-level firm with its questionable system of preying on the ignorant and the old. This was not what he anticipated five years back when he graduated with a master's degree from a prestigious business school and began sending his resume out to all the right investment firms.

The fact that he'd held the gold ring and all its perks, if only briefly, made matters worse. He'd tasted the best, and now its loss was bitter to his palate. Brief success was worse than no success. If only he hadn't--if only he had--

One day at this job now followed another without appeal or engagement other than to complete the tasks before him as quickly and efficiently as possible, lest he would find himself the victim of his own carelessness, resulting in another search for a position even less palatable than the present one. There were few noteworthy moments, and the ones that did come were only barely noteworthy.

For that reason alone, Sam's actions, after returning from a hurried and solitary lunch, were egregious in hindsight, even to him. Sometime during the afternoon, an old gentleman walked in with the assistance of a cane and was conducted to Sam's desk. Sam rose to greet him.

"Ben Ledford here, young man."

"Sampson MacDonald. Please have a seat. What can I do for you this afternoon, Mr. Ledford?"

By way of response, the old man handed Sam twelve, letter-length, yellowed envelopes. When Sam opened the first envelope, he counted ten one-hundred-dollar bills...a thousand dollars.

"They're all the same, young man. All twelve of them. Twelve thousand dollars in all." The old man smiled. "I got the name of your company off of the Internet. I like the promises you made. I know you people will invest my funds wisely and carefully, as they represent most of my savings." He reached across the desk, shook Sam's hand again and thanked him in advance for help in growing his little piles of money.

It was clear this was a man used to keeping his savings under his mattress until now. Sam could always tell when he had a novice client with no sharp edges, the easiest kind.

"We'll do our best, sir. We pride ourselves in taking care of our clients as we would our families here at Tann & Leisch Investments."

Getting cash from a client was rare. Usually investments came as checks, rollovers, other means of funds transfers, but not cash. Twelve thousand dollars...one hundred and twenty bills of a hundred dollars each in twelve envelopes...lay on Sam's desk.

An idea took root that surprised and appalled him. Almost without thinking, he acted on it.

A glance at the old man found him fumbling for his dropped cane on the floor beside of his chair. Sam's hands moved so fast, so smoothly, he was absolutely certain no one saw him secret the envelopes into the pocket of his suit coat.

Sam shuffled the necessary paperwork related to the transaction back and forth. By the time the old man was ready to leave with a glossy portfolio filled with confidence-building but virtually undecipherable pamphlets of projections and upward curving trend lines, Sam had covered his tracks.

Following a final handshake, the investor was gone. Sam sat motionless and quiet for some time, pretending to study a manual open on his desk. In actuality he was arguing sides of the ethics battle raging within him.

After all, by his previous standards, Sam was underpaid and underappreciated on this job. All the stress and overtime with no compensation...his company owed him a debt. This was his chance to make good on his collection.

It wasn't like it was pre-meditated theft. This was the only time he'd ever done something like this. The money and the opportunity were just there. Sure, he'd stretched the boundaries of honesty in his work practices before, but not like this. By taking the old gentleman's twelve thousand dollar investment, he'd crossed over some line.

Sam had little regard for what the money could eventually buy, not that he couldn't use such a nest egg. While not quite broke, Sam had never been careful to follow his own investment advice and store away for the future, even when he was making big money. No, it was not so much the money as the ability to get back at the profession that nearly ruined him.

As he sat and mentally replayed the scene again and again, disgust grew for his act of petty thievery. What had he done? And more important, why had he done it?

He could read the headline: *Discredited Investment Broker Guilty of Crime of Convenience!* But that was crazy. His secret was safe. He'd made sure of that. He knew the power of confusing paperwork, double talk about acceptable risks and doctored account entries.

Sam shook off these thoughts. Without knowing why, in the same way he failed to understand why he took the money in the first place, he removed one of the cash envelopes from his coat pocket. To this envelop he attached an altered record of the transaction with a forged signature. He stood and walked across the office toward the alcove filled with potted ferns where a large wall safe was hidden behind an even larger framed watercolor of the East River.

After procuring the access key, Sam paused long enough beside Alaine's desk to alert her that he needed to be accompanied to the safe to accommodate the two-person rule for all safe deposits. She followed and watched as he put the envelope into the deposit folder, nodding when he checked to see if she noted his actions. He closed the safe and, as she watched, turned the tumbler and tried the door again. Locked. She nodded once more and walked back to her desk without speaking.

It was a routine transaction to any other observers, simply safekeeping a client's cash until a bank deposit could be made. He stepped out of the fern shrouded alcove, feeling strange about the actions he'd just performed, and returned the key.

He waited to speak until they were within hearing distance of others to help mark his movements and scanned the room to catch any undue attention. "Thank you for your assistance, Ms. Albert. Enjoy your evening." Nothing seemed to register with his potential audience in any way.

Alaine's, "You're welcome," was barely discernable, but the slight smile she gave him as she said it was one of the few he'd seen her offer.

For the first time in a long time, Sam left his job site in the World Trade Center's North Tower thinking about something other than his own problems. The focus of his thoughts was not on the old man with the envelopes. It was on Alaine Albert.

He was hard put to pinpoint why. She wouldn't stand out in a room full of beautiful women. If she had a personality worth noting, it was not evident so far. But there was something about her, some little spark of mystery, that gave him a reason to look forward to work on Tuesday, if only slightly.

# # #

Tann and Leisch Investment Services opened for business at 9:00 a.m., and the doors closed at 5:30 p.m. Because being early and staying late were considered virtues in the uphill climb to longevity with the company, most of the cubicles were filled, with little evident enthusiasm, by 8:30. Though Sam lacked ambition to claw his way toward the top of a company he held in contempt, he kept his opinion to himself and played the corporate game well. If his boss, Rupert Tann, arrived at 8:00 a.m., Sam came at 7:30.

To Sam's amusement and discomfort, the boss began coming in at 7:00, making Sam's nights short and his commutes to One World Trade Center even earlier. Still, on this Tuesday morning, he'd entered the office at 6:45, hurrying to his cubicle to make it appear he was on the job for hours when his boss arrived. It had become a sport, one he believed he would eventually lose, but one that, nevertheless, provided a momentary diversion.

By 8:30 a.m., Sam already felt caged and restless, and the official workday hadn't even started yet. He'd never last to 5:30. He made a trip to the men's room and poured yet another cup of coffee in the break room, the only discernable perk available at this company.

One of Sam's pleasures, and they were pitiful and few of late, was to stand at the large expanse of glass windows comprising the walls of the massive office structure and gaze out over the panorama of the City, as he did on this Tuesday morning. He never stopped feeling vertigo from the exercise; he never stopped feeling a sense of his own insignificance when he saw the geography of The Big Apple spread around him. But he was moth-drawn to continue looking as he held his cup of bitter coffee and thought about the endless, mind-numbing day ahead of him.

With reluctance, Sam turned from the windows to confine himself within the cell of his cubicle when he heard a shout from somewhere across the room.

"It's coming straight for us!"

Unable to pinpoint the source of the uncharacteristic disturbance in the normally silent office, Sam moved once more toward the windows, squinting now into the brightness.

One moment the sun's light was alive in the ice blue sky. The next moment a shadow blocked the light as if a great bird bore down from on high.

The shadow of what?

The thought had barely come when the building gave an immense shudder that dashed the lukewarm coffee onto Sam's once-crisp white shirt as it tossed him across the potted plants near the windows and slammed him to the floor.

Spread-eagled on the dark gray carpet with his face burning from its contact when he fell, Sam felt a rush of vertigo as the building began to roll from side to side like a giant tree responding to a mighty wind.

Sam held his breath and waited for his demise.

So this, then, is to be the end? Am I to die in humiliation in a place I despise with people I hold in contempt?

The rocking continued for seconds that lasted forever. When the building stabilized, the bitter taste of coffee, or horror, mixed with blood in Sam's mouth. He was surprised to find he was still alive with only a cut lip from his own tooth and a rug-burned face to show for his hard fall.

The shadow was a plane.

As if answering his own question from seconds before, the thought shook him as he pushed to his feet. *An airplane has hit the building.*

As incomprehensible as it sounded, Sam knew it was true. He remembered the shout, "It's coming straight for us!"

He also knew...maybe from instinct...that to hesitate, to wait, was to die.

Sam took in his surroundings for the first time since the impact. Already, a stifling, noxious smell permeated the air. The once undistinguished but orderly office space was now in shambles. The detested cubicles were twisted bits of metal and fabric. Papers and debris littered the floor and the lights were off. Strangest of all were unexpected breezes coming from windows no longer there to separate conditioned air from that outside in the City.

His office mates, the ones he could see standing, began shouting to each other to understand what just happened. A further glance told him there were others who would never shout again.

He had to get out. He had to go now. Instinct again told him elevators would be too slow or impassible. *The stairs, find the stairs. Do it now!*

And then Sam saw Alaine. She was sitting on the floor behind her desk, covering her head with her arms. Her eyes were closed, and she held a small purse in one hand. In the other, she clutched a stapler, as if it were a life raft. She crouched like she warded off some invisible terror armed with only these weapons. Sam took the stapler from her as gently as he could in the hurry he was in and met her just-opened eyes.

"Come with me now. We have to go."

Without waiting for a response, he took her hand, helped her to her feet and began to run, pulling her toward the exit to the hall. A doorway from their office was near one of the stairways to the ground. Sam knew it was a long way down and their time was short. He pushed open the heavy door to the stairwell and dragged Alaine along behind him with a death grip on her wrist as they joined hundreds of their building mates on a race to the outside exits of the World Trade Center's North Tower.

Sam glanced at his watch. The time was just before 9:00 a.m. on September 11, 2001.

The actual descent from the 87th floor of the North Tower took forty-five minutes. The memories of those minutes would be largely lost to Sam, who moved as a machine as fast as his breathing and the crowd around him allowed. All the while he led, and sometimes nearly carried, a terrified and incoherent Alaine. His only thought, his only goal, was to rid them both of the smothering confines of the structure he feared would be their tomb.

At first, the group with which they descended was oddly silent. The sounds of occasional sobbing broke through his daze, but early on, there was no panic, no hysteria. New fellow travelers, joining them on their sometimes rapid and often snail-like downward journey, offered snatches of fresh and horrifying information.

"It was a bomb on the 100th floor. Everyone up there is dead."

"No, it wasn't a bomb. It was a plane. A very large plane."

And later, "The South Tower was hit, too...20 minutes ago. It was no accident either."

"I think it was terrorists."

"I think it's the end of the world. The Bible says--"

Each added wave of escapees, each piece of news or theory about what was happening brought a heightened sense of desperation and increased alarm to those on the long journey down.

The smells alone brought eye-stinging and gagging misery. The heat was intense, and some of the crowd began to shed pieces of clothing as they plodded along. The steps were wet with who knew what liquids...jet fuel, urine, blood, tears of the angels? From the condition of some of his fellow-travelers, Sam knew that only the angels could help them survive.

While their downward movement stalled to admit still others escaping from lower floors, Sam felt Alaine sag and begin to pull him down. One look told him she was exhausted and on the verge of passing out. Instead of lowering her to rest on the steps below them, a move that may have sealed their fate, he clamped his left arm around her waist, pulled her head to his chest and whispered directly in her ear.

"You will not give up. We will not die here. Open your eyes and breathe. Move your feet now. I will not leave you here to die."

Though a violent shudder went through her body in response, at that moment, the movement of the people downward began again, and Alaine moved her feet with them.

When it became clear that leaders on the stairs in front of them had reached the exit door to the lobby, near panic broke out as that final obstacle to life and freedom jammed for several horrifying moments. Whether from the sheer brute force of the crowd or because whatever gods there might be heard the curses and screams and tears of the people, Sam didn't know or care. But finally, the door from the stairwell cleared, pouring the contents of its travelers into the lobby of the North Tower.

Men and women, firm and some severely infirm, who walked down seventy, eighty, even ninety floors and thought they could go no further broke into shouts and what sounded like prayers as they headed for the outside walkways and freedom from their prison.

But the shouts that greeted them from the guards, policemen and firemen swarming the lobby chilled their euphoria, made them glance around in terror and break into a run, were they able.

"Get out! Get out of the building! Move now to the outside exits. Don't stop for anything!"

The news on the street was no better. They looked to the sky and held up their hands to shield themselves from fireballs, unidentified objects and all manner of toxic wreckage that swirled around them. Their brains barely registered the unspeakable sights in their pathways.

"The Pentagon. They got the Pentagon! Oh, God, Jesus, help us!"

Sam, from nervous habit, looked at his watch. It was 9:55 a.m. At 9:56, the South Tower began to fall, collapsing in on itself and spewing gray dust and debris in a fury some likened to Armageddon.

Sam became a madman. Crazed by his desire to be rid of the smothering, sickening holocaust that now surrounded the hated place where he'd but recently made his living, he moved his body and Alaine's as far and fast as he could go away from the burning cauldron he knew lay behind.

He dismissed all concern for the effects on their bodies of the desperate flight that had now taken them almost two hours. Without thinking beyond immediate survival, walking and running in no particular direction other than away and oblivious to his pain and Alaine's sobbing, he moved them forward.

2 SANCTUARY

Sampson

By the time the North Tower fell at 10:28 a.m., Sam and Alaine had covered a lot of ground. As if by a miracle, only he didn't believe in such, they finally stumbled into the lobby of a small hotel in lower Manhattan. Obviously old and visibly shabby, the Hotel Salima appeared reputable, as if that mattered here at the end of the world. Again, miraculously, the hotel was still open with vacant rooms. They had come just twenty-two blocks from the spot Sam now heard called *Ground Zero*.

He settled a dazed and confused Alaine in one of the rooms where he left her alone only after insisting, as if she were a child, that she shower immediately.

She, like he, wore the gray powder that covered everything for blocks. He didn't know exactly what the powder was, but it couldn't be good for them. He stood outside of the bathroom door to make sure she did it and didn't pass out during the process. He could hear her retching behind the closed door.

When Alaine finally emerged wearing a towel and a confused look, Sam steered her to her bed, covered her and turned off the lights. It was impossible to believe that little more than two hours ago, this had been a normal fall Tuesday morning with the sun shining, the sky blue and the air clear. No more. Maybe never again.

He moved through the door to his adjoining room, closing it behind him so as not to disturb Alaine's exhausted sleep. He turned on the TV. Terrorists.

Attacks on both towers of the Trade Center, both of which were now gone. An attack on the Pentagon. A plane down in a field in Pennsylvania. Not the end of the world, but almost as bad.

He couldn't follow his own advice to shower. He was simply too tired. Sam fell asleep across the bed in the small hotel with his rumpled conservative suit covered in the ash and debris from an event that, before it was over, would take the lives of God only knew how many people. He knew he would sleep hard, as if he'd joined them.

# # #

Sometime during the late afternoon, Sam woke with a headache and an awful taste in his mouth. He was hungry and thirsty, hot and uncomfortable. His feet ached. His whole body hurt. By the time he finished running through his list of physical complaints, he remembered where he was and why.

Wiping his hand across his face reminded Sam of the ash rain from the crumbling buildings. He still wore his clothes and those awful shoes, had slept in them for hours. He hadn't eaten since early morning, and his head had a thousand reasons to pound. Did the events of the morning happen in reality, or was his condition the result of some overindulgence and a bad dream?

Sam pulled himself up against protesting muscles and throbbing temples and turned up the TV. A visibly shaken reporter somewhere on the street as near as possible to what she called Ground Zero reviewed the timeline of the morning.

"At 8:45 a.m. Eastern Daylight Time a hijacked American Airlines Boeing 767, Flight 11, hit the North Tower of the World Trade Center in downtown Manhattan. By 9:03 a.m. another hijacked airliner, United Airlines Boeing 767, Flight 175, hit the Trade Center's South Tower. At 9:43 a.m. American Airlines Flight 77 crashed into the Pentagon in Washington, DC. By 9:50 a.m. the South Tower collapsed due to structural damage sustained from the impact. At 10:10 a.m. United Airlines Flight 93, presumed to be headed toward a target in

Washington DC, crashed in a rural area of Pennsylvania. By 10:30 a.m. the North Tower also collapsed. Scores of rescue and emergency medical workers are on scene to assist in the rescue and recovery efforts."

It was painful and clear that the morning had not been a hallucination. The horrors had happened in real time. In his heart, Sam knew from what he saw when the South Tower fell that there would be little rescue and maybe not much recovery.

"God, help them. God help us all." His own audible words to no one surprised Sam, who hadn't considered God in any form for ages.

And then he remembered Alaine in the next room. Hours had passed since he left her asleep. Would she still be there? Would she be alive?

He walked to the adjoining door and pushed it open enough to look in. She was there, smaller than he remembered and in a fetal position under the covers just as he left her. He didn't think she'd moved. She looked dead.

If she is, I can't help her now. I don't have any words of comfort to give her. Truthfully, I don't have any comfort to spare. Besides, I have to get cleaned up. Sam often methodically self-talked his way through hard situations. This would qualify.

He dropped his clothes on the bathroom floor and showered for at least half an hour in the hottest water he could stand.

I'm washing the dust of 110 floors off of my body. I'm washing off the cells of a thousand people. The shower may have lasted an hour; he really didn't care. There was nothing to do but re-dress in his dusty clothes, so he did the best he could to rid his pants of their distasteful covering. He put them on but left his coat lying where it fell. And the blasted shoes. *This is the last time. The last time.*

# # #

Alaine

When Sam finally got back to Alaine's room, she was awake and sat with her back against the headboard. She smiled as he entered.

"I was afraid you were dead. You looked dead." Sam didn't smile back as he spoke.

She laughed at his words, without joy, but she laughed. It came out as a hoarse croak. "No, I survived. And you did. How did you get us here? It's hard to remember. Is this a hotel? Are we still in the City?"

Her voice had obviously suffered.

"We walked. Together, you and I walked all the way from the Trade Center. Twenty-two blocks. I counted. It's gone, you know. Both towers gone."

"What? ...What do you mean *gone*?"

"Terrorists hit the towers with planes. The towers went down, the South first and ours next. The Pentagon was hit, too. There's more. It's bad, but you should know. Do you remember any of it?"

By now, tears slipped from her eyes. She shook her head.

"Not much. Just snatches. You pulled me up. You kept pulling and wouldn't stop. I remember walking...couldn't feel my feet. I begged you to let me rest. You refused. You hurt me, you know? I wanted to lie down and die in the street."

"But you didn't. We made it. No way we can leave here now. We should stay put until we're sure it's safe to move around. Then I'll take you home."

Alaine sat up straighter with a jerk, her pulse racing with fear.

"Not home, Sam. I won't go home. I don't know what else I'm going to do, but I'm not going back there."

Up to this point, he stood by her bed. At these words, he turned away to open the curtains closed earlier against the sun. As soon as the late afternoon outside light hit them, Sam closed the curtains again and reached to turn on the dresser light. He eased himself into a chair and made no audible reply.

"Sam?" It came as a whisper. "Did you hear what I said?"

"I heard."

More time passed.

"I can't go back home. He can think I'm dead, that's all. I can't go." It was so hard to talk that she wasn't sure he heard her over the hum of the air conditioner.

"Who's at home that you can't go back to?"

"The man I live with. Paul Mowher. We're not--I'm not--" She didn't finish.

"Married? I didn't think so. You said you were engaged."

"That was the nicest way I could put it. It wasn't true. He never asked me."

"What do you mean you can't go back? What is he to you? Are you in danger from him?"

Alaine slipped once more into a fetal position on her bed. She turned her back to him and started to sob. Not quiet, lady-like sobs but great, wracking ones that shook the bed and gave her trouble catching her breath.

Again, Sam didn't speak. Instead he ran warm water onto a washcloth in her bathroom, sat on the edge of the bed and bathed her face. It was something her mother had done, and it used to help, long ago.

After a while, she quieted and they sat silent while the afternoon wore on.

"I'm hungry, Sam. Are you hungry?"

He must have dozed sitting straight up. At her words, she watched him startle and stand up, as if to cover his embarrassment.

"It's been a long time since breakfast. Are you OK for me to go see what I can find?"

# # #

Sampson

It took a while to locate a place that was open and served take out that seemed suitable. Sam wasn't that familiar with the part of the city where they were, and most everything was closed anyway. Not that it mattered, but Sam didn't know her tastes, her likes or dislikes in food or what she could eat. He finally settled on deli sandwiches, bottled juice and some packaged things he thought wouldn't spoil for a while.

On his way back with his bags of food, he passed a small discount store that was about to close. By making some wild guesses and quick decisions, he gathered enough personal provisions and changes of clothes to get them through a couple of days, if not in the best of fashion. Sam hadn't bought ladies' things before except high-end jewelry in the old days or sweaters and bathrobes for his mother. A kind clerk offered help without commentary and made the job easier. He went home with his arms full for not much money, considering.

Home. Two rooms in an old hotel. Why did he call it home? Sam's most recent digs were rented rooms at the Lettie Baker Boarding House in Queens, an hour from downtown.

Alaine? He still didn't know where she lived or much about with whom.

When he entered his room with his purchases, he was met by the pinched and swollen face of Alaine. Still wrapped in the towel, he could tell she'd been crying again.

"I thought you were gone. It took you so long. I knew you weren't coming back."

"I'm here now, Alaine. I don't know my way around this part of the City, and I'm on foot. Not much is open. I stopped for food and some stuff we need. We're staying put for now. Unless you want --"

"No." The answer came before he finished. "I'm sorry. Thank you, Sam. You brought food?"

It might have been Christmas, complete with packages of presents and the simple feast Sam managed to find. A nightgown for Alaine. Toothbrushes. Underwear and simple clothes to last them a few days. Last he brought new non-work shoes for them both. Sam wore his, having left his old and uncomfortable ones in a dumpster in an alley. He brought things to show they survived and hoped to do so for at least another day, regardless of what had happened in this one.

After dressing in their new sweats, they attacked the meager fare. Questions hung in all of their quiet moments for which there was no energy to find answers. As soon as they finished the meal, Sam saw Alaine was fading, and he was near exhaustion.

"Sam, I think I need to tell you--"

Whatever it was had to wait.

"Not tonight. Tomorrow is good enough. Do you think you can rest now?"

"I think so. I'll try. I feel safe here. Thank you."

He closed the door between their rooms and readied for his own rest without returning to the television. Enough of that for now. He hoped he could feel safe here, too. He wasn't sure whether he'd ever feel safe again.

Just before sleep took him, Sam started awake and remembered he wouldn't be going to work tomorrow. There was no place to work anymore, only a big, toxic, smoking void. The relief he felt at not having to return to the demeaning world of his company was instantly offset by a profound revulsion for the events that freed him from his job. It was not the way he wanted to leave even the most disgusting of positions.

# # #

For four days Sam and Alaine cocooned quietly, in a state of semi-shock, in their two-room refuge only a handful of blocks away from the frantic beehive of around-the-clock activity that was the site of the late Twin Towers. They subsisted on junk food or take-outs Sam gleaned from brief, daily forages into a Manhattan that felt and smelled and sounded so unlike itself. A war zone he often heard it called from the TV.

Sam's movements outside were quick and alert, not unlike those of a soldier on patrol in enemy territory. He made surgical strikes to purchase their food and other needs, always avoiding personal engagement but ever listening to news from the City: which bridges and tunnels were open or closed, which streets were cordoned off or areas evacuated, which means of transportation were shut down or running. He moved, zombie like, collecting and sorting information that might be needed later. He hadn't begun to think of later.

By evening on September 14, after four days of talking little, thinking less, and resting for hours at a time, Sam began to feel small stirrings of renewed interest in life. He had faint flashes of hope that there would be a world out there to return to and weak, but real, desires to find it again.

It would soon be time to decide what he and Alaine must do, together or separately. The discussions they'd avoided would have to happen, the questions asked and answered by each. What would come next?

After dinner from the Chinese restaurant three blocks away and eaten on the round hotel table in Alaine's room, their makeshift dining area, Sam watched her tidy up as she might have in her own kitchen.

"Did you like it? I didn't even ask if you like Chinese," he said, as she wrapped the remains in the take-out bag, twisted the top shut and disposed of it in the bathroom.

"Yes, thank you. It was fine, really." The amount she ate belied her answer.

She avoided eye contact again as she had done, increasingly, since coming to the hotel. She talked little, answering when spoken to but with as few words and breath expended as possible, much like she did at her job. Her greatest outlay of energy always came through the fear she showed when he left her alone or came back later than she expected from one of his forays to the outside world.

That's the way he came to think of their circumstances, the outside world versus their safe hideout.

"Sam, I have a question for you."

This surprised him, the fact that she initiated communication on her own.

"Sure. What is it?"

"Do you believe in God? I mean someone out there bigger and wiser than we are? Do you?"

Alaine's eyes were large and dark. They had circles underneath, despite that she'd slept most of the past week. And they were scared. That she turned to him for strength and answers was an indication, to Sam, of how desperate she must be.

"I really don't know, Alaine. At one time I thought I did...when I was a lot younger. Now, I really don't much care either way. What about you?"

"I did...until last Tuesday. Where was God last Tuesday?"

Alaine started to moan. Wrapping her arms around her midsection, she sat down on the edge of her bed and rocked.

Sam didn't know what to do. He had no idea what to tell her.

He bent down, moved her further onto the bed, and helped her lie down, drawing the sheet over her and turning off the light over the bed, he pulled a chair close and sat with her. He didn't know how to help her mourn, so he waited.

He stayed near Alaine's bed long after she quieted, listening to her ragged intakes of breath even in sleep and thinking about her question. Maybe he would tell her, sometime, why God didn't figure in his life. He might tell her about his grandfather, who loved him, believed God was real and always took him to Sunday School.

The last time Sam was in a church was for his grandfather's funeral. He was nine. His parents had no interest in anything spiritual, so keeping up his attendance was not a priority. Besides, he was done with a God who would let his grandfather, the only one who seemed to give a care about him, die.

That was a long time ago before he became a successful stockbroker, before he fell from grace and had to take the job where they'd both worked. Like

Alaine, Sam couldn't explain why a God who reported to care about the events in human existence would allow the lives of hundreds of people to end in a horrendous dust cloud.

Sam was fairly sure, if God was real, He had left the buildings at One and Two World Trade Center a little before 9:00 a.m. on September 11, 2001.

After he left Alaine's bedside some time before midnight, he stood in his room and looked through the open curtains at the city lights reflecting against the night sky. It was time to leave the sanctuary where they had found refuge and rest. Staying any longer, so close to Ground Zero, wasn't a wise or healthy option. He was afraid Alaine would grow more morose and would eventually pull him down with her. They had to go.

Late into the night, he lay back on his pillows with his hands behind his head running over their various options. He had his rooms at the boarding house. He could always go back there. The rooms were furnished and also housed a few of his personal belongings. He didn't own much.

He knew nothing at all about Alaine except there was something bad going on with her boyfriend, something that made her frightened or ashamed...or both. It was obvious she wasn't planning to go back to him. As far as he knew, she hadn't tried to contact the man since coming to the hotel.

Despite his practice to avoid involvement in other people's lives, he needed to know where Alaine wanted to go next. For some reason, the thought that she might have somewhere else in mind made Sam uncomfortable. He wasn't used to thinking about anyone but himself. Over the last week, he'd had to consider what her needs were. It gave him a focus...a purpose he'd been without.

The idea of going alone back to the rooms at the boarding house wasn't inviting. He couldn't picture taking Alaine there either, even though his landlady usually had a vacancy. Maybe he needed some place different, somewhere away from a City that represented such failure for him.

In the midst of the dull, detestable existence that had become Sam's life, he'd often thought about just walking away. He'd gained some small pleasure from the idea that he could simply not show up at work one day, get on a plane or train and go...start over somewhere. He hadn't gotten as far as visualizing where, not that it mattered.

Sometime in the early morning of the fifth day after the fall of the World Trade Center, Sam realized the time for walking away from everything had come. Work was gone. Nothing and no one in his past life mattered enough to go back to. The ordeal of starting over couldn't be as bad as the effort it took to live his current life.

He didn't know where Alaine stood on any of this or how it would affect her. He knew he needed to get away to survive. Maybe she did, too. They'd have to talk...first thing in the morning.

# # #

Alaine

Alaine had been awake for hours. She'd been sick on her stomach several times. Now, one look in the bathroom mirror told her how pale she looked, and she felt even more listless than yesterday.

When Sam checked on her about 9:00 bringing breakfast, she was back in bed and feeling miserable.

"Alaine, I'm sorry. Afraid this is all I have to offer...day-old doughnuts and coffee."

When she turned away, a hand over her mouth, he set the food down and stood over her.

"Alaine, you're sick, aren't you? What can I do? Do you want me to find a doctor?"

"I feel awful. I'm sorry. I tried to hide it. But I just feel so bad."

Sam went out and came back with a Coke and a pack of cheese crackers. He poured Coke in a hotel cup and held her up to take some sips. He broke a cracker apart and gave her the half without the cheese. She knew Sam was doing all he knew to do.

"Tell me what hurts. What does it feel like?"

Not wanting to worry him further about her upset stomach, she turned her description in a different direction.

"Nothing really hurts. Not like my head or anything. It's...I think my mind hurts, Sam, and my insides hurt. I hurt so badly for all those thousands of people who didn't get out. I've seen their faces in pictures. I've heard their stories...their last words telling their families goodbye...knowing they were going to die. They could have been us, Sam. We could have been trapped there. I can't stand thinking about it anymore. It's making me crazy."

"How did you find out so much about what happened, Alaine? Not from me. I haven't told you any details. I didn't think you were ready to know that much about what happened yet."

"The TV. It's all over the TV. I watch it in the night when I can't sleep and during the day when you go out. There's nothing else on. Just the replays of the planes hitting and the towers coming down and the people running and screaming in the streets and jumping from the--" Her sobs stopped her.

"And now it's the searchers looking for the bodies. Looking and looking through that mountain of rubble with those hideous metal pieces sticking out. There won't be any bodies, Sam. Don't they know that? It was too horrible. There won't be any bodies."

Alaine cried while Sam sat on the edge of the bed with his head in his hands. He didn't try to touch her for comfort. She was glad because he couldn't reach where she hurt.

When she calmed, Sam told her they had to make some decisions. He opened her curtains for only the second time in five days and moved to a chair where she could see his face.

"We've been here almost a week. We both know that we can't stay. Anyway,

I'm headed to maxing my credit card and don't have a lot of back up in savings. I've been checking around, and I think we can get out of Manhattan now without any trouble."

Alaine sat up. The room wasn't cold, but she pulled the blanket close around her as if it were.

"I've been waiting for you to say that. I've been dreading to hear you say it. I'm scared to death to leave this place...and even more scared to stay," she whispered.

"Alaine, I have to know what you want to do, where you want to go."

She watched him without moving or talking. His voice sounded kind but neutral, like he didn't want to influence her response.

"Alaine, where do you live?"

"In an apartment on Long Island. Most of the time not alone. There's a man named Paul Mowher who comes and goes as he pleases. It's his apartment. I met him in the City, and we've been together a couple of years. At one time, I was sure I couldn't live without him."

She sounded, to herself, like a robot delivering the information. She hoped what she didn't say told Sam as much as what she did.

"Do you love him now?"

"I think I despise him. I know I'll never go back to that apartment. I want him to think I'm dead, that I died in the attacks. This is my only chance."

"Your only chance for what?"

"To leave him...to leave my life."

"Why do you want him to think you died?"

Silence again followed while she struggled with what to say.

"He's not a nice person, Sam. He's obsessively jealous and controlling. If he knew I'm alive and have been with you all this time, I don't know what he'd do. The fact that you rescued me and took care of me would mean nothing. We'd both be in trouble. He's smart and thinks everyone else isn't, especially me. He has a way about him that keeps people from seeing who he really is. I just want to be free."

She stopped and stared at Sam with narrowed eyes as if trying to see into what he was thinking. His face was unreadable.

"You're about to tell me you're leaving here, aren't you? If you want to go alone, then go. I won't try to stop you, and I won't beg you to take me with you. I'll find a shelter and go there. I'll sleep on the street or under a bridge. I will not go back to that apartment."

Alaine lay back in the bed and closed her eyes. Her speech, a long one for her, left her exhausted.

Sam stood up and walked to the window. Without turning around, he spoke.

"It's about 10:00 now. Check-out time is 11:00. We don't have much to pack. If we hurry, we can be ready to leave in time. I'll do what you don't feel like doing. We have to go somewhere. We can go together and worry later about where. We'll find someplace."

Sam turned to find her sitting up and watching him.

"Do you feel like getting dressed? Maybe a warm shower would help?"

"I'll be ready," was all she answered. At least he wasn't leaving without her.

# # #

Sampson

Sam's packing was brief. Over the past week he'd unconsciously prepared for this. He'd picked up enough cheap clothes and personal supplies to last them for a while and two duffle bags for everything they needed to carry, which wasn't much.

He found the suit he wore on September 11th lying on the floor of the closet. He'd tossed it there trying to decide what to do with it. It seemed a waste to throw it away. The suit was a Hickey Freeman left over from his glory days.

He'd paid $1500 for it. Maybe he should leave the suit in the room for somebody from housekeeping.

He picked up the coat to put it on a hanger and felt something bulky in the breast pocket. Until he held the yellowed envelopes in his hand, he'd forgotten they were there...the old man's money. He'd worn the same suit for his last two days at work before the planes hit, but the events that followed had overridden the knowledge that he was a thief. He now held the evidence in his hand.

Unable to deal with this truth, Sam crammed the envelopes to the bottom of his duffle bag and made a quick trip down to the dumpster in the alley behind the hotel with the suit. The suit was unsalvageable. He hoped he wasn't.

Sam made two phone calls while he waited for Alaine to get ready. One was to his landlady in Queens. He intended to tell her he was alive and would send the money to cover the cost of cleaning out his rooms. When she didn't answer, he hung up and phoned for a taxi. Their destination would be the Port Authority Bus Terminal on 8th Avenue in midtown Manhattan.

By the time Sam opened the adjoining room's door to check on Alaine, she'd showered, dressed in a running suit and tennis shoes, and was sitting on the bed with her purse and duffle bag beside her.

As he reached for her bag, she stood and gave the room one last look. Sam understood her reluctance to leave the refuge. He felt it too, but he also knew it was time to move.

"Let's go. The taxi's waiting."

Alaine didn't talk at all as they rode the several blocks from the Lower East Side to the bus station. The Port Authority Bus Terminal was a busy place any time. The post September 11th terminal was worse due to re-routed traffic patterns and heavy security. It was 12:30 p.m. before they entered the station, which didn't really matter as they had no tickets and no destination.

"Sam," her voice was low and quiet at his side, "where are we going?"

He smiled down at her, he hoped with confidence.

“I have no idea. Let’s go see.”

They found a travel information kiosk where a young man took in stride their naïve questions about what bus lines, of the three dozen available, went where.

He also didn’t look suspicious when, in answer to his question about their destination, Sam said, “We want to go someplace quiet to spend some quality time together. Maybe somewhere in Virginia. Do you have a list of destinations for...say...Greyhound to Virginia? We don’t really care, as long as it’s rural and peaceful.”

When Sam put his arm around Alaine and drew her close to lend credence to his request for any suitable destination, he felt her stiffen and draw back slightly. He covered with words directed to her but spoken so that their young helper could hear.

“Isn’t that right, darling? After the week we’ve all had, we just want to get out of town for a while.”

The young man responded on cue. “I certainly understand. I think this brochure will be of assistance. Greyhound serves a number of smaller Virginia communities. You might find one that interests you. Let’s see...Woodbridge, Farmville, Lynchburg, South Boston, Copper’s Run, Oak Hall...”

Sam made an executive decision he hoped he wouldn’t regret.

“Copper’s Run. Sounds good. Let’s try that one. Now if you will point us in the direction of the Greyhound ticket area, we thank you for your help.”

Alaine was feeling sick again, and he steered her toward the women’s lounge. When she came out, her pinched white face affirmed his fears. It was clear she wasn’t in good shape, and Sam could only hope that getting her out of the City would help.

The next bus to Copper’s Run by way of a number of other stops departed at 4:00 p.m. To kill time until then, they ate sub sandwiches and people watched. At least he ate and watched. Alaine shrank as small as she could beside him, making herself nearly invisible. She nibbled a few bites but mostly kept her eyes closed and her head resting on the back of the booth.

By departure time, Sam was having second thoughts about his impulsive choice of destination. Alaine's fingers, when he reached for her hand to lead her across the terminal, were cold and tense.

The bus trip from New York City to Copper's Run, Virginia, a place he'd never heard of, would take them almost 24 hours and 350 plus miles with all the stops. It would be good rest time for Alaine. Within ten minutes of finding a seat near the rear of their bus, she was asleep.

# # #

About half way, and sometime in the middle of the night, Sam woke with the realization that both his name and Alaine's might already appear on some missing and presumed dead list in the aftermath of the collapse of the Trade Center buildings. Was it illegal to keep it that way? Sam didn't know. He was sure no one would be trying to cash in any life insurance policy on him. He didn't have one. But what about Alaine? Getting quietly out of the City was one thing. Going to jail for fraud or faking one's death or whatever the charges might be was another. That possibility was not the sort of starting over he had in mind.

When the bus made a brief stop at a small town terminal the next morning, Sam ate a quick breakfast with Alaine and told her he had to make a phone call. He put her back in their seats with fifteen minutes to spare to make the call from the phone booth before the bus pulled out.

By the time he was finally able to reach someone at the New York City Police Department who understood what he was trying to say about possible missing persons who were not really missing, he was sweating through his tee shirt. His head was pounding, and it was three minutes before the bus would pull out.

"Sir, let me just clarify what you're telling me. Your name is Sampson MacDonald...spelled MACDONALD, you worked for a company in the

North Tower of the Trade Center, and you were able to exit safely on September 11th. Is that correct, sir?"

"Yes, and a co-worker got out, too. Her name is Alaine Albert. No, that's Alaine with an A. We got out at the same time, so I know she's safe.

"And may I ask the address where you are currently residing, Mr. MacDonald, and a number where you can be reached for our records?"

"I don't have either, at the moment. I've left the City. I'm en route to my new home, but there's no address yet. And no cell phone number, either. This is a pay phone."

"How can you be reached after you arrive, sir?"

"I'm sorry, I can't be. I also don't know where Ms. Albert will be living. I understand she is also moving away from the City. I can't give you any more information about where to reach her."

Sam's watch showed the bus would leave him in two minutes.

"Mr. MacDonald, it's very important that I have more—"

"Look, I appreciate your concern and your need to ask. I just wanted someone to know that these two people who were possibly on your missing persons list from September 11 are no longer missing. They're alive. I'm confirming that. That's all. Sorry, I have to go now."

He hung up as she was saying, "Please don't hang--," and he swung on board just as Alaine was struggling with their hand luggage, about to get off of the bus herself. She was quietly hysterical.

Sam steered her and their baggage back down the aisle to their seats. He folded his arms around her, hunching them both down and trying to be as inconspicuous as possible. When he glanced at his fellow passengers, it was clear he had failed. Heads turned away when he made eye contact, confirming they were the subject of curious scrutiny.

Alaine was silent with her panic, but her body shook nevertheless. It took him some time to get her to speak.

"Alaine, where were you going? What were you doing?"

"I...I thought you had...left me. I didn't think...you were coming back. I didn't know what--"

Talking was obviously too hard for her, so he just held her, saying calming things he couldn't believe himself.

"Shhhh, I didn't leave. I'll tell you later what I was doing. We'll be OK. You'll see. I won't leave you. Not until you're ready."

This last phrase brought fresh tears.

Alaine slept most of the day, her head on Sam's shoulder, rousing only to eat or be sick in the cramped restroom. By the time the bus pulled into Copper's Run, Virginia at 5:07 p.m., September 16th, they were worn out, disheveled and Sam still had no plan for how to proceed in their new town.

3 COPPER'S RUN

Sampson

It took them exactly four minutes to disembark and watch the Greyhound, their only tie to New York City besides their memories, pull away. It left them standing in front of a tiny bus station with evening only a couple of hours off.

There was, at least, someone still at the ticket counter obviously readying the place for closing when they entered the waiting room. The Copper's Run Greyhound station looked, to Sam, like the setting of a 1950s movie about a couple trying to escape their parents by eloping on a bus.

Sam saw that Alaine was oblivious to anything but her fatigue and discomfort. He deposited her and their few belongings on one of the two waiting area benches. There wasn't even a snack bar. Sam stepped up to the counter.

"Good evening, I wonder if you could tell me whether this town has a motel, and if so, how far away it is?"

"Yes, sir. Welcome to Copper's Run. This your first visit here?"

"It is, yes. About the motel?"

"Sure, sorry. Well, there is one place about two miles up the road toward Petersburg." The man pointed as if that would be helpful. Name's the Blue Star. It's a motel, for sure, but it's also a roadhouse."

He leaned over the counter toward Sam and lowered his voice. "Not too sure this is where you'd want to take the wife, though. Not the best clientele, if you understand what I mean." He nodded toward Alaine.

"OK, I see." Sam felt his shoulder muscles begin to tense. This town of Copper's Run might prove to be a bit different from what he had hoped. "Is there...anything else, anywhere to stay besides the Blue Star?"

The ticket agent studied Sam for a long moment before responding and even then continued as if he weren't sure he should.

"Well, we do have the Copper's Run Inn. It's big and old and has lots of rooms...kind of historic, I guess you'd say. It's not the Comfort Inn, if that's what you're looking for. But still, it's a nice place, clean. Good people run it.

"It's either that or the Blue Star if you're stuck here for the night. Two blocks over." He gestured behind himself. "You could check it out and see what you think." He went back to whatever he'd been doing behind the counter.

The tightness around Alaine's mouth and the purple splotches under her eyes told him how she was holding up. It was two miles to the Blue Star and two blocks to this Inn with no transportation. What real choice did they have?

Sam excused himself and entered the men's room. He had to have a minute to think without Alaine's frightened eyes on him. He pulled his wallet from his pocket. There was a hundred dollar bill, another hundred in twenties and three single dollar bills. He knew there was another hundred in the cash belt he always wore under his shirt.

That was it. This was what remained of Sam's withdrawals from ATM machines over the last week by increments and used to buy their supplies. He had this and the one credit card with a five thousand dollar limit that already had over three thousand in charges, including their rooms over the past week plus the bus tickets.

Then he remembered the investment money he had pocketed from the old man at work the day before the planes hit the towers. Ten thousand dollars in cash still in the five envelopes the man handed him, minus the one he put in the safe at work that no longer existed. The money was in his duffle bag. There was no clear record of it, and his office was buried in the rubble that was the North Tower. There was no one to know.

Still Sam looked around as if somebody did know and was about to close in on him. Rather than feeling secure with the knowledge that they were far from destitute, Sam just felt corrupt. It was a novel feeling for someone who had not been a poster child for high ethics in business dealings. Maybe he'd keep pretending that the money didn't exist.

Sam had no idea what Alaine's finances were like, but he did know she was in no condition to discuss them at the moment. He made the decision, for the time being, that his own three hundred and three dollars and credit card with the mounting balance was it for them. For the time being, there was no money that once belonged to the old man.

Sam walked out of the men's room to collect Alaine and head for the Inn just as the ticket agent was shutting the little depot down. It was 5:30 p.m. on Sunday evening.

They didn't talk as they walked the two blocks that moved them immediately out of the business district and into a neighborhood born in another era. Late afternoon sunlight filtered through deep rooted oaks beginning to show autumn colors. They passed old houses with edges worn by years of being lived in.

Sam saw fenced in yards, porch swings and vines climbing around doorways. He glimpsed gazebos in back yards and the remnants of gardens. The town they picked, it seemed to him, was about as far from Manhattan and the events of the past week as it was possible to come.

At the end of the second block, in a wide cul de sac, with its front facing toward town, stood the Inn at Copper's Run, as the sign on the post in the driveway announced. Odd name for a hotel, it occurred to Sam.

On first impression it was, indeed, big and old. Wide porches ran the length of the front for two of its three stories. It was painted white, not recently, but it bore grace and elegance that time and wear only enhanced. Solid, sturdy and welcoming, it promised shelter.

Sam took Alaine's arm and steered her toward the wide steps leading to double front doors. She stumbled as she started up. He dropped their bags to catch her. She was not good and going downhill.

Just as he lifted his hand to use the worn pewter knocker, the doors opened to a large black man in a Sunday suit and tie. In his right hand he carried a king-sized black leather book with *Holy Bible* inscribed in gold across the front.

The man frowned at the sight of the two visitors, and Sam had a bad moment considering what they would do if they were turned away from this place. The Blue Star Motel hadn't sounded like much of an option.

Before Sam could speak, the big man turned his head back toward the inside of the Inn and called out to someone in a voice as massive as he was.

"Ms. Charity, come out here! I need you. We have guests."

The man turned back toward Sam and Alaine, and before Sam could say a word, the big voice thundered again.

"Son, step on in here with that little lady. She looks like she's all done in. Put her on this couch." He moved back into an entry room and motioned for the couple to follow.

While Sam propelled and half carried Alaine to a long leather and wood chaise longue across the reception room, the big man gathered their scattered belongings and dropped them on a bench before shutting the outside door.

Alaine curled into a ball on the chaise with closed eyes as Sam bent over her. When he straightened, he saw a trim, middle aged black woman with expressive dark eyes and the creases of a permanent smile coming toward them with one hand outstretched and the other holding a dish cloth. She moved to Alaine, gently nudging Sam out of the way as she knelt beside her.

"Oh baby, what's the matter?" she crooned, and then more loudly to Sam, "What's the trouble with this pretty young lady? Is she sick? How can we help?"

Sam found presence of mind enough to speak. He turned toward the big man standing nearby and put out his hand.

"Sir, my name is Sampson MacDonald." The two shook hands, or rather the large hand shook Sam's with unusual force.

"This is Alaine Albert. I don't think she's sick exactly, just pretty tired out from our trip. You see, we came in on the 5:00 bus from--" Sam cleared his throat. "We've been on the road a couple of days. I was wondering if--"

"How do you do, son? Welcome to Copper's Run. I'm the Reverend Raymond T. Bright, and this lovely lady is my wife, Ms. Charity Bright. Most folks call us Rev. Ray and Ms. Charity for short.

Ms. Charity rose and turned to Sam, her face welcoming. "Sit down, young man. You look like you're ready to collapse, too. Are you needing a place to stay for the night?"

"Yes, Mrs. Bright, we are. The agent at the bus station mentioned your Inn. We may need a room for a few days. We're new to this area and don't know anyone. If you have a small room, maybe one with two beds, we would be grateful."

"Son," Raymond eyed him directly, "is this young lady your wife?"

"No, Rev. Ray, she's not. She's a friend. We're traveling together, and to be honest, I'm not too sure how she'll do if I'm not at least close by.

We've...ah...been through--" Sam coughed, unable to go further with his explanation.

"Sampson, we'd be happy to put you in a couple of comfortable rooms near each other and discuss the details later. Ms. Charity, where shall Sampson and I assist this young lady to rest? Ellen, you said?"

"Alaine. Her name is Alaine. We appreciate--"

"Raymond, you and Sam help Alaine and follow me. We need to get her in bed as soon as possible."

Charity Bright was all efficiency as she led the way down a long hall to a room on the back of the building. Flipping the overhead light on as she entered, she directed the men to help Alaine to a double bed covered in a white chenille spread that she pulled back as they eased the girl down.

"Sam, if you will please leave Alaine's luggage here with me, I'll get her settled while Ray takes you right across the hall to your room. Give me a few minutes and I'll be with you." Ms. Charity closed the door gently behind the men.

There was little Sam could do but leave her to see to Alaine's needs. He hoped Alaine would accept the older woman's assistance.

Raymond Bright didn't appear to be one who found needless conversation necessary as he showed Sam his room and bath. The room was spotless and spare in its accommodations, like rooms from another century. That posed no problem when he considered their alternatives.

Sam was searching about for a topic to fill the quiet when Ms. Charity rustled in, checking the watch she always wore on a chain around her neck as she came.

"Reverend Bright," she said with a fondness that was apparent to Sam, "it's almost 6:30. You best be on your way as you're running a little behind now. The early sheep in your little flock will be congregating to find you missing."

"But my dear," the man answered, "I've surely had a divine appointment right here." It was the first time Sam noticed the blue eyes in Rev. Ray's dusky face.

"Sampson, my son, please tell me. How long has it been since you've been to church?"

A week ago Sam would have taken offense at such a question and at the asker. Tonight he did not, and he shook his head in admission that it was such a long time he had no excuse.

"Raymond, do you think tonight's the best night? I'm sure Sampson here is almost as tired as his friend."

"I'm just the messenger sent to make the offer, my love. We'll let Sampson decide."

Sam's eyes moved from the broad face of Rev. Ray to the petite one of his companion as they waited politely for his response. Over the last twenty years, Sam could remember only two times that he'd been invited to church. Once by a blind date who declared herself a member of a gathering that sounded to him like some far Eastern cult. The invitation was enough to cement his decision that they had nothing in common.

The last invitation had been from his landlady back in Queens, a grandmotherly woman who tried to make him feel at home. She'd asked him to accompany her to church on the second Sunday after he moved into rooms at her boarding home. Sam, who only wanted to consider her rooming house an unfortunate stop on his road back to an apartment downtown and prosperity, refused kindly but so firmly that she didn't ask again.

Now here was unexpected church invitation number three.

"Thank you, sir, but maybe I shouldn't leave Alaine."

"She's sleeping, Sampson. I would be happy to look in on her from time to time. I'll also be happy to save you some supper for when you come back."

"Thank you, Mrs. Bright, but--"

"Ms. Charity. Everyone calls me Ms. Charity. Of course I love being called Mrs. Bright, but Ms. Charity is what I'm used to." Her voice was soft, and her smile was genuine.

"But I wouldn't keep you from your service with Rev. Ray on a Sunday night."

"He understands when I'm needed elsewhere, but do as you feel comfortable. Raymond, it's time. You know you aren't supposed to rush, and you'll have to if you don't leave now."

Her husband, still carrying the large black Bible, bent to kiss Ms. Charity's cheek and moved toward the hall. He turned back to look at Sam one more time, saying nothing.

"I guess I could tag along, if it's all right. I don't have a suit with me, I'm afraid."

"The Lord probably doesn't wear a suit either, son. Come on before the deacons send out someone to look for me."

Sam MacDonald was six feet and two inches tall. Still, he had to hurry his steps to keep up with the Reverend as he, at least three inches taller, took the Inn's front steps at a near run. He didn't talk during the brisk two-block sprint to his church.

The sign on the church's small front lawn verified Raymond T. Bright as the pastor and proclaimed:

CHURCH OF THE CARING AND MERCIFUL SAVIOR

SERVICES ON SUNDAYS

AT 11:00 a.m. & 7:00 p.m.

WEDNESDAY NIGHT PRAYER AND VISITATION

AT 6:30. p.m.

The church was not very large with white clapboards, simple stained glass windows, and a small steeple with a cross on top. Despite its welcoming simplicity, the thought of going inside of the building caused Sam's neck muscles to tighten and his heart rate to increase.

Another sign beside the front door read:

WELCOME FRIENDS AND STRANGERS

Surely, this is our God;

We trusted in him, and he saved us.

This is the LORD;

We trusted in him;

let us rejoice and be glad in his salvation.

Isaiah 25:9

As the pastor of the little church strode with purpose up the walkway to the open front doors from which streamed welcoming light and piano music, he was greeted with warmth by two women, one white and one black, in their church dresses and gloves.

"Good evening, Sister Louise. You are looking lovely tonight. Meet my fellow traveler, Sampson MacDonald. Sister Miranda, how is Ms. Jane?"

"She's holding on well, Pastor. How do you do, Mr. MacDonald? I'm Miranda McLean and this is Louise Lucas. We welcome you this evening to our congregation."

By the time Sam greeted the ladies and was passed on to the usher in the vestibule, he felt he'd been dropped in the middle of unknown territory with no compass or map. Rev. Ray left him behind as he moved down the church's center aisle, greeting as he went.

The one usher, who introduced himself as Elder Johnson Story, must have been at least eighty, and his hair was full and white against his dark skin. He peered up at Sam from his diminutive size out of eyes that twinkled with the mischief of someone a tenth of his age. He shook Sam's hand with obvious and hearty enthusiasm.

"Come in, son. Come in. I see that the Reverend Bright has been out in the highways and byways again, compelling folks to join us in Sabbath worship."

"I beg your pardon?" Sam thought Mr. Story might be a bit senile with his highways and byways talk. Should he answer or ignore the man and move on? Johnson Story, however, continued to pump his hand and smile his gnomish smile, looking directly into Sam's eyes.

"No, ah, we...that is...I'm a guest at the Inn this evening. Rev. Bright invited me to accompany him to the service."

"Just as I suspected, son, highways and byways. Welcome again and sit anyplace you please." He handed Sam a folded paper with a picture of a Shepherd surrounded by sheep. Sam started down the aisle and stopped at the second set of church pews from the back, slipping in and as far toward the outside wall as he could go.

More to keep from making eye contact with any of the other church goers than out of interest, Sam opened the folded brochure. He saw it must be some kind of agenda or order of events for the services of the day. He flipped back to the front cover where the Shepherd was standing with one small lamb on his arm and his hand on the head of another close by his side. At the bottom of the picture Sam read, "Rejoice with me; I have found my lost sheep. Luke 15:6." The smallest lamb's head rested against the chest of the Shepherd.

Sam focused on the lamb and remembered how tired he was. He thought about Alaine, asleep at the Inn, and worried that she might wake up and find him gone. He wasn't sure what she would do. His stomach growled, and he knew he should have stayed back, had some dinner and gone to sleep himself.

Instead he was here in this unreal place where the pianist had started to play for the people, about fifty in all, to sing.

They were standing and some were swaying to the slow music. He stood too, not sure of what to do, but not wanting to appear rude or ignorant. Sam didn't sing. The words and music sounded vaguely familiar, something about Jesus being a friend. A cold, hard feeling gripped him as he stood listening to the unblended voices of the singers. He thought how smug and naïve they were, singing about being friendly with the One he'd heard desperate voices cry out to on the day, less than a week past, when his world collapsed around him.

"Jesus, help us! Oh, Jesus, I don't want to die," he'd heard more than once as he and Alaine made their escape from the burning tower.

Jesus, whoever he was perceived to be, might have been here in Copper's Run on September 11th, Sam thought, *but He surely wasn't in New York City on that particular day.*

He slipped from his place near the side aisle and made haste out the front door of the church as unobtrusively as possible, hoping he could find his way back to the Inn alone.

# # #

Alaine

When Sam tapped on Alaine's room door and entered to Ms. Charity's invitation, Alaine sat in bed with a tray across her lap eating dinner. She was dressed in a white terry robe with her hair brushed, and she greeted Sam with a smile. Ms. Charity was sitting in a chair close beside Alaine's bed.

"Sam, you're back. Is church over? Ms. Charity said you went with Rev. Ray."

"I, ah, left early. I wanted to check on you. Looks like you're doing fine." He entered the room as he spoke and moved to the far side of Alaine's bed, away from where the other woman sat.

"Ms. Charity's taking such good care of me, Sam. And what a good cook she is. I haven't been this hungry since—since--"

Alaine stopped in mid-sentence and stared at Sam, unable to finish. She put her hands over her face and began to cry as Sam waited, his hands at his sides.

Ms. Charity stood and removed the nearly empty tray from harm's way. Then she sat on the edge of the bed and put her arms around the younger woman as if she well knew how to handle this awkward social situation.

"Honey, I know something big is bothering you. I don't understand just what it is, and I don't need to right now. But it must be important if it makes you this sad. You're safe here. No one will bother you tonight. We can talk about your problem later, if you want to. Tonight, I think it would be wise for you to get a little shut-eye time. Here, slide yourself down in this bed and let me cover you up. I'm going to turn this light out so you can sleep. Before you know it, a joyful morning will be here, Lord willing."

Sam watched, not interrupting Ms. Charity's kind ministering to Alaine. When she stood and moved away from the bed, taking the tray with her, he reached out, gently touched Alaine's shoulder and gave it a soft squeeze.

"Goodnight, Alaine. I hope you rest well. I'm across the hall if you need me," was all he managed. She was too weary and distraught to respond.

# # #

Sampson

Sam could see Alaine was almost asleep already, and there was no answer. He followed Ms. Charity out of the room. As she closed the door behind them, Sam felt a need at least to acknowledge the lady's skill in comforting Alaine's obvious distress. Her swinging emotions were a mystery to him; so many things about her were.

"Thanks for your help. When she does that, I'm never sure-- You just seem to know exactly what to do. Thank you."

"Think nothing of it, Sam. It's a skill that didn't come from me. It's one with which I've been blessed, as my husband always says.

Sam felt something close to envy. This lady, this near stranger, knew how to care for Alaine with such assurance and confidence when he felt so deficient in the face of her continuous tears.

Ms. Charity interrupted his troubled thoughts.

"Now, I'm sure you've not eaten for hours. You know we have both an Inn and a little Café, too. I've kept you a plate in the kitchen. Would you like to have it brought to your room or do you want to come down to the kitchen with me?" Ms. Charity's voice was soft and gentle, as was her hand on his arm.

Sam almost declined her dinner offer in favor of a shower and bed, but as tired and stressed as he was, he still didn't want to be alone. For some reason, the thought of solitude was not comforting. The warm presence of Ms. Charity was. He followed her to the Inn's kitchen.

The Inn's Café kitchen reminded Sam of what the cookery of a small baronial manor might look like. Nothing old or shabby here. It was large and spotless. High ceilings gave ample room for hanging pots, pans and baskets. It was easy to see this was both a welcoming and efficient work place. Sam knew he'd made the right decision.

As they entered the tiled room, two workers introduced by Ms. Charity as Andi and Danisha were finishing the chores for the evening and readying for the breakfast rush. Ms. Charity explained that although Copper's Run was a small town, its citizens included a lot of people who needed breakfast but apparently didn't like to cook. The Inn's Café was a popular spot to begin the day. It was also a well-liked lunch and dinner destination for townsfolk, outliers and travelers alike.

Sam responded to the friendly greetings of the two girls, one white and one black. He watched Ms. Charity's efficiency of movement as she took his plate from a warming oven, poured an icy glass of tea and prepared a place for him to eat at a small kitchen worktable.

"This service is none too fancy for a guest, young man, but it's warm and nourishing. Today's special was Beef Bourguignon...which is just an impressive way of saying beef stew. That's Danisha's specialty. We offer it at least once a week by popular demand. Alaine seemed to like it. Come on and sit down. Let me know if you need anything else. I'll just be over here helping the girls finish up for the night. When you get through with that, we have a bowl of banana pudding waiting for you."

Sam was patient during Ms. Charity's explanation of his supper. It took a supreme act of will, as the fancy beef stew smelled like the best comfort food known. When she left him, he allowed only a few seconds to savor the anticipation before he assailed the beef and crunchy brown bread served with it. They were as good as his senses promised.

Feeling stronger and more comfortable, Sam got up and walked over to the two young ladies, now folding napkins around silverware for the next day.

"Which one of you is Danisha?" The dark skinned girl looked up.

“I am. May I get something for you?”

“I just wanted to tell you how exceptionally good your fancy beef stew is. Thanks.” He turned to the other girl.

“Andi? What’s your specialty?”

The light skinned girl peered at him through uneven blond bangs. “Funny you should ask. I’m the dessert lady. Let me get you the bowl of that banana pudding Ms. Charity promised.” The dimple in her left cheek deepened when she smiled as she handed Sam a big bowl and spoon. He ate it at once, in front of the girls, and made appreciative expressions as he savored.

“Andi, I must say, this is exceptional banana pudding to match

Danisha’s prime Beef Bourguignon. Where did you both learn to cook like this?”

Sam heard a chuckle behind him and turned to see Ms. Charity with an enigmatic smile on her face.

“We had a secret ingredient,” Danisha said, moving to put her arm through that of the older woman.

“Ms. Charity taught us both,” said Andi, with a look of devotion toward her friend. “She taught us a lot of things. You might say, we’re still in school. When Ms. Charity is around, the lessons never stop.”

The affection among the three women was obvious to Sam. Watching it as a bystander made him hurt, by contrast, for his own lack of affection from anyone.

Sam finished the last of his tea, expressed his appreciation again for their provisions and bid them goodnight. Just before he got to the door of the kitchen, he turned to Ms. Charity.

“Would you please give Rev. Bright a message when you see him?”

“Why don’t you tell him yourself? He’s standing right behind you.”

Sam turned to find the pastor grinning at him. This was not what he expected...maybe mild rebuff at the least...full-fledged censure at the most.

Instead he got cordiality.

"Sam, my friend," the pastor said with amusement, "I see you prefer the company of three beautiful women and a bowl of banana pudding to one of my sermons. Ms. Charity, did you save any for me?"

"Rev. Bright--" Sam started.

"Rev. Ray, if you please."

"OK, Rev. Ray. Forgive me about tonight. I just couldn't--"

Rev. Ray clapped the young man on his back so hard it propelled him forward. "The apology is mine. I know you're tired, son. I rushed you. I get a bit overly enthusiastic at times, don't I, Ms. Charity? Maybe some other time."

"Thanks, maybe so," Sam said, not wanting to hurt the man's feelings but less than eager to commit.

Turning to his wife, Rev. Ray changed the subject, letting the matter drop. "Now about that banana pudding?"

"Not so fast, Reverend," she answered, taking off her apron. "Girls, give this starving saint of a man a small serving of his sugar-free version from the fridge. I don't want to be responsible for any diabetic comas on my watch."

# # #

Sam awoke the next morning before light. He stretched and lay thinking about the events of the last seven days. He'd come, experientially, about as far as possible from the New York City he'd known a few days ago. It was true only a bus ride and less than four hundred miles separated him from his former home, but to Sam, the distance was immeasurable.

Copper's Run. A quick choice of destination at the bus station had brought him and Alaine to this obscure town huddled in the heartland of Virginia. Judging from his limited exposure last evening, the landscape, the people, the lifestyles seemed dissimilar to anything he'd experienced in his twenty eight years.

Coming here was like entering some alternate reality. His old life, the demeaning job, the frantic lifestyle, evaporated on September 11th with the fall of the Trade Towers. Only he and Alaine seemed to remain, dropped down in a place he'd never heard of. It was almost too much, too fast, too strange to comprehend.

Alaine. What on earth was he doing in the middle of nowhere with a woman he hardly knew? What was he going to do with her? What was he going to do with himself?

The night sky was barely beginning to lighten when Sam left the Inn to walk the early morning streets of Copper's Run. He'd stopped and listened at Alaine's door but considered it good news that he heard nothing. The door at the end of his corridor seemed to lead to the outside with no obvious alarm. He eased it open carefully just in case, prepared to race back to his room adolescent-style and pretend to be sleeping should a hidden alarm sound.

As Sam stepped out onto a small side porch, he heard nothing and closed the door behind him. The air was cool and the moon waning. It was hard to see in the dusky start of dawn, but Sam descended to ground level and walked away from the Inn toward where he supposed town to be.

New York City never stopped; the sights and sounds never really shut down making quiet spots hard to come by. In Copper's Run at 5:15 a.m., even on a Monday morning, there was nothing abroad that he could detect except a shadowy cat that followed him as he left the yard of the Inn. For some reason, he felt more comfortable walking in the street itself, rather than on the sidewalk, at least through the residential area surrounding the Inn.

Sam's footfalls from the sneakers he stepped into barefoot after dressing in sweats sounded loud to him in the stillness. He walked letting instinct and indistinct memories from yesterday lead him. A dog barked when he was half way up the block by his estimation, but it soon stopped, and he and the cat walked on.

He came up behind a row of brick, two-story buildings that appeared to be the backside of Main Street. Dawn was coming steadily, and Sam could see more clearly as he entered the business part of town through a side alley.

Copper's Run, downtown proper, was barely two streets deep from where Sam entered. As he walked past store fronts still dormant from the night, he saw signs that the little town was a throwback, whether by design or default he wasn't sure, to a previous era. In Copper's Run, there was still a dime store, a movie theatre with an old-fashioned marquee advertising last year's movies...*Reindeer Games* and *Chocolat*. He walked past a laundry mat, a video store, an insurance agency. Across the street he could make out clothing and antique stores, all still dark, and a restaurant with lights on toward the back but not yet open for customers.

At the end of three blocks, Sam came to residences again, so he crossed the street and started back down the other side. The cat, by now, was walking fast alongside of Sam, and he could see it was yellow as sunrise neared.

He covered the first three blocks quickly and then counted two more before he again saw homes. There was a church on the far corner, and out of curiosity, Sam crossed the street again in its direction. When he was in the middle of the street, he noticed, to his left, a park-like green space, which he'd missed earlier. He veered his path toward the small area, which reminded him of an island in the center of Main Street.

Sam could now see that a wrought iron fence surrounded the area of green, and a small gate led to the inside. The east and westbound lanes of the street simply circumvented the enclosed area, one on either side, as if it were not there.

Intrigued by this unusual street configuration, Sam walked over to the enclosure and entered the iron gate. Inside he found a flat slab of granite on the grass and a large, strangely shaped copper container beside of it. It was now light enough to read the words inscribed on a copper plate on top of the granite:

Requiem for Moonshine

The contents of this pot built Copper's Run

and nearly brought on its demise.

May we not forget.

1925-1966

Sam recognized the spot as a tribute of sorts to the illegal homemade whiskey trade. The practice must have had some past connection to this area of Virginia. He'd never been especially interested in history... too busy trying to make his own until his luck changed in the last couple of years.

Sam reached out and touched the smooth, hard surface of the copper pot. He bent over the granite slab. What did the dates mean? Were they connected to some important period of history? Nothing came to mind, and the roar of a large truck brought Sam back to the present. It was now daylight, and the street around him was coming alive. He left the little park space at a run on his way back to the Inn and Alaine.

4 UNEXPECTED CHALLENGE

Sampson

Sam knocked lightly on Alaine's room door. He hoped she was up and feeling better this morning. His optimism was rewarded when she opened the door.

"You look like a new woman."

"And I feel like a new woman. Last night was so awful I didn't care if I lived or died. You saved my life again by bringing me here. The Brights are wonderful."

"Breakfast is served in the Café. I've been up for a while, but I didn't want to wake you. Do you think you can eat?"

"I think maybe I can. It feels good to be hungry. I...haven't felt much like eating lately."

Alaine joined Sam in the hallway and followed him to the far end of the Inn where an informal dining room, which Ms. Charity called the Café, was open to the public. He held out a chair for her at a table to the side, away from the traffic.

"I've had coffee, but I waited for you to order," Sam said. "I'm glad you're feeling better. Did you sleep well?"

"I am and I did. Thanks. I don't even remember falling asleep. I must have been exhausted."

Sam laughed. "I was there. You were."

"Sam," Alaine's voice was low and soft, "this is the first time I've felt this safe in a week. I didn't ever think I'd feel really safe again, after what happened to us. What about you?"

Sam sat in silence for a minute before he answered. "I think I was too busy all week just trying to make sure we survived. I'll admit, leaving the City was a relief. Being here makes all that went on back there unreal, maybe because we've been away from the non-stop coverage on TV for a couple of days."

"I think it's more, Sam. I like this place...these people. They don't act like City people."

"I've been looking around. Seems like a quiet enough town, a little backward maybe. Let me tell you about a monument I saw this morning right in the middle of Main Street.

# # #

Alaine

Satiated with a Café breakfast to remember of fruited pancakes and country sausage, Sam and Alaine drifted down a path that led from the Inn's back porch toward the creek which, according to Ms. Charity, bore the town's name and bordered the back lawn. The closeness of the big old structure and the sheltering of ancient trees behind it created a buffer from the outside world.

To Alaine, this shield was reinforced by a sense of strength and quiet emanating from the people who ran the Inn. It was a refuge Sam would likely call fragile and temporary, but it was one she didn't want to lose, at least for the moment.

They walked to the edge of the creek and stood looking over its steep bank at the fast running waters below. Sam spoke first.

"We have to decide what we're going to do next. We don't know yet what the long-term consequences of what happened last Tuesday are going to be. A lot could change everywhere."

"It already has," Alaine said, "with me, at least." She watched the water and didn't elaborate. Alaine did feel stronger this morning. She'd felt so vulnerable...so beat down and brittle in the last week. But talking about it might make it all come back.

"Alaine?"

"How long do you think we can stay here? I mean here in this town...at the Inn? I was trying to tell you before breakfast, I like it here. I feel protected around these people. Do you think we could stay for a while?"

"This Inn isn't real life, Alaine. We can't just be here indefinitely. I know it feels good now, after where we've been, but these people have their own lives. Remember, they run a hotel. They get paid for being nice to folks like us. It's their job.

She knew what Sam was trying to do. She knew he could still see the pinched effects of the horror on her face and didn't want to add to her discomfort. He was just wanting her to face reality. But she wasn't ready.

"It seems like the rest of the world is on pause except for what's going on right here, right now. I need this, Sam. I'm not—"

"But it won't last. Things are happening out there. We have to make plans. We can't just hide here indefinitely."

Alaine didn't respond for some time. Finally she met Sam's eyes, something she didn't do easily.

"Sam," her voice was low, "I haven't asked you many questions since we left the Trade Center building on that day. I haven't wanted to know the answers. I've existed in my own little knot of fear and let you take care of everything. I owe you.'

"Shhh...you don't have to—"

"Please. I'm grateful for what you did for me. In every way, I'm thankful. I'm sure I would have died in that Tower, not caring whether I got out or not. Even before the plane hit, I'd run out of ideas for how to keep living."

"It went both ways, Alaine. I had to have a goal, a purpose, to get us both out. You were it. We hardly knew each other, but you were the only one at that office who meant anything at all to me. Getting you out with me gave me strength to keep going. It kept me focused. Strange, all those people we worked with every day...we don't even know who made it out and who didn't."

"I'll never know how you did it. I can barely remember leaving the building and getting away. I know we stayed at that hotel for several nights. We had two rooms in the City...plus you fed us and bought what we needed...and the bus tickets. I have no idea what you spent, but it must be a lot. Tell me the truth, Sam. How much money have you spent for everything, including last night here at the Inn and breakfast this morning?"

"Alaine, it doesn't matter. Please, forget it. I had some cash, and I've tried to hang onto it as much as possible." Sam met her eyes. "I used my credit cards mostly. We're OK for now, but it's soon time to make our next move."

"But Sam, I have some money, just not with me. I didn't take more than a few dollars to work the day that--I brought my lunch that day. I have a debit card, though, and can get to some of my funds that way. It's money that's just mine. None of it belongs to ...the man I was living with." This was almost a whisper.

"I should have told you before, but I just couldn't think straight those first few days. If we can find a bank, I can get some of it out. I can only withdraw a set amount at a time this way, but it should help."

"How do you know the money's still there?"

"Paul Mowher didn't know I had the money, or it would be gone. I had a bank account he knew nothing about. My mother left me some money when she died, before we were together. I never told him. It's not that much, maybe about eight thousand, but it can help us. We could get some out and stay here a little longer. Please, Sam."

Sam smiled. She hadn't seen him do that before now. Or maybe she just hadn't noticed it.

"You're sure you want to share your inheritance, at least some of it, with a perfect stranger?" His tone was light.

She surprised herself by smiling back. "Sam, we've been together, or whatever you call it, for less than a week. You're no stranger. I might add you're not perfect either. I heard you sneaked out on Rev. Ray's church service last night before it was over. Couldn't take the heat?"

Her tone matched his. It was the closest she'd come to feeling anything close to cheerful since that day. She watched for his response.

"Churches make me nervous. I nearly got married in one once--caught myself just in time. I get edgy whenever I feel like I've returned to the scene of my near demise." This time he laughed out loud.

"I've always loved church...haven't been much in a long time. I wish I could have seen Rev. Ray's. Maybe next time, Sam?"

She was stalling for time, more time at the Inn. She hoped for now he would just go along.

"Alaine, if you want to be here a few more days, I think we could make that work. Build your strength and then we'll decide what to do. And maybe we can find some way for you to stay on...if you feel so strongly about it. And I could go--"

She interrupted the rest of what he was trying to say on purpose. "Let's just find an ATM machine and get some of my money. Will you help me do that?"

"I will, honey. Let's go in now so you can get some rest. When you wake up, we'll walk downtown to let you get your money."

She left him at the door to her room.

# # #

Sampson

Sam didn't want to hurt her, but neither did he want her to be shocked if her boyfriend had cleaned her out. The man probably thought she was dead, despite Sam's early Saturday morning call from that bus stop to the NYPD letting them know he and Alaine survived the Twin Towers' collapse...the phone call he hadn't told her about.

He smiled at the irony of Alaine's offer of money. He, who'd embezzled money from an elderly stranger less than a week ago that he didn't even want to touch, now preferred not to take any money from Alaine.

But if we do use a little of her money, it might give us a couple more days here to come up with a plan about where and how we could live.

Sam caught his own presumption that they would somehow stay together. Fate or coincidence had already thrown them with each other under less than usual circumstances. Sam knew that shared stress events often gave participants a temporary sense of bonding. But he also knew that after a while, life moved on.

It was entirely possible, given some time and thought, Alaine would want to go home. Or at the least, she might have a friend or relative somewhere she would prefer over following him around while he made up his mind about what to do next.

And who knows? In time I might decide I want to go on alone, make a new start without any encumbrances. Without Alaine?

The exposed and vulnerable look on Alaine's face during their discussion told Sam that time was not now. For now he needed to stay close to her...at least until she was stronger and less fragile.

When he left Alaine, instead of going across the hall to his own room, Sam decided to explore the old Inn.

From the history on a brochure he'd found in his room, Sam read that the Inn at Copper's Run was built in the middle 1700's to serve as a refuge for travelers daring enough to move through the sparsely inhabited pre-revolutionary war Virginia countryside.

He read about the chain of warm and hot springs that dotted the area and how early inns and taverns were built near the locations of these springs. The accommodations housed visitors who came to the spa-like waters for health cures, recreation or socializing. Many of these old wooden establishments had burned, been abandoned and fallen into decay or been razed to make way for modern construction. A handful survived into the modern century, and the Inn at Copper's Run was one of these.

In its early days, the Inn was named for the wife of its builder and original owner, Jedidare Jones. For almost a hundred years, it was called the Inn of Justice Jones. That name lasted through the period of the Civil War when it served as headquarters of more than one confederate general and as a field hospital on several occasions. Dark spots still staining the floors in some rooms gave credence to these reports.

What had once been a small settlement community was incorporated in 1925 as the town of Copper's Run. The town's founding fathers gave the name in honor of the copper distillation pots of the moonshine industry and the creek or run on which many of the illegal whiskey stills of the era were built.

The owner of the Inn at the time also used it as his personal mansion, which was procured with money he made selling clandestine moonshine liquor to the community. Not surprisingly, he also named his inn and home Copper's Run. The Inn at Copper's Run stayed in his family until Raymond and Charity Bright purchased it for a bed and breakfast enterprise in the early 1990's.

The brochure gave a layout of the rooms for the rambling three-story structure. Having read the Inn's curious backstories, Sam set out to see if he could find the Civil War era bloodstains on the entrance and front parlor floors and the minie ball holes in walls of the old servants' quarters on the top floor.

Sam found his explorations as intriguing as the people who currently inhabited the ancient Inn. Near the end of his wanderings, he read a note in the brochure about a chapel room in the underground cellar that had served as a church for the innkeepers and for occupying soldiers during the war. Two of the aides to General Robert E. Lee were said to have prayed here during the period of Lee's Retreat in the final days of the confederacy on the road to Appomattox.

Sam was thoughtful as he moved down stone steps into the cool, slightly clammy cellar under the back of the Inn. He tried to mute his steps as he walked the long, stone corridor. At about half the length of the Inn, Sam figured, he found a small sign indicating this was the site of the chapel. The double doors to the room itself were ajar. He was close to entering when he was stopped by sounds from inside.

Sam recognized the voices of Ms. Charity and Rev. Ray. He moved to join them and hear their recount of the historical significance of the chapel. As he reached to push the wooden doors further open, it became apparent that their communication was not conversational but rather that of prayer.

Sam stood waiting, uncertain about what to do next. Should he withdraw, hopefully unseen and unheard? Could he make deliberate noise so they would be aware they weren't alone? He might simply enter in the guise that he, too, was there to pray.

Sam rejected the last option outright as hypocritical beyond what even he was willing to do. Before he could choose another action, he heard words coming from Rev. Ray, obviously meant for his Deity, which caused Sam to move closer.

"My Father, who has protected my days and my ways for the years since the repentance of my youth, we need your light on our pathway today."

His words were echoed by a soft and serious, "Yes, Lord, yes, Lord," from Ms. Charity. Sam could see them now, through the partly open doorway, kneeling together with their hands interlocked over a prayer bench set at the front of the small room.

"This old place, this Inn, is yours, Lord," Ray continued. "You gave it to us.

You own it, and you can take it whenever you desire. We understand that, Father. But until that day, we need your help as soon as you have time, please Sir."

Again Sam could hear Ms. Charity's soft whisper of, "Anytime now, Lord. Yes please, Lord."

"You know I need help with the business end of this Inn, Father, and especially the finances. Things are getting a little above our heads, Lord. We need some help. Seems I'm a little too busy with my preaching and keeping this place going. My Charity can't do it all either, Lord, what with the cooking and cleaning and hostessing.

"Lord, now please send us the help right away, if you will, to keep things running. You know this is your ministry. We don't know why you send children along to us like Andi and Danisha, but you do, and we're here as your vessels, Lord.

"And then there're the new ones, Sam and his friend, Alaine. There's a story somewhere behind them, when and if you're ready for us to know it. In the meantime, Lord, give them understanding of you and show us your way. And if you please, send us some help. In your Son's name, Amen."

"Amen," whispered Ms. Charity.

Sam waited to be sure the two were going to stay in the chapel a few moments longer before he turned to move as silently as possible down the long hall and up the steps to the first floor hallway. Not stopping there, he found the nearest door to the outside and stepped into the sunshine of an early fall day.

He walked away from the Inn, wanting space between him and what he'd overheard in the tiny underground chapel. His face burned in spite of the mild weather, and he knew it was not from shame for his eavesdropping but from the awareness of hearing someone pray for him.

The first reason he could shrug off. He was no saint. Besides, no harm had been done by his presence. The second was more difficult. Why would these strangers take the time, energy or interest required to pray for him? Who had ever done that before in his life?

A memory flashed before his eyes...his grandfather, his mother's father, kneeling beside his bed at night when he was five, maybe six, his rugged hand on Sam's head. The voice came back as clearly as if he, long deceased, were next to Sam now.

"Father, bless this child and bring him to you. Protect him and let him know you love him." That's all the memory held.

Sam stopped on a small stone bridge that crossed Copper's Run. How he found himself there, or where he was in relation to the Inn, he didn't know. He just knew he was sweating and shaking. Sam gripped the side of the bridge, comforted by the cold, damp feel on his skin, glad for the contact with something hard that served to bring him back to reality. Sam leaned over to watch the water of the run flow gently below. Where did the water that passed beneath him end up? Where would he?

# # #

After lunch at the Inn's Café, Sam and Alaine set out walking toward town to find a bank with an ATM where she could withdraw cash from her account back in the City. She appeared refreshed from her rest and excited to see some of her surroundings. To Sam, having her in a positive frame of mind was an encouraging change from her usual withdrawn and passive self he'd come to know in the days after their ordeal.

"Do we pass Rev. Ray's church on our way to the main street, Sam?"

"If you're up to going a block out of our way, I can show you. It's not far."

In less than ten minutes the two stood in front of the Church of the Caring and Merciful Shepherd. In the daylight, it was pleasant and unassuming with fall flowers planted on either side of the front door, which was painted a welcoming bright red.

Alaine stood before the church for some time until Sam placed a gentle hand on her arm.

"Ready?"

She put her arm through his, and they walked toward the small town. Finding a bank was easy. There were two and each anchored a spot at an opposite end of Main Street. Using her bank card, Alaine withdrew her per diem limit of $500 from the ATM and handed all but $20 of it to Sam.

"We'll get more in a couple of days. I'm just keeping a little mad money for me, " Alaine said and laughed. "After all, who knows what I might be tempted to buy? Since I currently have virtually...nothing."

"Why don't you hold on to this cash? I told you, I'm fine for now."

"I want to start paying you back, Sam. I'm trying to help. Humor me, please. You...we'll need it. As a matter of fact, let's do find a department store. I could use a few things. Shopping makes a lady feel better."

It was almost time for dinner when Sam and Alaine strolled back to the Inn with her few bags. The afternoon had been a good one, and the companionship between them relaxed and open. Sam began to feel Alaine might be right about staying put for a couple of days to figure out what should come next. Maybe the dramatic change in their routines between the breakneck pace of New York City and the calmer tempo of life in a small town in the middle of Virginia was a good thing.

The afternoon's exercise left them hungry and ready for one of Ms. Charity's specialties from the Café's kitchen. Anticipating this and the welcoming company of their hosts, Sam never expected what greeted them as they came within sight of the Inn's entranceway.

Backed up to the double front doors with its emergency signal blinking in the early evening light was an ambulance. A first responder vehicle sat close by.

Sam grasped Alaine's hand, and they ran the last few yards toward the Inn. He left her outside and dashed in past the open rear doors of the ambulance. The scene in a sitting room of the Inn brought flashbacks of the awfulness of the morning of September 11.

Rev. Ray lay on the floor with four emergency medical technicians attending him. At his head, on her knees and holding his hand, was Ms. Charity, calm while tears streamed down her beautiful face. Rev. Ray's eyes were closed, and for a black man, his color could only be described as blue-white.

By the time Alaine reached his side, Sam understood he couldn't help Rev. Ray, and rather than hinder the efforts to save the man's life, he took hold of her arm and moved to the side of the room away from the EMT workers. Danisha and Andi were nearby, huddled together, arms around each other.

Other persons Sam didn't recognize gathered in the door to the hallway. All appeared to have their heads bowed, as if in prayer.

The room was perfectly quiet except for the exchanges among the EMT workers or with Ms. Charity. While it seemed to take an inordinate amount of time for them to transfer Rev. Ray to a gurney and ready him for the ambulance, Sam knew that medical protocol required them to stabilize their patient as much as possible prior to transporting him.

When finally Rev. Ray was about to be rolled to the waiting ambulance, Ms. Charity, now on her feet and walking alongside of the gurney still holding his hand, turned back to meet Sam's eyes. Her words shocked him more than any he had ever heard, more than hearing that he was fired from the lucrative job he'd once held and almost more than hearing about the tragedies that occurred simultaneously while he and Alaine fled the North Tower.

"I'm depending on you, Sampson. We're depending on you, Ray and I. We believe you can handle the Inn for us for a while. It's in your hands."

She walked a few steps toward the door and stopped. "The keys to our van are in the drawer of the reception desk."

Sam stood, unable to respond, as he watched Ms. Charity lift her chin and walk with dignity behind the responders who loaded them both into the ambulance and took the couple away into the growing darkness. He still stood as they all listened to the wail of the warning siren fade into the distance in the direction of the county hospital.

When he came to, Sam saw multiple sets of eyes turned on him as if asking in unison, "What now? You're in charge. What do we do now?"

A helpless, inadequate feeling washed over him, followed closely by an immediate need to turn away from the waiting faces and leave by the nearest exit as fast and as permanently as possible. He could do that. He could leave everything here and go. He'd done it before and recently. He could even leave Alaine.

She'd be all right, eventually.

For Sam, time was suspended while he considered his options. In reality, seconds passed and so quickly that no one registered his hesitation. It seemed to Sam that the rest of his life, not Rev. Ray's, was in the balance to be determined by his next decision. Go and start over yet again. Stay and...what?

"Sam?" It was Alaine's voice at his side holding the question.

"May I meet with everyone in the Café please? We have some business to discuss." Sam didn't recognize the sound of his own voice, raised to ensure that those in the room and outside in the hall could all hear. He especially failed to understand the unfamiliar ring of authority that resulted in those around him, including Alaine, moving in the direction of the Café.

When all were assembled, seated at the Café's tables or standing along the walls, Sam realized there was a mixture of both the Inn's patrons and employees. He hadn't considered that customers would be among the group looking expectantly at him with faces that reflected their concern for Raymond Bright. But of course there would be. Rev. Ray and Ms. Charity were the Inn, and whatever happened to them also happened to their loyal friends and co-workers.

What on earth was I thinking? What could I possibly say to help the situation here and not make it worse?

Alaine sat at a table near where he stood with her head in her hands, as if she tried to disappear.

Sam addressed the small group quietly. "It's difficult to know just what to say at a time like this. There's a lot we don't know about what just happened and what the outcome will be. But we do know Raymond and Charity Bright. We know what they mean to this town and to many of us here. Could we just have a moment of silence for them right now?"

Sam didn't know what good that would do, but maybe it would help them all steady themselves, and maybe it would give him a chance to think of something else to say. What happened at the end of the moment of silence surprised Sam. A soft voice interrupted the quiet of the room.

"Would it be all right if I said a brief prayer for Rev. Ray and Ms. Charity, son?" He hadn't noticed him before in the room, but the speaker was Johnson Story, the old man from Rev. Ray's church.

"Why yes, sir. Please go ahead." It was a brief reprieve.

Mr. Story might look over eighty, but to Sam's ears, he spoke with a strength and conviction of someone who believed in what he was doing. He began his prayer as if he knew he had a Divine listener.

"Our most holy Father, in your wisdom you have chosen to strike down one of your best. We don't know why, and that's all right, Lord, because we know that you are in charge. Still, Lord, we love Rev. Ray and his lovely wife. If it's OK with you, Lord, please let him live and bring him back to us soon. You know he means a lot to us, Father. We know he means a lot to you, too, but if it pleases you, just leave him here a bit longer to help us out with our journeys and troubles, Lord. Show us what to do in the meanwhile, Lord. And help this young man here as he leads us. In the end, whatever you decide is best is really all right with us. In Jesus' name, Amen, yes Lord."

And many in the room echoed after him, "Yes, Lord, Amen."

Again expectant eyes turned automatically toward Sam, and he said what seemed to be the only reasonable response.

"Since we have no idea what Rev. Ray's condition is, I'm getting ready to go to the hospital to find out. We do know this place, this Inn and Café, are his and Ms. Charity's livelihood. We need to do all we can to keep everything running smoothly while they are gone, or until--Andi, you and Danisha know the Inn and Café workings. Right?"

What he saw were nods of agreement.

"I've never run an inn before, but I do know finances. I think I could hold up that end of the business for a while. What do you think? Can we keep things here going?"

More nods, but this time from others besides Andi and Danisha. Sam saw agreement all around the room, Mr. Story, several of the Café regulars and Alaine. All were likeminded to do what they could to help.

"Then let's give it a try, starting now. But first, anyone who hasn't had dinner, it's on the house. While you eat, we'll make some fast plans. Then I'm going to the hospital to find out what's going on with Rev. Ray."

The group seemed to plan as one mind. In addition to overseeing the business end of things, Sam would handle the front desk and act as host, meeting, greeting, and making reservations, whatever public duties were needed. Andi and Danisha would handle the housekeeping and Café operations, with help from a group of recruits and a couple of part timers who were happy to step in more regularly.

Johnson Story, who Sam discovered lived at the Inn in a small room on the other end of his hallway, admitted that he specialized in cooking in the army. Even though it was over forty years previous, he offered to be a breakfast cook, and his eyes showed the challenge delighted him.

While the animated discussion sprang back and forth among the group members engaged in the effort to keep the Inn at Copper's Run and Café afloat, Sam noticed the contrasting silence from Alaine. She sat without moving, watching the arrangements being made with no comment as she followed each speaker with her eyes.

When the brief and spontaneous meeting was over, and Sam was satisfied that they all knew what their next steps should be, he drained the last of his coffee and stood up to leave for the hospital. He was conscious of Alaine with a characteristic worry frown on her forehead. She followed him down the long hall to the entrance room of the Inn, where Ms. Charity said he could find the van keys.

Sam knew by Alaine's actions that she was planning to go with him. He moved to head her off.

"I think you should stay here, Alaine. You need to rest. We don't know what we'll find at the hospital. I want you to wait here."

"Sam, I want to help. I don't know how. Let me go with you, or tell me how to help here. I'm tired of feeling useless."

Her eyes told him she meant it. This was not the Alaine he knew, the one from their old office or of the last few days.

"OK, mind the reception desk until I get back or call. You can take messages. Danisha can show you how to work the reservation calendar in the computer if there's time." He reached out to touch her hand. "I'll call as soon as I know something."

# # #

With directions from Johnson Story on how to get there and a short learning curve on how to manage a mini-van, a vehicle Sam had never owned, he arrived at the small county hospital with no problems. While he thought his experience at the Trade Center prepared him for any lesser emergency, Sam discovered on his way from the visitors' parking lot to the emergency room that he wouldn't classify the well-being of Rev. Ray as a lesser emergency after all. Sam was winded and unnerved following the short walk, and he wasn't that out of shape. Truth is, he was worried about what he would find.

Sam had practiced, over the last unfulfilling years, the art of distancing himself from those around him, even those who would have considered him their close associate. He knew how to communicate one message with his words and actions, but without involving his emotions. Experience taught him that if you didn't get too familiar and personal with your colleagues or acquaintances, then using them or leaving them behind when it was time to move on were less troublesome.

Something had gone awry with those previous practices when he met Ray Bright. He was a man who seemed to see right through the cover of Sam's surface charisma to the core of insecurities and self-doubts that defined Sampson MacDonald, the man. This was a feeling Sam had rather than something Rev. Ray voiced. Maybe Sam was intimidated in the presence of a man of God. Maybe it wasn't how Rev. Ray viewed him at all, but it was how Sam felt.

Still, Sam was aware of the authentic interest Rev. Ray had shown in him and Alaine from the first, in spite of the little they revealed about themselves. Ray Bright seemed a man who could know your darkest questions and still care, while helping you to find the answers. In the brief time they had been at Copper's Run Inn, Sam both trusted and respected the older man. Sam felt the same way about Ms. Charity, though she seemed less readable and more enigmatic.

It occurred to Sam, as he approached the small desk at the entrance to the emergency room, that it mattered a great deal what he would hear in response when he asked his next question.

"Good evening, my name is Sampson MacDonald. I'm a friend of Raymond Bright who was brought in here not long ago...his heart, I believe. Can you tell me anything?"

A pause occurred while the middle-aged woman at the desk studied him as if she had an internal screening device. When she seemed satisfied that he met whatever criteria she expected, she responded.

"Mr. MacDonald, Rev. Ray's not here. He was transferred soon after he came by helicopter to Richmond...the VCU Medical Center. Ms. Charity left a note for you if you came looking for them. I guess she thought you might."

Sam stood looking at the woman as if he hadn't heard her. She met his eyes and waited, the note in her outstretched hand, unsure if he had. His mind jammed with too many messages at once, like a computer with multiple simultaneous commands.

This woman used their first names. Everyone must know Ray and Charity Bright. She called me by name, too. Ms. Charity knew I'd be coming. How did she know that? If Rev. Ray had to be moved by chopper, it must be bad. Could he be dead and nobody wants to tell me? How far is Richmond? Can I leave Alaine alone that long? I don't know what to do.

"I don't know what to do." Sam didn't realize he'd said the last sentence out loud.

"Read the note, sir. It might help." The desk attendant spoke again, still holding the note in her hand. Sam locked in on her eyes, and their warmth helped him focus. As he reached for the note, he noticed a security guard beginning to show interest in him from near the doorway. Sam straightened, understanding he may have sent body language signals that he was not well himself.

"Thank you. Would you be able to tell me what's wrong with Rev. Ray, or if he were--?"

"No, sir, I would not. Not officially. But Ms. Charity said to let you know he was still with her when they left for Richmond."

"You have kind eyes," Sam answered.

"I beg your pardon, sir?" Sam realized he'd had been almost whispering. He cleared his throat.

"You have been most kind, thank you. Good evening," he said, a little louder to ensure she heard this version.

Sam turned to go, nodding as cordially as he could manage, to the security guard who continued to watch him closely.

He was still with her when they left for Richmond. Charity Bright's message gave him hope. Of course, anything could happen while Rev. Ray was being transported.

But for now, Sam would take the news as good.

He walked to the van holding Ms. Charity's note, not stopping to read it until he sat in the driver's seat and turned on the dome light.

The writing, on a hospital note pad, appeared scratchy as if hurried. The message was brief and to the point, just as Ms. Charity would have spoken it with her efficient, purposeful tone.

Sam, thank you.

I knew you would come. I think my Raymond will make it.

Don't follow us to Richmond. Need you at the Inn.

God sent you, Sam, for this time. Do what needs doing there.

You won't be sorry.

Charity B.

P.S. Andi can help you access any records you need.

Sam turned off the overhead light and sat for a time, looking up at the night sky. It was strange to be able to see stars. In the city, the lights were so bright that stars were hard to see, unless you were up on a rooftop.

Sam couldn't remember a time when he'd been in such a situation. So much trust had just been placed in his lap by people he didn't know two days ago. He, whose only loyalty until recently had been to himself, was now responsible for keeping a business going and a roof over the heads of the little group of the Inn's dependents, Danisha, Andi, and Johnson Story. Sam wondered if that was all. And Alaine and himself. While they weren't permanent, the Inn was all they had for now.

He could still leave. Sam could just drop off the van and take the next bus out of town. He had a little credit and a few dollars left, even if he didn't count the old man's hundred dollar bills hidden away. If he took Alaine with him, he would have even more money. She'd said she had savings. He couldn't remember how much. Leaving now, before he was more involved, would be the cleanest and safest action. Someone would step up to help Ray and Charity. Of that he was sure. They had a lot of friends.

Sam sat and seriously considered the option. He could see himself taking the out. In a few hours, as soon as the next bus left town, it could be reality. He mentally followed himself to his next destination, somewhere far away from Copper's Run. He considered what the Brights would think about his leaving like this, much less Alaine. It left a sour taste in his mouth.

He started the van and backed out of his parking space in front of the hospital. He hoped he could remember the right turns back to the Inn. He hoped Rev. Ray was still alive.

5 REVELATION

Sampson

It was three days before any further word came from the hospital in Richmond about Raymond Bright's condition. Three days during which the small cadre of workers at the Inn at Copper's Run and Café worked as if Rev. Ray's life depended on them.

The only assurance they had that Rev. Ray was still alive was that the dreaded phone call had not yet come telling of his passing. Every morning at 6:00 a.m. in the Café, Sam held a brief meeting of the help, the regulars and a shifting number of volunteers, depending upon the day. They ate toast and omelets, prepared by Sam and Johnson Story, while they planned. They drank pots of coffee, made lists, sometimes cried, worried, but kept planning.

Sam, who had never been in the military, ran his crew as if he had. He assessed the previous day's successes or errors with them like a colonel. He was direct but positive in his comments, and always asked for input on how to make things run more smoothly. He delegated assignments and asked how he could help make them happen. His final words at each brief meeting were always the same.

"OK, people. We're doing this for Rev. Ray and Ms. Charity. Let's go to work!"

And always Johnson Story cleared his throat and followed with, "Son, would it be all right if I prayed?"

Sam would have preferred to end the time with his call to duty. It was hard for him to understand how the God Rev. Ray served so faithfully would let him get into such a situation, if he could prevent it. Still, Sam wanted to cover all bases, and he didn't have the stomach to turn the older man down.

"Go right ahead, Mr. Story, if you please," Sam always answered.

"Father, the Good Book says you are in your Heaven doing what you please. We beg to let it please you to heal Rev. Ray and bring him and Ms. Charity home to us. Thank you for taking our plea under consideration. In your Son's blessed and holy name, Amen."

Danisha and Andi always followed with their echoed Amens.

On the evening of the third day after Rev. Ray's attack, the phone rang just as the supper crowd was beginning to thin at the Café. On a good night, twenty or thirty people stopped by for the daily specials. Andi was the first to reach the phone, and all eyes were on her as it became clear who was on the other end.

"Ms. Charity? Is that you?" The room became silent.

"We're all here. Everyone's here and a few customers, too. Please tell us what's going on up there."

The little group held its collective breath as Andi listened, making small interjections as she did.

"Oh, no! How bad? Was there damage?" Between each question, there was a pause as Ms. Charity gave her response. No one in the room spoke.

"How long did it take?...Is he still in ICU?...What are you doing?...We didn't think you wanted us to come, so we've just been working here as hard as we can. Sam's about to kill us all, but I'm happy to say, things are going so great you would hardly know yall were gone...Yes ma'am, he's right here. Before you go, Ms. Charity, what do you need? We'll bring you clothes or food or--yes ma'am, here he is," and she motioned with the phone in her hand to Sam.

"Ms. Charity, Sam here. I got your note."

For the next while, Sam stood silent, holding the phone and listening to the voice of Charity Bright while the rest of the little group waited.

"I understand," Sam answered. "We took care of it... Yes, it's done... There have been five guests and seven bookings for next month... We ordered those... I called and had the repairs made yesterday... There is a two week supply remaining... Mr. Baird said not to worry about it until you can get back to the Inn... Of course, I'll take care of it tomorrow... Andi is handling that... That's Danisha's job...Alaine's taking care of it... Well, I put Mr. Story on that one, and it seems to be working out fine."

As he continued to listen, Sam, who had been concentrating on what Ms. Charity was saying, now turned to the huddled group and smiled, giving them all a thumbs up to show Ms. Charity's pleasure at what she was hearing.

"Tell us about Rev. Ray," Sam continued. "Another week? No problem. We can do that. Tell him we can do almost anything but preach for him...Oh wait, I was wrong about that. Tell him Johnson Story said he could take care of the preaching, too."

"I'll tell them all. You take care of the both of you, and let us know what you need. Bye now."

Sam hung up the phone and raised his hand for attention before the questions started.

"It was a heart attack. He's had stints, but he's generally doing well. They have to monitor him closely due to his diabetes so it could be another week, maybe more. She's fine and will call Danisha and Andi if she needs anything. Ms. Charity said to tell you all how thankful they are for each of you. Let me add to that, I think you are doing an incredible job of keeping things here going without Rev.Ray and Ms. Charity. Thank you."

Johnson Story spoke for the little group. "Sampson MacDonald, you were born to be an inn manager. Ray Bright better hurry up and get well, because he might not have a job if he waits much longer."

Sam didn't want the group to see how Johnson Story's words of genuine praise affected him. He met the kind eyes of the older man briefly and turned away.

"OK, let's get this place cleaned up and ready for breakfast. Morning comes early around here these days."

# # #

Alaine

Morning did come early, and Alaine, who had been unable to sleep, eased herself down onto the cold stone steps at the back of the Inn. When Sam found her, she had her knees drawn up and her head buried in her arms. She was visibly shaking. He sat beside her, and she was relieved he didn't rush her with questions about what might be wrong. Instead, he was quiet and simply rested his large hand on her head. He slowly and carefully stroked her hair, letting her know he was near but saying nothing.

Sobs wracked Alaine's body for some time before she gained enough control to raise her head and meet Sam's eyes. Hers were red and swollen, her face tight and pale. She was dressed, but not well. She'd slept in her wrinkled sweats and stained tee shirt, clothes Sam bought in a hurry during their cloistered days in Manhattan after the Towers fell.

She struggled to speak. As she tried, the tears returned, and she covered her face with her hands. She'd rarely felt more miserable, even during the days she spent mostly in bed in the hotel room next to Sam's before they left the City.

Alaine knew now her behavior immediately after September 11 could likely be attributed to shock. The depression that followed had left her even more quiet and reticent than usual. The full awareness of what they escaped was just now making its full impact on her.

But this circumstance was different from the horror just past. This was a fresh shock that left her agitated and having trouble communicating why.

Sam reached for her hand in comfort, but she jerked away, stood up on shaking legs and stumbled down the steps. He caught her just as she reached the bottom step and broke her momentum as she threw herself down on her knees and retched again and again while he brushed her hair back and held her head.

When she finally stopped being sick, wiped her mouth on her tee shirt and sat back on the bottom step, she again pulled away from Sam, who was still holding on to her arms.

"I'm pregnant, Sam. I've been afraid of this, but now I'm sure. I'm going to have Paul Mowher's baby. What am I going to do?" Alaine leaned over the side of the steps, sick again.

When she finished, they sat in silence. She could feel Sam's astonishment. Alaine knew he'd felt good about his accomplishments of finding a refuge for them and successfully orchestrating the Inn's activities. She understood her announcement could significantly complicate matters for both of them. She had no words to respond to his unspoken concerns.

Sam broke the painful silence.

"Are you sure? How do you know?" Sam's voice sounded skeptical, accusatory, almost as if he didn't believe her.

"This is not food poisoning, Sam. And I took a test this morning. It was positive. This is no joke. I'm going to have a baby."

Sam followed with another question so insensitive and offensive that she couldn't believe the Sam she'd gotten to know would asked it.

"The father...are you sure it's--?"

She was tempted not to respond, but the wave of sickness that overcame her again prompted uncharacteristic sarcasm.

"Well, let's see," she said between retches. "Let me check my date book. Yes, sure enough, the father is Paul Mowher, the person of dubious character with whom I used to reside. Are there any more painfully intrusive questions you'd like for me to answer? Would a polygraph help?"

Alaine avoided Sam's outstretched hand, ran up the steps and inside the Inn, closing the door not quietly behind her, hoping the sound served to underline Sam's knowledge that he had not gotten good marks for his response to her revelation.

# # #

Sampson

Sam glanced at his watch. In ten minutes he would go on duty, meaning he needed to make sure everything was up and running inside. This job usually gave him a rush, a sense of expectancy, something to look forward to. This morning there was no anticipation, only dread. He had ten minutes to figure out what to do next.

And so he sat, considering Alaine and her situation. Since their escape from the North Tower, his role with Alaine had been somewhat paternal, with him serving as rescuer, provider, and guardian. He'd gotten used to protecting Alaine, but he hadn't considered the sense of ownership that came along with the job. How else could he explain his audacity in questioning her about the identity of the father of her baby?

Sam ran his fingers through his black hair, leaving it rowed and unkempt. What possessed him? Alaine had told him she lived with this Paul Mowher. She'd made it clear she didn't want to go back to him. That was why she agreed to leave the City with Sam, and she apparently had few other options.

A baby. He hadn't considered such a possibility. How would the prospect affect their circumstances, his circumstances? Now he was thinking paternally again.

The thought came to Sam that her condition didn't have to affect him at all. The truth was that Alaine and her pregnancy were not his ultimate responsibility.

He acknowledged that, on one level, he cared about her, had cared about her even while they worked together. Alaine was lovely. But she was also vulnerable and needy. Sam thought back to the first time he became aware of her in the office. What made him notice her more than in passing? Was it her fragile physical beauty? That...yes. But that wasn't all.

Sam had never been attracted to looks alone. There had to be more. What was the more with Alaine? Was it her helplessness? He'd never considered himself a rescuer. Did her defenseless spirit make him feel needed?

But then, attraction was one thing...a baby was another. Sam checked his watch again. His processing time was up. Just as well. This line of thinking was giving him a headache. He stood up and prepared to start the workday at the Inn.

# # #

By the end of that day, Sam had managed to take the level of operations of the Inn and Café from somewhat efficient to near hopeless, at least in his own eyes. Andi was reduced to tears and Danisha to threats of bodily harm...his. He hadn't seen Alaine all day.

It seemed that the only one who was speaking to him by the end of the relentless hours was Johnson Story, and that was to invite him to share two small glasses of wine for, as the man said, medicinal purposes. Sam was relieved that someone still wanted his company. In the end, he should have seen what was coming and declined.

"Son, you don't mind if I call you son, do you? You remind me of my own boy. He'd be fifty-six now. Had his own law firm down in Birmingham. I loved that boy. Been gone five years. You remind me of him."

"How's that, Mr. Story?" Sam asked, warming to the personal conversation and preparing for a compliment.

"Well, my boy was stubborn, headstrong and thickheaded is how. I had to deal with that boy many a time on how he came across to folks. He just got something on his mind and nothing could stop what came out his mouth, no matter how it sounded or who got hurt. I think he meant well. According to him, folks need to hear things straight out, no holds barred. He said it's better to get matters out in the open and not cover up with nice words like most of us do. How did he put it? Tell it like it is. That's what he'd always say. Yes sir, I loved that boy something fierce."

Sam couldn't believe the irony of what he was hearing. Johnson Story was sure telling it like it is to Sam while pretending to be talking about his late son. The situation was so transparent that Sam laughed.

Johnson Story looked at him with amusement and affection.

"You got my point?" he asked Sam.

"I certainly did, sir. No holds barred. You think I've been heavy handed with the help today."

"Is that the message you got, son?"

"From both sides. From you and from the ladies. Was it that obvious?"

"What came across was that you weren't yourself today, Sampson. Things have been going fine the last few days. Better than any of us expected, I'm sure. But today, you just weren't yourself. I'm not asking. The business is yours. But you need to pull yourself together soon for everybody's sake and the sake of this old Inn. We need you on your game, son, and we need to work together."

With this said, the old man stood, acknowledging the conversation was at an end. Sam could tell Mr. Story was tired, and he stood also, offering the old man his hand.

"Thank you, Mr. Story. I'm glad I make you think of your son. Thanks for treating me like one." They shook hands.

Sam did one last security check around the Inn before heading toward his room. It was almost eleven, and he was tired and hungry. There had been no time for supper, but he was too tired now to make the effort.

He stopped at the door across from his. Alaine must be asleep by now. She never liked staying up much past ten. Sam was surprised to see a light coming from under her door. He could hear what sounded like muffled music from within. Alaine was still awake.

Sam raised his hand to give a knock on her door, but stopped the movement just short of contact. What would he say? How far was he willing to go to fix the damage of the morning? He was too tired to answer his own questions, let alone deal with Alaine.

Sam crossed the hall and entered his room, closing the door silently behind him.

# # #

His body was tired, but Sam still spent a weary night awake as his mind replayed the clumsy and unthinking way he'd treated Alaine at her announcement of the pregnancy. It took him by surprise, but that was no excuse. Alaine needed support, and he failed her. His penance was a night without rest, but by morning, he had a plan to redeem himself in her eyes.

Sam's inability to sleep gave him an excuse to access the Internet in the Inn's office in the early hours before the activities of the day began. He spent the time researching area medical facilities, few in this rural portion of the state, which offered abortion counseling and services. He could do the legwork, check out the places, ask some questions, and then help Alaine set up the procedure whenever she was ready.

The activity of pursuing his plan made Sam feel as if he was already helping her take control of an unwelcome situation. He was now eager to make amends for his lack of finesse from the day before.

With plans in order, Sam made his way to the Café for the morning meeting. It was early yet, but Andi and Danisha were in the kitchen sharing preparations for the breakfast diners. The looks they gave him were wary and their greetings restrained.

"Good morning, ladies. I wish to apologize for my less than civilized behavior of yesterday. I would like to claim that I was temporarily insane, but in fact, I was a bit preoccupied with a problem."

He could see they weren't buying this line of apology.

"Actually, that's not a credible excuse. I was out of line, and I'm sorry."

His change of tack must have seemed more palatable as the two now responded more favorably.

"Sam, you're doing a good job. You just need to relax," Danisha spoke. "You can trust we know what to do and how to do it. We didn't just come to work here last week."

"That's right," said Andi. "No telling how long we'll all have to run this big old place by ourselves, so no use getting into a cat fight about it. We need to cover each other's backs, not be at each other's necks."

Sam laughed at Andi's turn of phrase. They were right.

"Message received," Sam responded. "Has anyone seen Alaine yet this morning?"

"She wasn't feeling so good, and we sent her back to bed. We have a couple of volunteers coming in and don't really need her today. Did you two have a disagreement or something?" Danisha could be direct.

Andi rescued him. "Danisha, that might not be a large part of your business. Leave the man alone and help me with these muffins. Won't be long before our public arrives."

Sam stayed long enough for coffee, a sweet roll and a brief morning meeting with the staff before going back to the Inn's office to see what the day would bring. It was late afternoon before he took a break from ordering supplies, responding to email inquiries and balancing accounts. He still had not seen Alaine, although he heard her voice in the hall as she and one of the volunteers passed by. She must be feeling better.

Sam had one last personal task to complete in the office before heading to the Café to help out with dinner. He typed in a final Internet search to complete the information he needed to carry out his plan devised in the early hours of the morning.

When finished, Sam went in search of Alaine. She had settled into a routine of filling in wherever the greatest need was from day to day as her way of helping the Inn run smoothly. This included assisting with hospitality when guests arrived and relieving Sam whenever he needed to be away from the office.

Sam sought her assistance now as he wanted to take the next morning off. He found her in the Inn's laundry room folding sheets.

"Alaine," he greeted.

"Sam," was all she answered.

"Listen, I have an important errand to run tomorrow morning. Could you cover the front desk for me? And maybe there'll be time later for us to have a minute?"

"Yes, to your first request," she responded, followed by a noncommittal, "and maybe to your second." With that exchange, she slipped out of the room.

6 SAM'S PLAN

Sampson

The lines of communication with Alaine were still not open, but Sam refused to let that fact dampen his determination to make things right. The next morning, he backed the Inn's van out of its parking space, and following the directions he pulled from online, he started toward his destination.

The New Phase Reproduction Planning and Counseling Center was in a town a little larger than Copper's Run about fifteen miles to the north. Once he located the main highway linking the two towns, he had no trouble finding the Center. Sam was impressed from first glance. The building, though not large, was new, and the landscaping was immaculate. He'd feared finding an establishment that was less than inviting, but its professional appearance boosted his confidence considerably.

Sam was adamant with himself that his approach would not involve conversation stating, "I have a friend who...," so when he approached the smiling receptionist, his request was forthright.

"Good morning, I would like to speak with someone about the process of setting up an abortion. My girlfriend is pregnant, and we have decided to terminate the pregnancy. I would like to discuss this with a person who might be able to assist us."

Sam found that, while his voice seemed bold and confident to his ears, his hands shook. He wondered if the young woman noticed.

She smiled as if his request was one she heard regularly and routinely.

"Yes, of course, Mr...?"

"MacDonald, that's M-a-c. Sampson MacDonald."

"If you will have a seat, Mr. MacDonald, I'll find someone who can speak with you."

The waiting room was well appointed and empty. He had just enough time to sit and reach for a magazine when the receptionist returned.

"If you will come with me, Mr. MacDonald, one of our nurse counseling staff will speak with you."

He followed to a small, well-kept consultation room. Sam was more sure with each piece of information gathered that he had chosen his abortion clinics well.

He was joined by an attractive and efficient looking nurse who greeted him with warmth, introduced herself and offered a chair. She came immediately to the point.

"I understand you have some questions about our services, Mr. MacDonald?"

Sam decided to follow her lead and be equally direct.

"I do. My girlfriend has just discovered she's pregnant. The timing and circumstances are inconvenient for us both. It's not that we don't like children (*why am I saying this?*), but now is not the time. I'm sure you've heard this often enough."

"You're correct, Mr. MacDonald; we certainly have. And we can assist you with your dilemma, I'm sure. Tell me, do your feelings express those of your girlfriend, as well?"

"Yes, I believe they do. While we haven't discussed it at length yet, I'm sure she is as concerned about her situation as I am."

"This is an abortion clinic, Mr. MacDonald. You do understand that our services entail the performing of abortions and related counseling for up to a month before and after the procedure."

"A month? She wouldn't want to wait that long. Do we have to wait a month for this...procedure?"

"Not if both of you are sure this is what you want. I'm confident you are aware there are alternatives to abortion, such as adoption. Have you discussed them?"

"As I said, a baby simply wouldn't fit into the picture at this time. I didn't want to mention it, but my girlfriend has just been through the September 11th ordeal first hand. She was in one of the Towers when the plane hit. I think that's enough trauma for the time being."

The nurse was quiet for a moment.

"I see. We'll need to meet with her, of course, before the procedure. There are papers to sign and medical history to gather. Shall I set up an appointment, or would she like to call for herself?"

"Why don't we just set something up? If she has further questions, then she can call."

When Sam drove away from the Center, he had the appointment card for a date in the next week. The interview had gone well, and the process seemed simple. There didn't appear to be undue red tape, no long wait, and the result would be that Alaine's problem would be solved.

Sam was tempted to drive straight back to the Inn and tell Alaine the plan. He was eager to patch up the apparent rift in their friendship and wanted to show that he was working proactively on her behalf.

He had, however, made plans to visit one other facility. Although a date had been set at his previous site, some small nudging caused him to re-consider returning home immediately in favor of making the additional stop. At least by doing so he could tell Alaine he had considered more than one resource.

This second place was located at an address in Copper's Run. As he followed his directions, Sam could see that they were taking him to a part of town with which he was unfamiliar. The houses and few businesses of the neighborhood were closer together, smaller and not as well kept as those downtown.

Pictures of the less than reputable abortion clinics he had read about began to flash before his mind, and he slowed the van in anticipation of finding somewhere to turn around so he could abandon the visit.

At that moment, Sam realized he'd reached the address of the second facility. The building was a storefront, small and old but freshly painted. A discreet sign announced that he had arrived at the Life Options Pregnancy Assistance Center.

He could park on the street or in a small dirt lot beside the Center. Sampson opted for a spot across the street. The building was white wood and cement, Sam thought it had once been a neighborhood shop. There was no large window in front, but rather a bank of small panes through which he could view a shallow display case visible to passersby. Sam stopped for a moment to see what was inside. There was a sign that read:

Pregnant? Don't know where to turn?

Please allow us to assist you with your decisions.

Underneath the words were a series of colorful pictures in an orderly display. When he stepped up to get a closer look, he could see they featured a progression of photos of a developing human fetus. That much he remembered from college anatomy.

The first picture showed a mass of tissue in which was barely discernible an enlarged head, eye depressions and the stumps of arms and legs. The labeling beneath stated:

Janine: Age 6 weeks out from conception.

The next, showing the fetus with features similar to a newborn, read:

Janine: Age 12 weeks out from conception.

There were several others, and the final picture was of a pretty young woman, blonde and smiling, who was maybe in her early twenties. The caption read:

Janine: Age 23 years–at her college graduation.

Sam stood reviewing the images. Something about the display was offensive. He felt anger working inside of him, anger and tension that he hadn't felt since escaping from the job that he found so oppressive.

Again, he considered turning back toward the van, but the anger held him in place, making him want to express his opinions to someone on the premises who might be responsible for this propaganda.

Sam turned the white glass knob to the old front door beside of the display windows and walked inside.

He expected to encounter an interior that was sleazy, run down and smelling of mold. He expected to find the building's occupants to be worse...severe, opinionated and outdated in their dress and actions.

What he found was a warm and inviting space that was a cross between den and reception room. It smelled of coffee and something sweet...cinnamon? There was a desk and computer area to one side and a welcoming sitting area on the other. The woman who sat at the desk was anything but severe.

"Hello, welcome to Life Options. I'm Jane Dabney." The woman stood. "Please come in and tell me how we may help you." Her smile seemed genuine.

Jane Dabney appeared to be in her mid to late forties, but her age didn't deny her soft beauty. There were fine laugh lines around her mouth and outside of her eyes that told Sam she smiled, or laughed, often and with pleasure.

Nothing about her appearance gave an impression of calling attention to herself. Her light brown hair was drawn back at the neck, she wore no jewelry except for a single gold band on her left hand, and her dress was unadorned. Her voice was clear and friendly. She was slight and graceful.

Sam, who had entered on a mission to voice his disapproval of the display outside, found it hard to remember why he was here.

Jane Dabney stood smiling at him as he groped to re-gather. Sam spoke as if unable to control his words. "Who is Janine? The pictures outside...(he pointed behind himself)...who is she?"

"She's my daughter. The pictures before she was born were taken because she was at high risk for a genetic disorder. We were being followed closely at a university hospital. She was one of the first to have such prenatal pictures made. Janine's twenty-five now and in graduate school."

Sam still was unable to help what he said.

"And the genetic disorder?"

"It never appeared. The risk was so great I'd been advised, pressured really, to terminate the pregnancy. Janine's fine. If I had done that, I wouldn't have her today."

"But how could you be sure? What if she--?"

"I'd have made the same decision. Being conceived was not her choice. Letting her be born was mine and her father's. Much of life is a risk, Mr...?"

"MacDonald. Sampson MacDonald." He'd composed himself enough to regain his displeasure at having to view this blatant attempt to proselytize a moral position. "I'm here to discuss Life Options available to my girlfriend. We're actually planning to have an abortion and are comparing facilities and plans."

Sam followed this speech with the most direct and challenging look he could give Jane Dabney, who was perhaps the most unchallenging opponent he'd ever faced.

"Mr. MacDonald, we would be happy to discuss Life Options with you. Would you mind if I called my associate to join us? You see, usually it's the ladies who come in. I think you would appreciate a gentleman's perspective. Am I right?" There was kindness in her eyes.

The only response Sam had to the lady's question was a curt nod of his head. He stood waiting while she stepped through the door at the back of the room.

In less than a minute, Jane Dabney returned with a man only slightly taller than she and about her age.

"Sampson MacDonald, this is my husband, David. David Dabney."

In spite of himself, Sam couldn't resist the outstretched hand and eyes that riveted him as if they knew his thoughts.

"Mr. MacDonald, why don't you follow me to my office where we can talk? Jane, you come too. I'll have Bet to cover the front."

David Dabney's office was as simple and organized as Sam knew it would be. Here was a no-nonsense man cloaked with a kind spirit. He chose one of the comfortable club chairs offered, and the Dabneys sat together on the couch. As Sam expected, Dabney came right to the point.

"You wanted information related to abortion and Life Options alternatives available for you and your loved one?"

Sam found it hard to rekindle the anger he'd felt earlier when first suspecting the Life Options operation was biased against abortions. Maybe he'd judged too quickly. This man seemed intelligent and reasonable. He would hear Dabney out.

"Yes, she's just discovered she's pregnant. My girlfriend has recently undergone severe stress due to her escape from one of the World Trade Center buildings where she was working just before it fell. I don't think she's in any condition to carry a child due to the mental trauma, and who knows what else she was exposed to from the fallout."

Why do I feel compelled to retell this story as if it were an excuse for the procedure?

The couple sat silent. David Dabney's eyes never left his, and Sam was not comfortable as the feeling returned that Dabney could see what he was thinking. After the pause, the man asked Sam a series of quiet questions.

"Mr. MacDonald...Sampson, please forgive me for asking, but are you this child's father?"

Sam frowned. This line of talk made him even more uncomfortable and was, in his opinion, none of Dabney's business.

"I don't see what--"

"Please bear with me. I'm trying to figure out why you're here alone. Usually it's the young woman who comes in for help, or at least the two. Often we never meet the baby's father."

"As I mentioned, the lady is my girlfriend." Sam locked eyes with Dabney, thinking he could convince him of his story by keeping eye contact and sounding forceful. The ruse failed in the face of Dabney's quiet strength.

"Actually, she's a friend. I'm not the father. He's not in the picture. I'm here for information on how to get her out of an impossible situation. I'm sure an abortion is the quickest and best way to wrap up a bad circumstance."

"The events of September 11th occurred a little more than three weeks ago. What brings your friend and you to Copper's Run?"

Sam hadn't planned to reveal any more than absolutely necessary to gain the information he needed and convince Alaine to end the pregnancy. Here he was answering questions that seemed extraneous to his purpose.

"Look, I don't want to bore you with the backstory. I just need some facts, and I'll be out of your hair."

It was Jane who responded this time. "We're not bored, Sampson. Your friend is obviously in need, and we'd like to help. It's what we do."

Silence followed. Sam had never been good at leaving silence in conversations. He'd also never encountered anything like this situation. In spite of the Dabneys' hospitality, Sam felt like he'd just been given truth serum and put on a chair under a naked light bulb in front of a panel of inquisitors.

"My friend and I worked together in the North Tower. We were in the building when the first plane hit. Our building was the last of the Towers to fall.

We escaped and found a place to stay put for a while, and then we got out of town. Both of us were through with the City. Copper's Run is where the bus brought us. We're staying at the Inn located there."

Sam couldn't believe how freely he was speaking. It embarrassed him, but he seemed unable to stop. He hadn't told anyone the details of his and Alaine's story until now. As the couple sat before him, waiting and expectant, he kept going.

"My friend got pregnant during a former relationship...not a good one and one that is now ended. She just let me know about her situation. I'm trying to help out."

"And what is your current relationship to the young lady, Sampson? Why do you feel it necessary to act on her behalf?" asked David.

"As I said, we're friends or acquaintances really. I helped her escape, and she depends on me, at least she has been. That's it."

"You said you're staying at the Inn? I know the innkeeper, Rev. Bright, has been out of commission for some time, and his wife's been in Richmond with him at the hospital. You're not by any chance the young man who's doing such an admirable job of filling in for them, are you?" Jane Dabney was looking at him with renewed curiosity.

"Well, it's a joint effort really. We're all sort of working together. Things seem to be going fairly well for now."

"We've heard they're going quite well," said David as he sat forward and changed the subject.

"Let me be clear with you about what we have to offer here at Life Options, Sampson. You mentioned an abortion. We don't offer that option or recommend it elsewhere for a number of reasons, which we'll discuss if and when you wish. What we do offer here is dictated by our name, Life Options. We offer parent counseling and various alternative approaches that preserve the life of the unborn child."

Sam nodded, and Dabney continued.

"Our options include assistance to the mother or the couple during the prenatal period and birth, both open and closed adoptions, and long-term support of the mother or couple if they decide to keep the child."

Sam reached the limit of his already stretched comfort zone. This was not going in the direction he'd planned.

"Look, David...Jane, I appreciate your interest and your time. I've taken enough of both. Fortunately, we aren't to the stage where we're talking about a child yet. This is an unwanted pregnancy we're discussing, and the fetus my friend is carrying is just that. It's not a baby or a child, as you're calling it. I think my friend will want to end this before it becomes one." He rose to his feet.

"How far along in her pregnancy is your friend, if I may ask?" Jane asked.

"I'm not exactly sure. She just discovered this dilemma herself. I'm thinking no more than about six weeks. Why do you ask?"

"Sampson, would you consider one request I would like to make? I know we've just met and that you have a plan. Still, I feel I must ask you one favor." Jane and David were also standing now. Jane Dabney's look gave him no doubt about the seriousness of her question.

"What do you have in mind?" Sam's response was cautious as if he suspected a trap behind her serious demeanor.

"Would you be willing to bring your friend to meet us for a brief conversation before you make other arrangements? We understand your urgency and are willing to meet at your convenience. We wouldn't ask or intrude into your affairs if we didn't consider this matter and both of you as important to us. Please allow us to speak with your friend, if she will come. Abortion is a complicated step and may not provide the solution to the problem that you're seeking."

Jane waited with her eyes on Sam's and her hand on his arm. Sam wavered and looked away. He'd come into this conference with absolute self-assurance that his position and decision were correct about how the pregnancy should be handled. Here were two polite and non-threatening people who presumed to have another approach. They'd known him for what...fifteen minutes? Yet they were politely challenging his judgment.

Who were they to put him in such a position? Were it not for him, Alaine might well be dead and her baby...whatever.. with her. How could he not know better than they what was best for her? Even as his self-righteousness grew, Sam could feel Jane Dabney's determination not to let him side step her request and something more. He saw authentic concern that was so unexpected, so foreign to him that it stopped the angry words he prepared to deliver.

He stood, mouth open, with no reply in mind despite his feelings. David added, in a voice that also betrayed emotion, "Sampson, did you happen to see the picture displays in our windows on the way in?"

"I did," Sam answered. "Your wife explained them to me."

"Twenty-six years ago we stood at the same crossroads where you stand now. We came within minutes of making the same choice as I sense you and your friend are about to make."

Jane's low voice followed. "We didn't go through with the abortion. We thank God for that. I'd like for you and your friend to hear our story. Will you bring her to meet us?"

Sam looked at the couple before him and wondered how he'd managed to get into the middle of this. All he wanted to do was be away from them as quickly as possible, to leave without responding to their request and without thinking about those pictures of their daughter. Their story wasn't his and Alaine's. His decision wasn't theirs to make...or to influence, for that matter.

Sam opened his mouth to thank the Dabneys, decline their offer and make his exit. Instead, his voice betrayed him once more by saying, "I'll try. I can't promise. I'm not sure she'll agree."

Jane smiled and took his hand.

"That's good enough," she said.

"May I pray for you?" David waited for Sam's reply with no hint of coercion.

As unaccustomed as he was to that happening, David's question made him uncomfortable. He had no reason to believe prayers went beyond the boundaries of the rooms where they were spoken. Even if the act of praying held some inexplicable therapeutic value, it was on such a personal level as to be invasive if another presumed to pray for you.

Still, the only graceful way Sam could see out of what had become a highly charged situation was to nod his head in assent.

David prayed. It was short and to the point. "Heavenly Father, please take control of Sampson's situation. Work your highest will for yourself, for Sampson, for his friend and for this little life. Amen."

David offered his handshake while Jane smiled and reminded Sam, "I look forward to meeting your friend. I'll pray she'll come."

When Sam reached what felt like the safety of his car, he pulled out of his parking space as quickly as possible without calling attention to his departure. He was not one to share emotions and intimacies freely. This encounter was too close and personal to suit him.

# # #

Once away from the Dabneys, events of the last hour convinced Sam his first choice of a solution to Alaine's problem was correct. She needed an abortion and as soon as possible. That would end the matter outright.

Going directly from the Life Options Center back to the Inn with its duties and people was not his preference at the moment, so Sam headed toward the edge of town where he'd seen a small park. He needed to regain some balance and prepare himself for his conversation with Alaine.

It was critical that he make her understand why she needed to have an abortion soon so she could get on with her life. It was the only sensible thing to do that didn't have strings attached...strings that would last for another 18 years, at least.

Sam sat in his car in the park's empty lot and began to devise his strategy and the words he would use to convince her. In fact, he'd find a way to take her to the clinic today if the abortion procedure could be arranged that quickly.

In spite of his promise to ask Alaine to meet with the Dabneys, Sam was convinced their past situation had been vastly different from Alaine's present one. He also had no desire to learn more about their story and no real intention of fulfilling his promise.

As soon as Sam made his decisions, he felt immediate relief. The feeling lasted until his mind replayed the pictures of the Dabney's daughter, Janine, displayed in the Center's windows. Especially difficult to erase was the contrast between the one of Janine at six weeks after conception and the one at her college graduation.

7 ALAINE'S RESPONSE

Sampson

It was almost noon when Sam drove the van into the employee lot at the rear of the Inn. He'd been away all morning. While he knew the crew would keep things running smoothly, he still felt guilty for such a long absence. One person out of place could stress the others.

He went directly to the Café, by-passing the front desk in case Alaine should still be on duty there. She was not in the Café. As he expected, Johnson Story, Danisha and Andi had everything well in hand. The Café's dining area was nearly full. The tables had fresh flowers, and Sam noted the obviously contented diners. Ms. Charity would be proud.

Sam circulated among the customers, greeting and refreshing tea and water glasses. Most asked about Rev. Ray. Many said they were praying for the couple, who were clearly well liked in Copper's Run.

"Long time no see, Mr. Innkeeper," Danisha whispered as they passed in the kitchen. "Maybe you need to see if Alaine will come and have lunch. We suspect she skipped breakfast, too."

"Sam, we're worried. She's pretty upset. It's obvious something's wrong. Please see if you can find out what." This came from Andi as she passed an order to him for table delivery.

He worked steadily for the next hour helping to clear out the main lunch crowd. There was a small tour bus that had scheduled four tables for 12:30, so there was little time to dwell on Alaine's predicament. It was almost 2:00 before things lightened up enough for him to slip out to find her, a portable meal in hand she might find tempting.

Sam found Alaine at the desk in the reception room. He watched her from the doorway without letting her know he was there. Her misery showed through her face and posture.

He set the food on the desk, reached around Alaine to activate the Inn's answer machine and put the sign telling walk-in guests to proceed to the Café for assistance on the counter.

"Alaine, please come with me. I have food, and I'd like to talk," Sam said as he put his hands on her shoulders and gently lifted. He was surprised when she complied, allowing him to help her stand. Carrying her food tray, he led her out the Inn's front door to one of the metal tables Ray and Charity had placed in a side garden.

Alaine didn't speak as he spread a cloth napkin down and placed her food and drink on top. She ate immediately and without argument but also without talking.

Sam waited, not interrupting her lunch.

When she finished, she finally spoke, sounding surprisingly normal. "Thank you. That was good. I was about to starve. Where were you all morning?"

He decided to attack the issue head on.

"Taking care of some important business...for you. I was a jerk yesterday. Alaine, I'm sorry. I was insensitive and unthinking...completely out of line. I hope you can forgive me."

She sat for a long minute, giving him time, he was sure, to feel the hurt he'd caused. Her response was a simple, "I do." She repeated her earlier question, "So, where were you this morning?"

"Alaine," Sam answered, "I have a plan. That's where I was. Working out some of the details. Look at this." He handed her the brochure on the first abortion clinic from his pocket. "I think this might be the solution to your problem."

Alaine took her time reading the front of the brochure. She opened it and read the rest of the information while Sam waited, watching for signs of the relief he knew he would soon see.

Her reaction shocked him.

Alaine closed the brochure without looking up. She then tore it again and again until the pieces were small enough to defy further shredding.

Only when the paper pieces were scattered across the table and ground around them did she look at Sam. He read anger and disgust on her face.

"Sampson--" she stopped, rested her hands flat on the table in front of her, and started again. This time her voice was measured and controlled. "Sam, I know you're trying to help. I don't want to be unfair. We haven't known each other for very long. I realize there's no way you can understand how I feel. So, please let me be clear now, with no mistake. I would never...ever...abort this child. Not for you, not for Paul Mowher, not for anyone. I don't know what I'm going to do, but I do know I will not kill my baby."

Alaine stood up, letting pieces of the brochure fall around her.

Sam spread his hands to her, keeping his voice soft and low as if talking to a child. "Alaine, please give me a minute. This is for your good. Think about it. With the stress you've been through and the toxins we breathed from those buildings coming down around us, there's no telling—"

He never got to finish his sentence. Alaine put her finger to her lips in a quieting gesture, turned away from the table toward the Inn and fainted dead away on the garden path.

# # #

Alaine

The nurse practitioner at the local urgent care clinic, where Alaine was transported after her episode in the garden, confirmed her pregnancy but said other tests didn't indicate any serious problem. She assured Alaine, and Sam who joined them after her examination, that it was not at all unusual for pregnant women to experience weakness, dizziness and even an occasional fainting spell.

While she believed the medical expert in principle, only Alaine understood the real reason she had passed out. That information she kept to herself, not knowing whether Sam understood the stress and distress he had put her under with his so-called abortion plan.

In all fairness to him, he had no way of comprehending the bond she had formed with this child she was carrying, even in the short time she realized she was pregnant. She knew Sam was just trying to support her. But that thought was overshadowed by both his insensitive reaction to her pregnancy and now by his insistence that ending the pregnancy was her path out of her *problem,* as he called it. The Sam who had sustained her during their ordeal in the City had just twice proven to be a source of hurt here in Copper's Run.

On the way back to the Inn, Sam tried in vain to engage Alaine in conversation. While she was thankful he avoided further mention of the abortion option, she could only respond to his efforts in monosyllables, if at all. At the moment, she couldn't bring herself to care that her unresponsive reactions left him with an unrequited apology on his lips.

Back at the Inn, Alaine declared her intentions of going to bed for the remainder of the day. When Andi and Danisha discovered she'd fainted and Sam had taken her to the clinic, they took over and shooed him away, marshaling her to her room.

# # #

Alaine slept late the next morning. When she emerged at noon, feeling refreshed and fit, Sam's was the first face she saw. It was not the same face from the previous day when he suggested she end her pregnancy, still, he didn't apologize. When she backed away to leave the room by the same doorway she entered, he spoke with pleading in his voice.

"Alaine, just hear me out." Sam talked fast, and held his hands out in supplication. "I don't want to upset you again. Please, just listen to the rest of what I have to say. I also went somewhere else yesterday morning. It was not like the other place in the brochure. It's right here in town. It's called Life Options Pregnancy Assistance Center. They don't do abortions. I met a couple of the counselors, Jane and David Dabney."

Suspicion kept her body tense as Alaine listened, with reluctance, to Sam's words. "What did you tell them?" she asked.

"I never used your name. I basically made up a story about having a girlfriend who was pregnant, and said we were considering ...alternatives. I let them know what you'd been through with the 911 attacks, and that I didn't think you should go through a pregnancy."

Alaine hoped her face showed with clarity how she felt about Sam's uninvited imposition into this most personal part of her life, regardless of how sincere his motives were.

"Go on. I'm listening." There was no warmth in her reply.

"That's all. They just asked if I would please bring you in to meet them. I'm fairly certain they want to talk you out of the abortion that you're not planning to have anyway. But I promised I'd ask you to meet them. I gave my word I would try, so I'm trying. What do you think about it?"

Sam's face showed his great surprise when her next words were, "I'll go. I need to talk to someone. I'll hear what they have to say. Sam?"

"What did you say?"

"I'll go. But your girlfriend? Why did you say that about me?"

"I just figured they'd take me more seriously. Even they said that most women come in alone. Look, this is new to me, too. Believe it or not, I really am trying to help."

"I know that, Sam. It's just that...we're not--"

"Look, don't worry. Before I left, I let them know we are...friends instead."

She thought that clarification would make her feel better. It didn't, and she didn't know why.

"I tried to make it right, Alaine. Now what's wrong?

"Nothing." Since it was not something she could explain, she had no response. "Please just call and make the arrangements."

# # #

Sampson

Setting the meeting up with the Dabneys didn't take long. When Sam punched in the number from a card Jane pressed into his hand at the end of his meeting with them, David answered. They wanted to meet Alaine immediately. He and Jane offered a time the same evening, when the supper hour at the Café would be ending.

The two couples met at the Life Options Center. It rained on the way. The street was deserted and dark, reflecting the van's lights and creating a sense that Sam and Alaine were the only two persons in the town. Just one small spotlight lit the front of the old storefront that was the Center.

The light was dim but the greeting Alaine and Sam received at the entrance was warm and authentic. The Dabneys exuded an infectious calm. Without ceremony, they welcomed Sam and Alaine into a meeting room, comfortable after the cool of the early October evening.

"Come sit next to me, Alaine. It's so nice to meet you." Jane took Alaine's hand in hers and drew her to their seats. Sam took David's handshake even as his automatic defenses and a reluctance to be drawn into a potentially vulnerable position settled over him.

David began. "Alaine, as you know, we asked Sampson to bring you here. He told us about your pregnancy and that you're considering your options. If you're more comfortable meeting separately with Jane while Sampson and I talk, that's fine. We want you to be at ease."

"No, I'm all right. This is fine. It's no problem for us to be together." Her voice was soft but firm.

Sam cleared his throat. "I need to say something." He forced himself to look directly at David and then Jane.

They waited for him to continue.

"I need to apologize for a statement I made when I was here earlier. I first told you Alaine was my girlfriend. While I did correct it, out of respect for her, I have to repeat that we aren't a couple. I...ah...wasn't sure how else to explain why I was here talking to you about her. We're friends. We've been through a lot together, but we aren't together, romantically I mean."

After a pause, David spoke.

"I understand. Thank you, Sampson. May I ask again, does that also mean that you are not the father of Alaine's baby?"

"It does," Sam answered. Alaine nodded agreement and spoke.

"The father was someone I once cared about. He's not in the picture anymore."

"Do you want him to be?" Jane asked, looking at Alaine beside of her.

"No, he doesn't know about the pregnancy. I just found out myself. I have no desire for him to know. He's back in...where I used to live."

"Alaine, Sampson told us what you two went through in the City on September 11th, how you made it out and got here. I'm thinking that you had divine help all the way." Alaine watched Jane as she spoke. "Tell me how you feel about this pregnancy."

Alaine laced her fingers together and clenched them in her lap. Her hands shook. It was some time before she could answer. Sam watched tears slide down her face.

When she did respond, it was as if she only directed it to Jane. "At first, I was horrified. The father...our relationship...was not good. He's...once I got over the shock of being pregnant and realized it was true, I started to think about what it would look like, what it would feel and smell like...the baby I mean."

David spoke next, and Sam thought he gently tested Alaine. "Sampson was afraid you'd been through too much to think about having a baby. You've had trauma most folks will never experience. And you likely were exposed to unknown contaminants. How about all of that?"

Alaine glanced first at Sam and then addressed David. "I've thought about it, even in the short time I've known about the baby. Maybe it's true this isn't going to be a good pregnancy. It might not last. Something could go wrong. I might not get to see this baby born. But I know I have to try."

David continued. "Alaine, it's true lots of people make another choice. It's neither unusual nor illegal. It's up to you. And I know that a body...your body...can only take so much stress. What will happen next with your pregnancy is only partly in your hands." His words were straightforward, but his tone gentle as he continued.

"But it's been my experience that we humans can take a whole lot more than we think we can. That goes for unborn babies, too. While you do have options, keep in mind you aren't simply choosing for yourself. You're also choosing life or death for your child. This child doesn't know anything about 9/11 or who its father is or anything else for that matter. This child is not even aware that it's depending on you to keep its life going as long as you can."

Sam broke into David's statements. "I just think Alaine needs to be able to put all she's been through in the past and start over. Here...somewhere else...anywhere but in New York City. She shouldn't have to start over facing this new crisis. A baby would only remind her of all that's happened. This can end...be finished and behind her. That's all I'm saying."

Jane answered for Alaine. "Sampson, there's a myth that says it's all finished when the abortion's over, that everything reverts back to pre-pregnancy normal. That's not usually the case. Abortion may solve one immediate problem, but the repercussions, the side effects, stay on. And usually they aren't simply physical in nature."

David spoke again. "We've seen many women, young like you and some much older, who've chosen abortion only to find the effects are long lasting. I'm being truthful when I tell you we've seen regret, shame, guilt, sorrow, and a profound sense of loss. Unfortunately, for both the mother and the unborn child, abortion is an act that can't be undone."

Sam began again, his persuasive speech about what she should do escaping him. "Alaine, I just want to be sure you've thought this through. Please think about what's best for you, too. Be sure you aren't punishing yourself for what you feel you've done."

Alaine followed the speakers with her eyes, ending with a focus on Sam. "I thank you for what you're trying to do, Sam. You want to help, and I'm grateful for that. For a lot of reasons, this pregnancy shouldn't have happened. This child has no father. To me, that's not the best plan. I don't know exactly what I should do yet, but I do know it's not my baby's fault. And I know I can't be the one to end this pregnancy."

Jane folded her arms around Alaine in comfort. "You don't have to decide everything right now. You have plenty of time to think about what to do next. It sounds as if you've made the most important decision." She continued to hold Alaine while the younger woman buried her face on Jane's shoulder.

# # #

Alaine

Alaine didn't talk on the way back to the Inn. She closed her eyes and rested her head against the back of the seat. The emotions of the meeting exhausted her.

To her surprise and relief, Sam also seemed to have nothing to say on the short trip. She suspected he had a lot he wanted to say but held back out of respect for her feelings. He pulled into the Inn's parking area with no words having passed between them.

He turned off the engine and moved around the van to open her door. Alaine opened her eyes and smiled as he reached to give her a hand.

"Thank you for going with me tonight. I know you don't agree with my decision not to have an abortion. I don't completely understand it myself. But think about this. You've already saved this child's life once. I'm pretty sure that, without your help, I'd be one of the casualties of September 11th and so would my baby."

The look on Sam's face told her this thought hadn't impacted him until now. But she was right. When they made their way through the horror and confusion that were the World Trade Center less than a month past, Alaine's baby was with them.

In the few days following when they sought refuge in the downtown hotel, she hadn't known about the baby yet and didn't care whether she lived or died. It was Sam who had forced her to keep going. He'd fed her and clothed her and gotten her away from the place that held memories of both the terror of the burning Trade Center and of her ex-lover, Paul Mowher.

"I have to do a lot of thinking about where to go from here. I'm not exactly in a position to rear a child myself right now. But like Jane said, I have some time. I am grateful for all you've done for me, Sam. I meant it when I said not only did you save me, but you saved both of us."

Her smile and clasp were warm as she took his outstretched hand and stepped down from the van.

# # #

Sampson

Sleep eluded Sam for half of the night, and 1:00 a.m. found him foraging in the Café's refrigerators looking for that one snack that might satisfy the emptiness within. He had run through three unsatisfying attempts before he realized hunger was not his problem. The outcome of the evening was. He headed back to his room, still thinking about the turn of events.

Despite the cordial meeting with the couple from the Center and their persuasive speech, it was hard for Sam to accept the frustration to his carefully laid plan to free Alaine from her pregnancy dilemma. The plan was a good one. He just hadn't seen his involvement with the Dabneys, or especially Alaine's aversion to an abortion, coming.

Like a Rubik's Cube, his mind manipulated the arguments he could have used to make his position clear. Each time, the outcome was the same. He could hear Alaine's words, "*...without your help, I'd be one of the casualties of September 11th and so would my baby.*"

While neither of them knew about the pregnancy at that time, it was true. He had helped to save two other lives instead of one from extinction in the ruins of Tower One. Sam was surprised to realize this was the first time he thought of Alaine carrying a *life* instead of an *inconvenience.*

"I'm beginning to sound like the Dabneys," Sam said out loud to himself as he rolled over yet again in an attempt to sleep.

# # #

Sam knew, after his alarm forced him from the bed he didn't want to leave, that it was time to travel the forty miles to Richmond to visit Rev. Ray in the hospital. He'd stayed away because he knew Charity and Ray wanted him to focus on managing the Inn. He did and they all had done a good job. The Inn was on solid ground even without the Brights. In fact, it was in better shape.

The hard work by the Inn's usual staff, combined with the help of the volunteers and Sam's hands-on leadership, paid off. Profits were up and debts were down. Sam was proud of the report he would give to Ray and Charity.

He wondered what they would say about the pregnancy. Ray was a pastor, and Alaine was an unmarried expectant mother. The combination just might be volatile enough for Rev. Ray and Ms. Charity to ask them to leave the Inn. They didn't seem to be that intolerant, but Sam wasn't sure.

Maybe he needed to wait a little longer before letting them know. Alaine was good with either telling them herself, or having Sam do it for her. But once anyone at the Inn found out, things had a way of getting around. Better he told the Brights first than they hear it from someone else.

He left just after lunch, when things were quiet at the Inn, to make the trip to Richmond. The hospital was in a crowded downtown section of the city, mixed in with historic sites, making driving difficult.

He'd decided that showing up would be better than calling ahead. Charity and Ray would try to talk him out of the trip. Sam finally navigated the unfamiliar city and the maze that was the hospital, arriving at Rev. Ray's room on the cardiac floor in a little over an hour.

Ms. Charity's soft voice answered, "Come in," when Sam knocked. Her face showed the surprise he anticipated when he entered the hospital room. She came to him with outstretched arms and authentic welcome in her eyes. He knew he'd done right by making the trip.

After greeting her, Sam turned his eyes toward the hospital bed half hidden by a privacy curtain, ready to greet Rev. Ray, expecting him to be lying there, still an invalid.

The bed was empty, and Ms. Charity's eyes were laughing when he looked at her for an explanation.

"He's walking the halls, building his stamina. He calls it working out, and he spends half of his waking hours doing it. It's about time for him to check back in. I can't keep up with him. Come and sit with me, Sam, and tell me the news."

Sam pulled a chair beside the recliner Ms. Charity used for a bed during the last weeks. They sat down, and she reached for his hand.

"Sampson MacDonald, you are a blessed sight. And from what I hear, we are very much in your debt. I've been talking to Andi and Danisha. They say you're a genius at organization and business. They also say you run a tight ship. It's a wonder you haven't had a mutiny."

"We've come close a couple of times, but sanity prevailed. Actually, things have gone pretty well, for the most part. But the crew misses you and Rev. Ray. Judging by what we hear, the whole town's ready for you two to be back home. Everyone's been a great help, Danisha and Andi, Alaine, Johnson Story and the other staff. And we've got volunteers who come in to give us all a hand. You'd be amazed."

"Actually, Sam, I'd probably not be surprised at all. We have some real friends in Copper's Run. The town's been good to us. Financially, how are things holding up?"

"We're in the black. Bills are caught up. We're making payroll. I'm banking all I can after expenses. Things seem to be in good shape right now, although I'm not sure--" Sam stopped, as if saying more would be trespassing into private territory.

"You're not sure what kind of financial footing the Inn was on before you took over. Is that what you started to say? It's all right. We rather dropped this job in your lap without any preparation. You have every right to be curious."

Sam looked at Ms. Charity and didn't see any signs that he'd overstepped his boundaries, so he continued.

"To tell you the truth, I was concerned. Let me confess why. One day soon after I came, I was exploring the building and came on you and Rev. Ray in the downstairs chapel. You were praying. I should have announced myself, or joined you or something, but I stood there listening. Rev. Ray was speaking, and he prayed for help with the business and financial aspects of the Inn."

"Yes, he did," said Charity. "What he prayed, as I recall, was for the Lord to send us some help to keep the Inn going. Is that what you heard that concerned you?"

"I must say, it is. What I overheard sounded to me like the Inn might be on shaky ground and in need of help to stay open. I apologize. I shouldn't have eavesdropped."

Ms. Charity smiled. "First of all, you probably couldn't help it, and second, I'm happy to say that you misunderstood Ray's prayer. The Inn was solvent and solid. I praise God and his goodness for that. He sends us business on a regular basis. He's done that from the moment we took over the Inn, almost fifteen years ago now."

Sam's interest in what Rev. Ray's prayer meant overcame concern for being discreet about the personal finances of the couple.

"Then why did Rev. Ray pray what he prayed, if the Inn wasn't in fiscal hot water?"

"Time and hands, Sam. Time and hands are the problem, not money. Ray's been pastoring his flock at the church and overseeing the Inn, two full time jobs. He's beginning to feel his limits. You've seen Ray's health concerns...diabetes, heart trouble. This time, we had a close call. I thought he was leaving us. There's been some heart damage complicated by his other issues causing his hospital stay to be longer than usual."

Because Sam was sitting close to Ms. Charity, he could see tears suddenly pool in her normally clear and competent eyes.

"Ray was praying for God to send him some more trustworthy hands to help him run the Inn, Sampson, to free him up a little."

Charity chuckled, reached over and patted Sam's hand. "Looks like his prayer may have been answered. The Lord works in mysterious ways."

Sam had to clear a catch in his throat before he could use his voice. T*rustworthy.* She had said *trustworthy.*

"I don't understand. Why not just hire somebody? If you need help, advertise, interview, and find the best person."

"We could do that. We decided to take a different route."

"But why me? You didn't know me. You had no idea I knew anything about finance. You took a huge chance putting me in charge."

"A chance? Not really, Sam. There's something we haven't talked about that you may not quite understand. The Inn belongs to the Lord. It's a ministry, of sorts."

"A ministry? You mean the Inn is owned by Rev. Ray's church?"

"No, it's bigger than that. Decisions about what happens there are made in collaboration with our Heavenly Father through prayer. You see, he'd already nudged us to offer you a job. We just didn't expect it to happen the way it did."

"I must say, no we did not."

The voice was that of Rev. Ray as he walked into the room, resplendent in a long red checked robe and red bedroom slippers. He pushed an IV rack ahead of him.

Sam rose to shake the older man's hand, and instead, Rev. Ray enveloped him in an embrace. The man was thinner than the day he'd left the Inn on the ambulance, but that was the only difference Sam noticed, to his relief.

"Rev. Ray, it's good to see you looking fit and fine. What do the doctors tell you?"

The big man seated himself as he spoke. "They tell me I can go home in a few days. They say I have to slow down, but I have to exercise more. They tell me that if my food tastes good, I should spit it out because it couldn't be healthy for me. My good life, as I've known it, may be over." He laughed. "Can't thank you enough for what you're doing for us at the Inn, young man."

"It's been a privilege, sir. I also thank you for providing a place for Alaine and me to stay while you've been away. The accommodations, I must say, are most suitable."

Their exchange was comfortable and easy, as if Sam had long been part of the Brights' circle of friends.

Then Sam remembered one of the main reasons why he'd come, and he stood to gain courage.

"Rev. Ray...Ms. Charity, I've something to talk to you about that may make our presence at the Inn less welcome, perhaps even unwelcome. I don't know how you'll feel about what I'm going to say. Regardless, we're willing to abide by your wishes on the matter."

"Son, whatever it is, just tell us. Then we'll all decide what should be done." Rev. Ray's eyes were serious. Ms. Charity rose and stood behind her husband's chair, her hands on his shoulders, as if supporting him.

"What is it, Sam?" she asked.

"We've just found out that Alaine is pregnant. She gave me permission to let you both know. The father of her baby is back where she used to live. She's left him. He was...is...from what I understand...not a very good person."

Ray spoke first. "Is Alaine married to the baby's father?"

"No. They lived together most of the time. Sometimes he would leave her, but they've been together a while until recently."

"When you say he's not a good person, what exactly do you mean?" Charity asked.

"From the little bit she's told me, I think he was cruel, bullied her, was verbally abusive, things like that. She hasn't said whether there was physical abuse, but I think there was. He must be a mean son-of--I'm sorry, Rev."

"If that's the case, it's easy to see why she decided to leave this man. How did you and Alaine come to be together? You haven't told us, and we didn't want to ask, until now."

Ray reached out his hand and took hold of Sam's arm. Sam dropped his head, knowing this conversation with the Brights was long overdue.

"I apologize. I should have told you before now. Alaine and I worked together in the same office in the North Tower of the World Trade Center in New York City. I didn't know her well. She was quiet and always seemed withdrawn and unhappy. I asked her out on a date once, but she refused...said she was engaged. We were in our office the morning the planes crashed the buildings. When the first one hit the North Tower where we were, it was obvious right away it was serious. We were only a few floors below the impact, and I knew we had to get out fast. I could see that Alaine was in shock, and I grabbed hold of her and started for the stairwell. We just managed to make it out before the South Tower fell and, of course, our building followed."

Ms. Charity put her hand to her mouth, but neither one of the couple interrupted.

"I found us a couple of rooms in a hotel where we stayed put for a few days. Alaine was in no condition to do anything but rest. We didn't call or contact anyone about where we were. We just sort of hid out. I had nothing to go back to, and starting over somewhere sounded good to me. Alaine made it clear she was not going back to her old life either.

"When she was able to travel, we went to the bus station with the intention of getting out of the City. It didn't matter where. An agent there showed us some small town destinations. We chose Copper's Run."

"So, no one knows you made it out safely? Who might be looking for you?" Ray's eyes pinned him, as if trying to decide what to believe about Sam's story.

"At some point early in the morning of our first day on the road, I called the NYPD, gave them our names and told them we were alive. I didn't let them know where we were. That's it. I'm an only child and my parents are dead. Sometime I'll call my former landlady to let her know. I liked her. Alaine may need to call someone eventually. I don't think she's been ready yet. I don't know what kind of family she has. As for the baby's father, she says she doesn't want to go back to him. I'm certain she hasn't made contact."

"So you both just dropped off the face of the earth?" Charity asked.

Sam shrugged without meeting her eyes. "I suppose we did, at that. I hated my job and my life. I was ready for a big change. I'm guessing Alaine felt the same way. The irony is that such a tragedy provided the opportunity for us to disappear."

Ray questioned him again. "What's the nature of your relationship with Alaine now?"

"It's hard for me to say. We're friends...I hope. I upset her rather badly with an ill thought out remark when she told me about the baby a couple of days ago. She was understandably angry. She'd just found out for sure herself. I made matters worse. When I tried to remedy my first mistake, I got myself in even deeper."

"What on earth did you do, Sampson, if I may ask?" Charity raised her eyebrows at him.

"I tried to get her to visit an abortion clinic. I thought the best solution to her problem was to get rid of the pregnancy. I had plenty of friends go that route in my old life. Let's just say Alaine wouldn't hear of my proposal."

"What does she plan to do?" asked Charity.

"She says she's not sure, but she made it clear abortion isn't an option. We've met a couple who run Life Options Center and--"

"David and Jane Dabney?" Charity interrupted.

"Yes. You know them? Alaine seems to like them, and they said they would help her with her decision about what to do next. I don't know if she's thinking about adoption or what. She hasn't discussed it with me."

Charity and Ray looked at him for a long moment before Ray spoke. "And you thought we would turn you both out because of Alaine's pregnancy?"

"I thought it was a distinct possibility. You're a minister as well as a business owner. You have a reputation to uphold."

"That's true. We do. And let me make it clear that neither Ms. Charity nor I condone intimacy outside of marriage. We both feel that allowing a child to be conceived without the boundaries of a stable and loving marriage relationship to protect it is selfish and irresponsible. It neither corresponds with God's laws or the principles of good judgment."

Sam lowered his head as Rev. Ray spoke. It wasn't his child, but he felt responsible for exposing Charity and Ray to his and Alaine's presence and related troubles. He knew what he had to do, although it hurt to do it.

"I understand your position. We won't let this compromise your principles. I'll make arrangements for us to move on as soon as you're able to come home. Sooner, if you want. I'm sorry for bringing our problems to your front door."

Sam felt the sorrow he expressed. He liked the couple and hated to leave them under these circumstances.

"Sampson?" Charity's voice didn't hold the judgment he expected. Neither did her eyes. "We have a confession to make to you also. We all suspected that Alaine was going to have a baby before you told us."

For a minute, Sam was speechless. "You all? How could you possibly--? You weren't even--"

"I confess that it was the girls, Danisha and Andi. We've talked to them. They knew something wasn't right with Alaine, and it seems they guessed correctly."

Seeing the look on Sam's face, she continued. "Now Sam, before you go getting offended for Alaine as the target of our conversation, you need to understand something. And I'm not telling tales out of school, because the girls would tell you themselves just as quickly. They've both been just where Alaine is now. Pregnant, confused, anxious and unmarried. That's why they could read the signs in Alaine. They wanted to help but didn't know how without being intrusive. That's why they let us know what they suspected."

It was Rev. Ray's turn again. He reminded Sam of words Ms. Charity spoke earlier. "The Inn does belong to the Lord, Sampson. It's a ministry."

Ray continued. "You need to understand that while we do run a bona fide Inn, we also have other ministries commencing as part of the work we try to do with the Lord. The Inn is the hub and the other ministries branch out from it."

Sam broke in. "Like taking in fugitives from America's worst terrorist attack."

Ray smiled. "Hadn't considered that one. Maybe, maybe...but for now more like providing a haven for mothers without husbands to feel safe and find a way to get on their feet."

Charity spoke next. "A place where seniors who have no one to care can find security and feel useful."

"Like Johnson Story." Sampson was beginning to understand.

"Yes, like Johnson Story." Ray put out his hand and rested it on Sam's arm. "The Inn is the Lord's to do with as He sees fit. He saw fit to bless us with the presence of Andi and Danisha, two young ladies in need who now contribute untold value to the Inn's community and services. He seemed happy to send us Johnson Story when his own family pushed him aside, making him feel old and helpless. If you've been around him more than ten minutes, you know helpless and useless hardly describe the man. I have to run to keep up with Brother Johnson when he gets going."

Rev. Ray's laugh was hearty and full of affection.

"And you, Sam," said Charity. "You and Alaine. The Lord sent you to us when you needed a safe place to land. Just when we were about to need the skills you both had to keep us going, you show up. So here we all are. Hard to understand, isn't it?"

Sam's skepticism showed, and he didn't try to hide it. "So you're saying that all of us being at the Inn is part of some larger cosmic arrangement, beyond our control, at work to bring us together for whatever purpose?"

"No, Sam," Ray responded. "I'm saying that God orders who comes and goes behind the scenes at the Inn. We ask Him to, and He's faithful to do so. Our lives can't touch everyone who needs a steady hand or a lift up for a while, but with His help, we can touch a few for his name's sake."

Charity continued Ray's thought. "Jesus said, 'I needed clothes and you clothed me, I was sick and you looked after me, I was in prison and you came to visit me.'"

Ray followed with these words, "Jesus also said, 'whatever you did for one of the least of these brothers of mine, you did for me.' The same thing applies to our sisters."

Sam walked over to look out of the hospital window. He didn't speak for some time. When he did turn back, his question was a challenge.

"Are the good works you do, the helping and housing, the caring, are they designed to allow you to get into the kingdom of God or enter Heaven or whatever you are working toward?"

As soon as Sam asked the question, he knew he'd gone too far...misjudged the motives of his host and hostess. He could tell by the looks on their faces and the jolt to his own conscience, weak as it was. He knew he'd better fix this faux pas immediately and directly.

"I'm sorry. That was totally out of order and inappropriate, especially in light of all that you've done for us. I know it's not true, and I apologize."

"I realize our motivations may seem odd to you, Sam. You aren't the first to question them. We don't love to get. We give because we love." Rev. Ray's explanation was simple, and his smile was genuine, even in the face of Sam's cynicism.

Sam shook his head. "Then in my opinion, you and Ms. Charity are atypical players in this day and age. Maybe that's why your approach to life is hard for me to understand. I've mostly had to look out for myself." His smile masked the uncertainty he felt.

"Don't fool yourself, young man," said Charity. "We see how you've looked out for Alaine. You're still doing it, coming in here taking care of business for her. You're not all out for number one," and she laughed, indicating she hadn't totally given up on him, despite his skepticism.

"Alaine would have good support systems in Andi and Danisha. They were both referred to us as young, unmarried women in need of a place to stay and work while they had their babies and decided whether to keep them or give them up for adoption. We don't normally work with those who have chosen abortion. Both girls had healthy babies, and they both stayed on to work with us at the Inn afterwards."

"What happened to their babies?" asked Sam. He found he had a genuine interest.

"Andi placed hers with a Christian adoption agency. She had some problems at first with separation, but she also knows her baby has both a father and a mother who are Christ followers. Danisha kept her baby. She lives with her grandmother in town. The baby's father is active in her baby's life, and it looks like they might marry soon. We're praying to that end, and they both have been in discipleship relationships with older members of the church." Charity's eyes filled with tears as she answered Sam's question.

"So you see, you and Alaine walked right into a place that specializes in pregnancies of concern," she said. Sam noticed that she didn't call them problem pregnancies, as he had been considering them. He listened as Ms. Charity continued.

"We want Alaine with us as she works through her situation. We can provide a safe refuge for her for the time being. Do you think she'll agree to stay?"

"I wouldn't be surprised, Ms. Charity, if she does agree. I think she craves safety and security right now. The offer will be hard for her to turn down."

Rev. Ray stood and clapped his large brown hand on Sam's shoulder. "You know we all thought the baby was yours, as well, Sampson."

"I can understand. But I assure you, sir, my relationship with Alaine isn't like that. I care about her a lot. She depends on me...at least she did until my judgment started to let her down."

"Human judgment will do that, young man, even with the best intentions. Now it's time for us to talk about some business details, like catching up on salaries for you and Alaine, before you head back to the Inn to keep an eye on things while I get my last few days of rest. I hear I'm going to be set free soon, if all goes well." Rev. Ray sounded ready.

8 HOMECOMING

Alaine

After his return from Richmond, Sam shared first with Alaine the details of his visit with the Brights, including his revelation of her situation. He gave her what information he could about Andi and Danisha's similar experiences, and she and Sam then officially told the girls about Alaine's pregnancy.

During the next few days, it was obvious that Andi and Danisha had closed ranks around Alaine. Seldom was she alone without one or the other of her keepers, as she came to think of them.

Alaine guessed her new best friends now committed themselves to being her emotional support system as she came to grips with her role of prospective mother. She welcomed the increased attention and the growing friendships. She found herself eager to hear any advice the two had to offer about her pregnant state and what decision she should make about the future of the baby to come.

Following the events in the City, Alaine first found herself confused and lost. For days, she only wanted to sleep and forget, letting Sam take all responsibility for their care. When she did re-surface, depression left her unkempt and distraught. Finding out about her pregnancy served to deepen the depression. Sam's reaction when she told him hadn't helped.

Strangely, it was Sam she credited with shaking her out of her negative state of mind. True, it was initially anger at him and then at his plan that motivated her move to take control of her circumstances. Far from worsening her depressed state, acknowledging her pregnancy seemed to free her from constant fear related to their recent ordeal.

The result was that Alaine took renewed interest in how she looked and in her interaction with those around her. She loved covering the reception desk of the Inn, responding to inquiries by phone or online and welcoming the Inn's guests as they arrived.

One afternoon, as she checked in young honeymooners caught up in the romance of spending the beginning days of their marriage at the old Inn, she sensed Sam listening through the partially opened door of his adjoining office.

She explained its history and invited the couple to become part of the Inn's family as the groom signed their names to the register. Alaine thrilled to the new found confidence she felt as she conducted her welcome and delivered the background material. Her interest in and study of the Inn's past paid off as she could respond with competence to the couple's animated questions.

After she returned from showing the couple to their room, her earlier feeling that Sam had watched her interactions was confirmed. When Sam emerged from his office, Alaine felt her body tense and her defenses raise. Would he criticize her efforts or, worse yet, continue his urging for an abortion?

That it was neither was unexpected.

"Alaine, I was listening as you talked to those two love birds."

"I know. I saw you through the opening in the door. Was there a problem?"

"No problem. I thought you did a great job. You've really picked up the history of this place. Who taught you all that information?"

"It's in a book that's right here in the reception desk. Ms. Charity wrote it herself, with the help of some folks from the Bouchard County Historical Society. Did you know the Inn is on the National Register of Historic Places?"

He shook his head and seemed surprised that she did.

"I didn't know you're a student of history."

"I am. And there's a lot you don't know about me. What about you? What are you a student of?"

She couldn't help the sarcasm in both her question and her voice. Something was making her stiff and ill at ease. Why did being with him bring out this side of her, like she couldn't help herself? Why couldn't she just relax and stay calm around him?

They faced each other. When he spoke, it wasn't to address her question.

"Now what have I done to upset you, Alaine? If you're still disturbed by what happened earlier about the clinic, I really am sorry. We may not agree on the solution to your situation, but I'm willing to go along with what you want. I'm not going to oppose you again."

This conversation was deteriorating fast.

"You're *willing* to go along with what *I* want?" Her voice rose. "You're *not going to oppose me*?"

"Wait...I thought that's what you wanted."

"Sampson MacDonald, you never cease to amaze me. Who do you think died and left you in charge of my life? Need I remind you that you're not the boss of me! Please stop trying to sound as if you are. It's patronizing and insulting."

She didn't back down or turn away, but looked at him, her lips in a firm, thin line, despite a pounding heart and feeling like she had just made an adolescent level speech.

Sam raised his hands, palm out, and stepped back.

"I wasn't trying to--"

"Look, Sam. There's something you need to understand. I can never repay you for what you've done for me. Never. But neither am I the same person you dragged with you from that wounded Trade Tower. I couldn't think for days after that, weeks probably. I'm just now coming to and realizing how changed everything is...how different I am. You saved me, but I have to figure out who the new me is. I'm overwhelmed and scared and excited. This is going to take a while. But what I'm not is the helpless, hopeless, nearly paralyzed girl you rescued. Please don't treat me that way."

"Alaine, please, I'm trying here."

"Forgive me for lecturing you, Sam. I guess you're doing the best you can."

The look on his face as she left the room let her know he was trying to decipher her, once again, sarcastic meaning.

# # #

Sampson

Charity sent word early in Rev. Ray's confinement that Sam and Alaine should draw paychecks and pay reduced room and board. Ray reconfirmed this directive during Sam's visit to his hospital room.

Alaine seemed glad to be busy, and Sam noticed her efforts to make the reservations, check-in and hospitality phases of the Inn run as smoothly as possible. She'd already moved from the guest room across from Sam to the third floor to be near Andi.

Sam soon moved his living quarters to a small second floor room beside the one occupied long-term by Johnson Story. He felt he'd tied up a first floor guest room for too long, especially now that he was an Inn employee.

It was good to be officially working again, and it didn't bother Sam that neither the job nor the pay resembled his at the World Trade Center. Being temporary innkeeper in Rev. Ray's absence suited him so much that he made a game of seeing how busy he could stay and how many tasks he could accomplish in a day, often upping the number for the next day. Where once he considered workdays as drudgery, here he rose early in anticipation of what the day would bring. There was satisfaction in knowing the Inn was operating efficiently.

Sam's comfortable work rhythm consumed his time and helped him forget his last, uneasy conversation with Alaine. He was, then, puzzled by her unexpected request that he accompany her to a counseling session with Jane and David Dabney.

The Dabneys seemed sincere in their views, even if he didn't share them. But still, he was wary of being drawn in and thrown off balance by them. He would be more comfortable with less persuasion and willingness to share their beliefs. He felt a need to protect Alaine from undue influence and pressure from the couple. She was vulnerable. Perhaps he should agree to go along to the meeting.

Alaine was quiet as they drove the few miles to the Life Options Center, and Sam thought about the role he might play once there. Would he and Alaine meet with the Dabneys together again? Was he along simply in the function of driver? Would it be best to let her do the talking, or should he serve as her open advocate?

Alaine appeared removed and absorbed in her own thoughts, and he hesitated to talk to her about his questions. He soon discovered that their time at the Center was carefully orchestrated from the moment of their arrival.

Both Dabneys greeted the couple at the door as if this were a social call. Jane embraced Alaine, and David shook hands with Sam while seamlessly drawing him into his own office. It took Sam a minute, while David was asking him questions, to realize that the ladies disappeared further down the hall and out of sight. He stopped mid-sentence and looked to David for an answer about where they had gone.

David smiled. "Jane wanted Alaine to herself for a bit, Sampson. In the early stages of pregnancy counseling, we prefer for both parties to have some privacy and be able to speak without undue influence from anyone. I'm sure you understand. I realize your position in this situation is not the usual one, but the principle is still a good one. It's hard to tell what can affect a young lady in Alaine's situation. Besides, I'd like a chance to get to know you better."

David indicated the comfortable chair across from his desk. "Would you join me? How about some coffee?"

Sam liked this man in spite of his conviction that they wouldn't agree on many topics. He could afford a few minutes to engage in small talk and maybe gain some insight into what the content of Jane's conversation with Alaine might be.

As if he could read Sam's mind, David began, as they drank their coffee, to tell him that in the initial stages of counseling, Jane's goal was to make Alaine comfortable and hear her story, as much as she wanted to tell.

This made Sam smile. He doubted that, this close to September 11th, Jane had ever heard a story quite like Alaine's.

David said they would also talk about Alaine's relationship with her baby's father. Just the mention of Paul Mowher, the man Alaine named as the father, made Sam uneasy. She hadn't said much about Mowher, but something in her manner when she did talk about him convinced Sam that Mowher would be neither a suitable husband for Alaine nor father to her child.

When Sam came to, he caught the end of Dabney's statement..."if time permits, Jane will talk to Alaine about any relationship she might have with Jesus Christ." This subject made Sam more uncomfortable than thoughts of her former lover.

Sam stood up.

"Look, ah, David. No offense, but I think I'll walk around the neighborhood a bit while I'm waiting."

Sam knew David could see through his excuse to remove himself. *Coward* was Sam's immediate self-assessment. He looked at David and sat down again. *Face him. Do it. Don't back away.*

"On second thought, maybe you can tell me something, David."

"Try me."

"OK, why Jesus Christ? Why not Ghandi or Chairman Mao? Why not

Mohammed? Why not Joseph Smith or L. Ron Hubbard? Or John Lennon for that matter?"

David took his time in answering. Because he did, Sam began to feel smug. Maybe his question hit home.

When the man did respond, it was without any outward signs of indecision or uncertainty. "I think it may be different for different people. For me, it's the resurrection. You can visit the tombs of Ghandi, Mao Zedong, Mohammed, Joseph Smith and Hubbard. The graves all have one thing in common. They are occupied.

"The tomb of Christ is empty. Granted we aren't sure exactly where it's located, but wherever it is, there is no body there. There were eyewitnesses to that at the time. The Bible records the accounts. I'm sure you'll agree that's unique among religious leaders."

"What do you mean *it may be different for different people*?" Sam wanted to draw David out even more.

"Well, I believe that it's God who actually prompts us to follow him through his son, Jesus Christ. But I also think that God uses different aspects of Christ and what he stands for to urge people to become Christ followers. Not everyone responds initially for the same reasons."

"For example?" Sam pushed further.

"Some are influenced to come to Christ because their families believe and encourage it. Some hear a sermon in church or on TV, and the message simply appeals to them. Others find him to be Truth through a concentrated study of Christ's teachings and what the Bible says about him.

"One of the most powerful things that helps persuade people to become Christ followers is the influence of others around them. By that I mean people living lives that exemplify Christ in their behaviors and values. These are just a few ways people come to choose Christ on whom to base their worldview. I'm sure there are others."

"Others? You mean other ways to find the truth?" Sam knew what David meant, but he played devil's advocate.

"No, sorry, I didn't intend to imply there were other truths. In my worldview, Christ is the embodiment of Truth. He said so Himself. In John 14:6, Jesus said, 'I am the way and the truth and the life. No one comes to the Father except through me.'" There are other hooks that draw folks to put their trust in Christ, but I believe he alone is authentic Truth."

Sam was still not ready to let it go. "But you base your beliefs, your worldview as you put it, on the Bible. Not everyone begins there. Some think Scripture's outdated, out of touch or fabricated from other ancient documents or beliefs." Sam's interest in the answers wasn't faked at this point.

David met Sam's challenge. "It's a worldview based on Bible teachings, yes, but also on history and research and testimony of those who've experienced Jesus first hand in their lives. And, Sampson, I can tell you that my own experiences affirm the validity of my choice daily. That's one of the strongest pillars of my personal faith...what it's meant to me continuously for the last 30 years."

There was a pause while Sam processed what he'd heard. "So you're convinced you're right? Despite all the other religions across the globe, all the other faiths, all the other people willing to die for what they believe, including those men who rode their planes into the World Trade Center? You think your way is the best way?"

"Not just the best way, Sampson, the only way. I didn't say it first, either. Jesus Christ himself did. And He convinced me."

It was with some relief that Sam heard Jane bringing Alaine down the hall toward them a few minutes later. He and David had continued to talk, but mostly about inconsequential things as they waited for the women. Sam was sure David knew he'd deliberately changed the subject, but he didn't care. He wasn't up for any more Jesus talk.

As they said their goodbyes and set another meeting between Jane and Alaine, Sam wanted once more to put distance between himself and the Dabneys. He was OK with them personally but not with their obsession, as he thought of their religion. Still, he was committed to help Alaine and would return for her sake, if she needed him.

# # #

Preparations for Rev. Ray's return home to his Inn at Copper's Run kicked into full gear after Sam's visit with him in the hospital. There was no grumbling when Sam sent out the request that the Inn be put in inspection-worthy order for the couple's return.

He had no further opportunity to talk privately with Alaine as they all worked to make the innkeeper's homecoming momentous. Charity and Ray's private suite on the second floor of the Inn was thoroughly turned out by volunteers under the direction of Danisha and Andi. The Café was scrubbed as if to serve the queen, and fresh menus were prepared.

It was a Sunday afternoon when Rev. Ray, Ms. Charity and the nursing assistant who would continue to help with Ray's care for the next few days arrived in a private transport to a welcome a celebrity would envy. The Inn family, including part time help and volunteers, stood around the perimeter with townspeople who knew and loved the couple. When Ray insisted on stepping down from the gurney on which he had ridden in the back of the vehicle to stand on his own in front of his home, onlookers clapped and cheered.

Johnson Story had been appointed first greeter, and instead of the handshake he planned, he hugged the much larger Rev. Ray to his frail little frame and would have been lifted off of the ground were it not for the intervention of the nursing assistant.

Andi was in tears and Danisha not far from them, despite her brave attempts to comfort her friend. Alaine at first hung back as Ms. Charity pulled Andi and

Danisha close but was soon drawn into the circle of arms. The couple was gently and carefully besieged by the well-wishers who openly displayed the thankfulness they felt at the return of their friends.

Sam watched all of this from his vantage point on the top step of the Inn's front entrance. He struggled with contradictory feelings. Pleasure that Ray and Charity were home and relief that he no longer carried the entire weight of the Inn's management competed with concern that his role in running the Inn would soon be unnecessary. He'd have to move on. Where joy should have reigned, Sam felt empty and despondent.

He stood at his post while the commotion continued, only making an effort to join the celebration when he saw that Rev. Ray was watching him. His eyes followed as Sam descended the steps and strode across the lawn to shake the older man's hand.

Rev. Ray continued to hold Sam's hand as he took his left arm and encircled the younger man's shoulders, drawing him close and speaking into his ear.

"What's wrong, son? If I didn't know better, I'd think you were disappointed to see me home. I thought you'd be relieved."

"Of course I'm glad you're home. What makes you think I'm not?" Sam made his voice jovial and louder than necessary to cover his disquiet.

Still holding Sam close with both hands on his shoulders and talking into his ear, Rev. Ray said, "I'm grateful to you, Sam. But I need your help more than ever now that I'm home. I won't be able to do all I used to do. I want you to stay on for a while. Will you consider that?"

Sam swallowed the fear that filled his throat, smiled and stuck out his hand again to his friend.

"I'll consider that carefully, Reverend."

9 TRANSITION

Sampson

Normalcy began again at the Inn at Copper's Run. It was apparent to Sam and the others who called the Inn home that Rev. Ray was not his old self. Recovery would take time. He was up and about, working some every day, but also spending much of his time resting or in exercise therapy to regain his strength. Ms. Charity reported that, while he had suffered permanent heart damage, recovery and a near normal life would eventually be possible. All who knew and loved Rev. Ray seemed determined to help make it so.

Rev. Ray and Sam consulted daily about the affairs of the Inn. The pastor resumed limited duties at his church, meeting with his elders and preaching at one service a week, although he sat as he did so. Always those around him, especially Ms. Charity, watched him closely. This became such a source of aggravation to Rev. Ray that he finally issued an edict that anyone caught hanging over him would be fired, and that included Charity Bright herself.

Ms. Charity ignored his ranting, as did Sam and the rest of the Inn's staff. The oversight continued, if more covertly. No one wanted the man to overdo on his or her watch.

Alaine selected an obstetrics practice in the next town to follow her pregnancy. She was always accompanied to appointments by Ms. Charity or one of the girls. Charity would serve as her birth coach and agreed to be godmother to Alaine's baby.

As Rev. Ray improved and Alaine's waistline expanded, the days at the Inn settled into a more predictable pace. The Thanksgiving and Christmas holidays drew near, and reservations and party bookings increased. Extra help would be needed for the duration.

Sam made it known a few days after Rev. Ray's return that he would like to stay on and help for the time being. Without making an official announcement, the older man began to relinquish his major tasks at the Inn to Sam. While he was always underfoot to lend a hand or share advice, Sam and others who loved Rev. Ray felt his relief at passing on the larger share of responsibilities.

Ms. Charity didn't say much about the new arrangement, but Sam knew she kept a diplomatic eye on his administrative methods. This brought added pressure, but he wasn't surprised at her surveillance. The Inn was her heart's work, as well as her husband's. The pressure made him work harder to avoid her disappointment.

Sam relished his leadership role at the Inn, and spent considerable time researching ways to improve the aged structure itself and the Inn's services without adding undue expenditures to its budget. His efforts left him exhausted at the end of most days but feeling accomplished unlike with any previous job.

Townsfolk and travelers alike reported their satisfaction with what the refreshed Inn had to offer.

Sam ordered a wholesale cleaning of the Inn's interior and exterior, parts of which had become more shabby than chic over time. He then closeted himself with Ms. Charity and Andi, who showed an interest in design, to find ways to make the Inn better reflect the restrained charm of the eighteenth and nineteenth century travelers' retreat it had once been. He was especially interested in having it come to renewed life during the upcoming holidays.

To Sam's surprise, it was Andi who suggested that he include Alaine in the decorating plans.

"Did you know that Alaine was an interior design major in college with concentrations in early American periods?" said Andi at their first planning meeting.

"She never mentioned it to me. But then, I never asked. She was an office assistant when I met her."

Andi glanced at him and then at Ms. Charity, and Sam caught a look of understanding between the two women before Andi continued. "There's a considerable amount you don't know about that lady. But let's include her. I think she would bring great ideas, and furthermore, I think she would benefit from the diversion."

"Andi's right, Sam." Ms. Charity added. "I've discovered Alaine's quite artistic. I think a florist, a fabric store and access to the attic and basement would let Andi and Alaine breathe new life into this old place."

"So, Andi would you like to talk to Alaine and see if she--?"

"Sam, if I were you, I'd discuss this with her myself. She needs to hear from you that you value her contribution to the Inn's facelift."

Sam prided himself for his efforts on behalf of the Inn and those put into refining his relationships with Andi, Danisha, and the other Inn regulars. The one exception, the one person who appeared to remain restrained and controlled when around him, was Alaine.

Alaine was polite, cordial, but remote in the face of any direct contact with him. It was noticeable, and he attributed it to more than the fact that he was now, to some extent, her supervisor at the Inn.

He tried to psychoanalyze the motive behind Alaine's reticence to interact with him more than necessary. Was it embarrassment over the pregnancy? She didn't act ashamed in front of the others.

Was it because she had been so dependent on him due to the bizarre circumstances of their early days together? Maybe. But Sam most disliked exploring this possibility. What if Alaine regretted her decision to flee the City with him and leave behind the father of her baby? Maybe, for some strange reason, she missed him and her life in New York. Maybe she was wishing for an opportunity to return, as hard as that was to imagine. He hoped that was not the case.

Sam's attempts to entice Alaine to talk about what was on her mind were all met with elusive courtesy that faded off into vague denials that anything was wrong. Still he knew better.

Andi's proposal to include Alaine in planning for the Inn's uplift and holiday decorating gave him hope for a new avenue to break through her polite stonewalling.

Alaine was taking a walk in the back yard of the Inn when Sam approached her with his request. From watching her movements over the last couple of days, he chose this time and place for a talk so they wouldn't be interrupted by phone duties at the reception desk or Inn workers and guests. The evening, though cool, was mild for late October.

"May I walk with you a while?"

She looked startled at his request and hesitated before responding. Alaine finally smiled and answered quietly. "Of course. It's a lovely evening out here. I love the Inn from this back view. Have you noticed the path that leads to steps going right to the river's edge?"

It was the most forthcoming Alaine had been with Sam in some time.

"I found it a couple of nights ago when I couldn't sleep. I don't advise going down the steps any more, but I think they lead to a concrete fishing platform used by guests in past years. Could we sit for a few minutes?" Sam asked, pointing to a stone bench nearby. "There's a favor I'd like to ask of you."

The guarded look returned to Alaine's eyes, but she moved, without answering, to the stone bench.

"Ms. Charity, Andi and I are working on a project to renew the look of the Inn's interiors. Nothing extravagant. People seem to like the Inn to look old and a little worn. But it's due for some upgrading, and we were thinking that now, just before the holidays, would be a good time. We want to make changes that won't be cost prohibitive but will make an impact."

Sam sensed her interest, although she wasn't making eye contact. He noticed, by her stillness, that she was listening.

"Andi said you studied decorating, that you know historical period decorating. She thought I should ask you to help out in our efforts."

Sam could see enthusiasm alive in her eyes when she turned to look at him. He decided to risk a more personal approach.

"You never told me about that side of you." Sam paused, trying to read what she was thinking. "OK, I know. I never asked."

He stood up, his back to her as he faced the river. Night was closing them in, and he could only hear, not see, the water below them. Turning, he looked up at the back of the Inn, long and large, sprawling out in front of him like a lighted ship on dark waters.

"Look, Alaine, I know I've never asked about a lot of things. And when I did ask, I was clumsy and out of order. I've underestimated you, and I'm sorry. You told me you've changed since we came here. I agree. You're not the same woman who rode the bus with me from the City. You're stronger...more sure of yourself."

Sam couldn't see her face well enough in the dark to read how she was taking this conversation, certainly more personal than they had talked in weeks.

"You've changed too, Sam. Do you realize that you show more purpose than I've ever seen you have before, including when we worked in the office at the North Tower? You're more settled."

"Settled?" He might not have described his feelings in those exact words, but close. He wanted to hear more from her. "What do you mean by that?"

"It's hard to pinpoint," she said, "but you were sort of like a caged creature before...a bear maybe or a tiger...you know in one of those awful old zoos that kept its animals confined in concrete spaces that were too small. That's exactly what you were like. Like you were cramped in a space that crowded and suffocated you. Now you seem... I don't know... more free and not as restless and troubled."

"Was I that awful? Really?" Sam was bothered by her words.

"Not awful. Just somehow restrained and fighting it. Maybe I'm just way out of my territory, but I think this place and being here with these people have helped to make you more comfortable. Forgive me if I'm out of line."

Alaine stopped talking and sat. Sam became uneasy with the silence but was afraid to push her for more. He tried another route.

"So, what do you think? Will you give us a hand? Ms. Charity, Andi and me? We need some ideas and expert advice. Are you in?" The wait before she answered was measured and painful.

"I'd like to help." He could barely hear her. "I'd be happy to."

# # #

By the first week of November, almost two months since the fall of the Towers, the rejuvenation of the Inn for the holidays was underway. Storage areas were rummaged for vintage decorations, cedars were brought in from the farm of one of the Café's steady customers and natural wreaths were crafted from holly and pine. The local florist was called in to do what the Inn's ladies couldn't do, all under the careful eye and direction of Alaine and Andi, who were in their element.

They called on all comers for help, including putting Johnson Story and Sam in charge of decorating small trees for the Inn's back porches. Sam would have decorated the White House to see the light stay in Alaine's eyes.

In keeping with the theme of mid eighteenth century, lights were strung that mimicked flickering candlelight. Dimmers on the other lighting gave the impression that time regressed and Civil War officers on leave from their Confederate regiments might ride up to the Inn's broad front doors at any minute to meet their ladies waiting inside. Sam was not from the South, but even he could almost hear the ring of horseshoes on the front walk.

The week before Thanksgiving, which Ms. Charity was determined would not be lost in all of the Christmas finery, the Inn was at its ready, and the reservations for Thanksgiving evening buffet were full.

For one week, turkey was king, and Andi and Alaine brought out huge pottery turkeys they found in the basement to grace either side of the front entrance to the Inn. The two rummaged old boxes of vintage fold-out honeycomb paper turkeys that were placed on each table in the Café and adjoining dining room which served the Inn's guests on formal occasions.

Early in the week of Thanksgiving, Rev. Ray and Ms. Charity pulled all of the Inn's staff together for a pre-Thanksgiving meeting. The focus of the brief devotional given to the close group of workers by the couple was gratitude. Ms. Charity spoke of the need to be grateful for blessings, great and small, and for relationships that bind individuals and groups together in mystic and lasting ways.

Rev. Ray's words from the book of Romans were those of the preacher that he was. He reminded the little group of the greatest blessing, that of the love of Christ toward men to such a great extent that, "While we were still sinners, Christ died for us".

"Why did he love us?" Rev. Ray asked the group in the ageless call and response of his people.

"Tell us, preacher," several members of the staff responded.

"To glorify himself," Ray answered.

"And why did he do this thing, this sacrifice of himself?"

"You tell us, Reverend," came the response.

"To bring everlasting glory to himself," was his answer.

"But I ask you, why Jesus? Why did Jesus have to be the one to die in such a way? Couldn't there have been some other sacrifice provided?" Rev. Ray's voice showed the emotion he was feeling.

"We want to know, Preacher. You tell us."

"You know it's his Father's business. His Father, the holy God, sent him to do a job. And the Son was all about his Father's business. Isn't that right?"

"That's right, Rev. Ray. That's surely right. About his Father's business."

"And his Father, the Holy God, found it needful to take his only Son and make 'him who had no sin to be sin for us, so that in him we might become the righteousness of God.' Amen."

"Amen, Reverend."

"The Apostle Paul taught us in I Corinthians 1:30, "It is because of him that you are in Christ Jesus, who has become for us...our righteousness, holiness and redemption."

"Yes, Lord, He is."

"He was the only One, the only link between me and the Holy God. For that, there isn't any way to be grateful enough. For that sacrifice, let us experience Thanksgiving at its highest. Amen and amen."

There were whispered and audible *Amens* all around the group. Sam saw the paths of tears down Alaine's face. It was clear Rev. Ray's words had moved her. Sam found that intriguing.

He couldn't argue that the man had a way with his message. The tone and manner were persuasive, but the content of the Thanksgiving challenge left him cold. Sam found Rev. Ray's words to be foreign to his own way of thinking.

It was difficult for him to interpret words like, "*He was the only One, the only link between me and the Holy God.*" He'd heard of Jesus Christ, of course. He'd never given God much thought. Sam bought into the notion that if you needed something, you got it yourself, and if you wanted something, you'd better be responsible yourself for going after it. There hadn't been much room for the spiritual realm in this philosophy.

As he glanced around the group listening to Rev. Ray, most faces revealed the impact of his words. Sam felt singular in his resistance. He had, for some time, resisted overt, masculine demonstrations of emotion. It appeared he was in the minority on this day, as he saw Johnson Story wiping tears away with no shame.

# # #

Usually on Thanksgiving Day, Sam slept until afternoon and then ate a frozen pizza as a personal protest against a day that discriminated against those who had no close family. Last year his landlady, Mrs. Baker, asked him to join her and her 45 year old ex-biker son who lived in New Jersey and only came to see his mother on the major holidays. She cooked a turkey casserole, and they sat around in red vinyl chairs at the same chrome and Formica kitchen table she'd used for years.

The son was mildly polite and sipped from a flask when his mother's back was turned until, by the end of the meal, he could barely pretend to eat his supermarket-made pecan pie. Just before Sam excused himself, thanking Mrs. Baker profusely for her hospitality, he helped her son to his old bedroom where the man collapsed on the bed of his youth to sleep off the results of the contents of his flask. His mother seemed thrilled he was staying with her, apparently overlooking the reason this was necessary. It was hardly a Hallmark occasion.

Sam's memory of last Thanksgiving made the contrast between his landlady's kitchen and the dining room of the Inn's Café striking as he surveyed the readiness for the impending holiday buffet. The decorating expertise of Alaine and Andi, coupled with Ms. Charity's liberal spacing of pumpkin spice candles, set the stage to ensure that guests came to the tables well on their way to having their best Thanksgiving memories replayed.

Everything seemed in near perfect order.

Sam went in search of Andi to congratulate her on her decorating prowess. He found her in the kitchen, and sincere pleasure in her smile thanked him when he told her how good everything looked. Then he went to find Alaine.

She was serving as hostess for the evening, greeting guests in the reception room of the Inn and directing them down the hall to the dining area. She was dressed in a flowing wine colored dinner dress that accentuated her hair and eyes and concealed her growing waistline.

Sam noted, with some surprise, how self-assured Alaine appeared. It was true that she was emerging from the shy and dependent person of two months ago into a poised and confident stranger. This thought disturbed Sam, and thinking about why it did bothered him more. He watched her briefly and moved away without completing his mission to thank her for her hard work.

Even as the guests for the evening descended on the Inn, Sam walked down the stone steps into the darkened back yard, taking a moment to look back at the candlelit windows where the Thanksgiving celebration meal was beginning.

He knew he should go in and check on everyone. He knew he should make sure Rev. Ray, who was mingling with the diners, wasn't overdoing it. Still Sam stayed, walking closer to the river until he could hear its sounds through the dark.

Inside he would be too busy, too needed, to contemplate what was happening to Alaine right before his eyes. She was steadily being transformed from one bruised and shaken by a life over which she had little control into a composed and self-assured woman. All of this was happening while she faced giving birth to a baby without a husband and without a clear plan for the future.

Her immediate circumstances were not ones in which Sam would expect her to flourish. And yet here she was, thriving despite her constraints. He couldn't account for the changes. Sam lingered outside when he heard a call in the darkness.

"Sam, is that you?" The voice was Ms. Charity's, and as it came closer, he turned to meet her.

"I'm here. Is anything wrong?"

"No. In fact, I came to ask you the same question." He could feel the smile she gave him in the dark.

"I'm fine. Just needed a few minutes before making my rounds. It's a perfect night. This little river always has a calming effect on me. I'm afraid it didn't have any substitute back in the City." Sam spoke into the night.

"I thought New York City had its rivers, too."

"The East and the Harlem are really just tidal straits connected to the ocean. The Hudson's the only true river in the City. And there the similarity ends. A river running past Manhattan and a river running through the back yard of the Inn at Copper's Run have nothing more in common than the label. I never drew much comfort from the Hudson, at least not downriver."

Ms. Charity took hold of Sam's arm and linked hers with it. "A lot has happened in the last three months, Sam. Big things. Once in a life events. I think they're still going on. You wouldn't want Alaine to stay where she was then. You don't want to either. Don't try too hard to figure it all out at once. Keep asking questions, keep examining the differences, but give it time."

"You're very perceptive. How do you do that?"

"Prayer...and I keep my eyes open. One day maybe I'll explain. But now I'm getting cold. Shall we join the feast inside?"

10 ALAINE'S STORY

Alaine

The week after Thanksgiving was unusually cold and dreary. The bite in the weather was in utter contrast to the warmth and camaraderie Alaine experienced with the Inn family during the holiday. To worsen the circumstances, Rev. Ray caught a cold from one of the buffet attendees, and Ms. Charity had him in isolation, which robbed them all of his much needed inspiration. It also left the staff shorthanded during a time when seasonal parties flourished at the Inn.

At the height of the hectic holiday season, Alaine appropriated Sam once more to accompany her to a counseling appointment at the Life Options Center.

In spite of his apparent desire and voiced commitment to support her, she knew the timing of this particular appointment taxed Sam's patience. He'd worked on Inn paperwork all morning, and she knew it was difficult for him to break his train of thought to make the trip. Still, he went, and his presence somehow gave her strength.

A chilled rain went with them through the streets of Copper's Run, making their short drive and the task of entering and exiting buildings and vehicles particularly trying.

As Sam handed a dripping Alaine to Jane for their session, she heard him mumble something about having work to do and excuse himself to wait in the van. She suspected his retreat had more to do with avoiding another conversation with David Dabney than working, as she had not seen him bring anything with him to do.

An hour later, Alaine opened the door of the van, her session with Jane completed.

She watched Sam pull himself awake and glance at her as she settled in her seat and pushed her wet hair from her face. It was raining more heavily now, and he apologized that he hadn't met her at the Center's door with an umbrella. She shook her head, giving him no sign that she was bothered by his inconsiderate behavior, and in truth, his actions dimmed in contrast to the emotions crowding her head.

Her eye makeup was blotched and streaked. She hoped Sam would attribute this to the rain, and not that she had been crying.

Sam turned the key in the ignition, starting the motor and the heater. Then, as she feared, he addressed his concerns about her appearance.

"What went on? I knew I should have gone with you. If those Dabney's have upset or embarrassed you, I will certainly-- No way would I have involved you in something that causes you distress beyond what you must already be experiencing." He turned to face her.

"What happened in there? Why were you crying?" Sam reached for the door handle, and she put a restraining hand on his arm.

"You're right. I've been crying, but not because I'm not OK. I'm...really fine."

"Then tell me what's going on." Sam's tone was insistent and his tone harsh, as if he didn't believe her.

"No one said anything to upset me. Please, just relax. Nothing's wrong, I promise."

Alaine saw Sam watching for any hint that she was covering something. She worked to ensure her face was calm and open, without a trace of having been mistreated. In fact, she was jubilant with news she wanted to share but didn't know how.

"What happened?" he repeated.

"It's hard to explain, Sam. You'll think I've become some kind of religious extremist. I'm sorry, but I know how you think. That's not the way this is. This is real. It makes the most sense of anything I've ever heard before. It's like I've been waiting my whole life for right now."

"What are you talking about? Are these folks brainwashing you? I thought that might happen."

"That's how I thought you'd react. If you really want to know, I'll tell you as best I can. If you're going to overreact and be critical, then I'll wait until you're ready to hear it. But this is important to me. At least you can believe that."

There was a momentary standoff as each eyed the other.

He broke the silence as he pulled his hand away from the door handle and turned off the ignition. "I'm listening. I want to hear what you have to say."

"Sam, I know we aren't at the same place right now. I really hope you'll try to understand. This is serious for me. I've made a decision to follow Christ. This is not a whim. I haven't been unduly influenced. It's a conclusion I've come to over several weeks and with much thought. Yes, I've been crying, but emotion didn't prompt me to make this decision. It's right for me. And my whole life is going to change."

Alaine finished speaking and sat waiting for his response. She braced herself for skepticism or worse yet, sarcasm.

"Tell me a little more about what you did." OK, he was trying, but he sounded like he was repeating some exercise from a counseling class.

Alaine chose not to react negatively to his prompt. "It's something I've had on my mind for a while. I've talked to Ms. Charity and the girls and Rev. Ray. And then it came up during my session with Jane Dabney."

He waited, but she could see the cynicism on his face.

"I've felt for some time that the life choices I've made were bad ones. I've been in a self-destruct mode, making decisions that hurt me, and I kept repeating those mistakes over and over."

"Aren't you being a bit hard on yourself? Everybody makes mistakes."

"No, that's part of the problem. I've not been hard enough. Look, you really don't know much about me. I mean my background. My mom and I lost my dad when I was seven. He was killed in a military training accident. I was their only child, and when Daddy died, Mama and I couldn't live alone. She was not a very strong person, physically or emotionally. I can see that now. Back then, she was just my mom."

"I didn't know. I'm sorry." Sam interrupted.

"So we moved to another state to live with my mom's mother. Grandmother Maxwell took care of us by working part time and using money she and Granddaddy saved or she got when he died. It was all Mom could do to watch me for the few hours each week when Grandmother was away. Mom finally had to go into an institution when her hold on reality got so bad that she wasn't safe at home.

"By that time, I was almost through high school and working part time myself. It was sad to see Mom leave us that way, but I had Grandmother. She was a good woman and tried her best to teach me what it meant to be good. As long as she was alive, I tried to live up to her expectations and prove to her I could make a success of myself. I really tried. I did."

Alaine dropped her head, struggling to go on. Sam filled the void with what, to her ears, sounded like continued psycho-babble.

"All of that must have been very hard for you at such a young age. Of course you still have some moments when it would upset you, even now."

Alaine raised her eyes to Sam's and shook her head. "I'm not telling you this to be psychoanalyzed. I've already tried that. And I'm not asking you to feel sorry for me. I'm just telling my story to help you see where I'm coming from with this new decision I've made."

Sam was now quiet, and she continued.

"I'm sorry. That was mean spirited. I just want so much for you to understand." She opened her hands in front of her as if to beg his comprehension.

"By the time I graduated from community college with my two year degree, both Mom and Grandmother were dead, and I was already earning my own way as an office assistant. The money wasn't great, but that didn't matter because I had moved in with a guy I met my freshman year."

Sam's face reacted to this news, and she responded to that reaction.

"That's right. Paul Mowher, this baby's father, wasn't my first live in. He was number two. Why would that surprise you? That's what I'm saying, Sam. As long as I had Grandmother to help keep me straight, I seemed to be OK, but as soon as she was gone, it's like all of my reasons to behave like a lady and make something of myself left with her."

"Alaine, look, you don't have to—"

"Yes, Sam, I do. It's part of my story. It's part of what I want...need for you to understand." Without waiting for a response, she continued.

"I only stayed with the first guy a few months, but long enough to know his problems were worse than mine. I moved out. By then, Grandmother's estate had been settled, and I had a little extra money to help with rent and living expenses. I planned to go on to school and get my four year degree. I did it, but then I made my next huge mistake. When I graduated, I changed jobs to the one in the Trade Center for what I thought would be better pay. That's what I'd been led to believe."

Sam's laugh was sarcastic. "I hated that job and most of the people there."

It was now Alaine who showed surprise. "I couldn't tell. You seemed pretty much like everybody else there...interested in money and schmoozing and using people. Sorry, Sam, but that's how it seemed to me. Only you were a little nicer. Nobody really cared about anybody else in that place, and the company certainly didn't care about the employees. I found out really fast how the raises I had been promised would be earned, so I just stayed on with entry level pay."

"Why didn't you quit...find something else?"

"Why didn't you?" There was mischief in her voice.

"Ah, that's a story for another day. Besides, I asked you first." His tone matched hers.

"I was on the verge of quitting and doing anything else when I met Paul Mowher. We were both in Central Park by a fountain on a beautiful spring day. It was a storybook meeting, at least to me. He was the handsome prince, and I was the lonely maiden waiting for the perfect man.

"It took me six months to find out he was really on a stakeout to catch a man cheating on his wife, and I got in the way. End of fairy tale."

"But it wasn't the end."

"Not of our relationship...what a euphemism. But of the fairy tale? Yes. It was about six months before I found out who the prince really was. Once I even made a list of his good and evil qualities in double columns on a piece of computer paper at work. The plus side had four items: charismatic personality, bathes regularly, likes good music, is a great cook."

Tears now ran down her face smearing already messed makeup, and she struggled for some seconds before she could continue.

"And the minus column?" He now seemed eager to hear her out.

"I quit after ten things. I could have gone on. Let's just say that hypocritical, sarcastic, dishonest, cruel, unfeeling, and mean were among the lesser evils I remember listing. Paul Mowher is not a nice person. I forgot to mention that he's smart. That makes him even less nice, combined with his other qualities."

They sat for a few minutes, watching a cold rain fall. They were going to be late to help with supper at the Café, but they couldn't stop now.

"So why didn't you leave both your dead end job and Paul Mowher?"

"Don't you see? I have. That's just what I've done. Isn't that irony for you?"

"You know that's not what I meant. Why now? Why not then? You knew long before September 11th that both were losers, right? Why not just get out?"

"Sam, my friend, you're thinking like a man. You're not thinking like a woman who needed to belong to someone to prove she was worth being with. You're not thinking like a girl who had lived most of her life without a daddy to look to as an example of what a real man is. It's no excuse. I see that now, but I was running on a rough sea with no rudder. Paul wasn't a lot of things, but he was a strong leader. If he'd led me in a positive direction, we might have been fine, for a while. As it was, his leading became tight control of almost every part of my life."

"What do you mean? How could he control you? You had your own job, your own money."

"Sam, maybe you don't know about emotional control, but every woman who has lived with some jerk because she didn't think she could do any better understands. I couldn't go out to graduate school in the evenings because he needed me at home with him, or he was afraid for me to be around the city on my own at night. It was for my own good...or so he said. I couldn't quit my dead end job because I needed to show I could stick with something. And he promised he would put the money I made in the bank, supposedly for our future, and we would live on what he made. He'd take care of us...he swore. On and on and on, and I believed all of it for a long, awful time.

"The only thing I didn't do was tell him about the little bit of savings I had left over from my grandmother. He would have found out sooner or later, but 9/11 happened sooner. I hope my money's still safe. Oh yes, and he doesn't know about my baby."

"Is this Mowher guy dangerous? I mean, is he violent?"

"He's dangerous, yes, to sanity and clear thinking. He definitely endangers a sense of well-being. Would he commit violent acts in anger? Let's just say I know he would. I learned early not to push him and find out. He keeps his actions under pretty tight command. Mostly he works his magic by intimidation, but violence is not out of the question."

"And the terror attack on the Trade Center provided you the perfect cover to make your escape."

"It did, and hopefully he thinks I'm dead. I'm counting on all of the confusion surrounding the collapse and the aftermath to make my little trail to Copper's Run hard to follow. I hope I'm not dreaming. He's a former police officer turned private detective, and he's good at his work."

"Police officer? Detective? I didn't realize-- You never said—"

"Oh, I thought I had. Why?"

"Nothing. It's nothing. Your life's had its challenges then. You've found yourself in some rough circumstances. But I'm curious about what you said earlier. You said something about your whole life being about to change. What do you mean by that?"

Alaine surveyed Sam as if to judge the motives behind his question.

"Sam, I'm tired of being in charge of a miserable life. I've pretty well proven I can make a disaster of it. I'm worn out from living to get by for the moment and hoping for more. Jesus said, 'Come to me, all you who are weary and burdened, and I will give you rest.' That's so me. That's what I need. I think I can find forgiveness and rest doing things God's way. As I told you earlier, I've made a decision to quit trying on my own and follow Jesus and what the Bible teaches." She re-checked Sam's face to see if she'd lost him.

"What exactly did you do?"

"I finally paid attention to what the Bible says about everybody having sinned and displeased God. It's both our human nature and our choice, and it certainly describes me. The Bible also says that Christ is the only way to reach God. He gave his life to make that statement true. I believe it." She stopped for a deep breath. "I told God I was sorry for my personal sins and my lifestyle as a sinner and asked his forgiveness. I asked Jesus to take control of my life and show me his purpose for my existence...and also to give me his rest. I've a long way to go to understand what all that means, but it's the first hope I've felt in a long time."

She saw Sam was not going to respond and continued.

"You may not understand or agree with me now, Sam. I hope and pray you will someday. It's a decision that made sense to me. I'm done with the direction I've been going. Thank you for asking me about it. I think I need to go back to the Inn now. I'm pretty tired." She rested her head back and turned her face toward the window.

Sam backed out of the parking space. She could imagine what he was thinking. While it was all right for her, religion had little appeal to him. She wished it could be different.

As he pulled onto the highway toward the Inn, he reached across and placed his hand over both of hers where they were clutched together in her lap.

"I respect your decision. I hope this works for you."

11 MOWHER'S STORY

Sampson

Christmas was three weeks away, and both the façade and interior of the historic old building were draped with natural greenery and decorated with vintage cloth and painted wood ornaments. The atmosphere was good, and Sam was proud.

The Inn's holiday activities were at fever pitch as most afternoons and evenings it became a venue for celebrations, both sizable and intimate. Copper's Run wasn't a large place, but its citizen's knew how to celebrate the season, as did those of the surrounding towns.

In addition to its lunch and dinner guests, the Inn's rooms were booked to near capacity through most of the holidays, with visitors coming from several states away to spend time with family or just to enjoy the ambiance and service of the Inn and its setting. The word was spreading, and this knowledge also made Sam happy.

Additional help had been acquired for the busy season, and the services of the entire staff were employed to the maximum. There was little time to spend celebrating with each other as everyone pulled together to make the guests' stays memorable.

Rev. Ray's job was to circulate among the hard-working staff to encourage, keep alive the Christmas spirit and remind his little group of the real reason Christmas was significant. He was good at his job, and his support went a long way toward keeping everything running smoothly at the Inn.

Charity and Ray Bright had discovered years back that personalizing their attentions to guests went a long way. They made sure Sam and the Inn's staff stayed reminded. Alaine shared their conviction and developed a guest list from the reservations of overnight visitors, which she shared with other staff members daily to help make them familiar with the names, at the least, of guests.

Alaine was usually the first contact with those staying at the Inn overnight, as she most often manned the check-in as part of her duties. On Tuesday, one week from Christmas day, she worked at the check-in desk while Sam worked across the reception room in his private office.

He heard the sleigh bells jingle on the front door announcing someone's arrival, but he didn't get up and look out as he knew Alaine was at her post. What he overheard in the next moments brought him to his feet.

"Good afternoon, sir. Welcome to the Inn at Copper's Run and Merry Christmas. How may I help you?"

There was a pause during which Sam heard no response. Then he heard a name spoken in a tight voice by Alaine, a name he'd hoped not to hear again from her.

"Paul...what are you doing here?"

Sam froze at the name. *She must mean Paul Mowher. What is he doing here?*

A hard knot formed in Sam's stomach when he remembered his early morning call from the bus stop on the road to Copper's Run informing the NYPD that he and Alaine made it out of the North Tower before it fell. He'd not known at the time that Mowher was a former police and now a private detective. And he thought about that credit card of hers they had used to withdraw her money.

Sam heard the other man's unwelcome voice.

"Hello, Alaine. You're looking lovelier than ever. I can't tell you how glad

I am to find you. I feared for so long that you were--"

"How did you know I was here? No...don't touch me, Paul. Just tell me how you found me."

At this point, Sam unfroze himself and nearly knocked over the desk chair as he moved to close the distance between his office and where Alaine stood. He had no idea what to say or how to say it, so he uttered the first words that came to his mind to check the progression of the situation in front of him.

"Ms. Albert, is there a problem I can assist you with?"

Two things struck Sam as he stopped next to Alaine and faced Paul Mowher, who was standing with his hat in hand and smiling at Alaine. Sam's dislike for Mowher was both immediate and intense.

Besides the distasteful knowledge he already had about the man, Mowher's impeccable appearance and arrogant air of self-confidence rattled Sam. Add in light of the amusement in the man's eyes, which reminded Sam of a cat with a helpless mouse under its control that would torment it for fun, Paul Mowher's first impression was not a good one.

Alaine was obviously struggling to maintain a professional decorum before the two men. Sam saw that her face was deathly pale and her hands were shaking as they clenched in front of her, but she managed a smile.

"Mr. MacDonald, I'd like for you to meet a friend from New York, Paul Mowher. Paul, this is Sampson MacDonald. Mr. MacDonald is the current innkeeper here."

Sam was as reluctant to show hospitality to Mowher by shaking his hand as he guessed, from watching Mowher's eyes, the man was to accept Sam's hand.

Knowing that it might make the visitor uncomfortable, he reached out first as an offensive challenge.

It was a challenge Mowher met, and he followed with his own.

"Nice to meet you, MacDonald. Are you the person I have to thank for rescuing my fiancée from the World Trade Center disaster? I've had quite a time tracking you both down, but you have my most sincere gratitude for her safety. Now that I'm here, we can put all of that behind us and enjoy the holiday season, right my dear?" Mowher reached out his hand and gently gripped Alaine's arm.

Sam turned toward Alaine to gauge her reaction to Mowher's overture, expecting to see her back away in horror. What he saw was Alaine acting as if Mowher held her under some spell. Her eyes locked with Mowher's, and she almost imperceptibly leaned in toward his touch on her arm.

Desperate to intervene in any way possible, Sam used his most authoritative voice when he spoke again.

"Ms. Albert, you've been on duty for some time now without a break. Why don't I relieve you for a brief rest? I'll be happy to assist Mr. Mowher."

Before she could respond, Sam turned to Mowher.

"If you're seeking a room, I'm afraid we're all booked for the next few days." This wasn't technically true as there were a couple of small and inconvenient rooms kept open for emergencies, but Sam didn't consider this man's needs an emergency. "Perhaps you'll be staying for dinner, or I could see if there are motels in the area that have a vacancy?"

Alaine hadn't moved, and Sam could hardly send her to her room like a child. He stood his ground as Mowher gestured lazily toward the computer.

"Oh, I have reservations here already. You should find me listed as Paul Monroe. I altered the name out of concern for not giving my fiancée a shock until I could see her in person. Sorry to be deceptive, darling." He directed this at Alaine. "It was for your good. I must say again, you're looking so well, not quite as thin and pale as I remember. The Virginia countryside must agree with you."

By the time Mowher finished his speech, Sam found the Paul Monroe reservation in the computer. He'd booked four nights. The act was either Mowher's supreme confidence or ultimate stupidity. Putting Alaine under this kind of stress was just not acceptable.

"I'm sorry, Mowher," Sam began, "But it seems that under the circumstances—"

"It's OK, Sam. Leave it like it is. I have no objections. Paul can stay, if he wishes. Would you be so kind as to show him to his room?" Alaine said her piece and turned to walk out of the reception room.

Both Mowher and Sam watched her go. Just before she disappeared into the hallway, Mowher called after her. "Perhaps we can visit over dinner this evening, Alaine. I've come a long way to see you. I'd really like for us to have a chance to talk."

Alaine stopped and looked over her shoulder at Mowher. Sam didn't hear her respond, but he caught sight of a slight nod of assent before she left the room.

The two men faced each other. Neither spoke, and the quiet was uncomfortable. Mowher finally shrugged and smiled.

"She always was a bit of a mystery. I guess that's what makes her so intriguing. Say, that must have been some deal with the Trade Center. You got her down from the 87th floor, isn't that right? North Tower? Second Tower to fall. You were lucky to get the both of you out in time."

"It took a lot more than luck to get us down, Mowher. And Alaine did her part. It took all we both had. I certainly didn't carry her out. She worked as hard as I did."

Mowher didn't look impressed. His scowl told Sam that the man's anger that she was here trumped his gratitude that Alaine was alive. Sam's own dislike for him deepened, and he scowled back in response.

"Tell me, MacDonald, how did you persuade Alaine to leave with you and come to this god-forsaken backwoods town?"

"She's a grown--" Sam began before he considered the possible conclusions of his statement. If he sounded like Alaine came with him of her own volition, thus rejecting Mowher, there's no telling what the man might do. Better he thought she came along from some outside influence.

"Actually, Alaine wasn't herself for some time after the tragedy. Once we got out of the Tower, I couldn't just leave her in Manhattan. I had no idea where she lived. I wanted to be sure she was safe while she pulled herself together, so I brought her here with me to recover."

Sam hoped the unconvincing explanation he threw at Mowher would find a mark. Maybe now was a good time to show Mowher to his room.

As soon as he left the man in his suite, Sam set out to find Alaine. He checked back in the reception room, but Ms. Charity was there greeting a couple on their honeymoon. If Ms. Charity handled Alaine's duties, she might know where she was. Sam lingered in his office, waiting for a chance to find out what Ms. Charity knew.

The couple was intrigued with the Inn and its history, and Sam would have to interrupt their question and answer session with Ms. Charity or else lose time searching for Alaine on his own. He chose the former.

"Excuse me, Ms. Charity, I'm sorry to break in, but it's critical that I find Ms. Albert as soon as possible. Do you know where she might be?"

The look Ms. Charity gave him flashed a warning, but her manner was mild as she smiled and said, "I believe you might find her in the chapel." He thanked her and didn't miss the slight frown and shake of her head. Clearly Alaine was not to be disturbed.

Should he ignore the warning and go to Alaine himself? Would he know what to say to calm her and counsel her through this unexpected and, Sam was sure, unwelcome reunion with her former lover? He most likely should go back to work...maybe check in at the Café to see if anyone needed him there.

Instead of heading toward the dining facilities, Sam turned the opposite way, moving at a near run along the hallway and down the stone steps to the Inn's cellar area. Here was the chapel, and here he hoped to find Alaine. He had to ensure she was all right.

Taking the none-too-safe steps two at a time and not taking care to quiet his own loud footsteps in the stone passageway, Sam arrived at the chapel's doors to see the small "In Use" sign hanging on its hook on the outside.

He listened but no sounds came from within the arched chapel door. Nothing was visible through the frosted stained glass panes. Unsure of what to do, Sam sat down on one of the wooden benches in the hallway.

Sam could have sat there minutes or nearly an hour. Without his watch, he couldn't tell. When he finally heard footsteps and saw the door handle turn, he stood, not knowing in what condition he would find Alaine.

What he saw surprised him, and it showed on his face, judging by the silent scrutiny Alaine gave him. Gone was the agitation he had sensed earlier while she talked with Mowher. She appeared calm and at rest. He hadn't expected hysterics, but he never anticipated her obvious lack of anxiety. Sam's planned rush to comfort no longer seemed appropriate.

He had to say something, as Alaine watched him expectantly. "I just wanted to be sure you were OK. It must have been a shock meeting Paul Mowher again like you did. Look, if you'd rather me ask him to leave, you know I will."

"That won't be necessary, Sam, but thank you for that. I don't know how he found me or what he's after. I'm going to talk to him at supper and find out. I think I'll be fine, but I'm not going to say anything yet about the baby."

Alaine's hand rested on her stomach, but she was still thin. It was early enough in her pregnancy that her hand had little on which to rest. She didn't look pregnant.

Sam felt awkward and juvenile in the face of a composed and collected Alaine. It was a reverse déjà vu. Unlike after 9/11, she was suddenly the strong one. This insight amused Sam, and he smiled at Alaine with more confidence than he felt.

I'm glad you're OK. Let me know if you need anything." He touched her arm briefly before they walked down the long cellar hallway toward the stairs.

# # #

Sam served as maitre d' for the evening in the Inn's dining room when Paul Mowher entered and requested a table for two. Sam forced himself to be civil and made small talk as he seated Mowher at the best available table. Ten minutes later, Alaine slipped past him while he was greeting another guest and joined Mowher.

Mowher rose to greet her, bent and kissed her on the cheek as he pulled out her chair. Once seated, he leaned back and watched her with a smile without speaking. Alaine faced him, also without speaking or smiling. Sam observed from across the room, an uninvited watcher, but a watcher nonetheless. He didn't trust anything about the polished and charming Paul Mowher.

Sam welcomed guests and later bid them good bye as the evening dragged on, and still Mowher and Alaine sat over their after-dinner coffee.

Sam, while pretending not to, watched Mowher's every move. Alaine hadn't smiled or warmed up all evening; he could tell by her body language. But she hadn't left Mowher alone at the table, either.

At five minutes before 10:00, just before the Inn's dining room closed for the evening, Sam saw Mowher assist Alaine from her seat and escort her toward the exit. He forced himself to offer obligatory polite gestures.

"Good evening, Mr. Mowher, have a pleasant night. Alaine, I hope you rest well."

"Thank you, Sam." And then she surprised him. "May I have a brief word with you?"

"Now?" Sam's voice came out in an adolescent croak. He hadn't expected her date with Mowher to end with a request to talk to him instead.

"Good night, Paul. I'll see you tomorrow. Please excuse me. I need a few minutes with Sam."

Sam stood with Alaine and watched Mowher leave the dining room. She faced him. "You've been watching me like a hawk all night. You're worried about me, Sam. That's obvious and I'm grateful, but please don't be. I can understand why you're concerned. But I wanted to let you know that I'm fine."

The two stood looking at each other in silence until she became visibly uncomfortable.

"Well, that's it. I think I'll call it a night. Thanks, Sam."

Sam was well versed in helpless frustration. He'd practiced it thoroughly through countless jobs and relationships, both professional and personal. Seldom had he experienced the irritation this brief conversation with Alaine caused him. He knew she was exiting so quickly due to his lack of something to say in response to her announcement.

But Sam did have something to say. He checked to ensure they would not be overheard.

"Alaine, is this not the same man who, less than six months ago, was abusing you? Verbally and emotionally? Physically, too, if truth be told? Is Paul Mowher not the one who found fault with everything you did and controlled and secluded you from everyone and everything but work? Is he not the same person you said you never wanted to see again when you left him and New York City behind?"

Sam understood he was berating Alaine at this point. Still, his aggravation at the situation egged him on despite the shuttered look about her eyes and the tightness around her lips.

"Look, I'll admit that the things I told you about him earlier were true. I didn't make them up. I wasn't delusional. I'm simply trying hard to be objective about Paul. When we were together, I was weak and immature...not much to love. I'm sure being with me wasn't easy, either. I need to be sure I'm not judging his past actions unfairly because of my own problems at the time."

Alaine stopped and watched him. His lack of response must have disappointed her.

"This isn't helping me, Sam. Please try to understand what I'm saying. The man I had dinner with this evening is not the person I used to live with. I know it's far too early to tell, but this Paul is utterly opposite to what he was a few months ago. Look, I've changed since 9/11. I'm sure a lot of others have as a result. Maybe he has, too."

Her voice, while hesitant at first, grew stronger as if she convinced herself of her position.

"What exactly do you mean?" Sam's tone was harsher than he intended, but it reflected his conflict. He tried to soften the effect he was sure showed on his face.

"All I can say for now is, he's nice. Nice was not a descriptor I would have used for the man I knew before. His manner is softer. The old Paul was hard, both inside and out. I even explained to him that I have become a believer in Christ, and he said he understood and was happy for me."

There was another pause as if she wanted Sam to say something. Other than shaking his head, he did not.

"I know you think I've lost my mind, Sam. You don't cover your expressions well. I'm sorry. That's the best I can tell you. He's different. He doesn't scare me like he used to."

"Why is he here, Alaine? What does he want? And just how did he find you? Think about that. People can change, I know, but change comes hard, and most people aren't willing to pay the price. My bet is that Mowher's like most people. I hope I'm wrong, but I don't think I am."

Sam ranted again, and he worked to soften his tone, if not his message.

"I know I can't tell you what to do. I can tell you what I wish you would do, but you're a grown woman. Please be careful. Please promise me you won't make any sudden moves just because he's here and you've had one good evening with him."

She'd tracked Sam's eyes while he spoke, but somewhere in the middle of his speech, she broke contact. He'd lost her. He'd pushed too hard. Score for Paul Mowher.

Sam had barely touched Alaine in all of the weeks since their escape on 9/11. He understood how fragile and vulnerable she'd been at first and hadn't wanted to frighten her. Later, as she grew stronger, there was no need to touch her. After she told him about the baby and he'd behaved with such lack of sensitivity, he sensed any physical comfort from him would be rebuffed as unwelcome. Now he acted out of impulse because there was nothing left he could say that she would hear.

He enveloped Alaine in his arms, careful to keep his hold light and gentle. She didn't pull away, to his surprise, although she didn't move toward him, either.

"I'm sorry, Alaine. I'm not your father. I don't know it all. I just pretend to. Just please take care. Let me know if I can do anything."

She smiled as she pulled away without any visible annoyance toward his actions. Just before she left him standing there, she whispered, "You have, Sam. Goodnight."

# # #

Sam was up early the next morning, determined to keep watch on Paul Mowher but equally determined to do so without the intrusiveness he'd exhibited the previous night. His vigil continued well into the afternoon but in vain, as there was no evidence of Mowher at the Inn. A quick inspection of his account showed no check out. It was Alaine's day off, and she also seemed to be absent.

By the time he played host at the Inn all day with half of his attention while with the rest he constantly scanned for the sight of the missing couple, Sam, who never suffered from headaches, had an old fashioned splitting kind. The early twilight of the pre-Christmas week was well underway when he made out two forms walking down the Inn's front entry drive. He could see just enough to know that it was Mowher and Alaine.

Sam's first impulse was to stand in the front doorway, outlined by the light coming from within the Inn, to let them know they were being observed, and not in a welcoming way. Judging that to be somewhat juvenile, he busied himself in his office but stayed positioned to know when anyone came through the Inn's front door.

Again his wait was unproductive as he exhausted any tasks he could find in the area, but still Mowher and Alaine hadn't come through the reception room.

Finally, feeling as irked as a parent whose teen is spurning curfew, Sam stalked out to the front doorway to look again, not caring who saw him standing there.

Just as Sam was about to go into the yard to see why the two weren't coming in, he heard Alaine's voice coming from the hallway opposite the front door. She was calling his name.

"Sam...Sam, are you in here? Oh, there you are. I was looking everywhere for you."

"Looking everywhere for me?" Despite Alaine's cheerful greeting, his voice came out sarcastic and severe. Before he could stop himself he followed with, "Where have you been? You've been gone all day," as if it were a crime or even his business.

To Alaine's credit, she didn't take his bait. Her tone was positive and her expression pleasant. "I've had the most wonderful day off. Paul and I decided to go for a walking tour around Copper's Run. He's never been here before, and there are a surprising number of interesting things to see in this town, not the least of which is that old copper whiskey still on the town square."

Without encouragement from Sam, she talked on. "We had the little deli on Third Street fix us a picnic, and we ate it in the park. I can't believe the weather is as nice as it is for December. We stayed outside almost all day."

Sam gained enough control to offer small talk when he decided that her chatter had more to do with letting him know she was all right than it did with her desire to tell him about her day. Or, on the other hand, maybe she was preparing him gently for a growing re-attachment to Paul Mowher.

Sam couldn't help himself. "So...how was he?"

"A gentleman. No negative talk. No anger. No pressure. I don't understand it, Sam. He's pleasant. In the old days...he didn't know the word."

He's not for real, Sam wanted to tell her. *He can't keep this up.*

What he managed to say was, "That's great, Alaine, but keep your eyes open. It hasn't been that long ago."

"He wanted me to ask you to join us for dinner. Can you spare some time?"

Another unpredictable turn of events. Dilemma. If he refused, he would risk hurting her and appearing uncivil. If he said yes, would he be complicit in endorsing a relationship he felt was doomed and destructive?

A glance at Alaine's face dictated his response. She wanted him to join them. For whatever purpose, she was silently seeking his assent.

"I think I could arrange that, at least for an hour or so."

Her face affirmed his decision.

Alaine and Mowher were already seated when Sam turned his duties over to another of the Inn's employees and joined them at their table. Her greeting held both anticipation and a fair amount of tension.

Mowher's greeting reminded Sam of someone accustomed to hiding his true feelings behind cordial and correct manners. On the surface, Mowher was genial and charming, but Sam sensed this act was a mask.

It was obvious to Sam that Alaine wanted him there and Mowher didn't, despite his invitation.

Sam decided that the best approach was to match charm with charisma. Years of disingenuous communication experience uniquely qualified him to play the part.

"Alaine, Paul, hope you both are doing well this evening." Sam shook hands when Mowher half rose to acknowledge his arrival. "Alaine, you look radiant. You had a nice day off, then?" Not waiting for her response, which he already knew, Sam continued, "So, Mowher, what's your line of business back in the City?"

There was an uneasy silence while the man clearly debated his reply.

"I'm in...security." The words Sam knew to be misleading were delivered clipped and sparse in the air between them.

Sam answered in kind, deliberately choosing to misunderstand Mowher's response. "Securities as in investments...stocks, bonds? I have a background in investments myself, as Alaine may have told you."

Again, an awkward pause. "No, not trading securities. Security, as in private investigations...detective work. I'm a private eye, as they say in the old movies." This little attempt at humor left Sam cold.

"Oh. Well. I'm afraid I don't know anything about that line of work. What's your specialty? Corporate spying, divorce, missing persons, criminal investigations? Hey, is that how you found Alaine? You must be pretty good at what you do. Copper's Run is a bit off the beaten track."

Sam was baiting Mowher, but better to do that and get a reaction now than let the man continue to fool Alaine into thinking he'd changed his ways. And Sam was fairly confident Mowher had not. He would have trouble explaining his reasoning, but nonetheless, his conviction stood.

Mowher's voice interrupted Sam's thoughts. "I'm good at what I do. And once in a while you get that lucky break. Somehow, after September 11th, I couldn't convince myself that Alaine was dead, and I had lost her for good." He turned to look at Alaine with an expression of tenderness that made Sam grip the sides of his chair to keep from responding physically.

To his annoyance, Alaine returned Mowher's look with some caution but no animosity.

Mowher continued. "I have to tell you, I was pretty torn up when I realized Alaine was most likely in the Tower when it was hit. And then I didn't hear from her after it fell. While I feared the worst, I had to be sure. Naturally, in my line of business, I have some contacts. I started in immediately doing everything in my power to find her.

"I couldn't rest until I did all I could. It was bad for a while, and then I got a lead. I found out from a buddy in the NYPD about an anonymous report phoned in a few days after the attacks. The caller stated that Alaine and another person whose name was on the North Tower missing list had made it to safety. That other person would, no doubt, be you, MacDonald."

The look Mowher gave to Sam was clearly not one of gratitude for assisting his girlfriend to escape. It was, rather, a look of envy or resentment. A glance at Alaine showed her surprise at hearing of the phone call for the first time. Sam chose no response, and Mowher continued.

"After I knew she was alive, then I could use the same methods I use to track any missing person. Were there any phone calls appearing on a cell bill or credit card charges or bank activities? Sooner or later, missing persons are usually found."

Mowher was studying Sam. Though appearing to be the poster of casual composure, Sam managed to slide his eyes toward Alaine.

What must she think after hearing of his phone call to the police confirming their survival on the way to Copper's Run? He'd not intended for her to know and worry that she would be tracked...which is exactly what happened.

Sam saw the answer in her restrained expression. He'd failed her again by not telling her of his actions. He could almost read the moment she remembered their use of her ATM card to withdraw money, just once, soon after their arrival in Copper's Run. That transaction, coupled with his own call, led to this moment. Understanding flashed between them about the significance of these actions, however desperate and well intentioned they were at the time. *How could we be so stupid?*

Mowher, too, seemed to feel their discomfort, as he smiled and continued. "So, while it took me a few months, here we all are. I have to say this is a gratifying occasion."

This time, Mowher reached across the table and dared to lay his hand on top of Alaine's. She flinched at his touch, and then appeared to hide it with a smile as she slid from her seat murmuring something about a trip to the ladies' room.

Her absence left the two men to sit, facing each other, at the table. Silence ruled for long and uncomfortable seconds as they studied each other with barely concealed animosity.

Mowher made the first move when he leaned in toward Sam and spoke in a voice so low Sam could hardly hear him. What he didn't miss was the intended threat in tone and message.

"Look, MacDonald, I don't know what your responsibility for Alaine is here in this backwater pioneer excuse for a town. I'm sure I'm obliged for any part in her rescue back in September, but dragging her off here away from home...away from me...was a mistake. If you have designs on her, forget them. She's with me, or soon will be again. She belongs where I can take care of her. I understand her where you can't begin to. I'm giving you fair notice. Stay out of her personal affairs. She doesn't need you any longer. She has me. Don't take my advice lightly. Consider yourself thanked and discharged. Your job as far as Alaine is concerned is concluded." Mowher jabbed the table with his forefinger to accompany his final words.

The audacity of the man and his hostility left Sam with no socially appropriate response. He fought to keep emotion away from his face and stared at Mowher, who rested back in his seat sipping coffee as if the encounter had not taken place.

Before he could plan a suitable rebuttal, Alaine rejoined them. Mowher rose to greet her, and Sam followed suit. He'd lost his window of response. He was left to smolder in silence while Mowher exhibited precisioned charm intended, Sam was sure, to deceive Alaine into believing his transformation was indeed complete.

Sam knew he should stay and buffer Mowher's influence, or moreover, offer physical protection against any imminent danger to Alaine, but Sam was sickened and disgusted by the man's threats and deceptions. He excused himself from the table as soon as possible.

How next to approach Alaine about his gathering fears would be a problem to be faced tomorrow.

12 IN CONFLICT

Sampson

Restorative sleep eluded Sam. Reading a boring book didn't help. TV only stimulated his already overactive mind. By 3 a.m. he resorted to lying completely still and refusing to move, hoping to fool his overtired body and mind into relaxation. Rest hadn't been this inaccessible since the days immediately following 9/11.

In the pre-dawn hours, Sam traced his churning thoughts to see if there were common threads causing his lack of calm. The concern competing for most of his attention came, naturally, from Paul Mowher and the unease he raised for Alaine's well-being. Acknowledging this led Sam to recognize the undeniable bond between Alaine and himself. This connection, he supposed, stemmed from their escape and the co-dependence that developed as a result.

That they'd formed such an attachment wasn't odd or unusual. Sam knew this often happened to survivors of catastrophic events...plane crashes and other escape experiences. It also occurred between rescuers and the rescued. Most of the time, the connections were strong and emotional for the immediate aftermath of the event. Some even lasted over time, but most such links slowly receded...faded...with remembrances at anniversary dates and other milestones.

Was that phenomena what he and Alaine experienced now, more than three months after their near death event on September 11th? It was a fact she'd needed him immediately following their escape...depended on him completely for everything in the dark days of her confused and helpless state.

When did that dependence begin to lessen? It was true their arrival at Copper's Run provided Alaine with a broader support system. She'd gained Ray and Charity Bright, Danisha, Andi and later the Dabneys. But Sam also knew that Alaine's move away from dependence on him was more than a natural transition due to the caring of others.

With near physical pain, he remembered the look on her face the morning she told him she was pregnant. He'd followed her announcement with the question for which he would be forever ashamed. When he'd asked Alaine if Mowher was the father of her child, it implied there were other candidates, making her seem promiscuous and unfaithful, even to her live-in partner.

Thinking about the damage his unthinking words caused her made Sam break his determination not to move until he fell asleep. He threw back the covers and sat on the side of the bed, his face again hot with embarrassment.

Why did it matter what Alaine thought? If people thrown together by disastrous events eventually drifted out of each other's contact anyway, why should he be concerned about something he said that could make their disconnect come sooner?

For the first time since leaving New York City, he thought seriously about the longevity of his time at Copper's Run. It came to Sam that he now considered the town and the Inn as home. Feeling at home anywhere was a novel experience for the man who had never felt that way, even with his own family.

The thought of quitting the Inn and its people jarred Sam's senses. He couldn't imagine deciding to leave on his own behalf, but what if he overstayed his usefulness to Ray and Charity? They depended on him now, but that could change. They could move on in their own ministry and no longer have a need for his services. Or Ray could die and Charity could sell the property. Sam forced his thinking to the possibility that one day he might have to go.

Sam stumbled in the dark as he moved toward the small refrigerator in his room looking for something cold to drink. His hand gripped a soda as the light from the appliance lit his way.

Three months ago, pre-September 11th, thoughts such as those troubling Sam now wouldn't have been a problem. He would have slept as if dead without dreams or distractions. He wouldn't have wasted time caring much about what he said or where he lived. He'd been on automatic, spending as little energy on what would come next as possible.

Had he discovered before 9/11 that Alaine, or any woman he pursued at the time, was pregnant, that would have ended his interest and his pursuit. Ladies with baggage were not on his list of obligations. In fact, people with needs of any kind that impacted his life would have been avoided by Sam MacDonald. His own needs were few, survival in the world of low finance being one of them. Since his nosedive from the big time in the field of investments, he'd been holding on, hoping for better times but without authentic motivation to make better times a reality.

It shocked Sam to realize that his perspective had indeed changed over the last three months. It mattered whether Alaine had respect or disgust for him now. It was of significance whether she stayed at the Inn where she was safe, content and thriving or whether she withered again into her fragile and vulnerable former self with Paul Mowher. The work the Brights were doing at the Inn and their success at it mattered to Sam so much that he worked far harder and longer to help it happen than he had ever contributed to his job in the Trade Center.

Engaged. For the first time in an unhealthy span of time, Sam found himself engaged in his life at the Inn. He was invested in what happened and in the lives of the people around him, including Alaine. Especially Alaine. He cared what happened to them, and further, he wanted the best for them, wanted to stay a part of them for the foreseeable future. This awareness, coming at 4 a.m. on a sleepless night, amazed Sam.

He'd talk to Alaine. He'd disclose his concerns and cautions about Paul Mowher. He'd get Ms. Charity and Rev. Ray involved if he had to. And Andi and Danisha, too, if it would help. Sam wanted to do his part, his fair share to keep things at the Inn running smoothly and prevent Alaine from making the second biggest mistake of her life. The first had been to waste her time on Mowher in the first place.

This long self-examination took some time. When Sam glanced at the red numbers of the digital clock beside his bed, it was 4:45 a.m. Sleep finally came, but it was short lived. His alarm went off at 6. Sam's first thought was that today was the last day of Mowher's reservations at the Inn. Then they were booked solid until after Christmas Day.

# # #

Andi and Ms. Charity had the coffee hot and the homemade cinnamon rolls ready. Sam took their offerings with gratitude.

"Ladies, you've saved my life, no doubt. At the rate I'm going, I surely won't make it through Christmas."

Sam sat at the counter and ate with his eyes closed, both in appreciation of the taste of the pastry and because his head pounded and his eyes ached. The hour and a quarter's worth of sleep were almost worse than none.

He usually loved this earliest time of the morning, the smells and the sounds of quiet breakfast preparation and service. Today the ladies seemed to sense his weakened state and left him alone to let the caffeine and sugar do their jobs.

When Sam could finally lift his head and open his eyes, enticed by the soft sounds of holiday melodies over the Café's sound system, he met Andi's eyes as she refreshed his cup.

"Have you seen Alaine yet today?"

The response was a questioning look from Andi.

"What?" Why that look?"

"Sam, haven't you even noticed that Alaine is never up at this time? She's barely four months pregnant. She still feels awful in the mornings. It takes her a while to get going."

"Oh, well, no. I hadn't noticed. She hasn't said anything."

"Not to you." A pause followed, long enough to let the implications of her point sink in. "She'll be fine soon enough."

"Andi, has she said anything to you about--?"

Another pause, this time broken by Andi.

"I don't know what she's going to do, Sam, if that's what you mean. None of us does. Rev. Ray and Ms. Charity are going to talk with her today. That's all I know. Now, if you'll excuse me, I have guests waiting." Andi and her life-giving coffee pot moved away.

Finally understanding that Alaine had problems with mornings, Sam didn't seek her out for a couple of hours while he worked on the Inn's end of year reports. The bookwork was not unpleasant, as the Inn and its Café had broken records in both reservations and meals served. A surge of growth had come under Sam's watch care, and it made him proud.

His lack of sleep reminded him about 10 a.m. that he hadn't had his second cup of morning coffee. He closed the files and rolled his chair back from the computer, ready to visit the Café again.

Alaine. The thought reminded him of his determination to face her straight on about his doubts associated with Paul Mowher. Check-out was in one hour. He would be more than glad to see Mowher on his way.

Sam's need to speak with Alaine immediately took precedence over his desire for coffee, and he went in search, hoping to find her but avoid the man. He did neither.

The staff was usually welcome in the Brights' living quarters at any time except when they found a small red card displayed in a wire basket on the door of their suite. Usually the card was green, which meant *Just knock and we'll let you in. You are most welcome.* A red card meant *Not now please, but do come back later.* The staff of the Inn collectively understood and honored the cards' messages unless there was an emergency.

Alaine was closeted away in Ray and Charity's private quarters, he learned from Andi, who was delivering room service as he passed her in the hallway. He found the red card in evidence when he got there.

Didn't he have a right to be included in private counseling the couple was giving Alaine about her involvement with Paul Mowher? Hadn't he been instrumental in helping her escape not only the North Tower but also her dangerous relationship with the repulsive individual?

After examining his unrealistic thoughts, Sam could see that his part in Alaine's rescue didn't give him universal rights to her private business. That would clearly be out of order. He couldn't justify an excuse to interrupt.

Sam had no way of knowing how long the session between Alaine and the Brights would last. There was nothing to do but go back to his office and wait it out.

He poured himself more coffee in the Café and made his way back to the Inn's reception area, wondering as he went where Mowher was now and when he would leave. His answer was waiting for him at the check-out desk.

Mowher was there and clearly impatient to go. The man appeared ill at ease, jumpy and more than eager to be on his way.

For perverse reasons, Sam slowed the check-out process down as much as possible in spite of the fact that he wanted Mowher off of Inn property in the worst way. It gave him some pleasure to watch Mowher fidget, drum his fingers, check his watch and finally exclaim, "Man, I've got a plane to catch!"

Sam handed the man his receipt for his stay, and just when he expected Mowher to tear it from his hand and bolt from the Inn, the man surprised him.

Mowher smiled his ingratiating and irritating smile and stuck out his hand.

Refusing to let Mowher know how ready he was to see him gone, Sam responded in kind.

"It's been good to meet you, my friend. Thanks again for your kind attention to Alaine. Look, um, I need to ask a favor."

Sam ensured his face was devoid of all expression when he met Mowher's nervous eyes and responded, "What can I do for you?"

"I have, um, a flight time. Earlier than I thought. Was supposed to see Alaine before I left. Understand she's tied up. Explain to her for me, will you? Tell her I'll be in touch. That's my good man." Mowher was out the door and stepping into the waiting taxi almost before he finished his last sentence.

That's my good man? No one said that any more. Sam, who had trailed Mowher to the door while the man verbally threw instructions as he left, watched the taxi depart the Inn's driveway at far greater than safe speed.

Abnormal. The man's behavior struck him as abnormal and somehow deceptive, as if his hasty departure was actually to avoid Alaine rather than to catch an earlier flight. Sam was conflicted as to whether he should be relieved or more concerned.

Something was not right. Sam's instincts confirmed what Mowher's erratic, nervous behavior implied, and he decided to err on the side of concern rather than bask in relief that Mowher was, at last, gone.

He needed to find Alaine, deliver Mowher's message and warn her of his concern before any more time passed.

The door to the Brights' apartment was just opening at Sam's approach, saving him the risk of embarrassment by barging in despite the red card. He could see Charity embracing a visibly upset Alaine while Ray stood by with deep concern evident on his face.

Sam stopped his forward motion, conscious of three pairs of inquiring eyes turned toward him. Alaine's were swollen and reddened. He wasn't sure how to start, but knew he had to try again to explain his misgivings about Mowher.

Sam was sure the man and his influence had also been the topic of the couple's conversation with Alaine.

Maybe this was the cause of Mowher's rapid departure. Could it be the man knew she was closeted with her mentors and feared the outcome of the session would not work in his favor? Possibly the man was not as confident of his power as he'd seemed.

Face this head on. Otherwise the outcome could be serious. This advice to himself steadied Sam long enough to slow his breathing.

"Paul Mowher's gone. He just left the Inn. His message was that he had an earlier than expected plane to catch. He'll be in touch. I was to tell you that."

"That's all he said?" Her voice was barely heard.

Her question gave Sam a window into the strength of Mowher's influence on her, even now.

"Just that he was supposed to see you before he left, and that's why he wanted me to explain his reason for leaving early. And that you'd hear from him."

Alaine closed her eyes and shook her head.

"I have to tell you that his actions seemed erratic and maybe a bit paranoid. I'm sorry, but I think something's wrong. I didn't believe his excuse. I don't think he's on the level. Something's not right. It was like he was desperate to get out of here."

"He was." Alaine dropped her eyes and waited before she could speak again. "I've seen...this before. His mood can go dark with little warning. When it happens in public, he tries to get away so he doesn't lose face. In private..." She couldn't finish.

"I don't think you should have any more to do with him."

"But, Sam, for the last couple of days, he was a different man. He was not the Paul from back in the City. I could almost believe--"

"Look, for all practical purposes, this is none of my business. But I have to be honest about what I feel...what I know. No matter what he seems to be, Mowher's nothing but big trouble for you. I sense it, and I'm glad he's gone."

His speech delivered, Sam could tell by their faces that Ray and Charity agreed with him, but chose not to add to his words. He could also tell that Alaine was still in conflict. So what if Mowher was the father of her baby? Even greater reason for her to run the other way.

Sam knew more was expected of him. Alaine's face showed it. He couldn't understand her confusion in light of her past experiences with the man. But even though he couldn't share her uncertainty, neither could he take her obvious dilemma lightly.

"Look, I'm sorry if I upset you. Maybe I'm reading too much into his actions. Maybe there's something I'm missing here, but your safety matters to me...and your baby's. Regardless of what change you think you see in him now, you know what that man is capable of. Please, let this go. Are you finished with your meeting? Would you like for me to walk you to your room for a rest? I can handle the desk for now."

Ms. Charity hugged Alaine once more and then put her arms around Sam in a brief embrace. Sam drew Alaine's arm through his own, holding her hand close to his side as they walked the hall and a flight of stairs up to her room. She said nothing until they reached her door. Sam took her key, unlocked it for her, and held it open.

As she moved past him, Alaine stopped long enough to whisper her thanks followed by a quiet sentence spoken so low Sam strained to hear. She didn't meet his eyes as she told him, "You're wrong, Sam. I don't think what happens to me is none of your business. I hope you believe that."

She shut the door behind her, leaving him standing in the quiet hallway.

Sam would leave her alone for now. He'd had his say. He knew that the Brights supported his position. Maybe Alaine would rest, think about their words and forget about Mowher in anticipation of coming Christmas festivities.

He turned away from Alaine's door and turned his mind to his next tasks at hand.

# # #

Sam wanted to feel relief and satisfaction that Paul Mowher was no longer in residence. What he actually felt was uneasy and troubled. He sensed the matter wasn't closed, and that was cause for continued concern--not a good mix with the Christmas holidays.

Sam discovered that his best antidote for inner disquiet was fervent activity. The Inn at Christmas might just provide the therapy he needed. Christmas was now two days away. For the Inn's staff, that meant no rest for the foreseeable future.

The annual Christmas Eve vesper service and buffet to be held at the Inn the next evening was on Sam's mind. Rev. Ray, who would host the vesper service from the front steps of the old building, filled Sam in on what to expect some weeks back. It would be, the older man said, both a happy and a taxing event, but one that was expected and anticipated by the folks of the small town.

Christmas vespers had been held at the Inn since Civil War days, and it was now a time when the churchgoers of the area came together from their different houses of worship and joined as one family to hear a brief message drawn from the Christmas story and view the nativity set up among the trees beside the Inn.

The front walk and lawn would fill with rented chairs plus every description of portable seating brought from the homes of Copper's Run citizens. Last minute lighting had to be strung around the seating area, and lanterns with real candles hung strategically to make the outside of the Inn welcoming to its visitors.

After vespers, all comers would be invited inside to enjoy a supper of Brunswick stew and cornbread cooked by Ms. Charity and the ladies of the Inn's Café. Sam was surprised to learn that the event was free to anyone who came. He, who spent so much of his time working to ensure the Inn operated in the black, at first mourned the opportunity to charge for the privilege of eating Christmas Eve dinner in such an historic place. It comforted him to learn that dessert offerings would be sent to the Inn throughout the day of the meal by community members to be ready when the buffet opened. No one would go home hungry, and the Inn's budget would not suffer.

This year would be the largest gathering to date, and the coordination fell to Sam and Ms. Charity. The logistics of an undertaking of this magnitude had Sam concerned.

"There could easily be 200 to 300 people here. Ms. Charity, what do you do about dinner seating?"

She laughed at his discomfort. "Sampson, my dear, we have plenty of seating in the Café and dining room for the elderly, the parents with small children and any who need special consideration. All the others fend for themselves. They sit on couches or chairs inside or bring more chairs in from outside. We find people sitting on stairs, leaning on mantels or going wherever they can find a comfortable spot. It's simple, the food is good, and it works. You'll see. Now quit fretting."

Working with Ms. Charity's experience as a base gave Sam a new appreciation for handling details without drama. Her gracious serenity in the face of any pressure made working with her a pleasure.

Between tasks, they sought the refuge of the Café's kitchen to refuel. This was the chance Sam had been seeking to talk to her about Alaine. How to begin was a problem.

"I may be out of order. If so, just say it. I understand I'm not in a position to--"

Charity put her hand on his arm and interrupted.

"If you need to talk about Alaine, it's OK, Sam. You have reason to be concerned. She had a hard time with the appearance of Paul Mowher, especially right now."

"What do you mean, a hard time? Was she afraid? Did he threaten her?"

Ms. Charity's lack of response told him he was on the wrong track. "She wasn't seriously considering going with him...going back to him? Not after--?"

"She was. She is, Sam. Considering it, I mean."

"But she can't. That relationship was destroying her."

"She's a grown woman. We mustn't try to think for her or dictate her decisions."

"But surely you and Rev. Ray can influence her. She trusts you both. She loves you and loves it here."

"You can be sure we've counseled with her, even warned her. She knows clearly how we feel and understands why. But her past is a strong pull, just as it is with all of us. Most everybody has a profound need to feel loved. Those of us who had fragile to no love growing up seem to be even more desperate to get it. That's one of the hard things about people like Paul Mowher. He and men like him give out just enough hope to keep women like Alaine, women like I was before I met Ray Bright, hanging around thinking this time will be different."

"This time won't be different." The flat of Sam's hand as he hit the worktable where they sat to drink their coffee caused his cup to overturn, and he stopped to mop up before continuing.

"I'd never met Mowher before this week, so I only knew the little she told me about him, which wasn't good. I've not been a very smart judge of character in my life, Ms. Charity, but even I could see through the act he put on here at the Inn. In my opinion, what you saw this week is not what you'll get from him in any other situation. Why can't Alaine see that?"

"Hope springs eternal, Sam. He is the father of her baby. I suspect that counts for a lot of it. There's always a slim chance we've misjudged him...that his change is real. Anyway, I can promise you that Ray and I are in constant prayer that Alaine will make the right decision. I know you don't necessarily share her faith, but she's better equipped to make the right choice than when she came here three months ago. She's a new creation in Christ. It just may take her a while to get used to that notion and understand what it means. She can make a clean break from Paul Mowher, if that's the right move."

"If her religion keeps her from that man, I'm all for it, whatever it is." Charity didn't respond, but Sam could tell by the way she bit her lip after this pronouncement that he'd said something ill advised. He didn't care. He felt what he felt. Sam changed the subject.

"Come on, let's get back at it. Santa Claus waits for no man."

"Nor woman," Ms. Charity said as she rose to rinse out their coffee cups.

13 BEAUTIFUL STAR

Sampson

Sam only saw Alaine in passing over the next few hours as the staff pulled together to ready the Inn for the Christmas Eve vespers, the supper and then Christmas day. Christmas morning offered an early prayer service in the small chapel for whatever staff and Inn family chose to attend. Later there would be a brunch of elegant simplicity in the Café for Inn family and overnight guests only.

At the moment, the focus was on preparing the lawn before the front entranceway to the Inn for the vespers service. The lights still needed to be strung and the rented chairs set up to supplement those attendees would bring.

Rev. Ray would speak from a simple podium on the covered porch at the top of the wide wooden stairs leading to the front doors. There were candles in strategic rooms on the Inn's first floor. On the balcony above the front doors a single, lighted star already hung, and lanterns cascaded down the steps.

The light from the star and the lanterns would create what Danisha predicted was a heavenly setting fit for a heavenly message. Sam didn't know about that, but he did want to be sure tradition at the Inn didn't suffer on his watch.

There was little sleep for Sam and two or three of his most faithful crew on the night before Christmas Eve, but when dawn broke, the Inn itself was ready. A quick check with Ms. Charity told him the food and serving preparations were also in good order for the next couple of days. It might be too early to let out his breath, but Sam felt himself begin to relax. They'd worked hard; it was about to pay off.

Christmas Eve day was quiet, all things considered. Guests had few needs and seemed intent on resting to build their strength, leaving staff breathing room to prepare for the evening's events.

Vespers began at 5:30 p.m., and those attending began to arrive quietly and unobtrusively a little before 5:00 to, as Sam overheard often, "get a good spot." The mood was subdued but anticipatory, as if the whole of Copper's Run held its breath.

His immediate responsibilities taken care of, Sam stood at a tall window in the Inn's reception room looking out at the growing crowd. He was impressed with how orderly the gathering was. And how quiet. He was most certainly not in New York City.

As Sam waited and watched, careful to stand back from the window so as not to spoil the view from outside, he felt a soft brush at his side. It was Alaine, her face pale and lovely against her black dress. She wore a long silver wrap indicating she was ready to join the visitors on the front lawn.

"Sam." Her greeting was soft but friendly.

"Alaine, you look beautiful this evening. You're going outside? Will you be warm enough?" In fact, the evening air lacked the biting cold of the North during the Christmas season.

"I'll be fine. Are you coming?"

Sam didn't really care to sit through a sermon, even from Rev. Ray. Because he knew this night would mean something to her and her new found religion, he relented in his response. "I am. Not just yet, but I'll be out there before Rev. Ray speaks. There's special music first from guest musicians, and I want to be sure they go on OK."

"There are a couple of places set aside on the end of the first row. Shall I save you a seat?"

The offer seemed genuine, even eager. Was she being polite, did she seek his company or did she want to make sure he heard the words of Ray's message? As willing as Sam was to make a positive response to her offer, he was not about to be shanghaied into sitting still for even a short sermon this night.

"Thanks, Alaine. You go ahead. I need to be able to move around out there in case I'm wanted somewhere."

Sam was surprised at the look of disappointment that flickered across her face following his rejection, however kind he tried to be. He almost...almost but not quite...gave in and agreed to join her. He couldn't bring himself to task and, to cover his hesitation, he reached to open one side of the Inn's double front doors for her.

Alaine smiled at him and walked out into the evening. Had he seen disappointment after all from the self-possessed young woman who moved carefully down the steps of the Inn? Too late not to make a scene, he realized he should have at least accompanied her to her seat. Her pregnancy still wasn't obvious to anyone who didn't know her, and her wrap covered the small midsection just beginning to show, but still he felt ungentlemanly not helping her navigate the stairs.

By 5:30 the crowd on the lawn was hushed and waiting. The lights in the bushes blinked a few times to indicate vespers was about to begin. The front doors of the Inn opened and members of a local gospel quartet came out. The lead singer led the citizens in prayer, and the group sang a medley of Christmas songs a capella, beginning with "Beautiful Star of Bethlehem" and ending with "We Three Kings of Orient Are."

Sam watched from the window as the singers proclaimed, "Star of Wonder, Star of Night." Sam felt a heavy hand on his shoulder and turned into the face of Rev. Ray, looking more fit and able than Sam had seen him in some time.

"Can I do anything for you before you go on, Rev. Ray?"

He stared at Sam for a long moment. Sam knew Ray was going to require something of him at this point, something unexpected and hard. He could see it in the man's eyes.

"Son, what I need is for you to listen with an open mind for the next few minutes. You mean a lot to me, Sam. Would you do what I ask?"

He reached out for Sam's hand and Sam took it. The long shake ended in an embrace as they heard the musicians close with, "Guide us to thy perfect light." The group members came inside, and Rev. Ray stepped out under the large star shining over the doors of the Inn.

The night around was dark and quiet. Rev. Ray raised his large right hand above his head and pointed upward, focusing the attention of all participants on the star above his head. He continued to point with his right hand, the other hand raised skyward, and bowed his head in silent prayer. The people waited, joining him in prayer.

When Rev. Ray opened his eyes, his right hand still raised high, he began.

"The star that led those Eastern wise men more than 2000 years ago to travel so far to spend a few minutes with one little Hebrew boy who came from Heaven's glory and would one day again be recognized as the King of Kings can teach us a lot, if we'll just look and listen. We don't know much about what kind of star it was. Was it a special star put into action for this one occasion only? Or had it been around for eons and was recruited for extra duty at this one time? We don't know the makeup of this star or what its orbit was, if it had one, or even how long it did its duty. But that doesn't change the importance of this star or make its work less significant."

"Tell us about the star, Reverend." "Speak to us," came voices calling from the audience, and Ray continued.

"Now, you might say, 'Rev. Ray, don't you know a star is an inanimate object and cannot speak? How is a star going to tell me anything?' Let me remind you that our Heavenly Father uses some unexpected things to do his bidding. Think about Balaam's donkey and Jonah's great fish. Don't forget Elijah's ravens or the sun standing still for Joshua. Those are only some of God's holy tools. We can learn from anything if we're willing to set aside our arrogance and pride and have teachable hearts.

"'Well,' you say, 'Reverend, getting beyond what we know about the physical characteristics of stars as large hunks of metal and chemical elements, what can we learn from them that we, in all of our human wisdom, don't already know?'"

As soon as Rev. Ray walked out on the porch of the Inn and began to speak, Sam slipped out a side door and moved quickly to the edge of the yard where he could be hidden by trees but see and hear everything that was going on.

He had not actually promised to listen to Rev. Ray's sermon, but he knew Ray expected him to, and he planned to give Ray that. Sam had no intention, however, of being seated where the preacher could see him to gauge his reaction.

Sam knew Ray and Charity were aware that he didn't share their religious convictions, nor those newly found ones of Alaine. He also knew from their open communication that they prayed for him often. Sam was touched by their concern, but unmoved by their position. He had no real need of a personal faith, as they expressed it. He was fine, better in fact than he had been for a long time. He had a job he liked, friends for whom he had great affection, and a sense that he was contributing something positive for a change. Religion wasn't a factor he felt inclined to consider.

Sam leaned against a tree where he wouldn't distract other listeners. He made sure he stayed in shadows, behind any lights that might profile his presence.

He could see Alaine on the front row. She was near the end and sure enough, there was an empty seat beside her as she had told him. Her full attention was riveted on Rev. Ray, and she seemed at ease in spite of sitting alone.

Sam listened, despite himself, as Rev. Ray spoke on.

"Imagine with me, friends, what it would be like if that Star of Bethlehem we sing about had human emotions and reactions. You know, the Star that led the Wise men had a designated job to do...one job, one chance...and it did that job well. Just suppose that star had told the Lord, 'I'm tired. I'm about to go on my coffee break. I just put in for vacation. Can't you get some other star to take my place? The time is just inconvenient for me right now.'

"No, that star took God's command seriously and did what it was told to do. It was that simple. Do we do what we are told to do when God sends us a call or do we beg to be excused?"

Again calls came from the audience, "We run the other way, Reverend." "We fall down on the job."

"What if that star had told the Lord, 'If you'll just wait a while, say 1500 years, I can become electric' (and Ray pointed upward again to the star shining over his head)? 'In a few hundred years, the timing will be better for me. If I'm electric, I can shine brighter, stronger. I can blink or strobe or even change colors. Why not just wait until somebody develops the technology to make me more efficient and impressive?'

"No sir, that star just shone as long and as brightly as it could with what power it had in obedience to the command of its Maker, knowing that its light would be as bright as the Lord wanted it to be. Do we want to wait for our obedience until we're smarter or have more awards or a string of degrees behind our name?

"You know, that star could have said, 'Lord, it's a long time you want me to set aside for this job. I'd have to make an appearance so the Wise Men could see me in the East and then reappear two years later to lead them from Jerusalem to Bethlehem. I really don't know if I can give you that much of a commitment. I'm pretty busy. I'll have to check and see if my schedule allows me to be tied up that long. I might miss some really important opportunity that comes my way.' How do we stack up against that star when we're asked to do a task?"

"Talk to us, Brother Ray." "You know we don't always want to be faithful. We surely don't."

"And finally, that little star might have said, 'I'm just not cut out for that kind of duty. It doesn't fit into my long-range life plan. What I had in mind was something a little more prestigious, maybe a key star in a constellation. But if you have a president or ruler of a great country to be announced, I might be available.'

"Just about now you may be saying, 'Rev. Ray is being absurd. What does this have to do with Christmas and with me? Stars can't think. They have no will. They just shine.' Well, fortunately, that is just what they do, because if stars were people like you and me, they would have all of the excuses we have for not being obedient to our Lord and Savior, Jesus Christ.

"This same Jesus, that little boy the Wise men traveled to visit, did His Heavenly Father's bidding by giving up His life that we may have eternal life. It was hard, yes. Remember that He prayed for another way to be found, but no other way was available. He was the perfect sacrifice. It most likely wasn't convenient to our Lord. Dying on a Roman cross with common criminals on either side would never be convenient, especially when He was innocent. Timely? Our Lord was a young man who had only been in ministry for about three years. He could have argued, 'Father, wait; give me more time. There's so much more I can do for you alive on this earth.'

"Ridiculous, isn't it? Of course He did His Father's bidding. When called upon to provide the only reconciliation between a righteous God and His sinful creation, He said, 'Even so, Thy will be done.' We are the most blessed of all creation because dying on that cross was a major part of our dear Lord's long-range plan. Isn't it, then, our reasonable service back to Him to be obedient when He asks something...anything of us? Isn't it just our reasonable service?"

Again the audience spoke, "Yes, Lord, it is." "Lord, our reasonable service."

"I'm glad our God didn't send one of His weaker creatures to lead the Wise Men to Him so many years ago. We might not have been up to the job. Because He chose a star, I can look to the shape of that star as a symbol to live as an obedient servant to my Lord and Savior, ready to do His bidding, ready to give up my own agenda to do what He asks."

Sam had to admit that even though Ray's words were simple, the star illustration was persuasive. Ray's presentation of the story was dramatic without calling attention to himself. As Ray spoke, it was obvious from the reactions of the listeners, young and old, that they were with him and moved by his message.

As Ray approached the part of the sermon that referred to Christ dying on the cross, out of a conscious effort to engage his attention on something other than Ray's uncomfortable words, Sam let his eyes rove over the faces making up the audience. He was struck by the diversity of the group. Persons from a range of ages and a mix of ethnicities were present and sitting, not as segregated groupings, but together as if their presence spoke of a oneness and commonality seldom observed.

To further block out Ray Bright's message but still be counted present, Sam let his gaze linger on face after face, gauging the level of interest each showed for the Reverend's story. In the nearly three months he'd been in Copper's Run, Sam had met a number of the townsfolk, and he recognized many of the attendees at the vespers. He noted David and Jane Dabney sitting with Charity Bright near the front of the audience.

Sam realized that Ray Bright's voice had become low and still, causing him to listen in spite of himself, as Ray repeated, "In light of what my Lord and Savior, Jesus Christ, did for me, isn't that just my reasonable service?

"Now if you'll all bow your heads and pray with me..."

Sam's visceral reaction, at this point, surprised him.

I can't listen to any more of this. He moved into the darkness and away from the influence of the preacher's voice. Just as he started to slip further into the trees, he caught a glimpse of a face among the visitors that halted his movement and shot adrenalin through his veins.

Paul Mowher was sitting on an end seat of the back row of folding chairs, directly in line with Alaine on the front row. He was dressed in a dark overcoat, was hatless in the crisp air, and was unmistakable even in the dim light.

Sam touched the tree beside him, as if feeling its hard surface would give assurance he was awake, aware and in reality having to deal with Paul Mowher again.

Vespers ended with the singers reappearing to lead the gatherers in a quiet children's chorus:

Away in a manger, no crib for His bed,

The little Lord Jesus lay down his sweet head.

The stars in the sky looked down where He lay

The little Lord Jesus, asleep on the hay.

Following moments of quiet, the worshippers broke into small groups for subdued conversation and greetings. Sam moved into the crowd toward the spot where Paul Mowher sat. When he reached it, the seat was empty. Mowher was not in sight.

The visitors made their way toward the front porch of the Inn where they would enter for the evening meal. By the time the first visitor reached the entrance, Sam was back inside and stationed by the double front doors to greet the vespers goers and watch for the reappearance of Mowher.

He must have welcomed two hundred people before he decided that Mowher wasn't going to show. Sam had one more undercover task and that was to find out from Andi and Danisha if Alaine had expected the man's attendance for the evening.

But no, Sam knew that was the wrong approach. He would have to be straightforward...talk directly to her if he wanted to know something, and he couldn't show evidence he suspected she was hiding anything from him either. Besides, if Alaine wanted to be with Mowher, what could he do to prevent it, even if it bothered him? And it did.

# # #

The Christmas Eve supper at the Inn for the townspeople was voted the most successful in recent memory by the weary but elated members of the Inn family. They shared stories as they finished the last bit of clean up from the night and preparation for the simple brunch that would be served to guests in residence late on Christmas morning.

Danisha gathered her coat and purse to end the evening in time to prepare Christmas surprises for her daughter. Andi sat on the floor, her head in Ms. Charity's lap and her eyes already closed. Alaine joined Johnson Story and Rev. Ray on the couch in the Brights' living quarters. Only Sam stood, sipping on a last tepid glass of tea. He was tired and at a loss for where to go from here.

His suspicion that Alaine was meeting Mowher on the sly changed to a certainty that she had no idea Mowher was nearby, as the man failed to make further appearance. That made the direct approach more critical than ever.

"Alaine, do you think I could have a word with you for a minute? In private?"

"Now, Sam? I'm dead on my feet. Can it wait?"

She must have sensed it couldn't. Alaine pulled herself to her feet and met him in the hall, the question in her eyes.

"Paul Mowher was here tonight. Did you see him?"

"What? Are you sure? Here where?"

Sam watched her face and listened for any clues in her tone that she'd expected to see Mowher. Or was disappointed that she hadn't.

"At vespers. He was sitting on the last row. I'm sure. Before I could get to him, he was gone. He never came to supper. I'm sure of that, too."

"Why would he come back, Sam? Why would he show up but leave without speaking to anyone?"

Sam took a chance. He could alienate her so easily.

"I thought you might know."

"I spoke to him by phone two nights ago. He was in the City. He called me but said nothing about coming tonight."

"Why did you talk to him? Whatever could you have to say to him?"

Alaine turned her back on Sam and gazed out a window in the hall despite that fact that the night was so black there was nothing to see.

"He asked me to think about coming back to New York to be with him. He said he needed me...that we belonged together."

She turned to face him.

"I told him about the baby, Sam. I told him the baby was his. I didn't want to, but I thought he had a right to know."

"A right? How could he possibly have a--?" Sam stopped himself in mid-sentence. "OK, forgive me. What did he say? How did he react?"

She didn't respond to his outburst but kept her answer matter of fact.

"He was surprised, I think. He wasn't expecting it. That was obvious. He said he was pleased. It seemed genuine, but with Paul, it was always hard to know what he was thinking. He told me once when we were together there was no room in his life for children."

"Alaine, I'm sorry, but after the way he treated you, how can you think for a minute he was on the level?" Sam knew he was both being redundant and interfering big time, but he couldn't understand why Alaine continued to waiver about Mowher. She'd told him once she had hated the man.

"Sam, you think I'm foolish. I get that. I know I told you how Paul used to treat me. Not in a million years would I have predicted this, but I tried to tell you how he seems genuinely different now. He told me he's not the same man

I left behind in the City. I think something's changed him."

"And you're sure he still wants you to go to him? Even with the baby?"

"Yes, that's one thing that makes this so hard to understand. He said the baby makes it complete...that he'll take care of both of us. He said we can be a family. Sam, he practically begged me to come. This makes it so hard to know what to do. This is a man I once cared about. And, after all, it is his child. He told me he wanted to 'do right' by me and my baby."

Sam couldn't help what he said next. It came out as easily as his breath. "Your baby? He called it *your* baby? Has he ever called it his baby?"

The silence that followed was lengthy and alive with emotion.

"He said he wanted the baby, but he never called it his. He's never admitted it's his baby. I don't think he believes it is."

From the flickers of concern in her eyes, Sam knew Alaine was uneasy about Mowher's omission and probably the news of his silent visit earlier in the evening. He saw her body begin to tremble.

Carefully, slowly...as if approaching a frightened child, Sam reached out and brought her into his arms. He wanted to provide comfort, offer safety. He hoped the strength he tried to convey with his touch would calm his own growing alarm over why Mowher would make the four hundred mile trip to see a woman but then not wait around to talk with her. Something didn't make sense.

For the brief moment he held her, Sam sensed the struggle Alaine was having to maintain control in spite of physical fatigue and emotional distress. Her trembling ceased within seconds, however, and Sam felt her move away from him.

"Thank you, Sam, for your support. It means a lot." She stood apart, but her eyes signaled sincerity. She reached her fingers and brushed them against his cheek.

In the face of such openness, Sam found an equally direct response difficult.

"Don't mention it." She met his eyes again before she turned to re-enter Ray and Charity's sitting area.

14 ENCOUNTER

Sampson

Sam didn't sleep at all the night before Christmas. He'd counted on being tired enough to rest, had hoped he would be too exhausted to think about Alaine and Paul Mowher until he had his wits about him. It didn't work. He was apparently not tired enough to turn off the *what if* scenarios that played in his closed eyes for hours.

He started the night in his bed and ended it on the couch in the Inn's reception room. Nothing worked. He was weary, but he still had to deal with the duel realities that it was Christmas Day and Mowher could still be in the area.

Christmas was normally one of the quietest days of the year at the Inn. Anyone in residence was offered brunch at midday and soup and sandwiches late in the evening. Otherwise, there were no organized festivities.

Behind the scenes, on-duty staff gathered in the late afternoon in the quarters of Rev. Ray and Ms. Charity for Christmas fellowship. There was eggnog, sweet wine and small gifts. The afternoon was lazy and pleasant. The fire in the aged fireplace in the Brights' sitting room drew the small group together as Ray traced the thread of the Christmas story from Genesis through Revelation.

Andi and Alaine sat together on the sofa beside Rev. Ray. Ms. Charity sat on a small stool at Ray's side while Johnson Story listened with closed eyes and nodded agreement, brushing silent tears from his wrinkled face. Sam stood looking out of the second floor window onto the front lawn of the Inn.

He'd never heard the Christmas story told from the Old Testament. It didn't make much sense, the part about the seed of the woman and the serpent's head. But then religion in general had never made much sense. Too much faith and not enough reality.

He watched the lawn as Ray Bright's voice told the story. No sign of Paul Mowher so far, and the day was over half gone. He turned from the window to look at Alaine as she listened to the Reverend's words. He wished believing in anything at all was as easy for him as it seemed to be for her.

Alaine caught Sam watching her. They hadn't had time for even a brief conversation since Christmas Eve. He wanted to talk to her more about Mowher, to find out how much he'd been communicating with her, to warn her again that the man might still be in Copper's Run.

She gave him a trace of a smile before looking again toward Rev. Ray.

Sam turned back to the window in time to see a figure walking in the dusk of the late December afternoon across the Inn's yard toward the front entrance. He was sure who it was.

By the time Mowher reached the front doors, Sam was in place, out of breath but standing at the check-in counter as if he'd been there all afternoon.

"Good evening, Mr. MacDonald. Merry Christmas."

"Mr. Mowher, what can I do for you?"

"I'd like to speak with Alaine, please. If you would be so kind as to tell me where I might find her. I have a gift for her."

Sam didn't figure that his response would work for long, but it was a first line of defense. "I believe she's in a meeting with the Brights at the moment. They're the owners of the Inn, and she's with them. I think she'll be tied up for some time. If you'd like to leave your package here, I'll make sure she gets it as soon as possible." Sam made a move forward as if to receive whatever

Mowher wanted to leave, even though no package was in sight.

Mowher backed toward the door, gripping his travel bag in one hand and reaching out his other hand, palm out, as if to keep Sam at bay.

"Don't crowd me, MacDonald. Just stay back. Stay right there, please."

Sam watched him closely, seeing the man struggle for control. Paul Mowher's extended hand shook slightly, and he pulled it back, slipping it into his overcoat pocket.

"Look, sorry, I'm a bit tired. Help me out here, man. I need to talk with Alaine just for a minute. I have something important to discuss with her. Do me a favor, please, and get her for me."

Sam was about to decline and suggest that Mowher leave quietly when he heard Alaine's voice behind him.

"It's OK, Sam. I'm right here."

Sam knew when he saw her face that standing in the way wouldn't work.

"Now, if you'll excuse us please, Paul and I can have a conversation right here. Would you mind getting him a cup of coffee from the Café's kitchen?"

Her request surprised Sam, and he re-checked her expression to see if he'd read her wrong. Her eyes said *please make this easy but don't go far*.

"I'll be happy to. Would you like some, too? No, that's right, cutting back on caffeine. I'll be right back."

Sam made the trip to the coffee station and back in short order. The less time Alaine spent with Mowher alone the better. His service to Mowher didn't include a smile.

Apparently Sam hadn't missed anything yet. The two sat in the Inn's reception room, obviously as ill at ease in each other's company as any couple Sam had ever observed. To Sam, Mowher feigned nonchalance as he accepted the coffee cup and nodded dismissively.

Alaine, from the edge of her chair some distance from Mowher, kept her eyes down. Sam could see the white of her knuckles as she clutched the seat.

"If you will excuse me then..." Sam turned to leave, but not before he caught the flicker of doubt in Alaine's eyes as she glanced up at him just before he left the room. He hoped she could read from his slight head motion toward the hall that he wouldn't be far away.

In his past, Sam never bothered with questions of emotion. He conducted his life and business dealings in whatever way seemed best to him, without undue consideration of the feelings of others. His experiences at the Copper's Run Inn changed all that. He now had a dilemma on his hands.

He walked with great willpower out of the room and down the hall from where Mowher and Alaine sat, all the while in conflict over his next move. Should he keep walking and find something difficult to do that would keep his mind off of the pair in the reception room? Or should he lower himself and ease into the adjoining room, a small storage closet, where he might be able to overhear whatever conversation took place between the two?

Which? Occupy himself or eavesdrop? The choice would be easy in his past life, and the decision would depend on what would profit him most. Why should it bother him now that spying on a private exchange might be questionable?

Still, Sam knew he didn't mistake the anxious look that came from Alaine. That she might need backup justified Sam's stealth as he eased the key into the storage room lock and moved soundlessly inside. The little room had no window, and only the small penlight on his keychain kept Sam from stumbling over boxes of cleaning products left to be unpacked in the center of the small space.

He guessed correctly that the locked door that led from the reception room into Sam's hiding place, most likely original to the old Inn, had healthy cracks under and around it which let in clear sounds from the next room. Detection was not an option; so, Sam positioned himself as close to the vertical crack in the adjoining door as possible and did his best to control his breathing.

# # #

Alaine

As startled as she was to find herself sitting with Paul again with no notice that he was coming, Alaine refused to allow him to see he had gained any advantage by the surprise. She loosened her grip on her seat and forced her shoulders to relax while she waited for him to speak.

"Alaine, please give me a little time. All I need is a few minutes to explain why I came back. I want you to understand what's different this time...what's happened to me." His voice was soft, soothing, as if she were a frightened child.

"Allie, baby, I know you're hurt and distrustful. You blame me for the way things were between us back in the City. I understand you still have a bit of a problem with me even now. But it doesn't have to stay that way. You know it can be better. We can get past all that. I've shown you by my actions how good things can be between us."

She didn't answer, and had a difficult time making eye contact.

"Allie, please look at me."

When she couldn't meet his eyes fast enough, he spoke again, this time louder and with an edge in his voice.

"Allie, look at me."

She flashed back to the control he once exercised over her and felt her blood pressure rise.

"Baby, I don't think you are aware of what was going on that explains the problems we had." The edge was gone now, and he reached out and touched her.

"I know you think I was hard on you. I was, baby, but not for the reason you think. I need to explain what I was trying to do. Honey, this is hard for me to say, but you were weak, and I wanted to make you strong. You needed to be able to stand on your own two feet. If I seemed tough on you, it was because I loved you and wanted to help you grow into the woman I knew you could be."

Alaine could no longer sit in the face of this explanation, and she stood and faced him, taking a deep breath to ensure that her next words were calm and measured.

"How can you expect me to believe that? You were harsh and mean, Paul. You were cruel and hurt me. How can you say you loved me?"

Her voice, quiet at first, became louder and stronger as she spoke.

Even as she dared Mowher with her eyes to respond, she heard a small bump from the direction of what she knew to be an adjacent storage area. *Sam's hearing this.* To divert attention, she made a show of turning her back to Mowher, scraping a chair on the floor as she did so.

"Alaine, listen to you. The way you look and act now and the way you speak proves that what I was trying to do worked. You're beautiful and strong. You never would have questioned me before. And now hear what you just said. You're acting like I knew you could all along."

If what she'd experienced recently wasn't so life-changing and personal, she would find his explanation laughable. She turned to face him.

"Paul, you have no idea what I've been through. If I'm different, it's no wonder. There's no way I can describe the horror of what happened after those planes hit the towers last September. Nobody could be the same after living through something like that."

"But that's just my point, baby. Look at how many people didn't make it that day, but you did. Maybe you should have died with the rest of them, but you didn't. I think it's because I made you strong. That's what kept you alive when you should have died."

"If anything kept me alive, it was the grace of God... and Sampson MacDonald. He dragged and practically carried me out of our building that day just before it came down around us. I was a wreck then and for days afterwards. Sam was the strong one, not me."

"Well, then, we have him to thank, don't we? But you did make it out after all, and now it's time to take all we've learned and start over. You should have come home to me right away that day so I could help you. But I'm willing to overlook that. And now I want you to come home to New York with me and let me take care of you the way you should be taken care of, especially now with a baby involved. I need to fix things for you and the baby for good. You won't ever have to work or worry about anything again. I can do that for you, Allie. All you have to do is come home to the City with me."

"I hate New York, Paul. The thought of going back there terrifies me. Besides, I have a new life. I'm happy here in Copper's Run. These people at the Inn are family to me. This is where I want to stay, at least for now."

Mowher's voice took on a pleading note, but there was an underlying self-assurance not lost on Alaine.

"I know you feel safe here with your new friends. They've been good to you. I'm grateful you found them, but this is not where you belong. Trust me, baby. I know you, and I know what's best for you and your baby. Come with me. Let me take you where you really should be. Come home to New York with me. I promise that everything will be different and your worries will be over."

"You're right, Paul. I have changed in so many ways. But how about you? Based on our past, the thought of leaving with you scares me. Why should I believe anything will be different? How could I know you wouldn't treat me the same old way? I'll never be good enough to suit you. I'll end up feeling stupid and inadequate. You'll make me believe I'm powerless and pathetic. *Pathetic* was the word you used, wasn't it?"

"Alaine, I've never—"

"Don't you remember calling me pathetic? Have you forgotten yelling at me that I couldn't do anything without you? I can't live like that again. That's not who I am. I have skills I'm good at. I can think for myself, and there are things I believe in for myself. I never felt like that with you."

The man stood, flung his arms out wide and then ran his hands through his carefully coiffed hair.

"Ok, please listen, Alaine. I have something to tell you. Believe me. I've not told this to anyone else. I was waiting to tell you first."

At this point, Mowher's voice broke, as if he was overcome by emotion. There was silence while he seemed to struggle to hold back tears.

"I'm a new me, Allie. I've found my connection with God. The day the attacks came and I knew you were in the Trade Center and probably dead, God spoke to me in a voice that I could hear. I was standing in front of the TV, had been standing there for what seemed like hours. I saw your building come down in that awful, smoke filled debris storm when I literally felt God's hand on my shoulder and heard his voice out loud right there in our apartment."

"Really, Paul, there's no need to--" Sam heard her try to interrupt without success.

"He said to me, as clearly as I am talking to you, 'Paul, she's alive. She didn't die in the Towers. I have a job for you to do. Look for her, Paul. Finish this for me. Find her no matter what and bring her home. This is what she deserves. It's what she needs. I have a plan for her. This is the way it should be.'"

Alaine again tried to speak, but he held up a hand as if to hold her off.

"Right then and there, I fell on my knees and began crying out and thanking God for letting me know. It was clear to me. I knew then what I needed to do, and I got up and began trying to find you that first day. And I didn't stop, even when it seemed impossible and I wanted to give in to the fear that you were lost to me forever. I couldn't stop. I kept hearing the very voice of God ringing in my ears, 'Find her, Paul. She's alive and needs you. Bring her back where she belongs.'"

Mowher's voice broke again, and this time Alaine was horrified to hear audible sobs coming from the man. A cold sweat broke out on her. Could this man who had been the source of such pain be on the level? Was there any way that the revelation Paul Mowher had just made was true? Was it possible that God's plan was for them to be together again, this time as a real family?

# # #

Sampson

Paul Mowher's revelation so unnerved Sam that he nearly fell over a chair as he turned to make his way out of the dark storage room where he hid. This religion thing was strange enough from what he'd already observed from the Brights and Alaine. But the actual touch and audible voice of God?

Either Mowher was a con artist of the first order or he was crazy or he was telling the truth about his encounter with God. Whichever way, Sam had heard enough.

He welcomed the light as he exited the dark room and made his way down the hall to an outside door. Whatever went on with Alaine and Mowher now would just have to go on, despite his determination to stay close to protect her. Sam had to get out of the Inn and away from the couple where he could think.

He walked for miles as fast as he could, with little thought for the cool air or the direction he took. He must have wandered up and down almost every street in Copper's Run before he found himself on Main Street again and stopped for coffee at a small diner, surprisingly open on Christmas night.

As Sam sat in a booth holding his hot cup, he could see out of the window onto the town's deserted street. Not usually given to emotions of any kind, he was now as stirred up and bitter as the coffee in his cup. All of his walking and thinking led only to more confusion and turmoil.

He closed his eyes and leaned his head against the high back of the booth. What he hoped would be a moment of respite turned into a nightmare flashback of his worst memories as his mind replayed, in slow motion, his movements right after the plane hit his building on September 11th.

He smelled the acrid smoke, and his throat closed again in sympathy at the choking stench of the death of a building and its occupants. Instantaneous sweat bathed his face and body when he sensed again the paralyzing fear that had threatened to doom him.

Never had he felt so dark and lost, misplaced beyond all chance of finding. What he hoped would be a chance to start life over after his escape from the inferno of the North Tower was, in reality, in danger of being as painful and dissatisfying as his previous life.

Sam sat motionless, without a sense of real time. Hot tears of utter despair wet his cheeks.

"Say, buddy, you OK?"

The diner was empty except for the man wearing an apron who was sweeping up.

"Excuse me?" Sam struggled to avert attention from his vulnerable state. "What did you say?"

The man with the broom turned away and continued his sweeping. "Just letting you know I'll be closing soon."

"Yeah, OK. Thanks." What could he say to appear normal? How could he shake from the stupor of his memories and drive himself to keep going in a life that now suddenly reflected total confusion?

He took a final gulp of his cold coffee and looked again out of the window. The first thing that caught his eye was a black shadow with an odd shape in the middle of the street. He realized he was staring at the darkened outline of the large copper contraption that sat in the median between the north and southbound lanes of Main Street.

He couldn't have cared less about the big metal container, but in a distracted attempt to assure the sweeper he was in control of himself, Sam blurted, "What's so special about that big pot out there that the town would leave it in the middle of the street as some kind of monument?"

At first he thought the sweeper hadn't heard him. He was ready to repeat his question when the man stopped and turned his way again.

"I know you. You help Reverend Bright over at the Inn. Ain't that right? If you want to know anything about that there big copper pot, why don't you ask him? The Reverend can tell you all about it. Yessir, he surely can." The man went back to his cleaning.

Sam wanted to ask more, but he noticed the clock on the wall above the cash register. It was much later than he thought. He seldom left the Inn for long unless he let someone know his whereabouts in case he was needed.

Sam threw a five-dollar bill on the counter next to the register, nodded to the sweeper who watched him leave and walked out into the night.

It was dark when Sam returned to the Inn. When he entered the driveway, he knew something was wrong. For this time of night, there were too many lights on. Sam condemned himself for staying away so long as he took the front steps two at a time.

Was it Ray Bright? Another heart attack? Maybe one of the guests was sick. *Alaine!* That had to be it. Something was wrong with her...or the baby.

Sam collided with Danisha in the hallway, grabbing her arms to keep her from falling. It was late for her to be at the Inn.

"What's wrong? I know something's wrong. Is it Alaine?"

"The rescue squad's on the way. We're afraid she's going to lose the baby. After that sorry guy from New York City left, she just fell apart. Then she started to have stomach pains, so Ms. Charity called the EMT's. They should be here any minute."

Danisha pulled Sam along the hallway to the stairs.

"She's in her room, and she's asking for you. Where on earth have you been, Sampson MacDonald? We've needed you here something awful!"

Sam didn't try to explain but ran up the three flights to the girls' hallway. He didn't bother to knock and opened the door to Alaine's room.

She was curled into a knot on her bed. Ms. Charity lay beside her, holding

Alaine in her arms, and Andi sat on the other side of the bed. Sam could tell by the looks he got from the two other women that they were scared and he was in for it.

“It’s about time you showed up.” When Charity Bright was angry, she didn’t mince words. “This child needed you.” She got up and stood with hands on her hips.

Sam came around to stand beside Charity. He ignored her anger as he knelt by the bed and reached for Alaine’s hand. He had to know.

“What did you tell him?”

It was hard to hear her, and Sam had to lean in to catch her words.

“That I’m done with him. Won’t see him anymore. Not now or ever.”

“Are you sure about that decision?”

“He tried to make me believe--I was almost--Yes, I’m sure. He didn’t take it well.”

Sam, still holding her hand, rested his forehead on the bed as if in prayer. He wasn’t praying, at least he didn’t think he was. But the relief that washed over him felt like a prayer.

The arrival of the EMT’s pushed Sam out of the way. He left Alaine to them and the women and went to find Rev. Ray.

Ray Bright was in his suite down on his knees in front of the sofa. The man was praying audibly and stopped only to motion Sam to come in and take a seat.

“Father, only you know how to untangle this mess our sister Alaine finds herself in. This baby she carries is in danger, Lord. You love it and you love her. Her life may be in jeopardy. Lord, reach down and touch them both. Protect them from anything that might rob us of them. We don’t feel so good about that Paul Mowher fellow, but surely he needs you, too. We love that girl, Father, and we already love her little baby. We ask you to look into this, and show us your best way out. Thank you, O Lord, for the wisdom you plan to give because we don't have very much on our own. Amen."

Rev. Ray stayed quiet and on his knees for a long time after the close of his prayer. Sam sat, head in his hands, and thought about how true Ray's last words were. He certainly didn't feel he had much in the way of wisdom to offer himself, much less Alaine.

He walked to the window in time to see the red lights of the Rescue Squad blinking as it pulled out of the driveway. Following it closely was the black SUV Sam knew would hold Ms. Charity, Danisha and Andi.

He sat back down near Rev. Ray, who was still on his knees, and waited.

After a three-day rest in the hospital, Alaine came home to the Inn. The early labor turned out to be severe dehydration coupled with exhaustion and a significant dose of stress. While the baby appeared to be fine, the doctor warned of a more serious outcome if Alaine were not kept calm and hydrated.

The doctor's admonition was enough for Charity to mobilize the entire Inn's staff to make sure his prescription was followed. It wasn't long before Alaine was complaining of a conspiracy to drown her in every known consumable liquid, but Sam noticed it didn't take long for her color and strength to return.

God, or somebody, had answered Ray Bright's prayers.

# # #

Celebration of the New Year was always an intimate and solemn event at the Inn at Copper's Run. New Year's Eve, 2001, was even more so. There were no noisemakers, no fireworks and no one crowded around the TV to see the ball drop in Times Square. But there were candles in abundance.

The Inn family along with any guests, who were so inclined, gathered at 11 p.m. in the ancient chapel in the underground passageway beneath the Inn. Sam was uncomfortable with his decision to participate, but more uncomfortable that he might disappoint the others with his absence.

According to custom, Ms. Charity and Johnson Story stood at the double doors marking the entrance to the stone steps leading underground, welcoming each participant with a handshake or an embrace. The mood was serious, but the greetings were warm and genuine.

Quietly, as if in meditation and anticipation, the participants moved carefully down the steps to the stone corridor below. Low lights in the passageway cast shadows on the walls as the people passed. Sam, who was the last one to follow, could hear the shuffling and clicking of footfalls ahead of him. No one talked or even whispered, but he could hear the soft strains of traditional dulcimer music coming from the direction of where he knew the chapel to be.

Nothing prepared Sam for the eerie sensation created by the coming of this New Year's celebration. He felt an unexpected and unwelcome tightness in his throat, and he coughed to clear away the feeling.

By the time he slipped into the back row of pews in the small chapel, Rev. Ray was standing before the little group of congregants with his hands raised. He waited in that position until Johnson Story, with Ms. Charity on his arm, walked the narrow aisle to sit on the front row.

"Let us join in a prayer to seek our Lord's blessing on our little celebration of the passing of an old year and the welcoming of a new. Shall we pray?"

Rev. Ray's voice was large, and his illness of the past year had done little to dampen it. His words, as he spoke to his God as if He was also in the chamber, rolled and bounced off of the stone walls.

The room was cold and felt a bit damp. Climate rarely concerned Sam, but he noticed most of the women in the room were swathed in heavy shawls. Alaine sat with Andi behind Ms. Charity. She was shrouded in a red wrap, and her head was bowed. She was beautiful in the light of the candles that also lined the walls of the chapel.

Sam shuddered and accounted it to the cold and the damp. He bent over, rested his forearms on his knees, dropped his head and searched for something...some pattern or lost artifact...anything on the floor to hold his attention for the duration of the event unfolding in front of him.

Rev. Ray's *Amen* thundered off of the walls and drew the eyes of the rest of the congregation to the man's face. Sam shifted his weight and continued to study the floor.

"New Year's Eve," began the Reverend, "is a time to think on the used and lost opportunities of the dying year and to look forward in hopeful anticipation of the renewed chances to be found faithful in the coming year. It's a time to celebrate when we've been good stewards of what the Lord has given us and a time to mourn those times when we fell short. But, thank God, His mercies are new every morning."

There were a number of soft *Amens* of agreement around the little room.

"For those of us who are blessed to wake up tomorrow morning, His blessings will be renewed again. We will have another chance to choose to trust His Son, another time to be obedient and do His will, another time to share His blessed name. Should the sun shine again tomorrow morning, and I truly believe it will, it will shine on a new day...a new year...that the Lord has made. Let us then rejoice and be glad in it."

There were a few raised hands around the room and again a murmuring of agreement that tomorrow would indeed be a glad day.

"I can think of no more fitting way to bid goodbye to this old year with all of its sorrows and joys and to welcome in this new year than to praise the name of the One who created both and sees fit to leave us here to endure the sorrows and embrace the joys. Join me in lifting up His name above all names."

Rev. Ray raised his arms high and began a call and response time of praise like a song, honoring the names of Christ.

"He's the Rose of Sharon."

The little congregation in the stone chapel beneath the Inn called out, "Oh, yes, He is!"

“He’s the Lily of the Valley.”

“Oh, yes.”

“He’s the Savior, Immanuel, the Lord our Righteousness.”

“He is.”

“He’s the Alpha and Omega, our King of Kings.”

“Oh, yes, He is.”

“He is God the Son...the beloved Son...in whom His Father is well pleased.”

“Oh, yes, well pleased.”

“He is the Seed of Abraham and the Seed of the woman who bruised the serpent’s head.”

“Oh, yes, He is.”

“He is the Man of sorrows, acquainted with our griefs.”

“Yes, yes, Lord.”

“He is the Good Shepherd and the Lamb of God that takes away the sins of the world.”

“Oh, yes, He is.”

“He is the Creator, the First-Born, our Mediator and the True Vine.”

“True Vine, yes, He is.”

“He is the Resurrection and the Life. He is the Way, the Truth and the Life.”

“It’s true, He is.”

“He is the Lord of Glory who will come soon in the clouds with a shout, the trump of God and the voice of the archangel. And all the people will say, ‘He is the Lord of Glory, He is the Lord of Glory. He is Lord of All, Lord of All.’ Hallelujah! Hallelujah! Hallelujah! Even so come, Lord Jesus!”

Sam watched, spellbound by the rhythms of Rev. Ray’s voice. He heard and felt the affirmation and agreement in the responses of his friends and those he now considered family around him. What did they have that he was missing? For the first time without condescension, Sam asked himself the question.

In the silence that followed, Ms. Charity rose and walked on the arm of Johnson Story to the doors of the chapel. The passageway beyond was now dark. As the group filed out in silence, she lit a single candle for each participant and handed it to the old man, who in turn, passed it to each outstretched hand with a nod, a smile and the words, "A New Year's blessing to you."

The lights from the candles lit the way upward into the Inn and into the New Year.

15 WARNINGS

Sampson

Traditionally, the two months after the New Year were quiet at the Copper's Run Inn. There were few guests by design so that they could be cared for by a skeleton staff. The Café was open only for breakfast except for Friday and Saturday when it also served evening meals. It was closed on Sundays, and the live-in help fended for themselves in a staff kitchen on the third floor.

Alaine's front desk duties were curtailed, both due to the season and the combined efforts of the Brights and Sam. Watching her move about the Inn, Sam was amused at the change in her physical appearance and more at his reaction to it.

He was once discriminatory in his taste in women and privileged in his selection of those he honored with his attentions. He only noticed those who were model-thin. While Alaine was by no means overweight when he met her in the office they shared in the City, she was not waif-like either. And now, while it was obvious that her waist was expanding, Sam was surprised at how pregnancy became her, enhanced her already natural beauty.

There was a softness about her, as well, which grew from her newly found strength, or so it seemed to Sam. This was not the Alaine who was barely able to leave her bed in those days in New York after 9/11. This Alaine made eye contact and smiled. She radiated hope and expectation.

He found himself studying her, wondering how she could be so calm. She was peaceful in spite of all she'd been through, and there was still more to come with the birth of the baby. It surprised him to realize he searched the room for her whenever she was not present.

It must be a learned protective reaction following their escape from the Towers. Maybe he felt responsible to see her through this next challenge, since he'd helped her get this far. Or it could be simple curiosity at being around an expectant mother and not knowing what was coming next. Sam laughed out loud at his own theorizing efforts.

For a man who likes action better than analysis, you're sure trying hard to over-analyze this situation.

Sam felt the reason in his gut before it reached his head. He cared about what happened to Alaine because he loved Alaine. It was that simple.

Why has it taken me this long to see it?

No answer was forthcoming.

The adrenalin rush from the new awareness gave him an instant headache, and he headed toward the Café to see if Andi had washed the coffee maker yet after breakfast. He needed his in a large cup and high octane black.

Sam forgot it was Andi's day off, and Danisha, who was mostly home with her child during the holidays, had come to fill in.

"I know what you want, and you're just in time. Dumping the pot was next on my list. You look awful this morning. You sick or something?"

Sam feigned a sleepy stupor to keep from meeting Danisha's eyes. She was too perceptive for his comfort at the moment.

"Thanks." He took the cup she held out and mumbled something about feeling a little off with maybe a flu bug when she noticed that his hand shook.

"Sampson MacDonald, you aren't fooling me one bit. You're sick all right, but it's not the flu. You think I don't know what's going on with you? You've had your head so high up in the sky for the last few weeks that you couldn't see what was going on right in front of you. Now I think it's bitten you on the foot."

"Danisha, I don't know what you're talking about. I have a headache, that's all. And you're making it worse with all of your rambling. What are you getting at?"

"You've got a bug, for sure. It's a love bug's got you. Am I right? It certainly took it long enough, but I'm pretty sure he's got his stinger in you now. Um huh. I knew it was bound to happen, but you resisted longer than I figured you would."

Danisha stood, hands on hips, looking at him, and she wasn't smiling. It did not look good.

Sam shook his head and dropped it into his hands.

"Let me tell you something. This is serious business, Sam. I've not been here much over the holidays, but when I did come around, it wasn't hard to see what was going on. You can hardly take your eyes off of Alaine. Andi's no gossip, but the way you've been acting doesn't go unnoticed. She's seen what I've seen, and she's concerned, too."

"What do you mean *concerned*, Danisha? What have you and Andi been up to? You haven't talked to Alaine?" The very thought that they might have said something sent a warning flash through him.

"'Course not. That's not for us to tell her. But there's more. I don't know how to say this other than just to say it. We love you like a brother, Andi and I, but I have to be honest with you. We don't think you should tell her how you feel either. Don't mess her up like that."

"What do you mean, mess her up? I wouldn't do anything to hurt Alaine."

"Sorry, honey, but that's just it. You already have. You and she aren't on the same road, Sam. Andi and I...we think it would be better for you just to pretend Alaine is your sister and leave her out of any romantic notions."

"First of all, Ms. Be-All-In-My-Business and Tell-Me-What-To-Do, who said anything about romance? You did...not me. And I don't remember soliciting your advice in the first place."

Danisha sat down at the table across from Sam and put her hand on his arm.

"OK, I apologize. I think I've mis-handled this little talk quite well. I'm sorry, but my heart's in the right place. I get points for that. We love you both. Everyone here at the Inn does. We just don't want to see either of you get hurt, and that's what's going to happen if you go after Alaine right now."

Sam looked at Danisha for several seconds before responding. "Apology accepted, I think. But what did you mean when you said, *right now*? Is that because of the way she is...I mean...pregnant?"

"No, Sam." Danisha's voice was low and serious. "It's because of the way you are. Look, I've said enough. Probably too much and in the wrong way. You need to talk to Rev. Ray about this if you're feeling what I think you are for Alaine and if you're considering acting on the way you feel." She turned away.

Sam waited, untouched coffee in his cup, hoping she would say more and not understanding what she meant. Something in Danisha's body language told him not to push her.

"Thanks for the coffee and the advice. Have a nice day." He scraped his chair back from the table, left his still full cup sitting there and walked out of the Café.

# # #

Sam found out first hand that even late February in Virginia can be cold, especially if it rains and the wind blows. The weather provided all three as he went for a walk after being too angry to go back to his room for his coat. He soon felt how thin his sweater was but refused to slow down or consider turning around to head back to the Inn.

I don't need this. Nosy interfering women. How could anybody think they know how I feel about Alaine? I didn't know myself until this morning. But if they knew, does Alaine know? What possible objections should Andi and

Danisha have about me being interested in Alaine, even if she is in the middle of a pregnancy by another man. And after all, those two should understand the predicament she's in. They've both been right there. Why wouldn't Alaine need all the help she could get, including from me?

Walking faster usually helped ward off the cold, but not this time. While his outside felt the wind and rain, the worst cold came from inside of Sam. He knew there was something more. He knew he wasn't getting to the heart of the reason why Danisha was concerned that he might get involved with Alaine.

Two miles from the Inn, the rain turned to sleet, the wind increased, and the cold air hurt Sam's lungs with each breath. He was on the highway leading out of town, and through the wet slush hitting his face, he could see the lights of the competition blinking nearby.

The small, rundown motel on the outskirts of Copper's Run offered rooms by the hour, the night or the week. The thought of spending any time in the place revolted Sam, but the thought of the two-mile walk back to the Inn disgusted him more. He was entering the empty parking lot when he heard the sound of a vehicle pulling in behind him.

S*omebody's more afraid of getting stranded on the road in this weather than of staying in this dump.*

Sam kept walking, eager to get to the motel office first, if only to get warm. He was surprised to hear his name over the sound of the wind and the vehicle's engine, which was now alongside of him.

"Sam, get in. Please, Sam, I'm sorry. Just get in, and let's get away from here."

It was Danisha. He was shocked that she'd come for him. She must have been looking a while and in spite of this nasty weather. He'd been gone from the Inn for some time.

"Come on. Please don't make me get out in this place and beg you to come back with me. Sam, get in."

Sam relented, and the warmth of her smile was better than the eighty degrees she must have the heater set on. She threw a car blanket across the seat to him and lost no time in exiting the parking lot of the Starlite Memories Motel, leaving the desk clerk standing in the doorway of the office looking wishful as they passed.

The two didn't talk on the way back to the Inn. Danisha had to watch the road, which was now getting treacherous. Sam sat hunched over in his seat, with his hands close to the heater vent, trying to warm them.

Danisha pulled her car into the Inn's drive and around back where she parked it near the ancient car shed. They sat for a minute more, reluctant to open the doors and lose the warmth.

"I really am sorry, Sam. Not so much for what I said but for not handling it differently. This whole thing is important. Please don't blow it off. Talk to Rev. Ray."

"Just tell me what the big deal is, Danisha. You think I'm interested in Alaine in more than a casual way. I'm not ready to talk about whether or not that's true. But let's say it was. What bothers you so much about that? She's growing stronger every day. Certainly I'm used to the fact that she's carrying another man's baby. And I'm not all that bad myself." He turned to look at her. "Am I?"

She looked down, and he could see her struggle to put an answer into words.

And then it hit him.

"It's religion, isn't it? Alaine's got religion now, and you don't think I do. Is that right?"

Danisha put a light hand on Sam's arm. He felt the pressure and warmth through his sweater. He also saw the regret in her eyes, but this time she didn't hold back.

"It's not religion I'm worried about, Sam. It's faith. I don't think you and Alaine share her faith in Christ. Whether you believe it or not, that's a big gulf between you and poses a significant problem."

# # #

The day grew darker by the hour. In late afternoon, the sleet turned to snow, falling fast with the kind of tiny flakes that could last all night. The wind found every un-insulated crack in the old Inn. The heating bill to keep the cold out would be staggering.

There were only two sets of guests in residence for the evening, a young family traveling to a wedding in Pennsylvania and a couple of brothers from up North, attending to business in a nearby town.

To make the place less grim, Sam, Rev. Ray and Johnson Story lit a fire in the large fireplace of the Inn's library. There supper was served, marshmallows were toasted, and Rev. Ray entertained the guests and staff alike with stories from the Inn's past. The atmosphere of intimate festivity inside made the cold and snow outside seem a planned backdrop for the evening.

While this took place around him, Sam found his usual place on the fringe, watching Alaine and the little group near the fireplace from a reading nook in a far, rather cold, corner.

She sat on the floor with one of the children, and her pale copper hair reflected the firelight. To Sam, she was beautiful.

That thought, and the cordiality of the gathering, should have brightened his mood, but the memory of his conversation with Danisha kept him away from the fire's warmth and from Alaine.

He slumped in his seat, the leather upholstery cold through his clothes. Sam hoped he appeared casual and relaxed, but he sensed the old fears moving into his dark corner. It had been a while since he'd been bothered by the remembered inadequacies his decline in fortune in the investment business had brought on, but they re-visited him now.

It had taken months, and the trust of the Brights, to begin the restoration of his self-confidence and sense of manhood. He'd almost started to believe his life had purpose and his abilities had worth. Running the Inn for Rev. Ray and Ms. Charity was the link that kept him away from the bottle, the needle and the other vices he'd found himself sliding closer to in the days before 9/11.

And now, that moment of honesty from Danisha had brought the dark thoughts back. The job in the Trade Towers taken in desperation, discovering he worked for a loser company, his act of thievery from the old man, all the old failures came crashing down on him. He fell short. He didn't fit. They all thought he wasn't a good match for Alaine, even though he'd rescued her and brought her to the Inn.

Sam sat with his head down, arms resting on his knees, careful not to make eye contact with anyone around the fire. He was bitter and knew it would show on his face.

He really didn't need any self-righteous, judgmental preaching from anyone here. He should be secure in himself without their approval.

After all, who was responsible for practically dragging Alaine out of that doomed building that almost became her grave? Who'd kept her going in those days after the Towers fell when she could hardly move or think?

Who had brought her here to Copper's Run when she had nowhere else to go...to this place where she found a family and a home? Who had tried to shield her from the man she feared, the father of her baby?

And now he wasn't worthy of her in their eyes just because she was in the Jesus Club and he was on the outside looking in? Who was Danisha to tell him anything? It was no secret she'd had her own shortcomings.

The more Sam let his anger talk to him, the more it stoked its own flame. By the time the real fire burned low in the fireplace, the stories were over and the campfire songs started with the children, Sam had enough. Looking obviously at his watch as if he had an urgent appointment, he walked out of the room. He was done for the night.

# # #

Not sleeping well had become a habit with too much on his mind, too many details to check and too many plans to make. And then there was Alaine. When he was with her, she was friendly enough, if a little quiet and in some odd way remote. He tried to talk about how she was feeling and about the baby. He wanted to engage her in conversation, get closer to her on a more personal level. A few attempts had convinced Sam that she was, indeed, holding him at a distance. Nice but not close.

He wandered about the cold halls of the old Inn at night when sleep failed, and that was often. He was a master of catching snatches of rest when he could and working out problems in his mind during middle of the night treks through the Inn. He'd developed a nocturnal routine. Start up on the third floor, walk the halls, listen for unusual sounds, check the elevators, make sure there were no heating hot spots or areas that were too cold. Move down to the second floor, check by the Brights' suite to make sure everything seemed right, walk the halls, look out the windows toward the back and front of the Inn for anything unusual, move on to the first floor, check the Café area, move on to the public rooms and check all doors to the outside and the cellar.

Walk, listen, think, check, think.

Everything was always OK, nothing odd or out of place. People around here really did their jobs.

But this night something *was* out of place, or rather in a place where nothing should be. It was a car, light colored against the darkness and not remarkable, but it was parked in the trees to the side of the Inn's front drive.

There was no comfortable explanation for why a car would be parked where it was at 3 a.m. Someone with car trouble would have left it on the street nearer a street light. None of the few Inn guests would have left a vehicle there.

Sam stood in the second floor hall window where there was no backlight and he couldn't be seen. He watched for a long time, but no light came from within the car, and he could detect no movement. He had just checked all doors, and they were locked. Sam waited. He was cold and finally getting tired, but uneasy enough not to say *forget it* and head back to his room.

He checked his watch. Twenty minutes passed and still not a movement or light from the car. At forty minutes, he was miserable and about ready to leave his post when the interior lights of the car came on, not for long, but just enough for the door to open and someone to step out.

To be sure he wasn't seen, Sam stepped further back from the window, no longer cold or tired.

The figure was dressed in a long overcoat. He couldn't tell the gender yet, but he could see the form standing by the front of the vehicle, facing the Inn.

Sam moved back again when he saw the figure move slowly toward the front doors.

Maybe it was a stranded traveler, after all, needing a safe place to spend the night. But one had to be purposeful to seek out the Inn in its location on a side street near the heart of the little town. A stranded motorist would have been much more likely to seek shelter in the sleazy motel just off the main highway.

The inner warning system that alerts one that all is not well started to sound in Sam's head.

The figure moved slowly and a bit unsteadily toward the Inn's front entrance. He'd checked it, right? Was he sure the double doors were secure?

The figure moved between the two post lamps that always shone on the front walk at night. Sam could see now it was a man. The man he recognized was Paul Mowher.

When Mowher's foot touched the first step of the Inn, an adrenalin rush second only to the one that helped him pull Alaine out of the doomed World Trade Center hit him. In a state of fury he didn't know he was capable of, Sam unlocked the Inn's doors and planted himself in Paul Mowher's path.

The look he found on the man's face, as Mowher stopped mid step and grabbed the railing to keep from falling, was surprise followed closely by anger.

"You, it's always you...the great gatekeeper in charge of all the doors. Get out of my way." Mowher's words were slurred and his tone belligerent.

Sam stood his ground. "Why are you here? We don't have any vacancies." It was a lie, but Sam's increasing anger overshadowed any thoughts of playing the role of host.

"Don't need a room. Here to see Alaine. Go get her." Mowher's tone became more confrontational and his words more run together. In spite of his own fury, Sam could still recognize the hot light of hatred...and alcohol...in the man's eyes.

"She's not here. She's gone. You're wasting your time and mine. I'm asking you to leave."

"You're a liar, MacDonald. She's here. I need to talk to her. She wants to see me, too. Just ask her. I'm warning you. Get her now."

"You're threatening me?" Sam moved closer to where Mowher stood.

"Take it any way you like, but I'm telling you for the last time, go get Alaine for me."

At that moment, Sam saw movement as Mowher's left hand slipped from the rail to fumble beneath his overcoat. He caught a glimpse of a gun strapped to the man's chest even while he tried to keep it hidden from view.

He had a choice and only seconds to assess the situation and make the right one. No way could he let the man get to Alaine. He could fight him here with no weapon and risk getting shot, or he could try to talk him down and convince the angry man to back away without trouble.

Intuition told Sam that talk wouldn't do it.

He saw Mowher's hand grip the handle of the gun. Time to think was over.

Sam took a giant step forward and gripped the rail. He raised his right foot and took advantage of the other man's momentum as Mowher moved further up the steps.

Sam planted the bottom of his foot firmly against Mowher's chest and gave the man a shove.

The force of Sam's push threw Mowher off balance. He flailed his arms wildly to stop a backwards fall down the steps. His thrashing flung the gun at Sam's feet.

Mowher crouched and scrambled up the steps again on all fours, aiming toward the gun on the wooden front porch of the Inn. With no time to stoop and pick it up, Sam took the next best choice. He kicked the gun through the rail into the shrubbery against the front of the Inn.

Mowher froze, his eyes locked with Sam's. Mowher's body was caught in suspended animation while Sam watched his face reflect the emotions he must be feeling inside...hate, uncertainty, fear.

"The gun is gone. I paged the police. They're on the way."

It was a bluff, but, no doubt due to Mowher's muddled thinking, it worked.

Paul Mowher's fear must have overcome his loathing for the one who blocked his way to Alaine. The snarl with which he uttered his response could have come from an animal.

"You won't win, MacDonald."

Sam didn't offer a response. He held his ground, fascinated as Mowher stood, brushed off his pants, straightened his overcoat and tie, turned and walked down the steps into the front yard with no further contact, as if nothing had happened.

The man's crazy. I really should call the police.

Sam watched him walk away and disappear into the darkness. The car still sat at the side of the driveway. No sounds like that of a motor starting interrupted the night's quiet.

After re-checking the locks on the Inn's entrances, Sam sat up all night watching the front lawn from the reception room window. He saw nothing, and in the morning, a white car was still there.

When the sky was light enough to see clearly outside, Sam opened the Inn's front doors with care, his eyes searching the yard area for movement. When he was as certain as he could be that no one waited to attack him, he eased out onto the porch to search for the piece of evidence from the night before that might spotlight Mowher as a threat to him, Alaine, and the others at the Inn...the gun.

Sam stood for a moment on the porch, recreating in his mind the events from the previous evening. While he hadn't felt fear then, due to his pumped state, he felt it in the cold haze of morning. It hit him now how easily his act of bravado could have been rewarded by sudden death had Mowher's instincts and reaction times not been impaired by alcohol.

He shook off an impulse to retreat behind the Inn's heavy doors and struggled to remember just where he was positioned when he kicked the gun off of the porch. *What trajectory? What force? Where would it land?* He remembered the thud as it hit the side of the Inn before it crashed into the bushes.

Where? Sam role played the kick again in slow motion, figuring where an imaginary object of the gun's size and weight would land. When he had some idea of where to search, he took another look around to be sure he was alone and moved from the porch to the narrow passage between the old growth boxwoods and the front of the Inn. He moved methodically down the side of the building, searching the ground, scanning the bushes, trying not to miss anything.

The front of the Inn to the right of the steps was long, and Sam searched far beyond where he was sure the gun could be found. No gun appeared on the open ground, was stuck in the bushes or lay hidden under them.

Sure he had simply overlooked it, Sam stood and scanned the yard, checking again for movement. Convinced once more that he was alone, he started back the way he came, this time crawling the whole way, taking his time, determined not to miss the gun.

Searching this way was slow and uncomfortable. The ground was damp. Sam's hands were bare and growing numb from the cold. As he closed in on the area closer to the steps where he knew the gun had to have landed, his searching became more frantic, as if haste would reveal what care and caution had not.

Four feet from the porch, Sam found something he'd missed the first time over...markings in the wet dirt as if something...someone had also been crawling there. He found the partial print of a shoe he quickly ruled out as being his own due to the distinct imprint marking it as a tennis shoe. Paul Mowher had been dressed up, under his overcoat, as if going out for the evening. That much Sam remembered from the night before. And he wore tennis shoes. Sam was sure because the shoes had struck him, even in the moment, as being incongruous with his outfit.

He bent to look more closely at the area immediately around the print and found small branches broken in the bush just above the outline of the ball of the tennis shoe. He was right. The gun had lodged in a shrub after ricocheting off of the Inn's foundation. Paul Mowher had come back and found it.

The thought of what happened right under his nose made Sam's heart beat out of rhythm. While he waited up and watched all night to protect the Inn's inhabitants from Paul Mowher's possible return, the man had, in fact, returned undetected. He'd obviously pretended to leave, then likely come back from another direction, crawled silently through the shrubbery...maybe using something as small as a pen light to find his way...and he'd found the gun!

# # #

As drained as Sam was after his ordeal, the overnight vigil and the disturbing discovery, he still felt he must tell someone, give some kind of warning about his encounter and Mowher's clandestine return. He knew it couldn't be Alaine. He didn't want to risk getting Rev. Ray's blood pressure up.

The police? No. What would he say? What proof?

Sam finally settled on Ms. Charity. He found her in the Inn's laundry folding guest towels.

"Could I talk with you a moment, Ms. Charity?"

"Sure, Sam. Do you mind if I keep folding? We've gotten sort of backed up here."

He leaned against the laundry room door while Ms. Charity continued at the work table, her back to him. As he told her about his middle-of-the-night encounter with Paul Mowher, Charity's folding got slower and slower. When he came to the part about the gun, now missing from the bushes, she stood still with arms crossed and her head down.

When she finally spoke, Sam wasn't surprised that she addressed an insignificant detail first. He guessed she was taking time to absorb the possible impact of the events on the Inn's family.

"We wondered whose car that was in the drive. Ray was about to call a wrecker but decided we'd better wait to see if anyone came around about it."

"I checked it out. It's a rental, but the paperwork left inside is not in Mowher's name. I called it in as abandoned. Someone will pick it up later today.

"Sam, I think you should've called the police last night. Obviously the man's dangerous. His actions don't make sense. I'll admit, I had my concerns about him from our first meeting, but now I'm pretty sure he's unbalanced."

"I know. Maybe you're right about the police. I thought I could handle it. And now I don't have any proof. Do you think I should tell Alaine? I don't want her upset."

Ms. Charity looked down and nodded. "It might upset her, but I think she should be told. If she's really in danger, she should know it. Do you want me to talk to her?"

"No, I'll do it if it has to be done. I just need to think of the best way."

"What about the police?"

"What would I say? Some guy came down from New York and sneaked up to the Inn and threatened me with a gun. He left his rental car in the drive. So the police will come and check it out. The car's rented under another name, and I'll just bet there are no prints. Mowher had on gloves, as I recall. So even if he's questioned, he'll have an alibi, and I have no witnesses. End of case."

"Do you think we can get a restraining order?"

"Again, what would be our evidence? We have nothing but a car in the driveway that could have been left by anybody. Mowher and Alaine have a rough history, but lately he's been nothing but charming around her. I'm afraid we'd be wasting our time."

"Well, I know the man is the father of Alaine's baby, but that doesn't make him upstanding. Something's not right. I don't know what, but I'm concerned. Maybe he's psychotic. Do you suppose Alaine's leaving unhinged him?"

"From what little she's told me, he was a jerk even prior to that."

"Sam, I want you to go to the police anyway and just tell your story. They may not be able to do anything, but if something else happens, at least there's a report on record about him. Will you do that?"

"I'll go now."

# # #

Sam returned from making his police report with his fears confirmed that there was little that could be done at this point about Paul Mowher's visit and threat. It was now urgent that he let Alaine in on what happened the previous night.

He found her straightening the reception room.

"Hello, Sam. You've been scarce lately. Have you been taking some time off? I know you need it after our killer holiday season. What's up?"

"Need to talk to you about something important. Can you spare a minute?"

The look in Alaine's eyes told Sam she didn't want to hear anything heavy and might bolt at any time. He took her hand and led her to his adjoining office.

She stood with evident uncertainty as he started to seat himself. He stood back up.

"Alaine, please. Sit with me. This is important. I need you to hear what I have to say."

She sat but on the edge of a seat opposite him. It was going to be hard to warn her without scaring her half to death. That she didn't need.

"The Inn had a visitor late last night. It was Paul Mowher again. He didn't come inside. I met him on the front steps. He was asking for you."

Sam paused and waited for her reaction. She hugged her arms to herself and waited.

"I made the decision that I wouldn't let him speak to you. I hope that was the right judgment, but he was really in no condition to talk to anyone."

"Why? How did he act?"

"Angry...belligerent...inebriated. He threatened me. There was a gun."

Sam didn't like what his message did to her color. She was visibly shaken, but he couldn't stop now. It was critical that she see just how dangerous the man was.

"What did you do?" Her voice was barely audible.

"I kicked the daylights out of him and sent his gun into the bushes. That's what I did!" He was bragging like a nine year old, but Sam didn't care. He wanted her to know to what lengths he'd gone to protect her.

"He left, as calm and dignified as you please. He just walked off and left his rental car. It's still here. Somebody's coming to pick it up. I've made a police report, but there's not enough evidence to get an arrest or restraining order. No one else saw him. Ms. Charity thought you should know. She thinks he's crazy."

"She's half right. He's mean and crazy. I must be crazy, too. I'm having that man's baby."

Alaine was now the color of chalk, and her hands were trembling. She bent over, holding her stomach.

"That man is your baby's father by a biological act. That's it. It doesn't make him qualified for the role. Do you really think he cares about this child?"

"Sam, in all the time we lived together, Paul only cared about Paul, Paul's needs, Paul's reputation, what Paul wanted. It wasn't like that for the few weeks we dated. But as soon as I moved in with him, it was clear that anything not completely self-serving to him was a highly skilled deception."

Sam's next question, to his distaste, was more for his sake than Alaine's, but he had to ask.

"Alaine, I watched him with you here at the Inn. I saw the chivalrous way he treated you. For your protection, I listened in the last time you two talked and heard him begging you to come back to New York with him, promising you a new life if you would go. I know you've struggled to know what to do. Why did you decide not to go?"

"I know you have no idea what it feels like to be in my situation, Sam. I've been desperate for some sense of security and permanence, for me and especially my baby. It sounded at first like that's what Paul was finally offering me. He knew exactly what to say and how to act to make me believe everything would be different if we got back together...that this is what he really wanted, even with the baby. He was good, very good."

"Then what made you back away from his offers? What was the final deal breaker?"

"Even though his talk of changing and making a life for us was very tempting, I remembered a Bible verse my granny used to quote. She would use it when she knew people were pretending to be nice, but she could see right through to the mean spirit they had. The verse is in Jeremiah 13:23, and it says something like, 'Can a leopard take away its spots? Neither can you start doing good, for you have always done evil.'

"That verse came to me as I was thinking about Paul's promises. I could hear Granny warning me that without long term proof of a change, which he wasn't offering, Paul could easily keep on being the Paul I knew before we left the City."

"Well, Alaine, I'm with Granny. I think that leopard has shown his spots clearly enough."

"I know now that the only reason Paul cares about me is to control me. He has to be the one in charge. No one can desert him without his permission. But I did. I left, and to him, that's intolerable. That was not part of his plan. That's why he came after me."

"And the baby? What about his rights to the baby?"

"My baby means nothing to him. He would say he wants it to get to me. In truth, we both mean nothing to him. As much as it hurts to know, I wasted a lot of time and emotion on someone who only wanted to control and use me. Now he wants to prove I was wrong in leaving him. He wants to win. And with Paul, when you stand between him and what he wants, you're in danger."

"You did that, Alaine. You defied him and disappeared, and I helped you. He may hate me more than he resents you because, in his eyes, I look like I have the upper hand, especially after last night."

"You outwitted him twice. That makes you doubly culpable, Sam."

Sam dropped his head in frustration. "He's not going to stop then, is he? He's going to keep trying to get you back, one way or another. He needs to regain control of you and get back at me."

"You may be right, Sam. He's tried to win me back with kindness and that didn't work. You may have seen a sample of his next approach. Thanks for your warning. I know you've let me know so I'll be on guard. I want to ask the same of you. You see how unpleasant the real Paul Mowher can be. I don't want you getting hurt because of me."

"Alaine...there's something else...I need to--"

Sam stopped. He wanted to tell her he loved her. He wanted her to know if she would have him, this baby would be his, and it would never have to know the name of Paul Mowher. He had saved Alaine from the end of the world at the Trade Center, and he could help keep her safe from her baby's father, if she'd let him.

"Sam, did you hear me? I don't want you hurt."

He couldn't tell her. Danisha's words stuck in his head and closed his mouth.

We don't think you should tell her how you feel...Don't mess her up like that...You and she aren't on the same road, Sam.

"Sam?"

"I know. I understand. I'll be careful."

16 HISTORY LESSON

Sampson

Sam's warning conversation with Alaine ended but not to his satisfaction. He didn't fear Paul Mowher, though he knew the man was a threat to both of them, and maybe to everyone at the Inn. What bothered him most was his inability to speak honestly to Alaine about his feelings for her, feelings he'd only just acknowledged to himself.

Sam, who'd become accustomed not to care who thought what about him, found he cared a great deal about what these new people in his life thought. Danisha's warning got to him. He had to have help.

"Charity here. May I help you?"

"Ms. Charity, its Sam. Is Rev. Ray available? I need to talk to him, if it's convenient."

"Sam, you sound funny. Is something wrong? Is it Alaine?"

"No, no, she's fine. I just left her. Look, I need some advice and I thought maybe--"

"Ray's right here. Shall I put him on? Where are you?"

"Standing outside of your door."

Ms. Charity opened the door of their suite immediately.

"Come on in. Ray's resting right here on the couch. Keep him company while I see to some things downstairs."

She left the room while Sam was still standing just inside the doorway. Rev.

Ray's booming voice welcomed him.

"Hello, Sam, sit there in my easy chair. If you don't mind, I'll just lie right here while we visit. What's on your mind, son?"

Sam sat and decided that the best approach was direct and straightforward. "Rev. Ray, I need help. I don't know where to start, and I'm not used to asking for advice. I felt like things were coming together...that I was getting a new start. I'm proud of what I...we've accomplished here. For the first time in a long time, I feel like I've contributed to something worthwhile."

"You most certainly have, Sampson. It's hard to think what we would have done without you, although I'm sure the Lord would have provided. But it was you that He sent when He knew our time of need was coming. I'd realized I had to have help here, and then I got sick. You've done a remarkable job. Do you doubt that? If you do, then we've been remiss in telling you how much you mean to us."

"Thank you, sir. You and Ms. Charity have been wonderful to me and to Alaine. Who else would have taken us in without a lot of questions and then made us feel like part of your family?"

"You are, Sam. You both are. Rest assured about that."

"I know you mean it, but I know also that something's not right. It's hard to put my finger on, but I can tell in your eyes I've come up short. I've put my heart into the work here, but I've missed the mark. What have I done wrong?"

"What makes you think something's wrong, son? What brought you to that conclusion?"

"I'm an outsider. I feel it every time the rest of you are together. I'm not in the circle. It's not that I think you all don't care or don't want to include me. It's just a sense I get. And then something one of the girls said the other day made me sure of it."

"Danisha? That girl's pretty straightforward."

Sam laughed. "It was Danisha, although it doesn't matter who said it.

Anyway, I think she was trying to help."

"What exactly did she say?"

Sam didn't answer right away. Rev. Ray let him sit in silence until he was ready to break the quiet.

"I hadn't planned to go into this part...hoped it wouldn't be necessary, but it's too late not to now. Danisha, well she and Andi together, figured out that I'm interested in Alaine."

"Interested as in--?"

"I think I love her. I've cared about her to some degree all along, but it was more like a brother taking care of a little sister. This is totally different. And new for me, I might add. I think I want to marry her and make a family with her and the baby, when it comes. This is all a surprise to me. I hadn't planned on it happening."

Rev. Ray raised up on one arm to face Sam. "Have you mentioned your feelings to Alaine?"

"No, I didn't talk about it to anyone, but Danisha brought it up. Instead of being happy for us, Danisha advised me not to say anything to Alaine. She mentioned something about both of us getting hurt."

"What else did she say?"

"When I pressed her, she said it was because I don't share Alaine's faith. I can't understand why that makes any difference. She can have whatever religious beliefs she wants. I won't try to stop her. I know I'm not perfect, but I'm not Paul Mowher, either. I don't get why Danisha was so adamant that Alaine and I shouldn't be together."

"Didn't she explain herself further?"

"No, she wouldn't. Just said I should talk to you. So here I am. It's like she thought I wasn't worthy of Alaine or something. OK, suppose I do love Alaine. I understand she might not feel the same way. But what if she does? Look, she has a past, too. That doesn't bother me at all, but I'm just saying she's not perfect either. I think we'd be fine together. So why is it such a problem?"

"Sam, do you remember what Alaine was like when you brought her to Copper's Run almost four months ago? Have you noticed anything different about Alaine now?"

"I do. She's stronger, more confident. She seems more centered or something. Alaine hardly talked at all back in September. Not that she has a lot to say now, but when she does, she seems much more sure of herself. Actually, she can be rather outspoken these days when she feels strongly about something. I'd say she's very different now. I think that's one of the reasons I feel like I do."

Rev. Ray swung his legs off of the couch, sat up and posed the type of question Sam was dreading.

"Why do you think she's changed?"

Something made Sam's throat tighten. He suspected he knew where Rev. Ray was heading. He'd sat through a couple of the preacher's sermons. He stalled for time.

"I'd guess it was partly the whole 9/11 experience. That would change anybody. And knowing she has a baby coming. Then she has this place and all of you to support her. With all that, it would be weird if she weren't different."

"I think you're right. I think all of those things contributed to the new Alaine. But, son, I think something else has had a more profound impact. Do you have any idea what I'm talking about?"

Sam's fears were right. He didn't want to go down this road with Rev. Ray. But then he'd come to Ray and not the other way around. Why not face it head on?

"You're talking about her religious experience, aren't you?"

Sam was surprised when Rev. Ray chuckled. He'd expected agreement, but not amusement from this religious leader.

"I'm sorry, Sampson. I'm not making fun of you, but you sound like she's gotten some ailment. Let's not call it a religious experience, how about it? Maybe we could say it was an act of faith. There's a big difference, you know."

Sam remembered *faith* was the word Danisha had used.

"Look, I don't mean to disrespect you or what you believe, but I don't see the difference. Isn't the exercise of faith the same as a religious experience?"

"It can be the same, or it can be very different, depending on a person's heart. Most religions and religious experiences don't start from a belief that you can't do anything to save yourself on your own. Most believe that redemption and betterment of self-come from something you have to do...like work harder, give more, do something worthwhile, perform certain rituals...save yourself. That doesn't require faith in anyone or anything but self. In essence, you become your own god."

"Isn't that the way it works?" Sam knew he sounded like a cynic, but he kept talking anyway. "From what I've observed, human nature is pretty depraved. I think people could do better, but most generally don't. The results are what I saw every day living in New York, topped off by what happened on 9/11. The only hope I see is for people to work harder at being less bad...and I doubt that will happen. The few good folks around like you and Ms. Charity can stand out more and keep the world from looking like such a depressing place."

Rev. Ray stood, walked out of the room and returned with a small picture in a rusted tin frame. He handed it to Sam and sat again on the couch.

"Sampson, I want to tell you a little story about the young man in that picture. I'll make it short, but this is something I've needed to share with you for some time. Will you spare me a few minutes?"

Sam hadn't come for a speech. He'd come for advice. Only his deep respect and gratitude for Ray Bright kept him seated and quiet.

"You've known me for a few months now. When you look at me, you see the Right Reverend Raymond T. Bright, esteemed minister of the church, beloved pastor of his flock, learned Bible teacher, astute business man, husband of one wife, friend to all." Rev. Ray laughed with ease at his own litany. "I know you understand that I, like everybody, have my faults, but I'd be willing to bet that you think I'm a good and somewhat pious man, a veritable pillar of the community. Am I right?"

Now Sam laughed. He saw the twinkle in Rev. Ray's eyes that made his description of himself arrogance free.

"If you do say so yourself, that's the way I would describe you, sir. You've been a preacher a long time, studied your Bible, and earned credibility in your field. That's easy to see from watching the way others respond to you. Johnson Story thinks you walk on water."

This time Rev. Ray's laughter was long and loud.

"What would you say if I told you Johnson Story and I have done time in a federal prison together? I did three and a half years, to be exact. The picture you hold was taken a month before I went to jail."

Sam looked at the picture in his hand, and the face of a young Raymond Bright stared back at him. Sam was used to being king of the straight face. He was not prepared for this. His look gave him away.

This brought another vigorous laugh from his mentor.

"I can see what you're thinking, Sampson. I guess that's one reason I've not told you my story before. I'm laughing now, but this is not something I'm proud of or make light of. Johnson Story, on the other hand, really was innocent and ended up on the inside because of a bad brush with some narrow minded folks back in the sixties.

"I can't say the same for myself. I ran afoul of the law with my eyes wide open, as they say."

He was going to tell his story, and Sam was now ready to listen.

"Son, have you noticed that big old copper pot that sits out in the median in the middle of downtown Copper's Run?"

"I saw it. Looked like an old moonshiner's kettle to me. Is that really what

I think it is?"

"I can vouch for it. It was mine. This whole area of Virginia was notorious for its illegal moonshine trade since way back before prohibition. We're rural so it's easy to hide a still, and there are plenty of creeks for water. The people around here made 'shine,' as we call it, for money. That's true, but it was also for the excitement it provided. Things could get pretty dull in the sticks, and we made our own fun."

Sam didn't interrupt Rev. Ray's narrative, and he tried to keep the disbelief from his face.

"Back in the early sixties, I was a major player in the illegal whiskey business. By the time I was 21, I had the reputation of being the toughest black kid in the county. My best friend was a scrawny, crippled white boy named Billy Strater. I needed him because he didn't care if I was black, and he needed me to protect him from the cowards who wanted someone weaker than they were to pick on. Billy was skinny and frail, but he had brains. I was bigger than I am now and not afraid of anything. We made a great working team."

Rev. Ray stopped long enough to look at his listener, likely checking his reaction. Sam couldn't say a word and only responded by shaking his head in disbelief. Rev. Ray continued.

"Billy Strater and I had a wealthy backer with lots of old Virginia money who wanted even more and loved to drink. He set us up in our own operation. We knew what we were doing because our daddies had been working moonshine together since before we were born. Billy ran the stills, and I ran the transportation of the whiskey to our markets. The operation was big. We employed more men part time than the local textile mill. At least half of the men in Copper's Run worked for us at one time or another. Our product was the best and our cars the fastest, with me out in front."

Rev. Ray's voice broke, and Sam watched in alarm as the big man's shoulders shook, and he wiped tears off of his glistening black face. It was some time before he could continue.

"For five years, we were on top, above the law, unstoppable...right up to the night that Billy talked me into letting him ride shotgun with me, something I never before agreed to. That one night I gave in. We came on a roadblock outside of a little town just over the North Carolina line. I thought I could run it. I'd done it many times before. This night I got us through the first obstacles, a set of wooden barricades, with no problem. What I hadn't counted on...nobody had...was that the roadblock was built at an intersection near a railroad crossing. The barricades didn't stop me, but the freight train that came earlier than usual that night did."

Ray dropped his head into his hands and sobbed audibly. Sam sat speechless for several long moments. Rev. Ray finally gathered himself and continued.

"Billy Strater died that night because I let him ride with me. As far as I know today, little, scrawny, crippled Billy, whom I loved like a brother, went out into eternal separation from God because I let my guard down that one time."

"Rev. Ray, you don't have to--"

"Yes, son, I do have to tell you this. I haven't finished yet, and I need for you to hear me out, if you will. Billy Strater wasn't the only one who died that night. If I hadn't been involved in what I was doing, other men might also be alive. You see, the roadblock was up because the law decided this would be the end of our moonshine enterprise in this part of the state. While Billy and I were on the road to North Carolina, a force with every outfit from the local sheriff's office to the state police and the federal officials were closing in on our stills. Once the big boys got involved, the county men were angry and embarrassed they couldn't shut us down alone. They hit eight stills at one time. There was little mercy shown to my men who were on duty. From what I could figure out later, any resistance at all was met with lethal force. Six more men besides Billy Strater died before the night was out, most of them from Copper's

Run. Because of my bad choices, seven men met a violent end that night, and I was spared to live with the knowledge that some of them, Billy included, will not be there when I reach Heaven."

Sam could not keep quiet at that conclusion from the man he'd grown to admire and love. "Rev. Ray, you can't possibly think that's true for sure. I can't believe --"

Ray interrupted his protest. "It's not about what I think or you believe, son. That's my point. It's about what God himself told us in his Word. Billy and I did not know God. I doubt some of the others did either, from the way we all lived. Oh, we all knew back then that there was a God, but we pretended He couldn't see us and the wild way we were living. We left God alone and hoped He would do the same for us."

It hurt Sam to see Rev. Ray taking so much of the burden for what happened. Ray Bright was a good man, and anyone who knew him could tell it. He had to say something to counteract Rev. Ray's negative line of thinking.

"Rev. Ray, Billy chose to ride with you that night. Those other men made their choices, too. Yes, they died, but how do you know where they are now? I think we just go out into nothing when we leave here, sort of like what happened to all those people who didn't get out of the World Trade Center, and their bodies were never found."

"I'd like to believe that, Sampson. I really would. That would give me great comfort when it comes to Billy and the other men, all my friends. But I can't. What I do believe is God's Word. Revelation 21:27 talks about Heaven and it says, 'Nothing impure will ever enter it, nor will anyone who does what is shameful or deceitful, but only those whose names are written in the Lamb's book of life.'

"Truth is, I still wake up sometimes and see Billy's face. And then I seem to hear the voice of Isaiah the prophet in the Bible saying to him, 'But your iniquities have separated you from your God; your sins have hidden His face from you, so that He will not hear.'"

To Sam, this all sounded cruel and unfair. "Who's to say that's true, Rev. Ray...that there's a real Heaven and Hell? Maybe there's neither. Maybe we just die, like I said, and that's it."

"If they're not real, Sampson, we're all off the hook. That would be great. But if you should be wrong and everything the Bible says is true, we're in real trouble unless we have someone to save us from ourselves. Consider this. The same God who created the universe sent his only Son, Jesus, to earth as a perfect baby to grow up and die so that my sins could be forgiven and I could live in Heaven forever. I don't think God would have done that unless this all is for real."

Rev. Ray got up and stood at the window overlooking the front yard of the Inn. With his back to Sam he said, "That's what I mean by faith. It took faith to believe all this is true and to act on it, to trust Christ alone to take my sins away. That's what I did that night, when I found out all the pain I had helped cause. I was at the end of myself."

When he turned back from the window, tears again streamed down the face of the big man.

"But you still went to jail. Your faith didn't keep you from that."

"I sure did, son, for three and a half long years. I deserved more. Did you notice the plaque on the copper still display downtown? Do you know what it said?"

"I think it was something like, 'This pot built the town and almost destroyed it.' I couldn't make sense of it."

"That's pretty close. The town and creek of Copper's Run took their names from the illegal whiskey business. The town was incorporated in 1925, one of the dates on the marker. The other date was 1966. The big bust happened on April 19th, 1966, a date I'll mourn the rest of my life. That night, besides my friend, Billy, the son of the mayor died, the nephew of the Baptist preacher, the high school football coach, two men who worked at the mill and my uncle, Marcus. The mayor killed himself two months later. They said it was because he couldn't get over his son's death and the shame of what happened. So you can see, can't you, Sampson, why that night almost ruined the town?"

"Rev. Ray, I don't know what to say. I had no idea."

"I pled guilty so there was no real trial. Some people later said I'd just gotten jail house religion...that I was only sorry because I was caught and hoped to have my time shortened by playing church. But I know in here, my head, and in here, my heart what really happened.

"I knelt down that night on the nasty floor of the county jail with my best friend's blood still on my clothes and cried out to the same Jesus who helped create the world and whose blood flowed down that old rugged cross for me. I told God, though He already knew, what a great sinner I was. I told Him that if He cared that much for me, I could trust Him with the near impossible job of taking all my sins and putting then as far away as the east is from the west. I cried all through that night, sitting in that jail, as they brought in one after another of my co-workers who'd managed to live.

"In the morning I was a changed man. Billy was still gone, I was headed to prison, but I would never be the same. That was 35 years ago, Sam. God stayed with me through prison, gave me a new friend in Johnson Story, and brought me out to find a life to serve Him with a feisty lady who is now Charity Bright."

Rev. Ray walked to where Sam was now standing and placed his huge hands on the younger man's shoulders.

"I'm a new man, Sampson MacDonald. I'm not that 21 year old outlaw who played God by running his own life. I'm not bragging. It was not by any righteousness on my part, but the mercy of the eternal God that saved me. He can do that for you, young man. I pray you let him."

The preacher walked over and lay down on his couch again, obviously exhausted from his revelations.

Sam walked to the door. It was time to leave Rev. Ray to rest. Anxiety tightened his chest. He now knew what Danisha was talking about. He turned back to the man prone on the couch.

"You never said what you think about me telling Alaine how I feel about her. You don't really need to. I'm sure I know your opinion, you and Danisha, Ms. Charity, Mr. Story, Andi, all of you, including Alaine. She has the faith you were talking about; you all do. I'm not there yet. That's why Danisha thinks Alaine and I shouldn't be together. At least now I know. I'll just let it go."

Sam reached the door before he heard Rev. Ray speak again. "We all love you, son. We're praying for you."

He closed the door to Rev. Ray and Ms. Charity's suite, fully intent on collecting his belongings and leaving the Inn with no goodbyes. He'd narrowly escaped making a capital fool of himself. The conversation with Rev. Ray saved him sure humiliation in the eyes of both Alaine and the Inn's staff.

Sam walked the hall with purpose. He was grateful for the man's frankness. While he would leave with no further communication, he would write back with thanks for all the Brights had done for him. He owed them that for their support over the past few months...and for their trust.

By the time Sam reached his room, he had a plan. He would call a taxi. By the time it arrived, he'd have his things together and be gone. He'd be fine. It would be hard for a day or two at the Inn until the Brights could find help, but they could manage. He was finally free with no one to rescue but himself.

Sam shut the door and was alone.

Alone. Who am I kidding? In the two minutes it took to walk to his room, he'd made a decision that would lose his home, his adopted family, his job and likely the confidence he'd gained in the last few months. He would leave as a failure to everyone here, including Alaine. And he had no place to go.

Now with little purpose and fading hope, Sam slumped in a chair, rested his head against its back and fought with the idea of ending his life.

17 DECISION

Sampson

Sam jolted awake and was flooded with relief as he realized the pain in his side was only a cramp and not from a self-inflicted attempt on his life. He was still alive.

A glance at the red numbers on his digital clock made the reason for the cramp clear. It was 3:20 a.m., and he'd apparently not moved in several hours. The room was cold. The conditions in the room matched his mood.

Sam smiled in the dark at the irony.

He'd slept, which may have saved his life, but now he didn't have any incentive to get up and move to his bed or call a taxi or do anything but let his mind replay with painful clarity the conversation with Rev. Ray from a few hours back.

Your sins have kept you from God. You can't see God's face because of your sins. Nothing that is sinful can enter Heaven. Only those can enter whose names are written in the Lamb's Book of Life.

A light tapping on the door interrupted his thoughts. He tried to ignore it. It came again. Moving his stiff muscles to get up required effort, but the soft taps wouldn't stop.

"Mr. Story? Why are you up?" Sam cleared his aching throat. "Is everything OK?"

"It is with me, son. How about with you?"

The kindness and caring behind those few words dislodged something stuck inside of Sam.

"I've been better, sir. Come in."

Johnson Story sat in the chair Sam just vacated, and Sam sat on the edge of his bed. He didn't have any words to say. He was just glad the old man had come.

"Having a little trouble are you, Sam? The Hound of Heaven after you?"

"What was that?"

"Oh, nothing. I just couldn't seem to sleep, and you came to mind. Thought you might like the company."

"I'm a fool, Mr. Story. I've been walking around in an arrogant, self-sufficient fog since I came here. I thought this place and Rev. Ray and Ms. Charity needed me and all the business skills I have to keep the inn going. I even thought I had something to offer Alaine Albert and her baby. I guess I figured I could keep rescuing her like I did back in September. Truth is, I'm a helpless jerk who can't do anything."

"Well then, I guess God has you right about where he wants you."

Sam expected commiseration, maybe even sympathy. He hadn't expected this response.

"If you don't mind telling me, sir, where do you think God wants me?"

"He works with us best when we come to the end of ourselves. I should know. He's kept me pretty much at the end of myself most of my adult life."

"Why would God have anything to do with people like me who don't buy into religion?"

"He made you, young man. Rest assured he loves you. My Bible says he loved me so much, even when I was hopelessly lost in my sins, that he sent his Son to take my sins onto himself. The Savior allowed himself to be sacrificed on that cross for my sins and yours. He certainly didn't have any. He was perfect. It is because of what he suffered that I can be forgiven."

"Mr. Story, I can't say I understand how this all works. I do know I'm at the end of all I know. I just don't have any idea what I'm supposed to do."

Johnson Story reached his hand across the space between them and laid it on Sam's arm. Sam could see tears in the old man's eyes.

"There's nothing you can do, son. You have to believe it's true and have faith. My Bible says, 'For it is by grace you have been saved, through faith, and this is not from yourselves, it is the gift of God.' He wants us to have faith that's strong enough to do what God says we should do. We have to repent to God, tell Him we're sorry for our sins and put our trust in His Son, Jesus Christ to take those sins away. There's a verse that says, 'Without faith it is impossible to please God.'"

"That's it?"

"That's all you can do, young man. The Lord Jesus did the rest. Just make a decision to follow Him. It's your choice."

Sam bowed his head. The tears on his cheeks matched Johnson Story's. Sam reached out and grasped the thin brown hand stretched toward his.

# # #

Sam didn't expect to sleep any more after the night's events, but he did, long and well. He stood beside his bed in the new day and wondered where it would go from here. Last night he was sure his step of...*faith,* as Johnson Story called it, was the clear and right move. He understood his need; he meant his decision. He knew his salvation was free. About that, Johnson Story made sure. Sam was forgiven. He finally got that. It was the *what next?* that concerned him.

As much as Sam wanted to tell Alaine what he'd done, he waited. He did manage to ask Ms. Charity for a few days off, saying only that he needed a break after the holidays. He asked her to explain to the others that he was taking some time so they wouldn't wonder.

Rather than leave the Inn during his hiatus, Sam scrounged the Inn's pantries for sustenance staples: peanut butter, jelly, bread ends, whatever seemed unlikely of being used and in danger of being tossed. Taking his stores to his room where he kept a small refrigerator, Sam withdrew behind his closed door.

He had felt ignorant before, but not like this. How could he know more about this God he chose to follow? There was so much to learn. Johnson Story showed him the promise of I Chronicles 28:9, "If you seek him, he will be found by you..." Mr. Story said to start reading the Bible in the book of John. Each Inn room housed a Gideon's copy of the Bible. For hours, Sam read and prayed. He struggled to understand what he read. He knew the words, but the language was strange to him, the ideas and content stranger. Still he kept reading.

When he became completely confused, he stopped to pray. When he tired of praying, he ate crackers and cheese or peanut butter and slipped out for a long walk before coming back to begin reading again. Johnson Story had also shown him in Hebrews that God "rewards those who earnestly seek him."

Sam read about the true Light that came to the world only to be rejected by the world. He measured his past life against what he read. He was guilty of rejecting the Light. Sam's life had been one of hard reality, right or wrong.

He thought long about the words of John the Baptist calling Jesus the Lamb of God who takes away the world's sins...including Sam's own sins.

He read about Jesus changing the water into wine and about the visit of Nicodemus to Jesus by night. He read the only verse he remembered hearing prior to coming to the Inn, John 3:16. He read Jesus' own words; "For God so loved the world that He gave His one and only Son, that whoever believes in Him should not perish but have everlasting life."

Sam read that men without Christ love darkness because they believe it hides their evil acts. He read that those who do right are not afraid to come to the Light and have their actions made public because they are pleasing to God.

He read about how Jesus fed 5,000 people and how he walked on the Sea of Galilee. He read about the adulteress who, rather than being condemned by the Savior, was told to go and sin no more.

And then he came to the passage in John 8 where Christ said, "Very truly I tell you, everyone who sins is a slave of sin." And "if the Son sets you free, you shall be free indeed."

He had never been one for self-reflection, but however painful, self-examination now seemed in order. Sam realized if he was to be really free, he had to face the shame of the things in his past that, though forgiven, still weren't made right. Some things were gone and could never be revisited. Other things would have to be rectified as much as possible, when and where he could.

Despite all of his shortcomings, one act in Sam's memory stood out above all the rest. While not typical behavior for Sam, the truth remained that he did steal the significant sum of money the day before the World Trade Center was hit from the old client, who likely could ill afford to lose it.

He'd never spent the money. It was still hidden away in Sam's duffle bag in the bottom of his closet, and he'd tried to forget the whole incident, what with the other drama in his life since September 11th. He remembered now, and he couldn't shake the thought of what he'd done.

It was time to talk to Rev. Ray again.

# # #

Rev. Ray didn't seem surprised to see him. "I've been waiting for you, son. Waiting and praying. Heard you had some good news for me." Rev. Ray first shook Sam's hand and then embraced him.

"I guess Mr. Story told you about my...about me...that I--"

"Got saved? Trusted Christ? Became a believer? There are lots of ways to say it, Sam, and they're all great. We've been praying for you since you got here...Charity and I, Danisha, Andi, Johnson and the members of my little church, and Alaine, too. You were lost, son, but now you're found. With all that praying, you never had a chance."

"Well, Reverend, I'm finding there's more to this new faith thing than I thought. I'm starting in pre-school. I have a lot to learn. That's all too clear to me now. But I didn't think I'd run into trouble with my choice to be a believer so quickly. I thought at least there would be some honeymoon time when things would go smoothly."

"What's the trouble? Are you regretting your decision already?" Rev. Ray was always direct.

Sam shook his head. "No regrets. I just need to run something by you. I can see this new road doesn't have room for shortcuts." He followed Rev. Ray's lead in taking a seat in front of the fireplace in the apartment.

Sam sat for a while looking into the fire. The older man waited, letting Sam have the time to process what he wanted to say.

"Rev. Ray, I'm a thief. You don't know what it costs me to tell you that. Don't misunderstand...I was used to being insincere and more than a little underhanded in the way I conducted my work back in the City. But barefaced stealing was beneath even me, until just before last September 11th."

"Tell me about it. I'm ready to listen." Rev. Ray leaned back in his recliner, his eyes closed. Sam knew he was in prayer.

Telling Rev. Ray about taking $10,000 from an old man who had entrusted him with his life's savings was a humiliating and painful process. It didn't help that he'd done the deed with no premeditation or that he left a portion of the money in the safe of the firm where he worked in World Trade Center 1. By anyone's definition, he was still a crook.

By now, Ray's recliner was upright. He watched with an unreadable look Sam could only assume was disgust. Sam couldn't help himself. He had to keep going despite the disappointment to his mentor.

"What was your plan to get away with this? How were you going to deal with the old man?"

"There was no plan. It was impulse. I doctored the firm's account of the money on the deposit information. Had he asked, I would have found a way to bamboozle the old man with talk of share prices, market conditions and future forecasts. He would never have known."

"How far did you get with that?"

"As it turns out, I stole the money on September 10th. By 10:30 a.m. on the next day, I assume all records of my company were buried in the rubble that was the North Tower. The only possible remaining evidence the transaction happened is a doctored agreement receipt signed by both of us showing he gave me one sixth of the money that actually changed hands. He never even noticed. I'm...I was that good."

"So, Sampson, what advice do you need from me?"

"What should I do now? The sin, and it was sin, has been forgiven. But--"

"But what? What's still bothering you?"

"I still have the money stored away. Never spent it. I think I have to return it to the old man, with interest, if I can find him. And he may want to press charges. He has every right to do that. I could go to jail."

Rev. Ray paused before responding. "You're right, you could. And what about your company? Would you consider that you stole from it, too?"

Sam's response was a slow nod.

"Do you remember the old man's name or anything that would allow you to trace him?"

"It's only been a few months, but I could never forget his name. If he's still living, I'll find him. I owe him his money. I've been pretty frugal since coming here and have some funds saved up for the interest. He'll get it and an apology. I'll ask for his forgiveness."

"And if he decides to press charges?" Rev. Ray raised his brows with the question. "What will you do then?"

"Pray he doesn't want to. Deal with it if he does. Unfortunately I have no excuse for what I did."

As Sam feared, Rev. Ray brought the discussion back to Sam's former company in the World Trade Center.

"Son, what kind of responsibility do you feel you have to your company for what you did?"

"The company doesn't exist anymore. I checked some time back. It went under after 9/11. I knew it was on rocky ground when I worked there. Competition was tough, and our track record wasn't great. I figured then it was a matter of time. I was right. September 11th was the final blow."

"So does that end it?"

Again Sam paused. "No, I need to find the CEO. From some research I did, he made it through the disaster. I need to apologize to him, too. Do you agree?"

"I agree. Sam, your plan's a good one. I'm proud of you for understanding what you need to do and why. These moves won't be easy, and the stakes are high. I should know. Prison's no fun. We'll pray with you that it won't come to that. But even so, you've shown a great deal of maturity and responsibility for meeting this thing head on and taking ownership for your actions."

"I'm ashamed. Even without Christ, I thought I was better than what I've done. No one knows but you...not even Alaine."

"Without Christ, Sam, we're all capable of most any evil. Few are exempt if the temptations are great enough or the enticements strong enough. With Christ, all of that can change. I know because I did."

Sam listened, trusting to learn from the older man's wisdom something that might relate to his own dilemma.

"Sam, there's a little more to my story I told you last night. Truth is, after I got saved and finally got out of jail, I've spent the next thirty something years trying to make right the wrongs I did as a young man."

"What do you mean? That was all a long time ago."

"It was, but like you, I remembered the names of a lot of my old customers and those I fought and wronged. I paid my debt to the law, but when I got out of prison, I tried to go to or contact those I took advantage of and ask for forgiveness. What I'm saying is, you're doing the right thing to go back to the City and talk to your boss and the old man. As a new person in Christ, making things right is the next step for you. Charity and I'll be praying, Sam. Whatever happens, your Heavenly Father knows about it and will show the way."

# # #

The next morning at 4:30 a.m at the Copper's Run Bus Station, Sam MacDonald got on the bus that would take him back to New York City in the same way that he came. He could have flown this time, or rented a car. He had the means, but going back by bus seemed right to Sam.

He left without talking to anyone but Rev. Ray, which meant that Ms. Charity would also know. He left word for her to explain things to Alaine, about his salvation and why he was going back to the City. And he told Rev. Ray to ask Johnson Story to pray.

Sam chose a seat on the bus and tried to sleep. When that didn't work, he tried to figure out why he'd left without talking to Alaine himself. He probably should have, but it was easier at the moment to let Ms. Charity speak for him. But Alaine still wouldn't know he loved her. The time just didn't seem right.

His first inclination had been to go to her before he left and tell her how he felt. It didn't take long for reality to convince him he needed to take care of a lot of overdue personal business first. As much as he wanted to do otherwise, Sam needed to think about Alaine later, if later allowed. Until then, she was in the best of hands at the Inn.

Rather than be distracted by the slow progress the bus made stopping at numerous little towns along the way, Sam used the time to pray for what lay ahead once he reached New York and to read his Bible, with which he was still largely unfamiliar. He'd been gone less than six months, but Sam felt as removed from the City as if he'd never lived there. He'd left as someone who narrowly escaped death. He was returning as one who had gained eternal life.

Somewhere around Washington, Sam dug the paper out of his duffle bag on which he'd scribbled several possible contact numbers for his former boss at his World Trade Center job and the old client from whom he'd stolen the $10,000. He'd tracked down the leads using a combination of the Internet and old fashioned New York City directory assistance.

Holding the paper with the leads to the two persons made Sam's mission become real. His stomach and neck muscles tightened from reading the information again. What had felt noble back in Copper's Run suddenly seemed like a fast track to prison.

He took out his cell phone and dialed the first number for his former boss, a man he remembered as gruff and unfriendly, named Rupert Tann.

"The number you have dialed is not a working number."

He hung up and dialed again. The message was the same. Sam scratched that lead off of his list. On the next try, he reached the right man. He could tell by the voice that answered the phone before Sam even spoke.

"Mr. Tann, this is Sampson MacDonald. I used to work for you at the World Trade Center. Could we talk for a minute?"

"MacDonald? I thought you were dead. We all thought you were dead."

"No, I made it out. Look, I won't take much of your time. I just need to meet with you for a few minutes. Do you think that might be possible? Sometime soon. I'm on my way to the City now. Should be there by tomorrow night."

"MacDonald, let's not waste each other's time. It's good you made it out, but there's nothing I can do for you if you're here about the firm. There's nothing left. Bankrupt. Everything's gone."

"I'm sorry to hear that, Mr. Tann. I'm not here to make any demands. I have something I need to talk to you about in person. It's important to me...won't take long. Do you think we could we meet somewhere?"

As it happened, there was a McDonald's within walking distance of Rupert Tann's home in Queens. To Sam's surprise, Tann agreed to the meeting.

He sat back in his seat with his eyes closed. He'd failed to pray before he made his call, but he didn't forget now. He would need help to explain his purpose to his old boss.

For some reason, calling Rupert Tann, as hard as it was, seemed easy compared to the thought of facing the old man from whom he had stolen the money. The man's face became clearer to Sam the nearer the bus came to New York City. His name was Ben Ledford.

Finally, it was only the knowledge that Ms. Charity, Rev. Ray and Mr. Story were back in Copper's Run praying for him that made Sam able to make the call to the first number he had for Mr. Ledford on his now wrinkled and creased list.

The first call resulted in a conversation with a voice that sounded young, Hispanic and unaware of anything about the man Sam described to him. Sam wiped the sweat from his face in spite of the 42 degree temperature.

The second number rang busy. The busy signal persisted across at least ten tries over two hours. Sam put a large question mark next to that number and tried the next and last number on his list, sending up a cry for help as he punched in the digits.

He misdialed twice. When the call finally connected, his mouth was so dry he could hardly talk and his heart pounded. A woman answered.

"Hello, my name is Sampson MacDonald. I'm trying to reach Mr. Ben Ledford. The Mr. Ledford I need is probably at least 75. I met him last year at the investment business where I worked. Do you know anything about this man? This is very important."

There was a pause. "I know him. May I ask why you need to speak with Mr. Ledford?"

How much should he tell this woman? Would she prevent him from reaching the old man?

"Mr. Ledford was a client at the company where I worked in the World Trade Center prior to September 11th. We had some business together. My need to speak with him involves our transaction, but I also have a personal message I need to deliver to him. It is very important that I have the opportunity to speak with him."

Another pause. "The man you are looking for is my father. He is not well, Mr... MacDonald was it? Is this a matter I could assist you with on his behalf?"

"If there is any way at all, if he is well enough even for a brief visit, I would much prefer to talk with your father directly. If that is out of the question, then I will certainly speak with you. Do you think he might spend a few minutes with me?"

"I will have to ask him, Mr. MacDonald. My father is in the hospital. I was just leaving for a visit. Is it possible for you to call me back tomorrow? Perhaps I'll have a response to your request by then."

"Yes, of course. I'll call you tomorrow night, if that's convenient. Please be assured that this is important or I wouldn't presume to bother your father at all. I give you my promise that I will respect his well-being in any conversation I have with him."

# # #

Sam was as exhausted by the phone calls as he'd ever been after a full workday in the Trade Center. Never had he felt as inept and exposed. While there was no doubt that his course of action was the right thing to do, the knowledge didn't prevent him from thinking about simply disappearing as he'd done after 9/11.

Running could get to be a habit. There were only so many chances to start over before his mistakes would follow and catch up with him. As tempting as it was, Sam rejected the plan.

It was an eerie feeling to arrive back in the City at the same bus station from which he and Alaine left more than six months earlier. It was a snap decision made in this very station, or in Heaven itself, that put Alaine and him on their journey to Copper's Run. Sam drew a long, slow breath. In a few short months, Copper's Run had become home. For how much longer, he had no guess.

18 CONFESSIONS

Sampson

It was 7:45 p.m., a little late for setting up a meeting, but Sam was going to give it a try. He found a men's room in the bus station and cleaned up before punching in Rupert Tann's number. The man answered on the first ring.

"Mr. Tann? It's Sampson MacDonald."

"I'm ready when you are. When do you want me there?"

"I can meet you by nine tonight. Is that too late?"

"I want to hear what you have to say. I'll be there."

Sam punched in the number to reach the daughter of Ben Ledford. He rejected his impulse to bypass her and try to find the man at an area hospital. On second thought, he remembered she hadn't given him the name of the hospital in a city of over 100 such institutions. Then there was the trust factor. The daughter was his inroad to see the old man, if he would even agree to it.

There was no answer on her phone. Sam left a message, found a taxi and headed out to meet his former boss.

The McDonalds in Queens where Sam's first uncomfortable encounter was to take place seemed busy for this time of night, but then Sam had grown accustomed to life in Copper's Run where 9:00 p.m. was considered late. He arrived ten minutes early, ordered a black coffee and sat where he could view both entrances.

At 9:05 Rupert Tann walked in and glanced around.

Sam rose to meet him, right hand extended. He dropped the hand when he remembered that the man never shook. His surprise when the man stuck out his own hand was multiplied when he heard his greeting.

"MacDonald, good to see you made it. No one heard anything from you. We assumed the worst."

"I didn't know you'd survived either until recently when I started looking for how to contact you. You may not think it's good when you find out what I have to say."

"Well, let's sit and hear it now. I told you, though, I have nothing to offer."

"Would you like anything? Coffee?"

"No. It keeps me up...when I can sleep." He laughed. Sam nodded at the irony, and Tann continued. "I see it doesn't bother you."

They sat and Sam didn't waste time.

"I know when I worked for you back before 9/11, there was no love lost between us. You knew I hated the job. I knew you thought I was a loser. Seems you were right on both counts."

"MacDonald, that was then. Old news."

"It's the truth. Please hear me out." Sam paused long enough to take a couple of gulps of his tepid coffee. It amazed him how relaxed Tann appeared in spite of all he'd gone through. Sam was anything but relaxed as he prepared to reveal why he'd come.

"I want you to know that the morning before the planes hit, I stole $10,000 from one of the older clients, Mr. Ben Ledford. He brought in $12,000 in cash. I recorded it as a $2,000 transaction and put that amount in the safe with a doctored record. The other $10K I slipped in my pocket. It's still there." He patted the breast pocket of his jacket.

"I also want you to know I've been in touch with Ledford's daughter. He's in the hospital. I plan to meet with him, if he'll see me, and let him know what

I did. I have his money. I plan to return it to him plus the interest he could have expected with us. I've been working. I'm good for it."

"What if that's not enough? What if he brings charges?"

"Then he does, and I'll deal with it. I deserve whatever happens. It would be his right."

They sat silent for a few minutes with Rupert Tann looking around and Sam focusing on his former boss. Then Sam spoke again.

"When I stole from Mr. Ledford, I stole from your company, too. You have the same right to turn me in for embezzlement from your firm. That was $10,000 that your company didn't have to invest and take your commission. You have to do whatever you think best to protect your investors and yourself."

"Why are you doing this, young man? You have everything to lose. What could possibly be your reasoning?"

"Mr. Tann, I've come a long way from that man who worked in your firm in the World Trade Center. I made it out of the North Tower and left the City after 9/11, hoping to start over in any place that wasn't New York City. I ended up in a small town in Virginia, as different from where and how I'd been living as possible. I needed more than a new start. I needed a new worldview. It took the help of a couple of aging ex-convicts to help me understand that where I was living wasn't the problem. I was the problem. I had to deal with how I was living...and for whom."

"You got religion, didn't you, MacDonald?"

"No sir, I wouldn't put it that way. I found Jesus Christ. After I did that, the next step was trying to make things right with people I'd wronged. You and Mr. Ledford are at the top of my list."

"Commendable. Often happens after a particularly stressful event. You may wake up one morning and feel foolish when you look back on this. Suppose one of us does decide to press charges?"

"I've considered that. I made the decision to see you with that very much in mind, believe me."

Rupert Tann watched Sam, saying nothing, for longer than Sam was comfortable.

"Well," Tann finally answered, "I wouldn't be too worried. On my account, that is. The business is gone. Everything. All destroyed in the building's collapse. You're surely aware we were never that careful about paperwork...or insurance, I'm afraid. I discovered a little too late about the benefits of backing up everything and making sure we kept up with our premiums."

"What about the clients?" Sam asked. "They had their monthly statements. Didn't that help to set everything back up? When they contact you, you could--"

"Bankruptcy, Sampson. If the clients do make contact, they're referred to the bankruptcy lawyers. I meant what I said. There's nothing left. It's all gone. Turning you in for embezzlement would be a joke, a waste of time. Forget about it."

"I won't pretend that I enjoyed my job at your firm, but I am sorry for what's happened to you. And I've figured up about what the normal earnings the company would have made on Mr. Ledford's money in the amount of time I've held it." Sam held out an envelope.

Rupert Tanner waived him off and rose to go. "I want nothing from you, MacDonald. You're off the hook. Go see the old man, if you dare. But I think you're crazy. I think your religion has gone to your head."

"Not my head, Mr. Tann. My heart. Thank you, sir, for your time. I apologize for my actions. I hope you will forgive me." Tann turned to walk away. "And Mr. Tann?"

"What is it?"

"Would you mind if I kept you in my prayers?"

The man took a long time to respond. Sam stood. Finally, Rupert Tann offered his hand. "On the off chance that it'll do some good, I guess I can live with that."

# # #

It was 11:00 p.m. before Sam reached the place where he was staying while in New York. Ironically, his landlady from before his exit to Copper's Run still had his old room available. He'd called earlier on the outside chance that she'd saved the personal effects abandoned at her home, even if they'd spent the last few months in her basement.

Sam was surprised when Lettie Baker greeted him with obvious pleasure and had, indeed, saved his belongings. She welcomed him back for the duration of his visit to the City.

Mrs. Baker was eager to stretch out the reunion, to catch up on what Sam had been doing since he left. But the collective weight of the trip and the meeting with Rupert Tann left him too exhausted to visit.

He slept for eleven hours and would have slept on had his cell phone not awakened him. It was Ben Ledford's daughter. The old man was feeling better and would meet with him in the afternoon.

Now wide awake, Sam agreed to be at the designated hospital at 3:00 p.m. The reality that the meeting with Ledford was imminent brought him face to face with the possibility that the outcome could be the end of his freedom. Alaine's face, which he had purposely suppressed during his trip, now flashed to the forefront of his mind.

For the first time in his life, Sam knelt beside the bed in his old rented room. He was growing accustomed to praying, but this time he prayed with a fervor stemming from shame and fear. His actions at the theft of the money months before still left him so ashamed that his faced burned when he thought about it, alone as he was. His fear of possible incarceration threatened to overcome him. Still he prayed on, first begging God for mercy and then asking for strength to take whatever God allowed. After all, he was guilty.

Elderly and somewhat lonely, his landlady insisted on preparing bacon and pancakes for Sam's breakfast, even though it was nearly time for lunch. He tried to dissuade her, as food was far from his thoughts. Finally, so as not to hurt her feelings, Sam ate two helpings in her kitchen while she questioned him about why he left town so suddenly, where he went and what he'd been doing.

Sam needed to be alone. Her genuine interest and motherly concern arrested his intention to escape as soon as possible. Unplanned, he found himself telling her his story. Mrs. Baker listened without interruption and without evidence of judging his actions. While he provided her the short version, Sam was struck for the first time with how bizarre the events and actions of the last few months sounded to his own ears, much less how they would to others.

When he completed his tale, Sam folded his napkin, laid it beside of his plate and reached into his wallet.

"Mrs. Baker, I want to compensate you in some way for the trouble you went to after I disappeared. Most landlords would have sold what was abandoned in the room and rented it out again as soon as possible. Tell me, what made you decide to store my things?"

"Something told me you'd be back for them, sonny. Must have been the Lord. I just didn't think you'd gotten yourself killed in the World Trade Center. I had faith you'd be back. Must have been the Lord, I'll say."

"I never asked you this before. I never cared before now. Mrs. Baker, are you a believer? I mean, do you follow Christ?"

"I do, sonny, for 65 years now, since I was a child. I prayed for you while you lived here, and even after you were gone, I still prayed for you. How about you? Have you been saved, Sampson?"

"I have. Only for a few days, but I have."

"Then you've just paid me all I need, child. My prayers have been answered. Hallelujah!"

Encouraged by Lettie Baker's enthusiasm, Sam called a taxi to deliver him to the Kings County Hospital Center in Brooklyn. As he exited the taxi at the hospital's main entrance, he checked around, once more half expecting to be greeted and arrested by representatives of the NYPD.

Whispering a prayer of thanks that his arrival was uneventful, Sam asked at the visitors' desk for the room of the gentleman he sought. Again, the elevator ride to the correct floor left him wondering if he would still be a free man when he walked out of the facility.

I'd never make it as a career criminal. I couldn't live life on the run.

Sam paused outside of Ben Ledford's room, asking for guidance to say the right words, to handle the humiliating situation correctly.

His light knock was met by the unsmiling face of a woman Sam presumed, from his phone conversations, to be Ledford's daughter. She nodded when he introduced himself, but didn't offer her hand. What she did do was walk to her father's side where he lay with his eyes closed.

"Dad? Sampson MacDonald is here."

The speed with which the old man opened his eyes and appraised him made Sampson know that his eyes were not shut in sleep.

I think he's been praying. The intuition hit Sam and left him shaking before he even spoke to the person lying with his hand outstretched, reaching for Sam's response.

Sam met him with his own hand closing around the one that felt frail but had a grip that warned Sam not to count him out yet.

"Hello, sir. Thank you for seeing me. I hope that what I have to say won't upset you. I give you my word from the start that I will do everything in my power to make things right."

"I remember you, Mr. MacDonald. You worked with the Tann and Leisch Investment Services before the Trade Center disaster. What could you possibly say to me this morning that would upset me? I've already lost my savings with your group when the Towers came down. When I inquired with the authorities,

I was notified that your firm is in bankruptcy and there's no formal record that I even invested my money, except for the receipt I have that's a bit hard to understand."

The voice was weak but had a hard edge to it. Sam guessed he would get no quarter from the old fellow. He'd made his bed, and now was the time to occupy it.

"Mr. Ledford, for what it's worth, I'm your witness that you gave me six envelopes with two thousand dollars, in cash, in each envelop on September 10th, 2001. Two thousand of it went into the safe for processing with my firm with doctored paperwork making it appear as if that's all you deposited. There was a reason the receipt you hold is confusing."

By now, the old man was struggling to sit up. Without taking his eyes off of Sam, he gestured for his daughter to move the bed into a more upright position.

Sam continued speaking despite the fact that his mouth was so dry he could barely talk and his heart rate elevated far above what he knew was normal.

"The remaining ten thousand dollars I put into my suit pocket without your knowledge and carried it home that evening. It remained in my suit coat and returned to work with me the next day. I did struggle at the time with why I did it and what I should do with the money, but there was no doubt that I had all intentions of keeping it for myself.

"That next morning, the planes hit the Trade Towers. I left the building safely, and a few days later, I left town. I've been living in another state since then. In reality, I have a new job and a new life. I never spent your money."

Sam extended six envelopes with Mr. Ledford's name scribbled on the front...five envelopes he had received from the man and one additional one.

"You will find here the ten thousand that I stole from you along with the other two thousand that you lost when our firm went down. I've tried my best to figure what a fair return on your investment would be had I deposited it all and had 9/11 not happened. I've included that amount also plus a small additional amount for your trouble."

Sam looked at the old man and his daughter. Both were watching him with the stunned and puzzled expressions of those who cannot believe information they are receiving.

"I promised at the beginning of this conversation that I'd do everything within my power to make this right. That includes allowing you to call the authorities and turn me in. I'll wait here until they come, if that's what you decide to do."

With that said, Sam turned to look for a chair, and finding two near the window, he took a seat and put his head into his hands. He was sweating and shaking worse than when he raced to escape death in the North Tower.

For several minutes there was no further conversation in the room. Sam worked to get his emotions and physical reactions under control and be prepared for whatever came next. When his breathing slowed and the pounding in his head subsided a bit, he raised his eyes toward the father and daughter across the small hospital room.

The old man was lying back against the pillows on his bed, which had been lowered again to recline. His daughter was bending over him holding his hands. To Sam's surprise, Ben Ledford was smiling as he asked a question.

"Why?"

Still struggling with composure, Sam finally responded, "I don't know why. I've had a hard time with that. Because it was easy and you were...or I thought you were...vulnerable. Because I was greedy. Worse yet, because I was just outright dishonest."

"No, Mr. MacDonald. Why did you come to return the money and tell me your story? You said you started over. Why are you here now?"

"If I tell you, you're going to think I'm trying to influence your decision about what to do. All I can say is, that's not true."

"Why don't you try me? I've nothing better to do than hear you out."

The daughter went to the window and stood with her back to the room, as if to remove herself and give Sam a measure of privacy. Or because she was too angry to face him. Either way, what he read into her actions didn't matter. Nothing mattered except to see this thing through to the end, regardless of the outcome.

"I did tell you I have a new life. That new life has recently included a faith in God and a personal commitment to Jesus Christ, His Son. I sinned against you, sir, and it certainly was not my first and only sin. I've asked for forgiveness for those sins and trusted Christ to give me a new start. Part of that new start is the need to make as right as I can the wrong I did against you. In light of that, I ask your forgiveness for what I did. By the same token, I don't ask you to forget my actions. They were wrong. I deserve whatever consequences you decide to bring. That's why I'm here."

The old man was quiet for so long, his eyes closed and his face serene, that Sam knew his revelation had killed him. When Sam moved toward the bed, the daughter intervened.

"Daddy's fine. Let him be."

Sam leaned against the wall in silence until the old man opened his eyes at last.

"This last year has been most disturbing for me, Mr. MacDonald. I lost my wife, my health and then the last of my savings. I've been feeling sorry for myself, a little like Job from the Old Testament. Do you know that story?"

"No, sir. Not yet."

"No time to tell it now. Look it up when you have a chance. Book of Job. Old Testament. I've been whining to God, whom I've followed as faithfully as I could for 50 years. He reminded me this morning that my life was his to do with as he pleased. A few minutes after that, my doctor told me I'm going to make it through this current crisis. And now you walk in with my money. Some people would call all of this a colossal coincidence. I call it God sitting in

Heaven doing as He pleases. I learned that from Psalm 115. Look that up, too."

"Dad, I think you've had enough excitement for today. Mr. MacDonald--" The old man gently interrupted his daughter.

"Thank you, honey, for taking such good care of me. You're probably right, but I need a few more minutes of Mr. MacDonald's time. Would you mind leaving us alone for a little while? I'll be fine."

The daughter left, with reluctance and a warning look at Sam.

"Mr. MacDonald, the time we have here on this earth is precious. I've learned that from my 75 years of experience. Heaven will undoubtedly be more precious, but the Lord told us to occupy ourselves while we are here. How old are you?"

"Twenty-seven."

"You've wasted most of that time, by eternity's standards, if you lived your life without the Lord. Maybe you should pay society for what you've done. Maybe I should turn you in. With all the evidence destroyed, you'd never be convicted, and to turn yourself in would just waste more of your time. From what you've told me, I believe you've learned your lesson. If you really came to know Christ like you say you did, you have a lot of time to make up. You need to start right now. Give me your hand."

Sam took Ben Ledford's hand.

"Lord, this young man has asked for my forgiveness. I believe you have already done that for him, so I can do no less. Give him wisdom to know how to live for you and opportunities to make up the time he's lost. I'm going to send him on his way now, Lord, but I look forward to spending more time with him in eternity. Amen."

The wrinkled hand gripped his and then gestured for him to leave. Sam started to speak, but the old eyes were again closed, and so he walked quietly out of the room, meeting the no longer unfriendly eyes of the daughter as she slipped past him to rejoin her father.

Sam's first thought, as he rode the elevator down to exit the hospital, was praise to his new-found Heavenly Father for the mercy He chose to extend in the events of the last few days. The second was exhilaration that the dread connected to his past wrongdoing was gone. No need to expect the NYPD to tap him on the shoulder at every turn. He was free, both from the sin and from the fear. For the first time Sam understood what Rev. Ray meant when he talked about being free indeed.

It was time to go home, and home was not the rooming house in Queens, as dear as Mrs. Baker had turned out to be. Home was Copper's Run, Rev. Ray, Ms. Charity...home was Alaine.

He'd have to go back and make arrangements to have his Queens' belongings shipped to Copper's Run. That wouldn't take long. Then, maybe a good night's sleep and an early morning bus were the only things between him and the Virginia countryside.

19 MISSING

Sampson

It was difficult for Sam not to stop strangers on the street to share how things had worked out beyond his highest hopes. As this was, after all, New York City, he restrained himself, but it was impossible to stop the flow of thanksgiving and praise he silently shouted toward Heaven. Thinking how uncharacteristic this inner behavior would be to the old Sam made him laugh aloud.

A taxi ride back to his accommodations took longer than expected. The traffic was heavy, even for New York standards. Sam refused to let the delays diminish his spirits.

His first act after reaching the privacy of his room at Mrs. Baker's was to call the Inn. He knew Rev. Ray and Ms. Charity would be ready to hear the outcome of his mission. He was confident their support and prayers had affected the conclusion.

It took seven rings for the Brights' private phone to answer. Sam knew after the first sentence from Ms. Charity that something was wrong. In order to delay asking her what, he ignored his instincts and jumped at the chance to respond to her question about his New York encounters.

"Here, let me put Ray on the other line so he can hear this, too, Sam. We don't want to miss a single detail."

He gave her what she wanted, too many details, about the meetings with his former boss and his landlady. They responded with predictable feedback, but something in their tone was off. Sam had just started on the story of his conference with Mr. Ledford when he interrupted his own monologue.

"What's wrong? Something's wrong, isn't it? I hear it in your voices. Rev. Ray, are you O.K? Tell me. Is it the baby?"

It was Ms. Charity who answered first.

"Sam, Alaine is gone. She left two days ago, not long after you did."

"What do you mean, *gone*? Ms. Charity...gone where?"

Rev. Ray answered. "Son, I'm going to give this to you straight up. It appears that Alaine may have left to join her baby's father. One of the guests told us he saw her get into a taxi at the street in front of the Inn."

"Not Paul Mowher!" Sam's response was explosive and unpleasant.

"I'm afraid so. Several hours after she left, Andi found a phone message on the reservation line. It came in the middle of the night. I think the call was made when there was little chance anyone would talk to her."

"What did she say?"

"That she knew we wouldn't understand or approve, but she's gone to be with her baby's father. That she'd considered her move carefully and felt it was the right thing to do, both for her and her child, who would need a father."

What? No!

This news made no sense to Sam, based on what Alaine told him about her decision to break all contact with Paul Mowher.

"Do you believe that? Do you really think she's left of her own free will? She's afraid of Mowher. Alaine knows him better than any of us. It's impossible to accept she would just go off with him without talking it over with anyone, knowing how we all feel about him...knowing what he's capable of."

"Quite frankly, Sam, we don't know what to think. We'd already advised her about our concerns over him before you left." Ms. Charity was uncharacteristically subdued. "We all thought we knew where she stood, but it's possible she changed her mind and made this decision on her own. She may have chosen to join Mowher. However unlikely, we do have to consider that outcome."

Sam didn't have a quick response. It was unthinkable that Alaine could choose Mowher. Maybe over him, yes. That hurt. But not over staying safe and cared for at the Inn. His respect for the Brights forced him to consider, at least, the possibility they raised. He tried, but silently and immediately shook his head.

"Sampson? Are you there?"

"I'm here, Ms. Charity. I just don't have a clue what to say. Look, I understand your uncertainty. There's no way we can know for sure why she left short of asking her. You may accuse me of not being realistic or failing to face the facts. But no way will I ever believe she left the Inn on her own...no way. Something's wrong. I'm sure of it."

"We don't know where she is, Sam. Even if we were sure she left under pressure or worse, we have no idea where they've gone. If Mowher took her, we don't know that they went back to New York. They could be anywhere."

Sam had never heard Ms. Charity this disturbed, even when Rev. Ray was sick. Sam tried to make his questions sound less uneasy.

"She didn't leave any clues at all? She didn't say anything else in her message or do anything out of the ordinary before she left?"

Ms. Charity was still on the line. "Not that any of us can think of, and we've been over the message and everything that happened since you left a hundred times. We can't come up with anything."

"What about her room? Has anyone been in there? Did she take everything? Maybe she left something that would help."

"We could try that. Her room's locked. We didn't go in before now because we were sure she'd come back. We didn't want to invade her privacy. Sam, I know it sounds like we've been bumbling around here since we got Alaine's message. Maybe so, but having her leave like this was such a shock. We did talk to our local police chief, and unless there is some reason to think she left under duress, there's not a lot the authorities can do."

At this point, Ms. Charity's voice quavered, and Rev. Ray took the lead.

"Sampson, the truth is, we don't know what to do. Only the Lord can give us direction now. We're trusting Him to do that. You do the same. We'll search out Alaine's room and call you back as soon as we're done. Since you're already in the City, you may want to stay put until you hear from us."

"Yes, sir, I will. And I'm trying to trust, too."

Sam closed his cell phone and sat on the edge of his bed. Just when his life had a chance of looking up in a way that hadn't seemed possible in recent memory, one of the main reasons had disappeared. This couldn't be happening.

Sam prayed... for Alaine and the baby, for the folks at the Inn, for God's will and for the strength to bear whatever it turned out to be.

And he prayed for help. He needed to think clearly about where Mowher might have taken her and what he had in mind because Sam didn't believe for one minute that Alaine would go to him on her own.

It was two hours before the next call from the Inn came...two hours during which Sam had time to find out in person what it meant to have the Holy Spirit pray in his place when he no longer could. Sam was prayed out.

"I'm here. Did you find out anything?"

"Oh, Sam." It was Ms. Charity. "I'm so glad you suggested we check Alaine's room. It doesn't look like she took anything. Her clothes are there, her cosmetics, her suitcase, looks like everything. If she took anything, it couldn't have been much."

"OK, that might mean she plans to start over with Mowher, which I don't believe for a second, or it could mean she left fast...didn't have time to pack. Was there anything at all out of place or unusual? Did she write something?

Any notes? Anything that might possibly help?"

"There was a notepad with a message scribbled on it. It appeared as if she wrote it fast. The writing wasn't neat like Alaine's usually is."

"Could you make out what it said?"

"It was to you, Sam. The note was for you."

"Alright. Alright." Sam found it hard to talk. "What did it say? Tell me now. What did she write?"

"I'm reading. It said, 'Sam, no way to thank you. You saved my life. Always grateful. Won't forget you. Know how you feel, but have to go to baby's father. Please understand. Don't follow me. Please. A.'"

No. She doesn't mean it. It's not right. It can't be right.

Sam had to know...had to ask.

"Did she know about me...my decision to follow Christ? And about why I went to New York? Did you have time to tell her?"

"She did. We shared it with her like you wanted the afternoon before she left."

"Listen to me, Ms. Charity. I hear her words, but I don't accept they're the truth. Maybe Alaine wrote it, but I know that she would never...she would never go by choice to that man. Something's wrong with the whole thing. I have to find out what."

"What are you going to do?"

"I'm going to start by trying to find out where Mowher lives in the City. Alaine never told me. I should have already started. It could take some time and might be useless, but I have to do something. I'll let you know how it goes."

"What should we do?"

"Stay by the phones in case Alaine calls again. Keep your eyes out for anything there that might help. Tell Rev. Ray and the others to keep praying. I don't have much experience at it, but I'm getting some fast."

# # #

Sam was surprised to find no entries for Paul Mowher in the New York phone book. He expected to find a long listing, starting with P. Mowher and continuing. He found Mower and Mowhir and Mowry...but not Mowher at all.

Directory assistance was willing but unable to help either. There was still nothing for Mowher, new or unlisted. Dead end.

The Internet might help, but the closest available one was at the public library three blocks away. Twenty minutes later Sam had checked in to the facility's computer access booth and put in a search for "Paul Mowher." There was an accountant in Little Rock by that name, but the picture online didn't match the man Sam knew. A physician in Philadelphia specialized in Gerontology, but again there was no way this was the man. No Paul Mowher showed up in the whole state of New York. Again, dead end.

Please, God. What do I do now? I believe he's got her. I think he's unbalanced. No telling what he might do. God, I could use some serious help now.

With hands jammed in his pockets and his head down, Sam started the three block walk back to the boarding house. It was 2:00 in the afternoon, his head pounded and Alaine was missing. That meant the baby was missing, too.

He wanted to run and hit things and yell out to the City that he needed help to find Alaine. Instead he was forced to hold himself in check and think.

Think. Where could he turn?

Not the police yet. There was nothing substantial to tell them. How could he explain what he felt...knew to be true with no real proof? He'd quickly be labeled a nut case himself. Nut case? Paul Mowher was the crazy one...wasn't he?

Maybe he was over-reacting. Maybe his vested emotional interests were influencing his ability to read the situation clearly. Could it be possible he simply didn't want to face facts that Alaine had changed her mind and now actually wanted to be with Mowher?

He needed to talk to somebody who could give him some objective information or advice.

Sam turned around and double-timed it back to the library. Somebody there would know where the nearest medical facilities were. He needed an opinion, however far removed, from a psychiatric professional.

# # #

"Good afternoon. How may I help you today?"

The receptionist at the front desk of the QuickMed Center glanced back at the large wall clock as she greeted him. It was now 2:30 p.m. What were his chances of finding anyone here with psychiatric training who could talk to him about Paul Mowher just from Sam's descriptions?

"Look, this might sound a bit strange, but what I need is..." In as few words and with as little emotion as possible, Sam explained his dilemma to the young woman. "I realize this is unusual, and I'm willing to pay for the conversation, but please understand that this is of critical importance. If there is any way you can help me, please do."

The young woman never broke eye contact with Sam during his request. Her reaction betrayed no indication that she thought his request out of the ordinary. She took his name and contact information before speaking again.

"Please have a seat, Mr. MacDonald. Let me see if there is anything we can do."

She was gone for fifteen minutes. When she came back, a woman in a white lab coat accompanied her holding a paper. The white coat lady addressed Sam.

"Mr. MacDonald? Could you follow me please?"

She took him to a small consultation room just beyond the main desk. She didn't sit or invite him to do so.

"Will you repeat your request to me again, Mr. MacDonald? I need to hear the same information that you gave to Ms. Vidik, our receptionist."

Again, Sam kept the summary of and reason for his request short. "I just need to talk to someone as soon as possible about a situation. You could call it hypothetical. I want, off the record really, some sort of opinion about whether a person who exhibits certain behaviors could be dangerous. I'm out of my league here. I need an idea of whether I should be worried about my friend or not. Is there anything you can do to help? I wouldn't be so insistent, but I don't think I have much time to lose."

The white coat lady handed him the paper she'd been holding. She still had not even introduced herself.

"Take this note to Dr. Bernard Weinstein. He's a psychiatrist with a wealth and vast range of experiences. Dr. Weinstein is retired and works as a consultant for us here at the Center. The address is on the note. His office is two blocks west. He's expecting you now." She led him out of the room and turned and disappeared into another room with no further conversation.

The receptionist merely smiled as he tried to thank her for her help. Two more blocks was a small price to pay for the chance to tell his story to a professional.

The office of Bernard Weinstein, MD, F.A.C.P., was only identified by a small brass plaque on the door with the doctor's name followed by an address and the instructions *Please Knock*. There was no receptionist, and the doctor himself admitted Sam to the waiting room and led him to a small adjoining office.

After an initial handshake and introductions, Dr. Weinstein began the conversation.

"Dr. Montrose at the QuickMed Center said that you requested a consultation. She indicated it was to be for a general opinion, off the record, with no additional follow up. Is that correct?"

"Yes, that's what I indicated." Sam was hoping, praying that the somewhat casual sounding request wouldn't be denied at this point simply because of its informal nature.

"Naturally, then there will be no formal diagnosis. I will simply be providing an informed opinion based on your hearsay description. Without much more in depth investigation on my part, I could not provide an official judgment. Am I being clear? Any actions on your part must be based on your best judgment of the circumstance."

"I understand you perfectly." Sam proceeded to provide all of the information he could remember about Paul Mowher, without using his name, from Alaine's first mention of him before September 11th through Sam's current concern over Alaine's disappearance.

He made every effort to provide the facts and his observations, even his fears, in a simple and straightforward way, without embellishment. When he finished, he put two questions before the doctor.

"Based on what I have told you, if the young lady, Alaine, were your daughter, would you be concerned? If she disappeared, would you think she went with the man I have described on her own?"

Dr. Weinstein didn't respond right away, rather he continued jotting notes as he had throughout Sam's account. Sam waited.

Weinstein met Sam's eyes, again not speaking for some time. Sam read his answers in the doctor's expression before he said a word.

"Mr. MacDonald, again I remind you that I am only providing an unofficial opinion to a hypothetical description which I would not stand behind without additional diagnostic information. But based on what I have heard, were it my daughter, I would be very concerned.

"You may have heard the term 'God complex' as referring to persons who are characterized by extreme arrogance and an inordinately inflated opinion of themselves. Stereotypically, these people often lack empathy and may treat others in an exploitive and callous manner. How others treat them, however, holds extraordinary importance to them as they may engage in fantasies about their unparalleled status and expect to be treated accordingly. Persons with a narcissistic personality disorder may be difficult to engage in therapy as they might consider therapeutic approaches to be criticisms, which they don't easily suffer."

Sam broke in, "Are these folks dangerous to others?"

"Without proper treatment, the disorder can easily cross the line into psychosis. If they feel threatened in any way, they can become volatile and violent. They can become, figuratively or literally, loaded guns. To respond to your question, in a word, *yes*, it is possible. In extreme cases, such persons can be exceptionally dangerous to those around them."

"What do you suggest I do?" Sam was starting to sweat even in the conditioned air.

"Find your friend as quickly as you can."

# # #

As Sam walked the seven blocks back toward the boarding house, he was enveloped in a blur of prayers and attempts to review each thing he had learned since Alaine's disappearance, although there was dreadful little that they knew.

He mustn't miss anything. There might be some detail that was important. He tried to keep it all straight. His brain treated it as a big puzzle with missing pieces. Each time he thought he'd matched two of the pieces together, his brain would scramble the puzzle, and he had to begin the matching process again.

Sam was exhausted, mentally and physically, and almost to the boarding house when his cell phone rang.

"Yes?"

"MacDonald?"

"Yes? Who's speaking?"

"Just listen. There's someone here I think you'd like to talk to."

Then, a voice he knew well.

"Sam, it's Alaine. I just wanted to tell you I'm fine. I...we're happy and together. I'm great, really. I'm sorry I had to leave the Inn so quickly. I wanted to be with Paul. He needed me and our baby. Thank you for understanding."

"Alaine, where are--?"

"MacDonald." Mowher took the phone. "That should put your mind at ease. Sorry, old boy. I guess the best man won. Well, nice talking to you. Catch you later."

And the connection was cut off.

20 JEOPARDY

Alaine

Thirty minutes out from the time Alaine's bus was scheduled to arrive at the Port Authority Station in midtown, she sat tense and cramped, considering whether she should slip to the front and beg the driver to let her off early. She didn't suppose he would. It was against the rules on this type of run, but maybe it was worth a try.

Alaine's mouth was dry, her head ached, and it was all she could do not to throw up. The fear she felt now was worse than she remembered from September 11th. But then she remembered very little of that day, and every second of this one seemed eternal.

Even as she clutched her handbag and small satchel that held the few things she brought with her and tensed her leg muscles in ready to move to the front of the bus, she knew she wouldn't do it.

Never had she faced a situation where only two options were open to her, and both would cause irreparable loss. Even when she lived with Paul Mowher back in the City, as horrible as that was, she always had the choice of walking away. It would have been risky, even dangerous, but the choice was there. She should have made it.

As it was now, to stop the bus and get off, even if she could, would signal the end for Sam MacDonald. Paul promised her that. To stay on the bus and be met by Paul at the station would subject her to God only knew what...ridicule, abuse, humiliation for certain...despite how he swore he would change.

"We'll go back and do it over, Alaine," he said. "It's important to me that we play it back and do it right this time."

Those were Paul Mowher's words when he'd called her to demand she return to the City to be with him. She had almost hung up on him, not believing for a second his promises. She hadn't broken the connection because of what he'd said next.

"If you don't come to me, Alaine, your new boyfriend, Mr. MacDonald, will die. If you don't agree to come now, and if you fail to make all your friends believe it was your idea, your heart's desire, then I will find him and kill him. I don't care about him. He's nothing to me. It's you I want. I want to make things right with you. I want you and your baby with me. If you aren't willing to agree to that, then Sampson MacDonald will die.

"You see, I know that he's on his way to the City now. I watched him get on the bus. I know everything that goes on with you and MacDonald and those fine folks at the Inn, thanks to my experience with New York's finest and my work as a private detective. I won't be responsible for what happens to any of those good people if you betray me. You did it once, and I'm willing to give you another chance. This time we'll get it right. But if you refuse me or go to the police, then MacDonald and your friends are in mortal jeopardy. The decision is yours."

"Paul, please just—"

"I repeat. The decision is yours. What say you?"

"Of course I will come." She knew tears would not help.

Mowher told her what to do next and when to do it. "Pack light. You can get new clothes in the City. Say goodbye to no one. Call a taxi within the hour. Pick up a ticket already paid for at the station and take a bus to New York. Meet me at the midtown Port Authority Station."

He would not be pleased to know she had left the note in her room. She knew the Brights would make sure Sam got the message.

This thing with Paul was like a business transaction...a terrifying nightmare wrapped in a cold, dry business transaction. It was only do-able because the consequences of not doing it were unthinkable. Sam's life was in the bargain, along with the lives of Charity and Ray Bright, Johnson Story and her other friends at the Inn. She had no choice. Alaine could not refuse Paul Mowher's commands.

The bus trip to the City was upsetting in its own right. At over seven months pregnant, she was already physically uncomfortable. Now she was stuck next to a passenger who tried repeatedly to interest her in some kind of ethnic foods from a paper bag, the smells from which made her sick.

When the bus finally arrived, rather than feeling relief, she could barely force herself to leave its relative safety and walk forward to meet Paul Mowher.

At least he didn't try to touch her, but took her small bag and muttered, "You made the right choice. This is the right thing to do, Alaine." He then turned his back to her, pushing through the crowd to the outside. Alaine had to move at a near run to keep up.

She knew when their taxi pulled up in front of the same hotel where she and Sam spent those cloistered days immediately following September 11th, before they left for Copper's Run, that it was not coincidence he brought her here rather than to his old apartment.

While she didn't know the name of the hotel and barely remembered the time she and Sam spent there due to being in shock most of the time, she was sure this was the exact hotel. *How did Paul know?*

"We're here, darling." She suspected the endearment was a show for the taxi driver and not for her. "You do remember the Hotel Salina, don't you? Of course you do. How could you ever forget your time here in refuge and sanctuary? How ironic that you're back again, this time with me."

Mowher paid the driver and ushered her solicitously into the lobby.

"How do you know about this hotel? What I mean is, how do you know that I've been here before?"

"My dear, I've tried to impress upon you the extent of my investigatory prowess. I will say, however, that this piece of information took me no small amount of time and resources to uncover, but uncover it I finally did. Welcome back!"

Mowher's smile was not welcoming. This was some kind of game for him. Alaine's internal alarm system activated an adrenalin rush that usually resulted in a pounding migraine.

Her anxiety spiked again when, after he checked them in as husband and wife, Paul Mowher led off of the elevator on the 8th floor and unlocked the door to the same set of adjoining rooms she and Sam occupied earlier. She had, at first, hoped beyond hope that the rooms only appeared to be similar. The view from the window of the room she was to occupy, when Mowher drew open the draperies, dashed that expectation.

"Paul, what are you doing? Why have you brought me here? I thought we were going to your apartment. You do still have your apartment?"

"Well, yes, my dear, I do. But I was thinking you needed a change since you didn't seem at all happy with me in that place. At least that's the conclusion I drew when I learned that you were, in fact, alive after the Towers fell and had simply decided to disappear rather than come home to me. I find that particularly difficult to understand since discovering you were expecting what you claim is my child at the time."

Instinct and experience told Alaine that reasoning with Mowher, in his present mood, was futile. She was tired beyond reason herself and needed rest to re-gather and try to figure out what he had in mind.

Without even asking Mowher's permission, Alaine picked up her bag and went into the bathroom. She showered, washed her hair, slipped on the one faded nightgown she brought and opened the door.

Surprisingly, Paul Mowher left her alone. The door to the next room was ajar, and she heard the TV mumbling. Alaine shut that door, turned out the light and crawled into bed.

When she woke, the clock on the bedside table said 2:30 a.m. Her first thought was to reach for the phone. But then Alaine remembered where she was and that the phone was gone. She saw Paul Mowher unhook it from the jack when they arrived. He already made sure he found her cell phone, too.

Alaine lay still. She was thirsty, but getting up to get a drink was out of the question. If she was as quiet as possible, Mowher might believe she was asleep and leave her undisturbed. She had to think this through and make a plan, some kind of plan, for the dilemma she had gotten herself into.

When she agreed to join him in the City, it was her only real option. Her freedom in exchange for the lives of those she loved.

Those she loved.

There was no question she loved Ms. Charity, Rev. Ray and her other friends back in Copper's Run. Of course she did. But that was not all. She loved Sam MacDonald. Not like the others. This was different. For the first time she admitted that she was in love with him. She *loved* Sam.

Alaine suspected he also cared for her in the same way. She'd felt it for some time, but pushed the knowledge into the background along with the growing awareness that he could be more to her than a rescuer.

Maybe it was the horror of what happened on 9/11. Maybe it was the fallout from her previous time with Mowher or her pregnancy. More likely it was the knowledge that Sam didn't share her new found faith. She had not been able to deal with even the possibility that they could fall in love with each other with no chance of a future together.

Just a few hours before Alaine got the call from Paul Mowher and left the Inn, Ms. Charity told her about Sam's choice to follow Christ. If that was real, if he was serious, his decision could change everything for them.

Except that now her decision to be here with Paul...and away from Sam...was the only choice she could make to keep him alive. How ironic it seemed, just as she discovered her love for him, that she must give him up to save his life.

Think. Put emotions and feelings aside. Think.

Alaine was willing to trade her happiness for the future of her friends, her newfound family. That would have been enough. If it were a matter of spending the rest of her life with Paul Mowher to keep those she loved safe, so be it. The last few hours, however, convinced Alaine of the naiveté of her thinking. Mowher had no intention of taking her and her baby in so that they, however miserably, could live happily ever after with him.

While she was unsure of what his plans for her and the baby involved, there was little doubt that his genuine regard for her was as low as hers for him.

Alaine was also nearly certain that his resentment and hatred toward Sam and the others who rescued her would not end now that he had her. By coming to New York alone, she had only endangered her unborn baby without securing the safety of her loved ones in return.

With no way to communicate and the weight of her mistake heavy on her mind, Alaine realized the deadly position they were all in. Without even knowing the words she was speaking, Alaine silently cried out in fear and desperation for Divine assistance.

She prayed and slept in alternate snatches until the neon-lighted night sky outside began to gray in preparation for morning.

# # #

"Alaine, are you awake? I've ordered up breakfast for half an hour. Join me in my room. Alaine...?" The door opened. "Did you hear what I said?"

"Yes, Paul. I'm awake. I'll be there shortly."

No answer had come in the night. There was nothing to do but wait, watch for some opportunity to get a message out and trust the heavenly Father was working on her behalf.

Alaine showered again, quickly, to calm her nerves and make her alert. She had to be on guard. With the little she brought with her, Alaine did her best to make up and dress to face Paul Mowher. Maybe looking as good as possible would keep her and her baby safe a little longer.

When she acknowledged that last thought, Alaine nearly threw up. It made real to her what Paul Mowher might have in mind.

"Good morning. I trust you rested well." She was shocked at how calm her voice sounded, despite her turmoil inside.

"Yes, indeed. And you?" Paul's manner was solicitous, but the evil amusement in his eyes was not hidden. He held out a chair, and Alaine joined him at the small table where a lavish breakfast was laid out.

It was all she could do to sip the coffee Mowher poured and nibble a bagel with eyes averted while he consumed bacon, eggs, cheese, sausage and a mountain of toast with obvious relish. Alaine's stomach churned.

When he rose from the table and stretched, not trying to hide a loud belch, Alaine met his eyes.

"How long will we be staying here at the hotel? I'm only asking because I'm wondering when we might go shopping. As you requested, I didn't pack much. You mentioned we would have time to shop for what I needed here." She followed the question with a smile. Contact with the world just might bring a chance to get a message out.

"I said that? Oh, right, I guess I did. Well, let's see. I guess we could go out for a while this morning. What sort of things did you need, just for now that is? Something to wear?"

"Yes, for now. Maybe a couple of changes of clothes, some underwear, a nightgown. Nothing much."

"Now that you mention it, that's a good idea. I have exciting plans for us, and you will want something special to wear. I believe there's a shopping area within walking distance. I can be ready when you are."

Alaine kept her tone light. "What's the event? What sort of dress will I need?"

"I think that will be my secret for the time being. Don't worry. I'll help you pick out something appropriate. You'll be beautiful...as always."

Just before he opened the door to the hotel's hallway, Paul Mowher took hold of Alaine's arm and gently but firmly pressed her body against the door. He spoke quietly but clearly, close to her face.

"You will want to be on your best behavior, my love. You might say that we are on a sort of private honeymoon, and we don't want to call undue attention to ourselves. Certainly you understand my meaning?" Mowher's breath in her face smelled like breakfast sausage, and Alaine again felt her stomach roll.

# # #

Rather than providing a chance to get a message to Sam or anyone at the Inn, the trip to the dress shop turned into an embarrassing ordeal for Alaine. Once they found a shop that sold maternity, Paul Mowher directed her purchases, playing the loving partner as he picked out each item. He kept her purse while she tried on his selections and checked the dressing room after she finished, alleging it was to see if she left anything behind. Alaine knew it was to ensure there was no note or clue for others to find.

Not that she cared, but their purchases were meager. They fell far short of what she would need if Paul were really preparing her to live happily ever after with him in the City...or anywhere for that matter. That fact nudged Alaine's anxiety level up a few degrees.

Paul did insist on one major item, a way too expensive and far too dressy black pants outfit with beading that would be much more at home at the opera than eating takeout pizza in a hotel room. Paul brushed her protests about cost and practicality aside, making a show of insisting that nothing was too much for his lovely bride-to-be.

Strange. It was another red flag that she was either misreading his intentions or was spot on in feeling he did not have her best interests in mind.

They lunched on grilled cheese picked up at a deli on the way back to the hotel, and she tried to rest in the afternoon. Alaine finally fell asleep. It was one of those sleeps so deep that she felt nearly paralyzed when awakened quickly by Paul Mowher's voice close beside her bed.

With his hand over his cell phone's speaker, he demanded her attention. "It's Sampson MacDonald. Make sure he thinks you are OK and happy."

Though barely able to hold her thoughts together, she forced herself to speak, "Sam, it's Alaine. I just wanted to tell you I'm fine. I...we're happy and together. I'm great, really. I'm sorry I had to leave the Inn so quickly. I wanted to be with Paul. He needed me and our baby. Thank you for understanding."

Mowher took the phone and moved into the next room. She heard him finish the conversation. Alaine rolled to the edge of the bed and tried to get up. The sick feeling in her head and stomach prevented further progress, and she clawed her way back to the middle of the bed, pulled up the covers and stayed there.

It was dark the next time Alaine awoke. Mowher was standing over her again, this time urging her to come into his room for the Chinese takeout just delivered. The smell of sweet and sour something teased her into thinking she could eat. By the time she washed her face and made it to the little table, the urge had passed.

Instead, she munched on the fried wontons that came with the little boxes of soup while, again, watching Paul Mowher eat both his food and what he'd ordered for her. His appetite seemed endless, and his enthusiasm for sating it made her avert her eyes in disgust.

"Well now, that was some of the best sweet and sour pork I've enjoyed lately." Mowher stood, loosened his belt buckle a notch and re-buckled it, rubbing his stomach when he was done. "Your sesame chicken was good, too. Sorry you didn't feel up to trying it. But maybe after a good night's rest you'll feel better tomorrow."

Alaine made eye contact to judge the authenticity of his concern. He seemed pumped and intense. This was another Paul with which she wasn't familiar.

He came around behind her chair, and she felt cold fingers on her back. He began to massage her shoulders and neck. Alaine bit the inside of her mouth to keep from screaming at him to stop.

"Look, Alaine, I know you've been a little tense. It's just an adjustment period. Things will be much better soon. Believe me. You know, I have something very special planned for you tomorrow. It will go a long way toward making everything all right between us. I promise."

"What do you mean?" She heard the distrust obvious in her own voice as she twisted to look up at him. "What is it you have planned?"

"Oh, now honey, that would spoil the surprise, and I've gone to a lot of trouble to make this very special. I'm afraid you'll just have to wait and see. But you can do one thing for me." He waited for her response, again kneading her shoulder muscles.

"What would you like for me to do for you?" She managed to keep the shaking she felt inside out of her voice. If he tried to touch her further, she didn't think she could stand it.

"When you get dressed in the morning, please wear that black suit I bought you. It's very becoming and will be exactly right for our special occasion."

"You want me to put that on when I get up? But it's more suitable for--"

"Wear it. It'll be fine. Wear it for me, please?"

He smiled down at her with a boyish beg on his face.

What difference would it make? She really didn't care what she wore.

"Of course, Paul, whatever pleases you. The black suit it is."

"That's my girl," he said and gave her shoulders a final squeeze that hurt, which she refused to protest.

21 HIDE AND SEEK

Sampson

Sam slept badly. Every time he woke up, which was often, he sensed he was standing with his face against an impenetrable and immeasurably tall stone wall in a cold drizzle. The feeling was so real that once he caught himself wiping the rain from his eyes. When the wet that came off on his fingers wasn't cold, he knew he'd been crying. He hoped it was silently.

At 6 a.m. his cell phone rang. His grab knocked it to the floor, so it was five rings before he answered it.

"Not an early riser, I see." The voice was Mowher's.

"Mowher, just tell me what you want and where Alaine is. Is she OK? Let me talk to her."

"Sorry, MacDonald, not this time, old man."

"Look, Mowher. Why don't you meet me somewhere? Why don't we just talk man to man? I know we've not been on the best of terms." Sam forced himself to keep talking despite Mowher's profane response. "I just need to be sure that Alaine's all right with this new arrangement. Let me see her. Let her tell me to my face that she's in good shape, and I'll be satisfied. What do you say, Paul?"

There was a lengthy pause during which Sam convinced himself that the man must be considering his proposition.

"Well, I have to give it to you, MacDonald. That's a most civil plan of action.

I would say that's even right Christian of you."

Again, there was a pause...followed by a hearty laugh.

"OK, MacDonald. Now it's time for me to let you in on my plan. I don't think you'll find it civil. I know for a fact you won't find it Christian. It is, however, the plan I mean to carry out this very day. Listen carefully, and you will be the first to know. Everyone else will have to hear about it on the evening news."

"Mowher, what are you talking about? If you're even thinking about--"

"What I'm talking about is undoing the terrible wrong you did on September 11th of last year. What I'm thinking about is fixing what you screwed up when you took matters into your own hands and dragged Alaine Albert and her illegitimate fetus out of that burning Trade Center Tower. You should have left her there to face what she deserves. For that matter, you should have thrown yourself out of a window, too, and done us all a favor."

"Mowher, please! Talk to me. I'll do whatever you say, only please just--"

"Listen and learn. That's all I need for you to do. Listen and learn. I've thought this thing through carefully and am now assured that I can undo this mess you put us all in. I can make things turn out right. I appreciate your offer of help. I understand you mean well. But rest in the knowledge that I now have everything under control. All will be well if I reverse every move you made, stay close to the script you wrote and come as close as I can to what you did, only backwards. Things will be put right."

"Mowher, what are you talking about? Make sense, man!"

Paul Mowher continued as if Sam had not spoken or as if Mowher had not heard him.

"I've mapped it out. I've gone over it step by step. All I have to do is re-run the film, just like you can do with a movie. You'll see. Everything will come out fine."

"Mowher, Oh God, Mowher--"

"No, Sampson, rest easy, man. I feel better just talking this through with you. You should, too. No hard feelings now. Happy ending. Thanks for listening. See you in church!"

Sam sat holding his cell phone long after Paul Mowher hung up. Without even trying first to decipher the ramblings of the man, Sam dropped the phone and slipped to his knees beside the sagging bed in the boarding house. He begged God for safety and deliverance for Alaine and her baby. He begged for courage. He needed wisdom and clarity of thought. He needed Divine direction.

# # #

Alaine

Just after 6 a.m. the next morning, Paul Mowher knocked on Alaine's door. He gave no time for her to respond before he entered and spoke.

"Alaine, my dear, rise and shine." He used a stage whisper that chilled her skin. Theatrics were not characteristic of the man. Blunt and abrasive, yes, but not affected. "Time to get up and face your special day. In fact, I would go so far as to say...our day. Your breakfast is ready. Why not just come as you are?"

She wasn't fooled by Paul's exaggerated cheerfulness. Whether his mood was a result of drama or derangement, the outcome for her was the same. She pulled back the curtain to the outside. Gray drizzle greeted her.

By the time she showered, put on the infernal black pants suit and joined Mowher, his demeanor had changed from jovial to agitated. He'd set out stale chocolate donuts that turned her stomach and luke warm orange juice in a can. She forced them down not knowing when or if there would be more.

While Alaine ate, Mowher paced, stopping a number of times to check his watch against the TV, and resuming the pace.

"Where are we going, Paul? It's raining. I have no raincoat. Can't this special day of yours wait? I really don't think I'm up to--"

"Oh no, oh no." He shook his head and paused his movements. "We really couldn't wait. That's not at all possible. I have orders...plans. You don't understand. I have it all worked out, step by step. I've worked very hard at these arrangements. I have to get it correct. When it works out right, everything will be fixed. I'll be able to rest."

"What about me, Paul? I could use some rest, too. I'm exhausted. Let's just stay in today and both rest. We can go wherever you need to go tomorrow."

Alaine was stalling, convinced that the outing Paul had planned would further complicate her predicament. If she could just put it off until... *what?* A sinking feeling in the pit of her stomach grew more pronounced. No one was coming to help her. No one knew where she was. She was alone and under the control of a man who appeared to be coming unraveled.

"Alaine, baby, you will soon be able to rest all you want. We just have this one thing to do today, and then it will all be straight and you can relax, for sure. The sooner we get this finished, the sooner you won't have to worry about a thing. I promise you that. Yes, I do. That's a promise." He touched her face lightly with his fingertips and feathered them down the side of her neck.

Paul's quick change from agitated to gentle unnerved Alaine worse than the pacing.

"Paul, why can't you tell me where we're going? I'd feel more comfortable if you would just let me in on your plans."

"Trust me, baby. I know I've sometimes given you a hard time, but I'm done with that. You can count on me. I'm going to take care of both you and your baby. Forever."

Alaine was convinced that Paul Mowher was losing touch. She also understood he would never let her walk away again. She was at a loss to explain what was happening and, more critically, what she could do about it to protect herself and her baby. He blocked all access to a phone except where he was in charge. She knew he was armed. She'd seen his gun.

Alaine stumbled into her bathroom to be alone, if only for a minute. She gripped the sink as panic enveloped her. Suppose she just locked the door and sank down to lie on the floor. How long could she stay there, even if he beat and banged on the door? What would he do if she simply refused to come out?

She pressed her hands tightly to her stomach. The baby kicked with such force that she cried out. It hurt. He kicked again, down low this time. The pain forced her to sit down hard on the side of the bathtub to keep from falling.

She held her breath and began to rock. The pain eased.

Suppose it wasn't a kick? No kick had hurt this much before. Suppose it was a labor pain. She was only a little over seven months pregnant. What if--? A dark cloud of fear threatened to consume her.

# # #

Sampson

Sam stood up, his prayer finished, and paced the small room. His mind was focused, his head clear.

Think. He had to think. *What exactly had Paul Mowher said? Something about listen. Listen. Listen and learn. And then something like he had a plan and could fix it. No, it was more like, "I can fix this mess you made."*

What mess had Sam made?

Remember. Stay calm.

He said people would hear about it on the news. What would hit the news? What would be big enough to make the news?

The terrible conversation was beginning to come back to Sam, and he grabbed for a pen and paper left behind in his desk.

Mowher had said something about righting a wrong that had been done on September 11th. A wrong that he, Sam, had done.

What else? What else? Please, God, what else?

Mowher wanted to take care of what I messed up by saving Alaine and her baby from the Trade Center building. He called the baby illegitimate. Mowher knew he was the father. Why did he say that? Didn't make sense. None of it made sense.

And then the rest of what Paul Mowher said came back, in all of its horror, as clearly as if he was repeating it slowly for Sam to get every word.

"All will be well.

"Reverse every step.

"Stay close to the script you wrote.

"Come as close as I can to what you did.

"Backwards...

"Things will be right.

"I've mapped it out.

"I've *gone over it.*

"Re-run the film just like a movie."

And finally*, "See you in church."*

See you in church! Now it made sense. The meaning was unthinkable.

Sam grabbed a jacket and left his room at a run. He knew what Paul Mowher was planning. He hoped...prayed he was wrong, but he was sure he could finally see into the twisted mind that was now in control of Alaine and her baby.

There was no time to debate the matter with himself. He had to act on the hunch as if it was true. No way could he call the police, or he might be arrested for being crazy.

He would see if he could borrow Mrs. Baker's old car to get down to lower Manhattan as fast as possible. But that might take lengthy explanations, and he remembered her car was not that reliable. Sam started out toward the nearest bus stop, but when a taxi approached, he threw that plan aside and flagged it down.

It took forty-five minutes to reach lower Manhattan and cost plenty, but to save time, Sam overpaid the tip and leaped to the curb. Ground Zero was six blocks away. Sam wanted to walk the rest of the way. He needed to collect his thoughts and make a plan.

By the time he'd gone four blocks, he was breathing hard and admitting to himself that he had no plan. He was still struggling with the small but real possibility that Alaine was here on her own. On the other hand, if that psychiatrist, Bernard Weinstein, was right, Paul Mowher was a time bomb and violence might soon be on the way.

Driven by the thought of Alaine and the baby being with Mowher when he blew, Sam made the last two blocks in record time. With no idea of what to expect, he'd just have to get there, see what happened and deal with it.

Maybe he had no plan, but he had a place in mind.

"See you in church."

There was a church...a chapel really, Sam remembered, that sat across the street from the Trade Center site. An old part of a larger, newer church complex, he'd seen the chapel many times in his coming and going during the months of working nearby. He'd even walked over one morning when he should have been at his desk.

The chapel was old and, by City church standards, small. It must have been there for at least two centuries. Sam only saw it from the back where a graveyard faced the Trade Center area. It was there, among the ancient graves, he'd gone to walk off his irritation at something that happened at his office.

St. Philip's Chapel was the closest church to Ground Zero, but it oddly hadn't sustained much damage when the buildings came down. Some called it a miracle. Sam had read about the Chapel now being used as a rest station for recovery workers, fire fighters, and National Guard.

The Chapel had a tall spire, a bell tower...*a tower*...of sorts. Sam remembered how cold and gray the day was when he visited. He'd stood, enraged at something his boss did, and looked up at the little church's tower. It seemed then to him like a good place to go if someone wanted to end his life.

"I've mapped it out...I've gone over it...re-run the film just like a movie...See you in church."

Whatever Paul Mowher was about to do, Sam had a feeling he would do it at the chapel. Mowher couldn't take Alaine to Ground Zero. The chapel would be Mowher's ground zero. Unless Sam was able to stop him, who else would?

# # #

Alaine

By the time Paul Mowher hustled Alaine out of the hotel, she knew this latest problem was more than her baby's extra strong kicks. Something was wrong.

"Let's go for a walk, my dear. It's a little wet out, but no problem. Just a bit brisk. A little walk will do you good."

"Paul, please, I've told you I hurt. Something's happening. I'm scared. I'm afraid it's the baby."

He took her by the hand, leading her as if she were a child out into a slow, cold drizzle.

"Alaine, I realize you've been under a lot of stress. We all have. I'm sure that you just need to relax and get a little exercise and fresh air. Come along now. We have several blocks to go. By the time we reach our destination, you'll be in good shape. You just need to walk the kinks out."

Alaine jerked her hand free and stopped in the middle of the sidewalk, tears running down her face as she bent double in pain.

"I can't walk blocks. I can hardly walk at all. I can't, Paul. I just cannot."

Paul Mowher threw his arms up in the air in apparent frustration and disgust, accompanying his physical reaction with a string of expletives. He motioned to a taxi passing slowly in anticipation of someone needing its services and steered Alaine inside with less than a gentle hand.

She thought about begging the driver to assist her, but realized quickly it could endanger his life and provoke Paul Mowher to violence. Instead, she hugged her arms across her waist and tried to distance herself from him as far as the cramped back seat of the taxi would allow.

"Where to, sir?"

"Church Street...across from St. Philip's Chapel. Near Ground Zero. How close can we come?"

"Hard to tell, sir. Things in that area are loosening up, it's true, but you can't be sure what might be open on any given day. Do you want me to get you as close as I can? You two sightseers?"

"You could say that. Yes, take us as near in as you can."

The taxi, after trying a number of alternate routes and passing through an alley or two, was finally forced to stop by a barrier set up by the NYPD. Alaine was horrified to recognize that they were within two blocks of the site of the downed Trade Center.

Whatever Paul Mowher was planning, it couldn't be good. Her stomach pains had eased, or maybe they were just overshadowed by a steadily growing sense of doom. Gone were thoughts that she would have to live her life, however unhappily, as Paul Mowher's wife. Forgotten were his promises that he wanted her and the baby with him to take care of them. In their place was an increasing awareness that, without Divine intervention, her life and that of her baby were in immediate danger.

Mowher threw money in to the taxi driver and pushed Alaine ahead of him out onto the street. The barrier to gaining closer access to Ground Zero was manned by members of the police force. Alaine made a quick decision to risk all, cause a scene and make an appeal for help.

Just as she was bracing to run for the anticipated safety of police presence, she felt Mowher's arm go around her waist and jerk her into the doorway of a closed business. Before she could protest, she felt the muzzle of a gun hard against her ribs.

"Whatever you're planning, forget it now. I'll take the cops out and then you. Trust me. This is not an empty threat. Do you want to cause the death of the City's finest before you go, too? Think about the baby. It won't make it long without you, now will it?"

Alaine's pains were coming back without mercy. She reached her hand down and pushed the gun barrel away. What did she have to lose?

"You don't need to worry, Paul. I'm not going to endanger anyone else's life. Tell me what you're going to do."

"Whatever do you mean? We are simply going to re-visit the site of the building where you used to work. Well, we can't actually get to the spot where the North Tower stood. It's still restricted. But we can get pretty close. I thought you might want to remember where you almost died, except of course for the valiant actions of your friend and mine, Sampson MacDonald."

"Leave Sam out of this. He has nothing to do with what's going on between us. I don't even know where he is. I left my new life back in Virginia to be with you. You said that's what you wanted."

"And I do want that, my darling. Don't forget that for a minute. But it's important, if we are going to be together now, that we do it right."

"What are you talking about?" She doubled over again with pain.

Paul Mowher took hold of her arm and reached into his breast pocket. The gun disappeared, but he pulled out badges, complete with photos, identifying them as Red Cross workers. He slipped one onto Alaine's coat and the other on his own. He pulled her arm through his and strode with purpose toward the area approaching Ground Zero, and she had no choice but to go with him.

# # #

Sampson

Sam knew the lower part of Manhattan was almost impenetrable in the days immediately following 9/11. It took ID and a need to be there to get even close to the site of the destruction. Business and transportation were disrupted for days, if not weeks, and many residents made an exodus from the area, some permanently.

Seven months had now passed, and while there was still a security presence, things were relaxing a bit as people became convinced another attack was not imminent. Sam took advantage of this knowledge and his understanding of the layout of this part of the City.

Because he was on foot and able to penetrate secure areas in ways a taxi was not, Sam threaded his way with little trouble and time directly to the site of St. Philip's Chapel. Walking into the open toward one of the Chapel's entrances brought on emotions so strong that Sam stopped and bent over, his hands on his knees.

Very close to this place he and Alaine nearly lost their lives. Almost 2000 others had.

He raised his head to see a stretch of fencing near the Chapel covered in flowers, flags, personal items and pictures. Sam's eyes focused on one scene depicting a happy family obviously celebrating a child's birthday. It formed the centerpiece of a yellow wreath on which was pinned a handmade card written in crayon and declaring, "We love you, Daddy." He was looking at a memorial wall.

Sam bent his head again, hands still on his knees, and struggled to breathe. Paul Mowher was here, or soon would be. Sam was sure.

He was also sure Alaine was with the man against her will, and Mowher intended her life and her baby's life would end here. "Oh, God, I need you now. They need you. Help us, Lord, please."

Sam felt someone take his arm and hold on.

"You OK, buddy? You must be a new volunteer here at the Chapel. Hits you hard, doesn't it? I felt the same way the first time I came down a few months ago. You'll be all right as soon as you get busy. See you inside."

Sam watched a young Asian man grin and wave to him as he headed toward the Chapel's doors. He'd been mistaken for one of the hundreds of volunteers that counseled and prayed with and served food and gave massages and medical attention to the firemen and construction workers working endlessly on the pile at Ground Zero.

Ashamed of his momentary weakness, Sam straightened and moved with determination toward the Chapel. Coming up close behind his Asian Samaritan, Sam was alert to any hindrance to entering the building itself. He had no credentials. It might be easier to slip inside if he was with someone who knew his way around for cover.

"Excuse me, hey, excuse me." The young man turned around.

Sam stuck out his hand to the man. "Thanks for your words back there. And for what you've been doing here."

The young man gave Sam another smile and a shake. "Glad to be of assistance. Name's Jason."

"Sam."

"Welcome to the Chapel, Sam. We can use the help. See you around."

By the time Jason disappeared into the crowd, they were inside the Chapel with no incident. Sam suffered no questions from the guard who nodded toward Jason and turned away to respond to someone behind him as Sam followed close behind his new acquaintance through the entrance.

Sam moved toward a wall and stood, getting his bearings and watching the order of comings and goings. He could see members of the NYPD, a few firefighters, and a bounty of construction workers who appeared not to have slept in weeks. He saw professionals and volunteers alike ministering to the needs of the ones on the front lines of the Ground Zero work force.

He didn't see Paul Mowher in the crowd. That could mean he was on his way, or he was already on site and putting his horrifying plan into action. This had to be the place.

Sam needed to find the door leading to the bell tower or spire or whatever it was as fast as he could, and he had to find it without getting thrown out or arrested. A needle in a haystack...and he couldn't ask for help. The best things to do were pray like crazy and move around like he knew what he was doing without calling undue attention to himself. No small tasks.

# # #

Alaine

Mowher spoke to the security officer at the checkpoint first. "Good morning, sir. Red Cross workers on duty today at St. Philip's Chapel. He pointed to his name tag and held out the two fake IDs and then made eye contact with Alaine.

Again she considered blurting her situation or simply falling to the ground as if she'd fainted. Again she rejected the idea, knowing such a move would almost certainly get the officer killed and probably herself, as well. Not dying yet, putting it off as long as possible and trying to keep others around her and her baby out of danger were her only goals.

"Have a nice day." The guard handed Mowher the cards and turned his attention toward others ready to enter the protected area.

Alaine allowed Mowher to pull her away some distance from the checkpoint before she stopped him by planting her feet and jerking away from him.

She paid for it when she felt the cruel pressure of his grip re-tighten around her arm as he pulled her close.

"If you refuse to follow me and cause a scene, I promise you, people will get hurt." His tone was deadly and his breath hot against her ear.

"Paul, please. Can't we stop just for a minute and talk about this? Let's go back to the hotel. I'm really hurting, and I don't want anything to happen to our baby." She wasn't lying.. Alaine's pains were strong, and walking was getting harder to do.

"Your baby, Alaine. Not mine. Yours and no telling who else's. Don't blame me for your situation, my dear. This is not my doing. But I can do something to get you out of it."

Alaine was crying now and desperate. "This is your baby, Paul. I promise you that. There was no one else but you. No one. I was pregnant before I left the City with your child. I just didn't know it. It's not too late for us, Paul. We can be together, all of us. We can be a family like you said. Let's go back and...start over...please, Paul."

Even while she begged, Alaine saw in his eyes that Paul Mowher was beyond reason. He'd convinced himself the baby wasn't his. He was also talking as if he had supernatural power to right whatever wrong he was sure had been done. Alaine knew her fears were well founded.

She stopped struggling as Paul Mowher shoved her ahead of him toward the void in Manhattan that used to house the Trade Center buildings. Her surrender came from pain that now rolled in waves leaving her nearly paralyzed mixed with the knowledge that struggle was useless. Paul and his hidden gun had the upper hand. Alone, Alaine might have kept resisting, but she wasn't alone. Her baby would die if she died, and others around the couple would die, too, if she pushed him too far.

Past the point of coherent prayer, Alaine remembered Rev. Ray saying when we didn't know what to pray ourselves, the Holy Spirit did it for us. He prayed with groans too deep for words. Alaine heard the groans but recognized her own voice surely mixed with that of the Spirit.

"Shut up!" Mowher jerked on her arm. "Act normal, do you hear me? If you don't want someone who hears you to suffer, you'd better be quiet."

She tried to ask him again where they were going...what he was going to do...but all she heard were moans as another, harder, pain hit her. The grasp of Mowher's hand on her arm tightened, and she clamped her hand over her own mouth.

The terror she felt at approaching the place where she almost died turned her mouth to cotton. The growing awareness that she would likely still die there brought back nausea. The rapid pace Mowher forced on her made the contractions, which is what Alaine now knew they were, come faster.

By the time she understood Mowher was now steering her away from Ground Zero, there was little comfort. She couldn't think why. She could barely think at all. Each step seemed more than she could stand, but she took it and then the next, hoping it would end soon. She didn't care how.

They crossed a street...there was a fence...a church cemetery beyond the fence...then a walkway. Alaine saw only what was close to the ground. She no longer raised her head to look up. Mowher pulled her on. She clung to his arm just to keep from falling.

They reached low steps, an entrance of some sort. It no longer mattered to her where they were. Mowher dragged her to the side of the entrance way and leaned down to talk in her ear, his arm around her so she couldn't move.

"If you cross me now, you'll be sorry."

"I don't care what you do." She started to slide down the wall, ready to collapse at his feet.

"Stand up straight." He jerked her upright and pushed her back against a very hard outside wall. "Maybe you don't care, but just know that a lot of other people will care if you cause trouble. That's a promise."

He brought his body close to hers in a way that might look like a caress to onlookers, but Alaine understood it was a cover. When he drew back, she forced herself to look at Mowher's face. It was contorted with contempt. He meant what he was saying.

"Where are you taking me?"

"You let me worry about that. Your job is to come along and not make a scene. Remember, if you do--" The pressure of his grip said the rest.

They passed through another loose ID checkpoint. Then they were inside the building. She could tell it had been a church, at some point. Now it was more like a busy mall. People in dusty uniforms rested on pews. Aid workers served coffee and food. Alaine could see what she thought might be medical personnel.

If she could just--but she couldn't. Too many targets for Paul Mowher's bullets.

He urged her on, away from the crowd, toward a set of doors that led to somewhere she knew she didn't want to go.

"Good girl. You're doing fine. Almost there. Just keep moving."

A new pain hit her so forcefully that she almost cried out. The pain was more intense now than the fear. Whatever was to happen, she prayed it would be soon...and fast. Alaine knew she'd not last much longer like this. Death might be the best way out.

22 PURSUIT

Sampson

Why Sam believed Paul Mowher would bring Alaine here to St. Philip's Chapel, he could not explain. That Mowher would do so, he was sure. Maybe it was the proximity to Ground Zero. Could be that the little Chapel overlooked where the Trade Center towers once stood across the street. More likely it was a desperate response to Mowher's promise to, *"See you in church,"* that set Sam in motion.

If he was wrong and Mowher never showed up with Alaine--he forced his mind away from how that could play out. He prayed it was God who had sent him here to face Mowher with the assurance that he was not alone.

Not calling attention to himself while searching for the pair over each foot of the Chapel's unfamiliar interior might be improbable, but what alternative was there? To ask someone would invite suspicion. He couldn't afford to be stopped at this point.

On his third circle around the crowded Chapel with no sight of them, Sam's chest tightened in frustration. What was he missing? Suppose he was wrong and Mowher wasn't coming here at all? Suppose Mowher's words were intended to confuse him while Mowher took Alaine somewhere else? And then the message could simply be the gibberish of a crazed mind.

Sam took a deep breath and ran his hand across his eyes. *God, help me. Let me think. Show me what to do.*

He looked up and saw the Asian guy from outside watching him. *Jason, was it?*

"Everything OK, man?"

"Thanks, I'm good. Just got a little turned around in all the confusion. First day and all."

"Sure thing. You'll get straight." Jason turned to move off into the crowd. Sam let out a slow breath. Jason turned back and walked over to Sam.

"Look, can I help you with something? You aren't here to volunteer, are you?"

Sam was out of options. Apart from a miracle, he wouldn't be able to pull this off alone. He could miss Paul Mowher in the crowd and lose Alaine for good. He was going to trust that Jason was his miracle.

"Jason...it is Jason, right?" The young man nodded. Sam moved closer to him to ensure Jason was the only listener.

"You're right. I'm no volunteer, and I do need help. I'm looking for someone. It's important...maybe life or death."

Jason watched him without questions or visible reaction.

"I know that's lame. Look, this is going to sound even crazier, and I have no proof of what I'm about to say. I have good reason to believe that a woman who means a lot to me is being held against her will. I think the man who has her will bring her here to kill her. They could be in the church now. It may already be too late. There's no time to explain. I have to stop him."

Sam saw the skepticism on Jason's face. He didn't blame him.

"Look, Jason, I know you're thinking I should have alerted the police. If you don't believe me...I said I have no proof...can you imagine what hassle I would get from them? I can't take a chance on that."

Sam stopped talking, ran his hand through his hair, and raised his hands over his head in despair, turning with his back to the other man. When he turned around, he met Jason's calm appraisal with a question. "So is there any way you can help me look for them?"

"What was your name again, man?" Jason asked.

"Sam MacDonald. I may be wrong, Jason, but I'm not lying or nuts. I hope you can help me try to save my friend's life. And the life of her unborn baby. At the least, please don't get in my way."

"Her unborn baby? She's pregnant."

"She is. Why?"

"What does she look like?"

"Medium height, slender except for the baby part, long reddish brown hair, real light skin. Pretty in a kind of delicate way. Tell me why you ask."

"I think they're here. I think I saw them. He's a skinny dude with blond, almost white, hair?"

"That's him. You saw them together? Are you sure?"

"Sure enough, and I'm all you have to go on now, right? Follow me...fast," the young man said, and crossed the short space to a set of stairs leading to another level of the Chapel. As they moved, Jason talked.

"If you're crazy or wrong and this blows up, I'll go down with you, for sure." Jason stopped short and Sam nearly hit him from behind. He turned around to face Sam with his right hand outstretched.

"Look me in the eyes and shake my hand that you're telling me the truth. I think I'll know if you are lying, and I don't want to spend the rest of my life in jail, or worse, for helping you if you plan to blow this place up. Or if you're really the bad guy."

Before Jason finished his speech, Sam gripped his hand hard, staring him down, willing him to understand.

"Jason, I'm on the level. Where are we going? What did you see?"

Jason moved again and fast, talking to Sam over his shoulder. "I saw the couple you described. They caught my attention because she didn't seem well, and he looked crazy. He was holding on to her really tight and almost pushing her along ahead of him. She looked rather out of it. Right or wrong, I decided not to say anything. This is New York City, and I've learned the hard way it's usually best not to get involved."

As scared as Sam was, he smiled at the irony of Jason's words.

"You mean until now?"

"I'm trusting this is different. I watched them head to the stairs of the gallery level. The man seemed to know where he was going. I lost sight of them while they climbed the stairs. Took a while because she seemed to be having trouble walking. Then they came back in sight above the main floor. They were moving toward that big pipe organ over there."

By this time, Sam and Jason were on the gallery level themselves and moving in the direction Jason described.

"Where could he be taking her? What's up here?"

"The entrance to the old bell tower is behind the organ. Not many people know about it, and hardly anybody ever goes up there. It's nine floors high, and the only way up is ladders. I've heard some of it's really in bad shape."

"How do you know this?"

"This Chapel has been part of our family all of my life. My aunt works here. She likes a challenge and has gone up by herself all the way to the seventh floor, finding all kinds of history. Beyond that, it's too dangerous to climb."

"That's it, Jason! I think that's what Paul Mowher's doing with Alaine. I think he's taking her up there to kill her. Show me how to get in."

"Come this way and let's hope nobody sees us. Why would he do something like that?"

Sam talked as they moved. "Alaine and I got out of the North Tower together on 9/11. I didn't know it at the time, but she was pregnant with Mowher's baby. We've been living with new friends outside of the state, but he found us. Mowher's deranged for real. I believe he thinks she should have died in the North Tower on 9/11. Without time to explain why, my theory is he's brought her back to redo that day with what he believes is the right outcome. He's going to kill her right here...as close to where the Towers stood as he can get and as high as he can pull it off."

# # #

Alaine

When Alaine saw the ladder Paul Mowher ordered her to climb in the dark, cloistered room, for the first time she gave real physical resistance, flinging herself away from him against a wall.

"Paul, this is senseless! I can't climb that ladder. I can barely stand."

"Alaine, my dear, you have no choice." His voice was detached and matter of fact. When Alaine looked at his face, it was as if humanity had been replaced by a machine. "Should you continue to refuse, I will be forced to encourage you by dropping these little motivators into the Chapel below. If you doubt I will do it, delay any further."

To Alaine's horror, he pulled his coat to the side revealing not only more than one firearm but also what appeared to be very real grenades attached to a strap across his chest. To underline his words, Mowher gripped his hand around one of them, smiling as if he were showing her a prized object.

Understanding he would carry out his threats without regret, Alaine turned and took hold of the wooden ladder. Pain hit her with such fury that she screamed, and immediately she tasted the stifling hand of Mowher across her mouth.

"Not another sound." His voice hissed in her ear.

When the pain eased for a moment, she wrenched her face clear to respond. "Paul, I'm in labor. I'm hurting. I need help."

Again, his lips came close. "Don't you understand? I am helping you. Do what I say, and you'll soon be out of your misery. I promise. Please climb now." Again, his hand cupped a grenade on his chest.

With the first step up the ladder, the terrible nature of her situation overwhelmed Alaine. She was in labor, climbing straight up an ancient wooden ladder in the top of a church, under the control of a mad man who wanted her dead, and no one knew what was happening to her.

She closed her eyes and gripped the rungs as more pain attacked her.

God, this can't be happening. Am I at the end of my life? I don't want my baby to die like this. Where are you, Lord? Help me, please.

"Alaine, climb. You must move more quickly. We have no more time to lose." She felt his hand on her hip pushing upward. A wave of revulsion washed over her.

Sam, if I never see you again, how can I tell you I love you?

As long as they were climbing, she figured they hadn't reached whatever destination he had planned, so Alaine climbed. She climbed past floor after floor, always expecting Mowher to tell her to stop. It was cold and dark, little light making its way through boarded over louvered windows to show her surroundings.

This can't be my life, and I know I'm not dead. This is like hell, but I know I'm not going there. God, help me now or take me quickly.

She climbed through unimaginable pain and tears that blocked what little she could see. She climbed with arm and leg muscles cramping harder than her labor. She climbed with Paul Mowher behind her saying she should have died when the Towers fell and that a messenger from God had given him the duty of making things right by taking her to a high place and finishing the job the correct way.

Alaine climbed until she could barely hold the rungs and, from the way the ladder began to shake, it could barely hold her. She rejected the added fear that thinking brought and prepared to climb further when she sensed Mowher was no longer directly behind her.

There was more light now. Alaine turned her head to see its source. On this level, there were no inside coverings over the decorative louvers, and daylight streamed in onto bare floorboards. She looked down to see Paul Mowher standing on the small wooden platform just below her. His arms were outstretched, and he was reaching up to her.

This is it. I know what he's going to do.

# # #

Sampson

"You've got to be kidding." Sam addressed this to Jason in a whisper. "You think Mowher brought her in here?" The space beyond the doorway was small, dim and like they had entered another era.

"They headed this way, and there's nowhere else for them to go. I have no idea how he got the key, or maybe he knew how to break in. This door is always locked. Quiet! Listen."

"I don't hear anything. I'm going up that ladder. What kind of lead time do you think they have?"

"Not more than five...ten minutes at the most. I'm right behind you. Let's climb."

With no real assurance they were on the right track and no time to pursue any other option, Sam moved up the ladder with as much speed and stealth as he could. He could feel Jason's movements matching his at his heels.

When Sam stopped to catch his breath after what seemed a long stretch of climbing non-stop, he heard his new friend caution quietly, "You'd better pace yourself. No telling how far we have to climb to find them. Or make sure they aren't here."

"I'm trusting God they're here. Do you believe in God, Jason?"

"That I do, my brother. That I do. Let's get going."

The brief rest had helped, and they climbed steadily without talking. The noise of a bump somewhere above them interrupted their progress.

Jason lowered his voice. "Sounded like someone jumping from the ladder onto a platform. What do you think?"

Sam's voice broke when he answered. "Or falling from it."

Before they could climb again, a man's voice sounded from higher in the spire. It was measured and authoritative, as if addressing a child.

"Alaine, come to me. I want you to come down off of the ladder now."

A woman's voice responded. The words were chilling.

"I...will...not...come...down...for...you...to... push...me...out."

"Oh, God, that's Alaine. They're up there!" Sam whispered, and it sounded to him like a shout. "They can't be more than two or three floors above us."

They climbed, faster but quieter now. Sam prayed to know what move to make next.

Mowher's voice sounded again, closer, more insistent and less patient.

"Alaine, there's no need to be oppositional. You can trust me. I know what is best. Come down and let's get this completed. It's the right thing."

There was a moan and cry, followed by a plea. "Paul, get help, please get me help. I can't do this anymore. The baby's coming!"

Sam could contain himself no longer. "Alaine! I'm here. Hold on! Don't give up now!"

"Sam?" She screamed his name. "Sam, how did you...no! No! Stay down! Don't come any higher. He has weapons. Go...please go!"

# # #

Alaine

Sam's voice, his nearness, penetrated the haze of pain and despair that paralyzed Alaine. She knew the baby was coming and any minute someone could die. She didn't want it to be Sam, and she determined it wasn't going to be her baby.

She wedged her arm at an awkward angle through the rung of the ladder to keep from falling, and it shifted precariously with her weight. The anchored arm hurt, but the pit of her stomach hurt worse.

Alaine twisted her head to see what Paul Mowher was doing. She could see him reach out to grab the ladder. He was coming after her.

As he clutched the ladder, she tried to move higher but was stopped by her twisted arm. Mowher came up quickly, and she felt his hand go around her ankle.

"This is it, little lady." He pulled on her leg. "Don't fight it. Come down and let me take care of you and your baby once and for all. I promise you won't feel a thing."

Paul Mowher wrapped his free arm around both of her legs and jerked with all of his weight. Alaine heard her wedged arm snap and felt herself sliding down the ladder into the arms of the man who would end her life.

With little strength remaining, she grabbed the side of the ladder with her good arm and pulled against Mowher's strength. The motion dislodged the unstable structure, and the ladder swung sideways, one side pulling loose. It didn't shake Mowher's hold on her, and they both fell the few feet to the narrow floor of the spire.

Mowher, unhurt, was up in a flash and dragging her toward the side of the small space. Without hesitating, he kicked at the decorative louvers forming the wall panels of the little room. The ancient boards split without resistance.

Alaine's last sensations were Paul Mowher's voice telling her it was time to die and the feel of cold air and sunshine on her face from the hole in the side of the spire.

# # #

Sampson

When his head cleared the floorboards of the landing onto which he and Jason heard Alaine and Mowher fall, Sam was horrified to see the man pulling her body toward the yawning hole nearly 200 feet above the City below.

"Mowher, stop!" Sam pulled himself up onto the platform. He saw Alaine wasn't moving, and the man turned to face him.

"Well, well...Mr. MacDonald. How fitting."

Sam realized that when Mowher was talking, he wasn't pulling Alaine nearer the jagged opening. "It's a pleasure having you here to watch me finish the job you interrupted back in September. Perhaps you'd like to accompany your lady friend."

Desperate to extend the time when Mowher wasn't attending to Alaine, Sam played dumb. He didn't have a plan, but maybe Jason hidden below the floorboards did.

"What are you talking about, man?"

"I told you before. Alaine wasn't supposed to survive the fall of the North Tower. If it hadn't been for you playing God, she wouldn't have. She and her fatherless baby would already be gone. But you had to interfere. I'm about to correct all of that. You're just in time. You can join them, if you wish."

"What do you mean about me 'playing God'?" Don't you think you're playing God by deciding they have to die? Why do you have a right to make that decision any more than I had a right to save them?"

"Why do I have a right, you ask?" Mowher's voice took on a superior tone. There was a lengthy pause during which a transformation came over Paul Mowher that, while visible, was hard for Sam to believe. The man became very still, arms to his sides. His eyes slowly lifted to the ceiling. A smile that could only be called celestial creased his face as he began to stretch out his arms, palms upward.

"I have a right because I have an extreme edict from the Almighty. I am one of only two chosen ones who have the right to receive such communication. I alone am given messages for the earth's western hemisphere. Only recently have I obtained this promotion. My extraordinary gifts are finally recognized. I have, as they say, been elevated."

The hairs on Sam's arms stood up. He could tell by the look in the man's eyes that Mowher wasn't acting.

Knowing that Mowher could push Alaine's inert body through the opening into space before he could possibly prevent it, Sam continued to stall for yet another miracle.

"Your messages...who sends them to you?"

"You don't know?" Mowher seemed genuinely surprised at the question.

"No, Paul, I don't know. Can you tell me? Where do they come from?" As he spoke, Sam made small and what he hoped were natural moves closer to Mowher and Alaine.

Again Mowher moved his eyes upward. Again he lifted his arms over his head. "They come from the Most High Almighty. He sends his messages to me. I am one of the chosen ones."

"Do you mean God?" Sam inched closer while pretending to look toward heaven himself. "How do you know it's really God speaking to you?"

"Oh, the Most High doesn't deign to speak directly to any man. He speaks through his servant, Gabriel. The royal order is God, Gabriel and the chosen ones. I am one of only two. What a grand and glorious honor is mine to do his bidding."

Sam was too terrified to pray. The Holy Spirit was again handling that job. Although he'd closed the gap a little between him and where Mowher stood over Alaine's unconscious body, Sam judged there was still no way he could overpower the man before he could push Alaine to her death.

He didn't know what Jason was doing on the ladder below them, but the only thing Sam knew to do was to keep Paul Mowher talking.

"Have you ever met this Gabriel face to face? Isn't he an angel? I've never seen an angel. What does he look like?"

Mowher paused and watched Sam closely, as if to judge the honesty of his question. "The angel, Gabriel, is much too sanctified to appear in person in today's evil world. He communicates with me by the spoken word, but I've never seen his face. In modern times, he never leaves the side of his master."

"So he talks to you...in plain English...just like we're talking to each other? What kinds of messages does he give you from...the Most High?"

Sam put all of the sincerity he could gather into the questions. As demented as Paul Mowher sounded, the man had to be convinced Sam's questions were on the level.

Mowher acted more wary with each question. Still, he seemed flattered by Sam's inquiries.

"He tells me who is doing the Almighty's good works and who is not. He sends me out to reward and punish according to those works. That..." and he stared down at Alaine, who was beginning to stir, "is why I am here."

He nudged Alaine's shoulder with his shoe. "This woman has done evil works. She bears an unfit child of an evil man. She was scheduled to die but was unjustly rescued. I am entrusted to see to her death in a manner similar to that which she escaped. I have heard the message. Her time has come."

Sam knew the time had, in fact, come...for him to act. Alaine was coming to. There were now two dangers. She could become disoriented and roll off of the platform herself or Paul Mowher could act in his demented state and push her through the opening.

Oh, God, what do I do now? Without your help, Alaine is going to die.

Sam's choices were to rush Mowher and risk a reaction that would end in her death or do nothing and watch what played out in front of him. To go for Alaine might be the best attack. If he could just pull her away from the broken wall, she might have a chance to protect herself while he worried about Paul Mowher.

There seemed little hope either way, but to do nothing was unthinkable. Sam took two deep breaths and tensed his muscles in preparation for his move.

He and Mowher faced each other like opposing animals.

A loud and authoritative voice broke the silence.

"Chosen one, hearken to me."

The voice came from below, but with unearthly volume, power and majesty. The sound startled Sam. *Jason!*

It appeared to have a profound effect on the man standing in front of Sam.

"Who addresses me?" Mowher held out his hands in front of him, as if to ward off a menace.

"It is I, Gabriel, the messenger. I bid you listen to my words."

Mowher now backed up and almost tripped over Alaine, who struggled to rise. He appeared not to notice her, but glanced around as if to see the source of the sound.

The voice continued, deep...slow...measured. "I have a message for the chosen one from the Most High. You must heed his words. You must obey."

The man raised his hands in supplication. "Speak, great one. I am here to do your bidding."

"You have mistaken the message from the Most High. He is displeased. You must not harm the woman. You are to protect her. She is not evil. She belongs to the Most High. Do not harm her or her baby. The Most High has spoken. You must obey."

Sam watched confusion wash over Paul Mowher's face. He saw the man become visibly agitated and begin to wring his hands and run his fingers through his hair.

"Oh, great one, I no longer understand. I was told--I was ordered to--"

"Do you question my words? Do you question the message of the Most High? Have you forgotten my power? I can appoint another chosen one who does not hesitate to do his bidding."

The faceless voice increased in volume and power. Jason played his part in the drama with masterful intensity, and Mowher's obvious anxiety heightened.

He placed his hands on either side of his head and swayed from side to side.

Sam watched with grave fascination as the man came unraveled before his eyes. Mowher mumbled words of response to the unseen speaker. He staggered about, again almost stumbling over Alaine as he moved toward the tear in the wall of the spire.

With both hands, Mowher gripped the top of the broken boards and stood with his body outlined in the empty space. A movement from Sam caused him to turn back around. Sam saw with alarm the light of awareness flash back into Paul Mowher's eyes.

With one hand holding onto the jagged side of the hole, Mowher reached down with the other and wound his fingers into Alaine's hair. The man was going to pull her out of the open hole.

A hot wave of anger erupted through Sam's veins serving as a catapult as he leaped across the remaining space and threw himself toward the woman whose body was being jerked closer to the brink.

Alaine's screams mingled with Sam's shouts as he grabbed her clothing and wedged his foot against what he hoped was solid wood to give him a hold against Mowher's steady pull toward her end.

Now fully conscious, Alaine clutched wildly at Sam for strength before twisting her body back to face the man bending over her whose hand was tearing at her hair. In one fluid movement, she folded her legs under her body, and raised herself up inches from the edge of nothing.

With one arm useless, she slapped Paul Mowher in the face with a swing from her good arm before sliding again to the floor. The blow was vicious and caused Mowher to loosen his hold on her hair.

Mowher brought his freed hand to his face. For a moment he seemed frozen while his eyes sought first Alaine's and then Sam's. The man knew who he was. He understood what was happening. He got it that he had lost.

Paul Mowher straightened slowly, turned, raised his arms to the sky and stepped out into nothing.

Sam threw himself down and wrapped his arms around Alaine, rolling them both away from the opening. He felt the strong hands of his friend, Jason, dragging them to safety. For a long time the three huddled together, mumbling prayers of thanksgiving and shedding tears of gratitude.

23 THE WAY HOME

Sampson

Alaine's baby boy was born on the rough wooden floor of the small room near the top of St. Philip's Chapel high above New York City, across the street from where the North Tower once stood. The NYDP and the FDNY were on hand in the cramped space as a first responder handed the tiny boy covered in an emergency blanket into the eager arms of Sam MacDonald.

Jason had made the call for help as he and Sam climbed. When pressed, he confessed that high school drama classes prepared him to play the role of his life as Gabriel, an act that Sam knew saved them. This hurried conversation came just before Jason slipped away to begin the bouts of questioning about the events that took place high above the old Chapel and the man whose body landed in the fenced graveyard below.

Sam climbed the long ladder down on his own steam with little assistance. Getting Alaine and the premature baby safely to street level proved challenging, even for the NYFD. When a basket and other plans failed, one burley fireman placed her over his shoulder and eased her down the seven floors as gently as another nestled the baby in a sling on his chest and followed his mother down the ladders.

Ambulances were waiting to take the three of them to St. Vincent's Hospital, Sam in one and Alaine and her child in another, only because Sam was gently redirected when he tried to climb in with them.

# # #

Sam was checked out and released within hours, but Alaine and baby John, almost two months premature, stayed on for three weeks. In spite of valiant efforts to the contrary, for the second time in a year Alaine teetered on the edge of Post-Traumatic Stress Disorder.

Sam spent his time, when not answering questions from the police, near Alaine and John. Mostly, she slept, sometimes from exhaustion and sometimes for medically induced respite from her memories of the preceding days as she recovered from the violence to her body and mind, as well as the baby's birth.

When the NICU allowed, Sam held baby John. The rest of his time, he spent with Alaine, only leaving her to eat, sleep at Mrs. Baker's or answer questions from the authorities.

Sam's story, according to the police, closely matched that of Jason's, as he knew it would. Sometimes the truth prevails. Investigation uncovered Paul Mowher's history of intimidation, abuse and increasingly bizarre behaviors, dating back to his days on the police force. His death, as predictable as it was, closed a chapter on a lost and tragic life.

St. Vincent's had been their home base for so long the time blurred for Sam. He was asleep in the uncomfortable hospital lounger with baby John, newly released to his mother's room, on his chest when he felt the baby stir and heard him making hungry sounds. Shifting John to the crook of his arm, he looked over at Alaine, expecting to see her in her usual fetal position with the sheet covering most of her head.

What he saw made him straighten in his seat and reach out his hand to touch the fingers that were reaching out to his. Alaine's eyes were clear and present.

"Hey, you. You look wonderful."

She laughed and ran her hand through her greasy hair. "Who's that you're holding?" She smiled.

"Your son."

"What did you name him?"

"He's yours, Alaine. You should--"

"What did you name him?"

"I think...Johnson Thomas Albert. Johnson's for Johnson Story. Rev. Ray's middle name is Thomas. I thought you'd want your last name instead of--"

"Mowher?" She took in a deep breath and shuddered. "You're right about that. But it's over now, isn't it, Sam?" Her look said she thought so but wasn't sure.

"It's over."

The room was quiet for a long time while tears ran down her face. Sam shifted the baby and worried that she didn't ask to take John into her arms.

"I've been calling him John. I think he looks like you."

"Johnson Thomas Albert. John Albert. I don't think I like that. It doesn't sound right."

"It doesn't matter, honey. He's yours now. You can call him anything you want to. That was just my idea, while you were--no problem. No papers have been signed."

"I was thinking about maybe Johnson Thomas MacDonald. That seems better to me. What do you think? He's yours, Sam. You saved him twice."

He knew she was speaking from emotion. Naturally, there was gratitude. He'd have to be careful not to read into what she was saying. He couldn't take advantage.

"I'm glad you feel that way. He's a special little guy. I'd be proud to give him my name. In fact, I think I'm going to like being his Uncle Sampson."

Sam stood up and moved to sit beside of her on the narrow hospital bed, lowering baby John so she could see him better, wanting her to reach for him.

"That wasn't what I meant. Did you misunderstand, Sam. Or is this your very kind way of declining my offer?"

Her question was as far from what he expected as New York was from Copper's Run. He wiped his own sudden tear off of baby John's face before he could speak.

"Are you saying--?"

"I'm saying I love you, Sampson MacDonald. I love you because you rescued baby John and me once and then did it again. I love you because you didn't desert me when you could have left Copper's Run months ago. I love you because of your new heart. Yes. Ms. Charity told me before I left the Inn. I love you for all of those reasons."

"Alaine, you have no idea. You deserve--"

"Those aren't the only reasons I love you, Sam. I love you because you are a part of me and my baby now. I know I'm not playing safe to say this, but we can't even imagine living the rest of our lives without you. If you feel differently, I'll understand and find a way with my child, but you will never leave my heart."

Before he kissed her, Sam slipped his free arm around her. With Alaine in one arm and baby John in the other, he prayed. He prayed out loud for her to overhear as a promise to her.

"Father, you have saved us all again. For that I thank you. You saved us when the Towers fell, you saved us from Paul Mowher, but best of all, you sent your Son to save us from ourselves when we were lost in our sins. Lord, it looks like you'll give us a chance to be a family. For that I thank you, too. Help me to be the best husband and father I can be. Amen."

And then he kissed her.

# # #

Charity Bright held off on coming to New York only because Rev. Ray restrained her with his words of wisdom. "Let Sampson take care of them for a while, Charity. He can work things out. It'll make them both stronger."

Sam knew this because Rev. Ray told him so in his daily updates to them.

"She wants to be there to take charge, Sam. I've asked her to stay here until you're ready to come home. She'll fly up to be with you all then. Can you handle things? I know you can."

Sam smiled. Ray Bright had him in his sights...the Sampson MacDonald Discipleship Program 101. It would be tough to measure up, but if he was going to become the man he needed to be, Sam would do whatever it took to pass.

"Yes, sir, I can handle it. Alaine's much better and the baby's fine. Tell Ms. Charity to pack her bags. I think we'll be free to leave here in a couple of days. Alaine is crazy to see her, but it's been good, now that she's better, to have the time for her to bond with little John."

"How's that going? I know you were concerned."

"The only thing that worries me now is how to get enough time with him myself. They're stuck to each other."

Rev. Ray laughed his approval. "We miss you, Sam, and we miss Alaine. We're all ready for you two and little John to come home. The Inn needs you, Charity and Johnson need you, and I need you. Is this home, Sam, at least for now? I certainly hope so."

"It's home, Rev. Ray. It definitely is home. And we have something important to discuss with you when we get there."

Sam came off of the plane first carrying the baby carrier and followed by Alaine, whose hand he was holding. Her other arm was still in a soft protective covering. Charity Bright was next clutching baby John in her arms and wearing a granny smile on her face. The greeting party in the terminal consisted of most of the Inn's staff and Rev. Ray, who wept as he embraced Sam and Alaine and pried the baby from Charity's arms.

"Come to Big Papa, little darling. Come home to Big Papa."

Baby John slept while his ready-made grandparents showed him off to Danisha, Andi, Johnson Story and anyone else in the terminal who would look.

The evening lights of the Inn at Copper's Run invited its extended adopted family home. A special meal served in the Bright's apartment completed the welcome.

Ms. Charity fussed over Alaine, and Rev. Ray and Sam competed for holding time with little John. As they finished their dessert and coffee, the conversation became serious.

"You said you had something to discuss with me, Sampson. Is this a good time?" He leaned back in his easy chair.

"Alaine, why don't I go with you and help you get baby John settled? We'll let the men folks talk." Ms. Charity ushered a tired mother and son out of the apartment, leaving Rev. Ray and Sam alone.

Rev. Ray closed his eyes and folded his hands over his chest, as he often did when he had serious thinking to do, and waited. This was a signal Sam knew well. The man was ready to listen.

"As you already know, I made things right in the City," Sam began. "My former employer...and the man from whom I stole the money...I talked to them both. No charges. I gave the money back with interest. I don't deserve it, but I got mercy."

"Mercy and grace. None of us deserve them, son. I'm happy for you. But that's not all you wanted to talk to me about. Am I right?"

Wait time never bothered Rev. Ray, and Sam took advantage of it now. It mattered what the older man thought, what his advice might be.

"I want to give Alaine's baby a real father. I want to be little John's daddy. I want to marry his mother."

"You're willing to do this for the child? That's commendable. But what about Alaine? What's in it for her?"

Sam laughed at Rev. Ray's way of putting it.

"I'm serious, Sam. Would you marry her as a means of staying in the little boy's life?"

"I love her, sir. I'd want to marry her if there were no baby. Let me be clear.

I do love her very much. But I also love them both. I need them in my life, and I think they need me. I want the three of us to be together for good."

"Are you ready for this? It's the biggest job you've ever had. You're a new believer. Do you think you're equipped with what you need?"

Rev. Ray was right. He'd known what Ray would say. He wasn't ready yet. It would be a mistake to move ahead too quickly. The silence grew heavy.

But then, he could get ready. He could do whatever it took, if Alaine was willing to wait.

"Would you work with me? I'm serious about this. What do I need to do? I want to do this right. Alaine and the baby are worth waiting for."

Rev. Ray moved his recliner upright and put his feet on the floor. He stood and faced Sam.

"We love you, Sam. Charity and I have loved you and Alaine since you came to us last September. I've watched you work hard and become a man. I've seen you come to the Lord. We think you two belong together. We want that for you as soon as you both are ready. Charity will work with Alaine. Johnson and I will disciple you. I believe God puts young men with a willing heart on a fast track. Let's get started."

Ray Bright put his long arms around Sampson MacDonald, rested his forehead against Sam's shoulder and started to pray.

###

Alaine agreed to wait. As she told Sam, when he put the situation to her, her cup, her arms and her heart were all full. What were a few weeks more? She also agreed with enthusiasm to be discipled by Ms. Charity while Sam was undergoing his Believer Boot Camp, as Rev. Ray liked to call it.

Sam wished for the patience Alaine displayed as Rev. Ray gave him no quarter. Sam had his regular duties at the Inn, met with Ray or Johnson Story for instruction at lunch or after hours and was left to study on his own late into the evenings after spending time with Alaine and baby John.

Ray would never discuss time frame. He'd turn aside all questions about when Sam's boot camp would end, and he and Alaine would be free to marry.

He might say, "Trust me, son. You have to learn to trust the Lord and wait on Him. You might as well practice on me." Or he might tell Sam," When I know, you'll know. Keep working hard and you'll get there. Remember how long Jacob had to work for the woman he loved in the Book of Genesis?"

"I'm afraid to ask."

"Seven years and a week, son, seven years and a week. And then it took him another seven years to pay for her."

Rev. Ray laughed when Sam groaned.

# # #

Alaine

It was early October in Copper's Run. The weather was still warm but the slant of the sun and the color change in the trees marked the coming of autumn. In a week, on the one year and one month anniversary of their escape from the inferno of the North Tower, Sam and Alaine would be married.

Alaine found her new reality hard to believe. Who would have imagined such change would transform two lives that, a year ago, could be described as without discernable hope. When she was tempted to feel she didn't deserve such blessings, Ms. Charity reminded her that "every good and perfect gift is from above."

Planning a wedding with a six-month-old proved to be challenging as baby John seemed to time his eating and changing needs with wedding planning sessions. But she always had a willing surrogate granny or aunt to lend a hand from the ladies of the Inn.

Still the planning progressed. The ceremony would be held in the stone chapel beneath the Inn. Rev. Ray would marry them, Ms. Charity would provide the music, Danisha would hold baby

John and Andi would be Alaine's only attendant. Johnson Story would serve as best man. It would be a small ceremony with only a few close friends, and the honeymoon would have to wait. It was busy season at the Inn.

There was little disappointment at postponing their private celebration as the newly joined family would move together into a renovated suite on the second floor of the Inn that had once served as a popular retreat for visiting notables of the 19th century.

During the planning, Alaine discovered from the Brights that these rooms had a notable history of their own. Rumor held that the President of the Confederacy, Jefferson Davis, once spent two nights there with his wife, Varina, during the War Between the States. The old records couldn't verify the visit, but there was a register indicating that Mr. and Mrs. S. Howell stayed there in early 1862. Could it be coincidence that Davis's father's name was Samuel and Varina's maiden name was Howell? In any case, it was a story that Rev. Ray always told with a twinkle in his eye, making sure the irony was not lost on his listeners.

Disregarding tradition not to see each other prior to the ceremony, Alaine and Sam met there for a quiet moment just before they were to appear in the chapel. She wore vintage lace from a trunk in the Inn's attic. Baby John slept in her arms. He wore a suit and shoes as different from his New York days as he could find. They stood together, looking around them at the rooms they would soon share as a family.

Sam spoke. "We've come a long way together. And beginning today, I hope we will have a long way to go. I will do my best, Alaine, with God's help, to be a good husband to you...a good father to John."

Through Alaine's mind flashed pictures of the past year...the falling Tower, arrival at the Inn, Rev. Ray's heart attack, awareness of her pregnancy, meetings with the Dabneys, her salvation, discovery by Paul Mowher, terrors surrounding her return to the City, John's birth, her lengthy recovery...all that had happened to bring her to this time. And with her through it all, for bad or good, had been Sampson MacDonald.

She responded. "If the delight in watching you grow as a man of God these past few months is anything like the joy I will have from being your wife, I am ready for this day."

ENCORE

[an additional performance at the end]

Sampson

Charity Bright played wedding music on the chapel's ancient organ through happy tears. Johnson Story wiped the wet from the wrinkles in his brown face. Ray Bright's strong, firm voice broke as he pronounced the couple man and wife. No one seemed to mind that baby John cried through the whole service. He finally quieted when his daddy took him from Danisha's arms. Holding his son in one arm, Sam placed the other around the baby's mother. With all of their adopted family looking on, Sam treasured the welcome in his bride's eyes before he sealed their vows with the first kiss of a new life together.

The End

SEPTEMBER TWELFTH

The death-planes flew,
The buildings fell.
Smoke clouds blocked the morning sun.
America held her breath and wrung her hands and watched her people die.
Hope took a forceful blow as the nation staggered,
shaking her mighty head in disbelief.

It was as if God had decreed,
"On the eleventh day, I will destroy the earth and all those who dwell therein."

People gathered
By twos and threes,
By tens and hundreds, by thousands.
The earth waited, in silence, and watched for what would come.
Fear reached its hand into the hearts of the watchers,
spawning doubt and cold uncertainty.

It was as if the Enemy had mocked and screamed,
"Look at me, I am great and I have won a grand victory!"

The dark hours passed.
The fiends of fear
Began to flee at the promise of a new dawn.
September twelfth.
The worst had happened. And yet...the sun rose once again.
Hope struggled, threw off its irons, raised its head
and rushed to meet the coming of the day.

It was as if the People rejoiced and cried with one voice,
"We are changed, but we are not broken.
With a strength forged from the hottest fires
we have survived;
we will go on." J.J.

ABOUT THE AUTHOR

In another life with another name, Jenny Johnson wrote non-fiction as a university professor in the field of Special Education. She has a BA from Wheaton College (Literature), an M.Ed. (Speech Pathology/Audiology, UNC-Greensboro) and a Ph.D. (Special Education, UNC-Chapel Hill). Jenny prefers writing faith based fiction, and now pursues that objective seriously. Her poetry and short stories have won local/state awards. *The Taxi*, her first romance-suspense novel, was published by Oaktara (2012). Her second novel, *The Inn at Copper's Run,* was born from interests in travel and history.

Jenny's goals as a writer are simple. "I want to write faith-based romantic suspense fiction that provokes thought about authentic Christianity through the actions and experiences of my characters, tells a good story, promotes values consistent with my beliefs as a Christ follower, and leaves readers feeling positive about their investment of time and resources."

Jenny's website and blog are available at:
  http://www.jennyjohnsonauthor.com/
  https://jennywjohnson.blogspot.com/

If you have enjoyed getting to know the characters at the Inn at Copper's Run and following their lives, please consider leaving a review of the book on the Amazon web site.

59653001R00217

Made in the USA
Columbia, SC
07 June 2019